THE STRANGE CASE OF DR. JEKYLL AND MR. HYDE AND OTHER STORIES

THE STRANGE CASE OF DR. JEKYLL AND MR. HYDE AND OTHER STORIES

ROBERT LOUIS STEVENSON

Race Point
PUBLISHING

Quarto is the authority on a wide range of topics.

Quarto educates, entertains and enriches the lives of our readers—enthusiasts and lovers of hands-on living.

www.quartoknows.com

© 2016 Quarto Publishing Group USA Inc.

First published in the United States of America in 2016 by
Race Point Publishing, a member of
Quarto Publishing Group USA Inc.
142 West 36th Street, 4th Floor
New York, New York 10018
www.quartoknows.com

10 9 8 7 6 5 4 3 2 1

ISBN 978-1-63106-242-1

Editor: Milton Creek Editorial Services
Cover Design: The Book Designers
Cover Pattern: Creativo Surface Design Studio

Printed in China

CONTENTS

INTRODUCTION

When respectable Dr. Henry Jekyll first consumed his transformative chemical potion in 1886, he changed not just his body and personality, but also literary history. Few works of Victorian literature have had the lasting appeal and cultural influence of Robert Louis Stevenson's novella *The Strange Case of Dr. Jekyll and Mr. Hyde*. The story has been retold and recast countless times since its first publication, and we can find echoes of Stevenson's creation in contemporary film, drama, television, fiction, comics, cartoons, and even psychological theory. Part allegory, part science fiction, part tale of terror, *Dr. Jekyll and Mr. Hyde* was wildly popular in its day, and it remains a favorite of college students, horror fans, and fiction-lovers in general.

Born in Edinburgh in 1850, Robert Lewis Balfour Stevenson would change his name to the more familiar Robert Louis Stevenson when he was a young man. An only child, Stevenson was raised in a comfortable middle-class home. His father, Thomas, had a successful career in the family business of lighthouse engineering; the Stevenson family had built many of the lighthouses along Scotland's rocky coast. Stevenson's mother, Margaret Isabella, came from a family of clergymen, maritime engineers, physicians, and attorneys. Stevenson and his mother both suffered from respiratory ailments, and throughout Stevenson's career as a writer, he traveled the globe in search of an environment that would not aggravate his health. As a boy, his mother's ill health made it difficult for her to care for him, and much of his childhood was placed under the care of Alison Cunningham, a nurse he called

"Cummy." Cummy's frequent story-telling most likely inspired Stevenson's own love for writing fiction.

Stevenson's early schooling was frequently interrupted by periods of poor health, but with the help of private tutors, he was able to enter the University of Edinburgh in 1867. At the university, he displayed little desire to follow in the footsteps of his family of engineers, and an attempt at a career in law did not inspire him either. Stevenson's passion was writing, and by the mid-1870s he had abandoned all other professions. His political, social, and religious beliefs were also undergoing great change during these years as Stevenson joined a socialist club, rejected Christianity, frequented brothels and pubs, dressed as a Bohemian, and traveled to France to surround himself with other artists. It was in France that he met Fanny Osbourne, a married woman eleven years his senior who had three children with her estranged husband. Fanny was forced to return to her husband in San Francisco in 1878 when he threatened to cut off her finances. The next year, Stevenson traveled to join Fanny in California after her husband left her. She divorced in 1879 and married Stevenson in 1880.

The remaining years of Stevenson's life would be spent writing and traveling the world for his health. He and Fanny lived in California, Scotland, England, France, and New York. He also spent many years at sea visiting places like Hawaii and Tahiti, and he eventually bought property in Samoa where he died suddenly in 1894, not long after his forty-fourth birthday.

Stevenson's writing career spanned two-thirds of his life, and he published over a dozen novels, numerous short stories, and a range of essays, poetry collections, and travel narratives. Four of his works, all novels written in the 1880s, are still widely read today: *Treasure Island* (1883), *The Strange Case of Dr. Jekyll and Mr. Hyde* (1886), *Kidnapped* (1886), and *The Master of Ballantrae* (1889). Three of these novels draw heavily on Stevenson's close relationship with the sea. *Treasure Island*, an adventure story written for boys, follows Jim Hawkins, a teenager whose encounter with an old seaman sets of a quest for buried treasure hampered by mutiny and the one-legged pirate Long John Silver. *Kidnapped*, another novel for boys, tells the tale of the orphan David Balfour whose uncle Ebenezer, grasping for an inheritance that is not rightly his, has the boy kidnapped and taken to sea. The tale follows David's adventures at sea, in the Hebrides, the Scottish Highlands, and Edinburgh. *The Master of Ballantrae* chronicles the lives of two Scottish brothers who frequently feud over money, women, and, as one might expect in a Stevenson novel, hidden pirate treasure.

Compared to these other works, *The Strange Case of Dr. Jekyll and Mr. Hyde* is indeed strange. The novella takes place entirely in London, a city in which Stevenson had never spent significant time. Readers looking for any sea-faring or Highland adventures would have been disappointed. But the novella certainly did not disappoint its initial audiences. The work was immediately successful in both England and the United States. A review in the January 25, 1886, edition of *The Times* claims that "Nothing Mr. Stevenson has written as yet has so strongly impressed us with the versatility of his very original genius as this sparsely-printed little shilling volume." A reviewer in the April 1886 *Contemporary Review* describes *The Strange Case of Dr. Jekyll and Mr. Hyde* as a story "which the reader devours in an hour, but to which he may return again and again, to study a profound allegory and admire a model of style." The poet and critic John Addington Symonds wrote to Stevenson to declare the work "the finest you have done—in all that regards style, invention, psychological analysis, exquisite fitting of parts, and admirable employment of motives to realize the abnormal." The first printings of the work quickly sold out in both England and the United States, and by the end of the century hundreds of thousands of copies had been sold.

According to Graham Balfour, who interviewed Stevenson's widow for his 1912 biography of the author, the central idea for the story—the transformation of the respectable Dr. Jekyll into the notorious criminal Hyde—came to the author in a dream during a period of ill health. Stevenson was so enthralled by the story's concept that he completed the first draft in a few days. That Stevenson would have such a dream is not entirely surprising. In the years leading up to the writing of *The Strange Case of Dr. Jekyll and Mr. Hyde*, Stevenson had been exploring the dual nature of humanity. He had become interested in the case of Louis Vivet, a psychiatric patient who, in 1885, became the first person for whom the diagnosis "multiple personality disorder" was applied. Vivet's personality would change from deferential and amiable to caustic and aggressive. While Vivet embodied one personality, he had no memory of the other. This type of psychological phenomenon—today called "dissociative identity disorder"—provides one useful lens through which we can read Dr. Jekyll's dual personality.

Stevenson, however, was well aware that a dual nature did not need to be the result of mental illness. In 1880, he had published *Deacon Brodie*, a play about William Brodie, a respectable eighteenth-century Scottish tradesman by day who was by night a gambler and womanizer who burgled the houses of his clients to pay his debts and support five mistresses. Stevenson's short story "Markheim," published in the *Pall Mall Gazette* in 1884, features a man who looks at himself in a mirror in an antique shop only to see in his reflection the ugly criminal lurking beneath his respectable exterior. In anger, Markheim tells the shopkeeper, "Why, look here—look in it—look at yourself! Do you like to see it? No! nor I!—nor any man." The theme of these works—that respectability and propriety are simply a performance masking criminality and animalistic behavior—was nothing new for Stevenson when it made its appearance in *The Strange Case of Dr. Jekyll and Mr. Hyde*.

Nevertheless, few works so effectively critique Victorian propriety as Stevenson's novella. Jekyll's transformation into Hyde certainly makes literal the idea that respectability is just a veneer beneath which lurks the monstrous, but this idea pervades the work even without the use of a transformative chemical concoction. When Jekyll explains the motives for his experiment, he notes that he was "fond of the respect of the wise and good among [his] fellow-men," but that he also had a "certain impatient gaiety of disposition" at odds with his need for respect. Long before he ever transforms into Mr. Hyde, he "stood already committed to a profound duplicity of life." In many ways, he already had a Hyde before he ever began his experiment.

Other men in the novel further advance this theme. The story opens with Gabriel John Utterson and Richard Enfield, two respectable gentlemen, going for a walk. As Enfield tells the story of his disturbing encounter with Hyde, we are left wondering why exactly he was "coming home from some place at the end of the world, about three o'clock of a black winter morning" in a deserted part of town. Even Utterson, who is one of the more serious and upright characters to be found in any work of fiction, reflects upon his own past with horror: "few men could read the rolls of their life with less apprehension; yet he was humbled to the dust by the many ill things he had done." If Utterson has behavior he must hide, all men do. Stevenson makes this point explicit when Utterson bursts into Jekyll's lab at the climax of the story. He is not greeted by Gothic horrors, but by a whistling tea-kettle in a quiet room described as "the most commonplace that night in London." In the Victorian world Stevenson has created, the duality of man represented by Jekyll/Hyde is not the exception. It is the norm.

Whether or not Stevenson also thought women were inherently duplicitous is another question. In the August 1894 edition of the *Idler*, Stevenson reflected upon his writing of *Treasure Island*. He stated that "It was to be a story for boys... Women were excluded." Indeed, many male writers of the Victorian period came up with strategies for either avoiding or marginalizing female characters. Herman Melville and Joseph Conrad, like Stevenson, set many of their works onboard the all-male environment of ships. Other works such as Rudyard Kipling's *Kim* (1901) place the action in colonial regions like India where European men interact with women who are marginalized, exotic foreigners. Stevenson's *The Strange Case of Dr. Jekyll and Mr. Hyde*, however, has neither a foreign nor a maritime setting. London in the 1880s was a thriving metropolis inhabited by more women than men, so the novella's lack of central female characters is remarkable. One would be hard-pressed to conduct a meaningful feminist reading of the story. The novel takes place in the sitting rooms, bedrooms, and laboratories of well-to-do professional men, none of whom seem to have wives or families. The few women we do meet are not presented favorably, from the women in the opening scene who are "wild as harpies," to the "romantically given" maidservant who faints upon witnessing one of Mr. Hyde's horrendous crimes. If *Treasure Island* was a book for boys that excludes female characters, *The Strange Case of Dr. Jekyll and Mr. Hyde* follows in its footsteps. The book arguably appeals to an older audience, but it is similarly male-centered.

The lack of women, however, has not hindered the story's popularity. Part of the appeal of *The Strange Case of Dr. Jekyll and Mr. Hyde* is that it is much more than an allegory of man's dual nature. Even at its most basic level as a story about good vs. evil, the work is far more complex than it might appear at first glance. Jekyll, for one, does not represent "good." Like each of us, he is a composite character with both good and bad characteristics. He cannot be reduced to one-half of a simple binary. Even Mr. Hyde—the embodiment of all those undesirable qualities that Jekyll attempts to separate from himself—is not easily reduced to the label "evil." In psychological terms, we might consider Hyde the "id," those animalistic and instinctual impulses that we all work to keep in check in a civilized society. Even here, however, the description doesn't quite fit. Hyde isn't entirely uncivilized. He pays restitution for the accident in the opening chapter, and we also learn that he conducts business about town and had visited the master of the maidservant in the chapter "The Carew Murder Case." Hyde may be destructive, but he is also a man who enjoys a cup of tea and participates in society.

The richness of the novella does not end here. Yes, it is about good and evil, Victorian propriety, and man's dual nature. The novel's often deliberately vague language, however, allows it to be read in many other ways. Jekyll notes that he "concealed [his] pleasures," but he does not identify what those pleasures are. Perhaps he uses drugs or alcohol, for the tale can easily be read as a cautionary tale about addiction: Jekyll drinks a concoction that makes him feel young, strong and uninhibited; he enjoys the feeling and continues to imbibe; soon the habit gets out of his control and leads to his destruction. Whether referring to alcohol or opium, it is a familiar story of substance abuse. Or perhaps his pleasures are sexual. Stevenson himself frequented brothels. Might his character Jekyll as well? And where exactly was Enfield coming from at three in the morning in the novella's opening scene? If the "pleasures" are sexual, they need not be heterosexual. Written at a time when homosexuality was criminal, the novella presents an apt allegory for a same-sex relationship: Jekyll is forced to keep his desires hidden in the closet, and he has a pleasurable but illegal and destructive relationship with Mr. Hyde.

The novella also lends itself to a study of theatricality. If we do not read the change from Jekyll to Hyde as an actual supernatural transformation, might it simply be Jekyll changing his appearance to indulge his desires without being identified? Poole, Jekyll's butler, even raises this possibility when he asks, "Sir, if that was my master, why had he a mask upon his face?" Adding more credibility to this interpretation, and as a testament to the wonderful ambiguity of the tale, the medical laboratory in which Jekyll conducts his experiments is multiple times referred to as a surgical "theatre." The word was commonly used in the nineteenth century in reference to a science classroom, but in Stevenson's work, it takes on an additional layer of meaning.

Given both the rich complexity of Stevenson's novella and its theatrical and dramatic elements, it should come as little surprise that the work has been adapted for the stage, radio, film, and television dozens of times. The first production is perhaps the most notorious. Within a year of *The Strange Case of Dr. Jekyll and Mr. Hyde*'s publication, the Bostonian novelist Thomas Russel Sullivan adapted the novella for the stage. The play met with a favorable reception in Boston, and travelled to England in 1888. As fortune would have it, the timing of the play's opening in London corresponded with the first of the Jack the Ripper murders in the Whitechapel district. The nature of the murders made investigators think that the Ripper was someone with medical experience, perhaps a respectable doctor by day and serial murderer by night. Stevenson's tale seemed to have come to life in the streets of the city. Richard Mansfield, the actor who played the lead role, was so convincing and horrifying in his portrayal of the transformation between Jekyll and Hyde, that one theatregoer even accused the actor of being the actual Ripper.

Since Sullivan's play, adaptations of Stevenson's work have remained popular. Many productions stay relatively true to the original novella, while others are only loosely inspired by it. Television and movie characters ranging from the Incredible Hulk to the Nutty Professor all owe a debt to Stevenson. On stage, the story has been presented with a female Dr. Jekyll, as a silent play, and as a musical. Film has seen famous actors such as Spencer Tracy, Christopher Lee, and Anthony Perkins play the role of Jekyll, and the 1996 film *Mary Reilly* starred John Malkovich as Jekyll with Julia Roberts as his maidservant. Stevenson's story also lends itself well to comedy and parody. Abbott and Costello, Scooby-Doo, Tom and Jerry, Bugs Bunny, Daffy Duck, Phineas and Ferb, and even a few erotic films have all found inspiration in *The Strange Case of Dr. Jekyll and Mr. Hyde*.

The popularity of Stevenson's novella is not likely to wane any time soon. Indeed, advances in psychology and our ever-increasing understanding of the complexity of human identity make the work all the more relevant. Stevenson's central themes of duplicity, addiction, and the indulgence of secret pleasures speak to readers today just as much as they did in 1886. Indeed, as long as readers have something to hide from the world, they will find a kindred spirit in Stevenson's Henry Jekyll.

Allen Grove is professor and chair of English at Alfred University. He holds a Ph.D. in English from the University of Pennsylvania, and his teaching and research focus primarily on the eighteenth- and nineteenth-century British novel.

THE STRANGE CASE OF
DR. JEKYLL AND MR. HYDE

Story of the Door

Mr. Utterson the lawyer was a man of a rugged countenance that was never lighted by a smile; cold, scanty and embarrassed in discourse; backward in sentiment; lean, long, dusty, dreary and yet somehow lovable. At friendly meetings, and when the wine was to his taste, something eminently human beaconed from his eye; something indeed which never found its way into his talk, but which spoke not only in these silent symbols of the after-dinner face, but more often and loudly in the acts of his life. He was austere with himself; drank gin when he was alone, to mortify a taste for vintages; and though he enjoyed the theatre, had not crossed the doors of one for twenty years. But he had an approved tolerance for others; sometimes wondering, almost with envy, at the high pressure of spirits involved in their misdeeds; and in any extremity inclined to help rather than to reprove. "I incline to Cain's heresy," he used to say quaintly: "I let my brother go to the devil in his own way."[1] In this character, it was frequently his fortune to be the last reputable acquaintance and the last good influence in the lives of down-going men. And to such as these, so long as they came about his chambers, he never marked a shade of change in his demeanour.

No doubt the feat was easy to Mr. Utterson; for he was undemonstrative at the best, and even his friendship seemed to be founded in a similar catholicity of good-nature. It is the mark of a modest man to accept his friendly circle ready-made from the hands of opportunity; and that was the lawyer's way. His friends were those of his own blood or those whom he had known the longest; his affections, like ivy, were the growth of time, they implied no apt-ness in the object. Hence, no doubt, the bond that united him to Mr. Richard Enfield, his distant kinsman, the well-known man about town. It was a nut to crack for many, what these two could see in each other, or what subject they could find in common. It was reported by those who encountered them in their Sunday walks, that they said nothing, looked singularly dull, and would hail with obvious relief the appearance of a friend. For all that, the two men put the greatest store by these excursions, counted them the chief jewel of each week, and not only set aside occasions of pleasure, but even resisted the calls of business, that they might enjoy them uninterrupted.

It chanced on one of these rambles that their way led them down a by-street in a busy quarter of London. The street was small and what is called quiet, but it drove a thriving trade on the weekdays. The inhabitants were all doing well, it seemed, and all emulously hoping to do better still, and laying out the surplus of their grains in coquetry; so that the shop fronts stood along that thoroughfare with an air of invitation, like rows of smiling saleswomen. Even on Sunday, when it veiled its more florid charms and lay comparatively empty of passage, the street shone out in contrast to its dingy neighbourhood, like a fire in a forest; and with its freshly painted shutters, well-polished brasses, and general cleanliness and gaiety of note, instantly caught and pleased the eye of the passenger.

Two doors from one corner, on the left hand going east, the line was bro-ken by the entry of a court; and just at that point, a certain sinister block of building thrust forward its gable on the street. It was two storeys high; showed no window, nothing but a door on the lower storey and a blind fore-head of discoloured wall on the upper; and bore in every feature, the marks of prolonged and sordid negligence. The door, which was equipped with nei-ther bell nor knocker, was blistered and distained. Tramps slouched into the recess and struck matches on the panels; children kept shop upon the steps; the schoolboy had tried his knife on the mouldings; and for close on a gener-ation, no one had appeared to drive away these random visitors or to repair their ravages.

Mr. Enfield and the lawyer were on the other side of the by-street; but when they came abreast of the entry, the former lifted up his cane and pointed.

"Did you ever remark that door?" he asked; and when his companion had replied in the affirmative, "It is connected in my mind," added he, "with a very odd story."

"Indeed?" said Mr. Utterson, with a slight change of voice, "and what was that?"

"Well, it was this way," returned Mr. Enfield: "I was coming home from some place at the end of the world, about three o'clock of a black winter morning, and my way lay through a part of town where there was literally nothing to be seen but lamps. Street after street, and all the folks asleep—street after street, all lighted up as if for a procession and all as empty as a church—till at last I got into that state of mind when a man listens and listens and begins to long for the sight of a policeman. All at once, I saw two figures: one a little man who was stumping along eastward at a good walk, and the other a girl of maybe eight or ten who was running as hard as she was able down a cross street. Well, sir, the two ran into one another naturally enough at the corner; and then came the horrible part of the thing; for the man trampled calmly over the child's body and left her screaming on the ground. It sounds nothing to hear, but it was hellish to see. It wasn't like a man; it was like some damned Juggernaut.[2] I gave a view halloa, took to my heels, collared my gentleman, and brought him back to where there was already quite a group about the screaming child. He was perfectly cool and made no resistance, but gave me one look, so ugly that it brought out the sweat on me like running. The people who had turned out were the girl's own family; and pretty soon, the doctor, for whom she had been sent, put in his appearance. Well, the child was not much the worse, more frightened, according to the Sawbones;[3] and there you might have supposed would be an end to it. But there was one curious circumstance. I had taken a loathing to my gentleman at first sight. So had the child's family, which was only natural. But the doctor's case was what struck me. He was the usual cut and dry apothecary, of no particular age and colour, with a strong Edinburgh accent, and about as emotional as a bagpipe. Well, sir, he was like the rest of us; every time he looked at my prisoner, I saw that Sawbones turn sick and white with desire to kill him. I knew what was in his mind, just as he knew what was in mine; and killing being out of the question, we did the next best. We told the man we could and would make such a scandal out of this, as should make his name stink from one end of London to the other. If he had any friends or any credit, we undertook that he should lose them. And all the time, as we were pitching it in red hot, we were keeping the women off him as best we could, for they were as wild as harpies. I never saw a circle of such hateful faces; and there was the man in the middle, with a kind of black, sneering coolness—frightened too, I could see that—but carrying it off, sir, really like Satan. 'If you choose to make capital out of this accident,' said he, 'I am naturally helpless. No gentleman but wishes to avoid a scene,' says he. 'Name your figure.' Well, we screwed him up to a hundred pounds for the child's family; he would have clearly liked to stick out; but there was something about the lot of us that meant mischief, and at last he struck. The next thing was to get the money; and where do you think he carried us but to that place with the door?—whipped out a key, went in, and presently came back with the matter of ten pounds in gold and a cheque for the balance on Coutts's,[4] drawn payable to bearer and signed with a name that I can't mention, though it's one of the points of my story, but it was a name at least very well known and often printed. The figure was stiff; but the signature was good for more than that, if it was only genuine. I took the liberty of pointing out to my gentleman that the whole business looked apocryphal, and that a man does not, in real life, walk into a cellar door at four in the morning and come out with another man's cheque for close upon a hundred pounds. But he was quite easy and sneering. 'Set your mind at rest,' says he, 'I will stay with you till the banks open and cash the cheque myself.' So we all set off, the doctor, and the child's father, and our friend and myself, and passed the rest of the night in my chambers; and next day, when we had breakfasted, went in a body to the bank. I gave in the cheque myself, and said I had every reason to believe it was a forgery. Not a bit of it. The cheque was genuine."

"Tut-tut," said Mr. Utterson.

"I see you feel as I do," said Mr. Enfield. "Yes, it's a bad story. For my man was a fellow that nobody could have to do with, a really damnable man; and the person that drew the cheque is the very pink of the proprieties, celebrated too, and (what makes it worse) one of your fellows who do what they call good. Black mail, I suppose; an honest man paying through the nose for some of the capers of his youth. Black Mail House is what I call the place with the door, in consequence. Though even that, you know, is far from explaining all," he added, and with the words fell into a vein of musing.

From this he was recalled by Mr. Utterson asking rather suddenly: "And you don't know if the drawer of the cheque lives there?"

"A likely place, isn't it?" returned Mr. Enfield. "But I happen to have noticed his address; he lives in some square or other."

"And you never asked about the—place with the door?" said Mr. Utterson.

"No, sir: I had a delicacy," was the reply. "I feel very strongly about putting questions; it partakes too much of the style of the day of judgment. You start a question, and it's like starting a stone. You sit quietly on the top of a hill; and away the stone goes, starting others; and presently some bland old bird (the last you would have thought of) is knocked on the head in his own back garden and the family have to change their name. No sir, I make it a rule of mine: the more it looks like Queer Street,⁵ the less I ask."

"A very good rule, too," said the lawyer.

"But I have studied the place for myself," continued Mr. Enfield. "It seems scarcely a house. There is no other door, and nobody goes in or out of that one but, once in a great while, the gentleman of my adventure. There are three windows looking on the court on the first floor; none below; the windows are always shut but they're clean. And then there is a chimney which is generally smoking; so somebody must live there. And yet it's not so sure; for the buildings are so packed together about the court, that it's hard to say where one ends and another begins."

The pair walked on again for a while in silence; and then "Enfield," said Mr. Utterson, "that's a good rule of yours."

"Yes, I think it is," returned Enfield.

"But for all that," continued the lawyer, "there's one point I want to ask: I want to ask the name of that man who walked over the child."

"Well," said Mr. Enfield, "I can't see what harm it would do. It was a man of the name of Hyde."

"Hm," said Mr. Utterson. "What sort of a man is he to see?"

"He is not easy to describe. There is something wrong with his appearance; something displeasing, something down-right detestable. I never saw a man I so disliked, and yet I scarce know why. He must be deformed somewhere; he gives a strong feeling of deformity, although I couldn't specify the point. He's an extraordinary looking man, and yet I really can name nothing out of the way. No, sir; I can make no hand of it; I can't describe him. And it's not want of memory; for I declare I can see him this moment."

Mr. Utterson again walked some way in silence and obviously under a weight of consideration. "You are sure he used a key?" he inquired at last.

"My dear sir . . ." began Enfield, surprised out of himself.

"Yes, I know," said Utterson; "I know it must seem strange. The fact is, if I do not ask you the name of the other party, it is because I know it already. You see, Richard, your tale has gone home. If you have been inexact in any point, you had better correct it."

"I think you might have warned me," returned the other with a touch of sullenness. "But I have been pedantically exact, as you call it. The fellow had a key; and what's more, he has it still. I saw him use it, not a week ago."

Mr. Utterson sighed deeply but said never a word; and the young man presently resumed. "Here is another lesson to say nothing," said he. "I am ashamed of my long tongue. Let us make a bargain never to refer to this again."

"With all my heart," said the lawyer. "I shake hands on that, Richard."

Search for Mr. Hyde

That evening Mr. Utterson came home to his bachelor house in sombre spirits and sat down to dinner without relish. It was his custom of a Sunday, when this meal was over, to sit close by the fire, a volume of some dry divinity on his reading desk, until the clock of the neighbouring church rang out the hour of twelve, when he would go soberly and gratefully to bed. On this night, however, as soon as the cloth was taken away, he took up a candle and went into his business room. There he opened his safe, took from the most private part of it a document endorsed on the envelope as Dr. Jekyll's Will, and sat down with a clouded brow to study its contents. The will was holograph, for Mr. Utterson, though he took charge of it now that it was made, had refused to lend the least assistance in the making of it; it provided not only that, in case of the decease of Henry Jekyll, M.D., D.C.L., L.L.D., F.R.S., etc.,[1] all his possessions were to pass into the hands of his "friend and benefactor Edward Hyde," but that in case of Dr. Jekyll's "disappearance or unexplained absence for any period exceeding three calendar months," the said Edward Hyde should step into the said Henry Jekyll's shoes without further delay and free from any burthen or obligation, beyond the payment of a few small sums to the members of the doctor's household. This document had long been the lawyer's eyesore. It offended him both as a lawyer and as a lover of the sane and customary sides of life, to whom the fanciful was the immodest. And hitherto it was his ignorance of Mr. Hyde that had swelled his indignation; now, by a sudden turn, it was his knowledge. It was already bad enough when the name was but a name of which he could learn no more. It was worse when it began to be clothed upon with detestable attributes; and out of the shifting, insubstantial mists that had so long baffled his eye, there leaped up the sudden, definite presentment of a fiend.

"I thought it was madness," he said, as he replaced the obnoxious paper in the safe, "and now I begin to fear it is disgrace."

With that he blew out his candle, put on a greatcoat, and set forth in the direction of Cavendish Square,[2] that citadel of medicine, where his friend, the great Dr. Lanyon, had his house and received his crowding patients. "If anyone knows, it will be Lanyon," he had thought.

The solemn butler knew and welcomed him; he was subjected to no stage of delay, but ushered direct from the door to the dining-room where Dr. Lanyon sat alone over his wine. This was a hearty, healthy, dapper, red-faced gentleman, with a shock of hair prematurely white, and a boisterous and decided manner. At sight of Mr. Utterson, he sprang up from his chair and welcomed him with both hands. The geniality, as was the way of the man, was somewhat theatrical to the eye; but it reposed on genuine feeling. For these two were old friends, old mates both at school and college, both thorough respectors of themselves and of each other, and what does not always follow, men who thoroughly enjoyed each other's company.

After a little rambling talk, the lawyer led up to the subject which so disagreeably preoccupied his mind.

"I suppose, Lanyon," said he, "you and I must be the two oldest friends that Henry Jekyll has?"

"I wish the friends were younger," chuckled Dr. Lanyon. "But I suppose we are. And what of that? I see little of him now."

"Indeed?" said Utterson. "I thought you had a bond of common interest."

"We had," was the reply. "But it is more than ten years since Henry Jekyll became too fanciful for me. He began to go wrong, wrong in mind; and though of course I continue to take an interest in him for old sake's sake, as they say, I see and I have seen devilish little of the man. Such unscientific balderdash," added the doctor, flushing suddenly purple, "would have estranged Damon and Pythias."[3]

This little spirit of temper was somewhat of a relief to Mr. Utterson. "They have only differed on some point of science," he thought; and being a man of no scientific passions (except in the matter of conveyancing),[4] he even added: "It is nothing worse than that!" He gave his friend a few seconds to recover his composure, and then approached the question he had come to put. "Did you ever come across a protégé of his—one Hyde?" he asked.

"Hyde?" repeated Lanyon. "No. Never heard of him. Since my time."

That was the amount of information that the lawyer carried back with him to the great, dark bed on which he tossed to and fro, until the small hours of the morning began to grow large. It was a night of little ease to his toiling mind, toiling in mere darkness and besieged by questions.

Six o'clock struck on the bells of the church that was so conveniently near to Mr. Utterson's dwelling, and still he was digging at the problem. Hitherto it had touched him on the intellectual side alone; but now his imagination also was engaged, or rather enslaved; and as he lay and tossed in the gross darkness of the night and the curtained room, Mr. Enfield's tale went by before his mind in a scroll of lighted pictures. He would be aware of the great field of lamps of a nocturnal city; then of the figure of a man walking swiftly; then of a child running from the doctor's; and then these met, and that human Juggernaut trod the child down and passed on regardless of her screams. Or else he would see a room in a rich house, where his friend lay asleep, dreaming and smiling at his dreams; and then the door of that room would be opened, the curtains of the bed plucked apart, the sleeper recalled, and lo! there would stand by his side a figure to whom power was given, and even at that dead hour, he must rise and do its bidding. The figure in these two phases haunted the lawyer all night; and if at any time he dozed over, it was but to see it glide more stealthily through sleeping houses, or move the more swiftly and still the more swiftly, even to dizziness, through wider labyrinths of lamplighted city, and at every street corner crush a child and leave her screaming. And still the figure had no face by which he might know it; even in his dreams, it had no face, or one that baffled him and melted before his eyes; and thus it was that there sprang up and grew apace in the lawyer's mind a singularly strong, almost an inordinate, curiosity to behold the features of the real Mr. Hyde. If he could but once set eyes on him, he thought the mystery would lighten and perhaps roll altogether away, as was the habit of mysterious things when well examined. He might see a reason for his friend's strange preference or bondage (call it which you please) and even for the startling clause of the will. At least it would be a face worth seeing: the face of a man who was without bowels of mercy: a face which had but to show itself to raise up, in the mind of the unimpressionable Enfield, a spirit of enduring hatred.

From that time forward, Mr. Utterson began to haunt the door in the by-street of shops. In the morning before office hours, at noon when business was plenty, and time scarce, at night under the face of the fogged city moon, by all lights and at all hours of solitude or concourse, the lawyer was to be found on his chosen post.

"If he be Mr. Hyde," he had thought, "I shall be Mr. Seek."

And at last his patience was rewarded. It was a fine dry night; frost in the air; the streets as clean as a ballroom floor; the lamps, unshaken by any wind, drawing a regular pattern of light and shadow. By ten o'clock, when the shops were closed, the by-street was very solitary and, in spite of the low growl of London from all round, very silent. Small sounds carried far; domestic sounds out of the houses were clearly audible on either side of the roadway; and the rumour of the approach of any passenger preceded him by a long time. Mr. Utterson had been some minutes at his post, when he was aware of an odd, light footstep drawing near. In the course of his nightly patrols, he had long grown accustomed to the quaint effect with which the footfalls of a single person, while he is still a great way off, suddenly spring out distinct from the vast hum and clatter of the city. Yet his attention had never before been so sharply and decisively arrested; and it was with a strong, superstitious prevision of success that he withdrew into the entry of the court.

The steps drew swiftly nearer, and swelled out suddenly louder as they turned the end of the street. The lawyer, looking forth from the entry, could soon see what manner of man he had to deal with. He was small and very plainly dressed, and the look of him, even at that distance, went somehow strongly against the watcher's inclination. But he made straight for the door, crossing the roadway to save time; and as he came, he drew a key from his pocket like one approaching home.

Mr. Utterson stepped out and touched him on the shoulder as he passed. "Mr. Hyde, I think?"

Mr. Hyde shrank back with a hissing intake of the breath. But his fear was only momentary; and though he did not look the lawyer in the face, he answered coolly enough: "That is my name. What do you want?"

"I see you are going in," returned the lawyer. "I am an old friend of Dr. Jekyll's—Mr. Utterson of Gaunt Street—you must have heard of my name; and meeting you so conveniently, I thought you might admit me."

"You will not find Dr. Jekyll; he is from home," replied Mr. Hyde, blowing in the key. And then suddenly, but still without looking up, "How did you know me?" he asked.

"On your side," said Mr. Utterson, "will you do me a favour?"

"With pleasure," replied the other. "What shall it be?"

"Will you let me see your face?" asked the lawyer.

Mr. Hyde appeared to hesitate, and then, as if upon some sudden reflection, fronted about with an air of defiance; and the pair stared at each other pretty fixedly for a few seconds. "Now I shall know you again," said Mr. Utterson. "It may be useful."

"Yes," returned Mr. Hyde, "it is as well we have met; and *à propos*, you should have my address." And he gave a number of a street in Soho.[5]

"Good God!" thought Mr. Utterson, "can he, too, have been thinking of the will?" But he kept his feelings to himself and only grunted in acknowledgment of the address.

"And now," said the other, "how did you know me?"

"By description," was the reply.

"Whose description?"

"We have common friends," said Mr. Utterson.

"Common friends?" echoed Mr. Hyde, a little hoarsely. "Who are they?"

"Jekyll, for instance," said the lawyer.

"He never told you," cried Mr. Hyde, with a flush of anger. "I did not think you would have lied."

"Come," said Mr. Utterson, "that is not fitting language."

The other snarled aloud into a savage laugh; and the next moment, with extraordinary quickness, he had unlocked the door and disappeared into the house.

The lawyer stood awhile when Mr. Hyde had left him, the picture of disquietude. Then he began slowly to mount the street, pausing every step or two and putting his hand to his brow like a man in mental perplexity. The problem he was thus debating as he walked, was one of a class that is rarely solved. Mr. Hyde was pale and dwarfish, he gave an impression of deformity without any nameable malformation, he had a displeasing smile, he had borne himself to the lawyer with a sort of murderous mixture of timidity and boldness, and he spoke with a husky, whispering and somewhat broken voice; all these were points against him, but not all of these together could explain the hitherto unknown disgust, loathing and fear with which Mr. Utterson regarded him. "There must be something else," said the perplexed gentleman. "There *is* something more, if I could find a name for it. God bless me, the man seems hardly human! Something troglodytic, shall we say? or can it be the old story of Dr. Fell?[6] or is it the mere radiance of a foul soul that thus transpires through, and transfigures, its clay continent? The last, I think; for, O my poor old Harry Jekyll, if ever I read Satan's signature upon a face, it is on that of your new friend."

Round the corner from the by-street, there was a square of ancient, handsome houses, now for the most part decayed from their high estate and let in flats and chambers to all sorts and conditions of men; map-engravers, architects, shady lawyers and the agents of obscure enterprises. One house, however, second from the corner, was still occupied entire; and at the door of this, which wore a great air of wealth and comfort, though it was now plunged in darkness except for the fanlight, Mr. Utterson stopped and knocked. A well-dressed, elderly servant opened the door.

"Is Dr. Jekyll at home, Poole?" asked the lawyer.

"I will see, Mr. Utterson," said Poole, admitting the visitor, as he spoke, into a large, low-roofed, comfortable hall, paved with flags, warmed (after the fashion of a country house) by a bright, open fire, and furnished with costly cabinets of oak. "Will you wait here by the fire, sir? or shall I give you a light in the dining-room?"

"Here, thank you," said the lawyer, and he drew near and leaned on the tall fender. This hall, in which he was now left alone, was a pet fancy of his friend the doctor's; and Utterson himself was wont to speak of it as the pleasantest room in London. But tonight there was a shudder in his blood; the face of Hyde sat heavy on his memory; he felt (what was rare with him) a nausea and distaste of life; and in the gloom of his spirits, he seemed to read a menace in the flickering of the firelight on the polished cabinets and the uneasy starting of the shadow on the roof. He was ashamed of his relief, when Poole presently returned to announce that Dr. Jekyll was gone out.

"I saw Mr. Hyde go in by the old dissecting-room door, Poole," he said. "Is that right, when Dr. Jekyll is from home?"

"Quite right, Mr. Utterson, sir," replied the servant. "Mr. Hyde has a key."

"Your master seems to repose a great deal of trust in that young man, Poole," resumed the other musingly.

"Yes, sir, he does indeed," said Poole. "We have all orders to obey him."

"I do not think I ever met Mr. Hyde?" asked Utterson.

"O, dear no, sir. He never *dines* here," replied the butler. "Indeed we see very little of him on this side of the house; he mostly comes and goes by the laboratory."

"Well, good night, Poole."

"Good night, Mr. Utterson."

And the lawyer set out homeward with a very heavy heart. "Poor Harry Jekyll," he thought, "my mind misgives me he is in deep waters! He was wild when he was young; a long while ago to be sure; but in the law of God, there is no statute of limitations. Ay, it must be that; the ghost of some old sin, the cancer of some concealed disgrace: punishment coming, *pede claudo*,[7] years after memory has forgotten and self-love condoned the fault." And the lawyer, scared by the thought, brooded awhile on his own past, groping in all the corners of memory, lest by chance some Jack-in-the-Box of an old iniquity should leap to light there. His past was fairly blameless; few men could read the rolls of their life with less apprehension; yet he was humbled to the dust by the many ill things he had done, and raised up again into a sober and fearful gratitude by the many he had come so near to doing, yet avoided. And then by a return on his former subject, he conceived a spark of hope. "This Master Hyde, if he were studied," thought he, "must have secrets of his own; black secrets, by the look of him; secrets compared to which poor Jekyll's worst would be like sunshine. Things cannot continue as they are. It turns me cold to think of this creature stealing like a thief to Harry's bedside; poor Harry, what a wakening! And the danger of it; for if this Hyde suspects the existence of the will, he may grow impatient to inherit. Ay, I must put my shoulders to the wheel—if Jekyll will but let me," he added, "if Jekyll will only let me." For once more he saw before his mind's eye, as clear as transparency, the strange clauses of the will.

Dr. Jekyll Was Quite at Ease

A fortnight later, by excellent good fortune, the doctor gave one of his pleasant dinners to some five or six old cronies, all intelligent, reputable men and all judges of good wine; and Mr. Utterson so contrived that he remained behind after the others had departed. This was no new arrangement, but a thing that had befallen many scores of times. Where Utterson was liked, he was liked well. Hosts loved to detain the dry lawyer, when the light-hearted and loose-tongued had already their foot on the threshold; they liked to sit awhile in his unobtrusive company, practising for solitude, sobering their minds in the man's rich silence after the expense and strain of gaiety. To this rule, Dr. Jekyll was no exception; and as he now sat on the opposite side of the fire—a large, well-made, smooth-faced man of fifty, with something of a slyish cast perhaps, but every mark of capacity and kindness—you could see by his looks that he cherished for Mr. Utterson a sincere and warm affection.

"I have been wanting to speak to you, Jekyll," began the latter. "You know that will of yours?"

A close observer might have gathered that the topic was distasteful; but the doctor carried it off gaily. "My poor Utterson," said he, "you are unfortunate in such a client. I never saw a man so distressed as you were by my will; unless it were that hide-bound pedant, Lanyon, at what he called my scientific heresies. O, I know he's a good fellow—you needn't frown—an excellent fellow, and I always mean to see more of him; but a hide-bound pedant for all that; an igno-rant, blatant pedant. I was never more disappointed in any man than Lanyon."

"You know I never approved of it," pursued Utterson, ruthlessly disregarding the fresh topic.

"My will? Yes, certainly, I know that," said the doctor, a trifle sharply. "You have told me so."

"Well, I tell you so again," continued the lawyer. "I have been learning something of young Hyde."

The large handsome face of Dr. Jekyll grew pale to the very lips, and there came a blackness about his eyes. "I do not care to hear more," said he. "This is a matter I thought we had agreed to drop."

"What I heard was abominable," said Utterson.

"It can make no change. You do not understand my position," returned the doctor, with a certain incoherency of manner. "I am painfully situated, Utterson; my position is a very strange—a very strange one. It is one of those affairs that cannot be mended by talking."

"Jekyll," said Utterson, "you know me: I am a man to be trusted. Make a clean breast of this in confidence; and I make no doubt I can get you out of it."

"My good Utterson," said the doctor, "this is very good of you, this is downright good of you, and I cannot find words to thank you in. I believe you fully; I would trust you before any man alive, ay, before myself, if I could make the choice; but indeed it isn't what you fancy; it is not as bad as that; and just to put your good heart at rest, I will tell you one thing: the moment I choose, I can be rid of Mr. Hyde. I give you my hand upon that; and I thank you again and again; and I will just add one little word, Utterson, that I'm sure you'll take in good part: this is a private matter, and I beg of you to let it sleep."

Utterson reflected a little, looking in the fire.

"I have no doubt you are perfectly right," he said at last, getting to his feet.

"Well, but since we have touched upon this business, and for the last time I hope," continued the doctor, "there is one point I should like you to understand. I have really a very great interest in poor Hyde. I know you have seen him; he told me so; and I fear he was rude. But I do sincerely take a great, a very great interest in that young man; and if I am taken away, Utterson, I wish you to promise me that you will bear with him and get his rights for him. I think you would, if you knew all; and it would be a weight off my mind if you would promise."

"I can't pretend that I shall ever like him," said the lawyer.

"I don't ask that," pleaded Jekyll, laying his hand upon the other's arm; "I only ask for justice; I only ask you to help him for my sake, when I am no longer here."

Utterson heaved an irrepressible sigh. "Well," said he, "I promise."

THE CAREW MURDER CASE

Nearly a year later, in the month of October, 18—, London was startled by a crime of singular ferocity and rendered all the more notable by the high position of the victim. The details were few and startling. A maid servant living alone in a house not far from the river, had gone upstairs to bed about eleven. Although a fog rolled over the city in the small hours, the early part of the night was cloudless, and the lane, which the maid's window overlooked, was brilliantly lit by the full moon. It seems she was romantically given, for she sat down upon her box, which stood immediately under the window, and fell into a dream of musing. Never (she used to say, with streaming tears, when she narrated that experience), never had she felt more at peace with all men or thought more kindly of the world. And as she so sat she became aware of an aged beautiful gentleman with white hair, drawing near along the lane; and advancing to meet him, another and very small gentleman, to whom at first she paid less attention. When they had come within speech (which was just under the maid's eyes) the older man bowed and accosted the other with a very pretty manner of politeness. It did not seem as if the subject of his address were of great importance; indeed, from his pointing, it sometimes appeared as if he were only inquiring his way; but the moon shone on his face as he spoke, and the girl was pleased to watch it, it seemed to breathe such an innocent and old-world kindness of disposition, yet with something high too, as of a well-founded self-content. Presently her eye wandered to the other, and she was surprised to recognise in him a certain Mr. Hyde, who had once visited her master and for whom she had conceived a dislike. He had in his hand a heavy cane, with which he was trifling; but he answered never a word, and seemed to listen with an ill-contained impatience. And then all of a sudden he broke out in a great flame of anger, stamping with his foot, brandishing the cane, and carrying on (as the maid described it) like a madman. The old gentleman took a step back, with the air of one very much surprised and a trifle hurt; and at that Mr. Hyde broke out of all bounds and clubbed him to the earth. And next moment, with ape-like fury, he was trampling his victim under foot and hailing down a storm of blows, under which the bones were audibly shattered and the body jumped upon the roadway. At the horror of these sights and sounds, the maid fainted.

It was two o'clock when she came to herself and called for the police. The murderer was gone long ago; but there lay his victim in the middle of the lane, incredibly mangled. The stick with which the deed had been done, although it was of some rare and very tough and heavy wood, had broken in the middle under the stress of this insensate cruelty; and one splintered half had rolled in the neighbouring gutter—the other, without doubt, had been carried away by the murderer. A purse and gold watch were found upon the victim: but no cards or papers, except a sealed and stamped envelope, which he had been probably carrying to the post, and which bore the name and address of Mr. Utterson.

This was brought to the lawyer the next morning, before he was out of bed; and he had no sooner seen it, and been told the circumstances, than he shot out a solemn lip. "I shall say nothing till I have seen the body," said he; "this may be very serious. Have the kindness to wait while I dress." And with the same grave countenance he hurried through his breakfast and drove to the police station, whither the body had been carried. As soon as he came into the cell, he nodded.

"Yes," said he, "I recognise him. I am sorry to say that this is Sir Danvers Carew."

"Good God, sir," exclaimed the officer, "is it possible?" And the next moment his eye lighted up with professional ambition. "This will make a deal of noise," he said. "And perhaps you can help us to the man." And he briefly narrated what the maid had seen, and showed the broken stick.

Mr. Utterson had already quailed at the name of Hyde; but when the stick was laid before him, he could doubt no longer; broken and battered as it was, he recognized it for one that he had himself presented many years before to Henry Jekyll.

"Is this Mr. Hyde a person of small stature?" he inquired.

"Particularly small and particularly wicked-looking, is what the maid calls him," said the officer.

Mr. Utterson reflected; and then, raising his head, "If you will come with me in my cab," he said, "I think I can take you to his house."

It was by this time about nine in the morning, and the first fog of the season. A great chocolate-coloured pall lowered over heaven, but the wind was continually charging and routing these embattled vapours; so that as the cab crawled from street to street, Mr. Utterson beheld a marvelous number of degrees and hues of twilight; for here it would be dark like the back-end of evening; and there would be a glow of a rich, lurid brown, like the light of some strange conflagration; and here, for a moment, the fog would be quite broken up, and a haggard shaft of daylight would glance in between the swirling wreaths. The dismal quarter of Soho seen under these changing glimpses, with its muddy ways, and slatternly passengers, and its lamps, which had never been extinguished or had been kindled afresh to combat this mournful reinvasion of darkness, seemed, in the lawyer's eyes, like a district of some city in a nightmare. The thoughts of his mind, besides, were of the gloomiest dye; and when he glanced at the companion of his drive, he was conscious of some touch of that terror of the law and the law's officers, which may at times assail the most honest.

As the cab drew up before the address indicated, the fog lifted a little and showed him a dingy street, a gin palace, a low French eating house, a shop for the retail of penny numbers and twopenny salads, many ragged children huddled in the doorways, and many women of many different nationalities passing out, key in hand, to have a morning glass; and the next moment the fog settled down again upon that part, as brown as umber, and cut him off from his blackguardly surroundings. This was the home of Henry Jekyll's favourite; of a man who was heir to a quarter of a million sterling.

An ivory-faced and silvery-haired old woman opened the door. She had an evil face, smoothed by hypocrisy: but her manners were excellent. Yes, she said, this was Mr. Hyde's, but he was not at home; he had been in that night very late, but he had gone away again in less than an hour; there was nothing strange in that; his habits were very irregular, and he was often absent; for instance, it was nearly two months since she had seen him till yesterday.

"Very well, then, we wish to see his rooms," said the lawyer; and when the woman began to declare it was impossible, "I had better tell you who this person is," he added. "This is Inspector Newcomen of Scotland Yard."[1]

A flash of odious joy appeared upon the woman's face. "Ah!" said she, "he is in trouble! What has he done?"

Mr. Utterson and the inspector exchanged glances. "He don't seem a very popular character," observed the latter. "And now, my good woman, just let me and this gentleman have a look about us."

In the whole extent of the house, which but for the old woman remained otherwise empty, Mr. Hyde had only used a couple of rooms; but these were furnished with luxury and good taste. A closet was filled with wine; the plate was of silver, the napery elegant; a good picture hung upon the walls, a gift (as Utterson supposed) from Henry Jekyll, who was much of a connoisseur; and the carpets were of many plies and agreeable in colour. At this moment, however, the rooms bore every mark of having been recently and hurriedly ransacked; clothes lay about the floor, with their pockets inside out; lock-fast drawers stood open; and on the hearth there lay a pile of grey ashes, as though many papers had been burned. From these embers the inspector disinterred the butt end of a green cheque book, which had resisted the action of the fire; the other half of the stick was found behind the door; and as this clinched his suspicions, the officer declared himself delighted. A visit to the bank, where several thousand pounds were found to be lying to the murderer's credit, completed his gratification.

"You may depend upon it, sir," he told Mr. Utterson: "I have him in my hand. He must have lost his head, or he never would have left the stick or, above all, burned the cheque book. Why, money's life to the man. We have nothing to do but wait for him at the bank, and get out the handbills."

This last, however, was not so easy of accomplishment; for Mr. Hyde had numbered few familiars—even the master of the servant maid had only seen him twice; his family could nowhere be traced; he had never been photographed; and the few who could describe him differed widely, as common observers will. Only on one point were they agreed; and that was the haunting sense of unexpressed deformity with which the fugitive impressed his beholders.

INCIDENT OF THE LETTER

It was late in the afternoon, when Mr. Utterson found his way to Dr. Jekyll's door, where he was at once admitted by Poole, and carried down by the kitchen offices and across a yard which had once been a garden, to the building which was indifferently known as the laboratory or dissecting rooms. The doctor had bought the house from the heirs of a celebrated surgeon; and his own tastes being rather chemical than anatomical, had changed the destination of the block at the bottom of the garden. It was the first time that the lawyer had been received in that part of his friend's quarters; and he eyed the dingy, windowless structure with curiosity, and gazed round with a distasteful sense of strangeness as he crossed the theatre, once crowded with eager students and now lying gaunt and silent, the tables laden with chemical apparatus, the floor strewn with crates and littered with packing straw, and the light falling dimly through the foggy cupola. At the further end, a flight of stairs mounted to a door covered with red baize; and through this, Mr. Utterson was at last received into the doctor's cabinet. It was a large room fitted round with glass presses, furnished, among other things, with a cheval-glass[1] and a business table, and looking out upon the court by three dusty windows barred with iron. The fire burned in the grate; a lamp was set lighted on the chimney shelf, for even in the houses the fog began to lie thickly; and there, close up to the warmth, sat Dr. Jekyll, looking deathly sick. He did not rise to meet his visitor, but held out a cold hand and bade him welcome in a changed voice.

"And now," said Mr. Utterson, as soon as Poole had left them, "you have heard the news?"

The doctor shuddered. "They were crying it in the square," he said. "I heard them in my dining-room."

"One word," said the lawyer. "Carew was my client, but so are you, and I want to know what I am doing. You have not been mad enough to hide this fellow?"

"Utterson, I swear to God," cried the doctor, "I swear to God I will never set eyes on him again. I bind my honour to you that I am done with him in this world. It is all at an end. And indeed he does not want my help; you do not know him as I do; he is safe, he is quite safe; mark my words, he will never more be heard of."

The lawyer listened gloomily; he did not like his friend's feverish manner. "You seem pretty sure of him," said he; "and for your sake, I hope you may be right. If it came to a trial, your name might appear."

"I am quite sure of him," replied Jekyll; "I have grounds for certainty that I cannot share with anyone. But there is one thing on which you may advise me. I have—I have received a letter; and I am at a loss whether I should show it to the police. I should like to leave it in your hands, Utterson; you would judge wisely, I am sure; I have so great a trust in you."

"You fear, I suppose, that it might lead to his detection?" asked the lawyer.

"No," said the other. "I cannot say that I care what becomes of Hyde; I am quite done with him. I was thinking of my own character, which this hateful business has rather exposed."

Utterson ruminated awhile; he was surprised at his friend's selfishness, and yet relieved by it. "Well," said he, at last, "let me see the letter."

The letter was written in an odd, upright hand and signed "Edward Hyde": and it signified, briefly enough, that the writer's benefactor, Dr. Jekyll, whom he had long so unworthily repaid for a thousand generosities, need labour under no alarm for his safety, as he had means of escape on which he placed a sure dependence. The lawyer liked this letter well enough; it put a better colour on the intimacy than he had looked for; and he blamed himself for some of his past suspicions.

"Have you the envelope?" he asked.

"I burned it," replied Jekyll, "before I thought what I was about. But it bore no postmark. The note was handed in."

"Shall I keep this and sleep upon it?" asked Utterson.

"I wish you to judge for me entirely," was the reply. "I have lost confidence in myself."

"Well, I shall consider," returned the lawyer. "And now one word more: it was Hyde who dictated the terms in your will about that disappearance?"

The doctor seemed seized with a qualm of faintness; he shut his mouth tight and nodded.

"I knew it," said Utterson. "He meant to murder you. You had a fine escape."

"I have had what is far more to the purpose," returned the doctor solemnly: "I have had a lesson—O God, Utterson, what a lesson I have had!" And he covered his face for a moment with his hands.

On his way out, the lawyer stopped and had a word or two with Poole. "By the bye," said he, "there was a letter handed in today: what was the messenger like?" But Poole was positive nothing had come except by post; "and only circulars by that," he added.

This news sent off the visitor with his fears renewed. Plainly the letter had come by the laboratory door; possibly, indeed, it had been written in the cabinet; and if that were so, it must be differently judged, and handled with the more caution. The newsboys, as he went, were crying themselves hoarse along the footways: "Special edition. Shocking murder of an M.P."[2] That was the funeral oration of one friend and client; and he could not help a certain apprehension lest the good name of another should be sucked down in the eddy of the scandal. It was, at least, a ticklish decision that he had to make; and self-reliant as he was by habit, he began to cherish a longing for advice. It was not to be had directly; but perhaps, he thought, it might be fished for.

Presently after, he sat on one side of his own hearth, with Mr. Guest, his head clerk, upon the other, and midway between, at a nicely calculated distance from the fire, a bottle of a particular old wine that had long dwelt unsunned in the foundations of his house. The fog still slept on the wing above the drowned city, where the lamps glimmered like carbuncles; and through the muffle and smother of these fallen clouds, the procession of the town's life was still rolling in through the great arteries with a sound as of a mighty wind. But the room was gay with firelight. In the bottle the acids were long ago resolved; the imperial dye had softened with time, as the colour grows richer in stained windows; and the glow of hot autumn after-noons on hillside vineyards, was ready to be set free and to disperse the fogs of London. Insensibly the lawyer melted. There was no man from whom he kept fewer secrets than Mr. Guest; and he was not always sure that he kept as many as he meant. Guest had often been on business to the doctor's; he knew Poole; he could scarce have failed to hear of Mr. Hyde's familiarity about the house; he might draw conclusions: was it not as well, then, that he should see a letter which put that mystery to rights? and above all since Guest, being a great student and critic of handwriting, would consider the step natural and obliging? The clerk, besides, was a man of counsel; he could scarce read so strange a document without dropping a remark; and by that remark Mr. Utterson might shape his future course.

"This is a sad business about Sir Danvers," he said.

"Yes, sir, indeed. It has elicited a great deal of public feeling," returned Guest. "The man, of course, was mad."

"I should like to hear your views on that," replied Utterson. "I have a docu-ment here in his handwriting; it is between ourselves, for I scarce know what to do about it; it is an ugly business at the best. But there it is; quite in your way: a murderer's autograph."

Guest's eyes brightened, and he sat down at once and studied it with passion. "No sir," he said: "not mad; but it is an odd hand."

"And by all accounts a very odd writer," added the lawyer.

Just then the servant entered with a note.

"Is that from Dr. Jekyll, sir?" inquired the clerk. "I thought I knew the writ-ing. Anything private, Mr. Utterson?"

"Only an invitation to dinner. Why? Do you want to see it?"

"One moment. I thank you, sir"; and the clerk laid the two sheets of paper alongside and sedulously compared their contents. "Thank you, sir," he said at last, returning both; "it's a very interesting autograph."

There was a pause, during which Mr. Utterson struggled with himself. "Why did you compare them, Guest?" he inquired suddenly.

"Well, sir," returned the clerk, "there's a rather singular resemblance; the two hands are in many points identical: only differently sloped."

"Rather quaint," said Utterson.

"It is, as you say, rather quaint," returned Guest.

"I wouldn't speak of this note, you know," said the master.

"No, sir," said the clerk. "I understand."

But no sooner was Mr. Utterson alone that night, than he locked the note into his safe, where it reposed from that time forward. "What!" he thought. "Henry Jekyll forge for a murderer!" And his blood ran cold in his veins.

Remarkable Incident of
Dr. Lanyon

Time ran on; thousands of pounds were offered in reward, for the death of Sir Danvers was resented as a public injury; but Mr. Hyde had disappeared out of the ken of the police as though he had never existed. Much of his past was unearthed, indeed, and all disreputable: tales came out of the man's cruelty, at once so callous and violent; of his vile life, of his strange associates, of the hatred that seemed to have surrounded his career; but of his present whereabouts, not a whisper. From the time he had left the house in Soho on the morning of the murder, he was simply blotted out; and gradually, as time drew on, Mr. Utterson began to recover from the hotness of his alarm, and to grow more at quiet with himself. The death of Sir Danvers was, to his way of thinking, more than paid for by the disappearance of Mr. Hyde. Now that that evil influence had been withdrawn, a new life began for Dr. Jekyll. He came out of his seclusion, renewed relations with his friends, became once more their familiar guest and entertainer; and whilst he had always been known for charities, he was now no less distinguished for religion. He was busy, he was much in the open air, he did good; his face seemed to open and brighten, as if with an inward consciousness of service; and for more than two months, the doctor was at peace.

On the 8th of January Utterson had dined at the doctor's with a small party; Lanyon had been there; and the face of the host had looked from one to the other as in the old days when the trio were inseparable friends. On the

12th, and again on the 14th, the door was shut against the lawyer. "The doctor was confined to the house," Poole said, "and saw no one." On the 15th, he tried again, and was again refused; and having now been used for the last two months to see his friend almost daily, he found this return of solitude to weigh upon his spirits. The fifth night he had in Guest to dine with him; and the sixth he betook himself to Dr. Lanyon's.

There at least he was not denied admittance; but when he came in, he was shocked at the change which had taken place in the doctor's appearance. He had his death-warrant written legibly upon his face. The rosy man had grown pale; his flesh had fallen away; he was visibly balder and older; and yet it was not so much these tokens of a swift physical decay that arrested the lawyer's notice, as a look in the eye and quality of manner that seemed to testify to some deep-seated terror of the mind. It was unlikely that the doctor should fear death; and yet that was what Utterson was tempted to suspect. "Yes," he thought; "he is a doctor, he must know his own state and that his days are counted; and the knowledge is more than he can bear." And yet when Utterson remarked on his ill-looks, it was with an air of great firmness that Lanyon declared himself a doomed man.

"I have had a shock," he said, "and I shall never recover. It is a question of weeks. Well, life has been pleasant; I liked it; yes, sir, I used to like it. I sometimes think if we knew all, we should be more glad to get away."

"Jekyll is ill, too," observed Utterson. "Have you seen him?"

But Lanyon's face changed, and he held up a trembling hand. "I wish to see or hear no more of Dr. Jekyll," he said in a loud, unsteady voice. "I am quite done with that person; and I beg that you will spare me any allusion to one whom I regard as dead."

"Tut-tut," said Mr. Utterson; and then after a considerable pause, "Can't I do anything?" he inquired. "We are three very old friends, Lanyon; we shall not live to make others."

"Nothing can be done," returned Lanyon; "ask himself."

"He will not see me," said the lawyer.

"I am not surprised at that," was the reply. "Some day, Utterson, after I am dead, you may perhaps come to learn the right and wrong of this. I cannot tell you. And in the meantime, if you can sit and talk with me of other things, for

God's sake, stay and do so; but if you cannot keep clear of this accursed topic, then in God's name, go, for I cannot bear it."

As soon as he got home, Utterson sat down and wrote to Jekyll, complaining of his exclusion from the house, and asking the cause of this unhappy break with Lanyon; and the next day brought him a long answer, often very pathetically worded, and sometimes darkly mysterious in drift. The quarrel with Lanyon was incurable. "I do not blame our old friend," Jekyll wrote, "but I share his view that we must never meet. I mean from henceforth to lead a life of extreme seclusion; you must not be surprised, nor must you doubt my friendship, if my door is often shut even to you. You must suffer me to go my own dark way. I have brought on myself a punishment and a danger that I cannot name. If I am the chief of sinners, I am the chief of sufferers also. I could not think that this earth contained a place for sufferings and terrors so unmanning; and you can do but one thing, Utterson, to lighten this destiny, and that is to respect my silence." Utterson was amazed; the dark influence of Hyde had been withdrawn, the doctor had returned to his old tasks and amities; a week ago, the prospect had smiled with every promise of a cheerful and an honoured age; and now in a moment, friendship, and peace of mind, and the whole tenor of his life were wrecked. So great and unprepared a change pointed to madness; but in view of Lanyon's manner and words, there must lie for it some deeper ground.

A week afterwards Dr. Lanyon took to his bed, and in something less than a fortnight he was dead. The night after the funeral, at which he had been sadly affected, Utterson locked the door of his business room, and sitting there by the light of a melancholy candle, drew out and set before him an envelope addressed by the hand and sealed with the seal of his dead friend. "PRIVATE: for the hands of G. J. Utterson ALONE, and in case of his predecease to be destroyed unread," so it was emphatically superscribed; and the lawyer dreaded to behold the contents. "I have buried one friend today," he thought: "what if this should cost me another?" And then he condemned the fear as a disloyalty, and broke the seal. Within there was another enclosure, likewise sealed, and marked upon the cover as "not to be opened till the death or disappearance of Dr. Henry Jekyll." Utterson could not trust his eyes. Yes, it was disappearance; here again, as in the mad will which he had long ago restored to its author, here again were the idea of a disappearance and the name of Henry Jekyll bracketted. But in the will, that idea had sprung from the sinister suggestion of the man Hyde; it was set there with a purpose all too plain and horrible. Written by the hand of Lanyon, what should it mean? A great curiosity came on the trustee, to disregard the prohibition and dive at once to the bottom of these mysteries; but professional honour and faith to his dead friend were stringent obligations; and the packet slept in the inmost corner of his private safe.

It is one thing to mortify curiosity, another to conquer it; and it may be doubted if, from that day forth, Utterson desired the society of his surviving friend with the same eagerness. He thought of him kindly; but his thoughts were disquieted and fearful. He went to call indeed; but he was perhaps relieved to be denied admittance; perhaps, in his heart, he preferred to speak with Poole upon the doorstep and surrounded by the air and sounds of the open city, rather than to be admitted into that house of voluntary bondage, and to sit and speak with its inscrutable recluse. Poole had, indeed, no very pleasant news to communicate. The doctor, it appeared, now more than ever confined himself to the cabinet over the laboratory, where he would some-times even sleep; he was out of spirits, he had grown very silent, he did not read; it seemed as if he had something on his mind. Utterson became so used to the unvarying character of these reports, that he fell off little by little in the frequency of his visits.

INCIDENT AT THE WINDOW

It chanced on Sunday, when Mr. Utterson was on his usual walk with Mr. Enfield, that their way lay once again through the by-street; and that when they came in front of the door, both stopped to gaze on it.

"Well," said Enfield, "that story's at an end at least. We shall never see more of Mr. Hyde."

"I hope not," said Utterson. "Did I ever tell you that I once saw him, and shared your feeling of repulsion?"

"It was impossible to do the one without the other," returned Enfield. "And by the way, what an ass you must have thought me, not to know that this was a back way to Dr. Jekyll's! It was partly your own fault that I found it out, even when I did."

"So you found it out, did you?" said Utterson. "But if that be so, we may step into the court and take a look at the windows. To tell you the truth, I am uneasy about poor Jekyll; and even outside, I feel as if the presence of a friend might do him good."

The court was very cool and a little damp, and full of premature twilight, although the sky, high up overhead, was still bright with sunset. The middle one of the three windows was half-way open; and sitting close beside it, taking the air with an infinite sadness of mien, like some disconsolate prisoner, Utterson saw Dr. Jekyll.

"What! Jekyll!" he cried. "I trust you are better."

"I am very low, Utterson," replied the doctor drearily, "very low. It will not last long, thank God."

"You stay too much indoors," said the lawyer. "You should be out, whipping up the circulation like Mr. Enfield and me. (This is my cousin—Mr. Enfield—Dr. Jekyll.) Come now; get your hat and take a quick turn with us."

"You are very good," sighed the other. "I should like to very much; but no, no, no, it is quite impossible; I dare not. But indeed, Utterson, I am very glad to see you; this is really a great pleasure; I would ask you and Mr. Enfield up, but the place is really not fit."

"Why, then," said the lawyer, good-naturedly, "the best thing we can do is to stay down here and speak with you from where we are."

"That is just what I was about to venture to propose," returned the doctor with a smile. But the words were hardly uttered, before the smile was struck out of his face and succeeded by an expression of such abject terror and despair, as froze the very blood of the two gentlemen below. They saw it but for a glimpse for the window was instantly thrust down; but that glimpse had been sufficient, and they turned and left the court without a word. In silence, too, they traversed the by-street; and it was not until they had come into a neighbouring thoroughfare, where even upon a Sunday there were still some stirrings of life, that Mr. Utterson at last turned and looked at his companion. They were both pale; and there was an answering horror in their eyes.

"God forgive us, God forgive us," said Mr. Utterson.

But Mr. Enfield only nodded his head very seriously, and walked on once more in silence.

THE LAST NIGHT

Mr. Utterson was sitting by his fireside one evening after dinner, when he was surprised to receive a visit from Poole.

"Bless me, Poole, what brings you here?" he cried; and then taking a second look at him, "What ails you?" he added; "is the doctor ill?"

"Mr. Utterson," said the man, "there is something wrong."

"Take a seat, and here is a glass of wine for you," said the lawyer. "Now, take your time, and tell me plainly what you want."

"You know the doctor's ways, sir," replied Poole, "and how he shuts himself up. Well, he's shut up again in the cabinet; and I don't like it, sir— I wish I may die if I like it. Mr. Utterson, sir, I'm afraid."

"Now, my good man," said the lawyer, "be explicit. What are you afraid of?"

"I've been afraid for about a week," returned Poole, doggedly disregarding the question, "and I can bear it no more."

The man's appearance amply bore out his words; his manner was altered for the worse; and except for the moment when he had first announced his terror, he had not once looked the lawyer in the face. Even now, he sat with the glass of wine untasted on his knee, and his eyes directed to a corner of the floor. "I can bear it no more," he repeated.

"Come," said the lawyer, "I see you have some good reason, Poole; I see there is something seriously amiss. Try to tell me what it is."

"I think there's been foul play," said Poole, hoarsely.

"Foul play!" cried the lawyer, a good deal frightened and rather inclined to be irritated in consequence. "What foul play! What does the man mean?"

"I daren't say, sir," was the answer; "but will you come along with me and see for yourself?"

Mr. Utterson's only answer was to rise and get his hat and greatcoat; but he observed with wonder the greatness of the relief that appeared upon the butler's face, and perhaps with no less, that the wine was still untasted when he set it down to follow.

It was a wild, cold, seasonable night of March, with a pale moon, lying on her back as though the wind had tilted her, and flying wrack of the most diaphanous and lawny texture. The wind made talking difficult, and flecked the blood into the face. It seemed to have swept the streets unusually bare of passengers, besides; for Mr. Utterson thought he had never seen that part of London so deserted. He could have wished it otherwise; never in his life had he been conscious of so sharp a wish to see and touch his fellow-creatures; for struggle as he might, there was borne in upon his mind a crushing antic- ipation of calamity. The square, when they got there, was full of wind and dust, and the thin trees in the garden were lashing themselves along the railing. Poole, who had kept all the way a pace or two ahead, now pulled up in the middle of the pavement, and in spite of the biting weather, took off his hat and mopped his brow with a red pocket-handkerchief. But for all the hurry of his coming, these were not the dews of exertion that he wiped away, but the moisture of some strangling anguish; for his face was white and his voice, when he spoke, harsh and broken.

"Well, sir," he said, "here we are, and God grant there be nothing wrong."

"Amen, Poole," said the lawyer.

Thereupon the servant knocked in a very guarded manner; the door was opened on the chain; and a voice asked from within, "Is that you, Poole?"

"It's all right," said Poole. "Open the door."

The hall, when they entered it, was brightly lighted up; the fire was built high; and about the hearth the whole of the servants, men and women, stood huddled together like a flock of sheep. At the sight of Mr. Utterson, the house- maid broke into hysterical whimpering; and the cook, crying out "Bless God! it's Mr. Utterson," ran forward as if to take him in her arms.

"What, what? Are you all here?" said the lawyer peevishly. "Very irregular, very unseemly; your master would be far from pleased."

"They're all afraid," said Poole.

Blank silence followed, no one protesting; only the maid lifted her voice and now wept loudly.

"Hold your tongue!" Poole said to her, with a ferocity of accent that testified to his own jangled nerves; and indeed, when the girl had so suddenly raised the note of her lamentation, they had all started and turned towards the inner door with faces of dreadful expectation. "And now," continued the butler, addressing the knife-boy, "reach me a candle, and we'll get this through hands at once." And then he begged Mr. Utterson to follow him, and led the way to the back garden.

"Now, sir," said he, "you come as gently as you can. I want you to hear, and I don't want you to be heard. And see here, sir, if by any chance he was to ask you in, don't go."

Mr. Utterson's nerves, at this unlooked-for termination, gave a jerk that nearly threw him from his balance; but he recollected his courage and followed the butler into the laboratory building through the surgical theatre, with its lumber of crates and bottles, to the foot of the stair. Here Poole motioned him to stand on one side and listen; while he himself, setting down the candle and making a great and obvious call on his resolution, mounted the steps and knocked with a somewhat uncertain hand on the red baize of the cabinet door.

"Mr. Utterson, sir, asking to see you," he called; and even as he did so, once more violently signed to the lawyer to give ear.

A voice answered from within: "Tell him I cannot see anyone," it said complainingly.

"Thank you, sir," said Poole, with a note of something like triumph in his voice; and taking up his candle, he led Mr. Utterson back across the yard and into the great kitchen, where the fire was out and the beetles were leaping on the floor.

"Sir," he said, looking Mr. Utterson in the eyes, "was that my master's voice?"

"It seems much changed," replied the lawyer, very pale, but giving look for look.

"Changed? Well, yes, I think so," said the butler. "Have I been twenty years in this man's house, to be deceived about his voice? No, sir; master's made away with; he was made away with eight days ago, when we heard him cry out upon the name of God; and *who's* in there instead of him, and *why* it stays there, is a thing that cries to Heaven, Mr. Utterson!"

"This is a very strange tale, Poole; this is rather a wild tale, my man," said Mr. Utterson, biting his finger. "Suppose it were as you suppose, supposing Dr. Jekyll to have been—well, murdered, what could induce the murderer to stay? That won't hold water; it doesn't commend itself to reason."

"Well, Mr. Utterson, you are a hard man to satisfy, but I'll do it yet," said Poole. "All this last week (you must know) him, or it, whatever it is that lives in that cabinet, has been crying night and day for some sort of medicine and cannot get it to his mind. It was sometimes his way—the master's, that is—to write his orders on a sheet of paper and throw it on the stair. We've had nothing else this week back; nothing but papers, and a closed door, and the very meals left there to be smuggled in when nobody was looking. Well, sir, every day, ay, and twice and thrice in the same day, there have been orders and complaints, and I have been sent flying to all the wholesale chemists in town. Every time I brought the stuff back, there would be another paper telling me to return it, because it was not pure, and another order to a different firm. This drug is wanted bitter bad, sir, whatever for."

"Have you any of these papers?" asked Mr. Utterson.

Poole felt in his pocket and handed out a crumpled note, which the lawyer, bending nearer to the candle, carefully examined. Its contents ran thus: "Dr. Jekyll presents his compliments to Messrs. Maw. He assures them that their last sample is impure and quite useless for his present purpose. In the year 18—, Dr. J. purchased a somewhat large quantity from Messrs. M. He now begs them to search with most sedulous care, and should any of the same quality be left, to forward it to him at once. Expense is no consideration. The importance of this to Dr. J. can hardly be exaggerated." So far the letter had run composedly enough, but here with a sudden splutter of the pen, the writer's emotion had broken loose. "For God's sake," he added, "find me some of the old."

"This is a strange note," said Mr. Utterson; and then sharply, "How do you come to have it open?"

"The man at Maw's was main angry, sir, and he threw it back to me like so much dirt," returned Poole.

"This is unquestionably the doctor's hand, do you know?" resumed the lawyer.

"I thought it looked like it," said the servant rather sulkily; and then, with another voice, "But what matters hand of write?" he said. "I've seen him!"

"Seen him?" repeated Mr. Utterson. "Well?"

"That's it!" said Poole. "It was this way. I came suddenly into the theatre from the garden. It seems he had slipped out to look for this drug or whatever it is; for the cabinet door was open, and there he was at the far end of the room digging among the crates. He looked up when I came in, gave a kind of cry, and whipped upstairs into the cabinet. It was but for one minute that I saw him, but the hair stood upon my head like quills. Sir, if that was my master, why had he a mask upon his face? If it was my master, why did he cry out like a rat, and run from me? I have served him long enough. And then . . ." The man paused and passed his hand over his face.

"These are all very strange circumstances," said Mr. Utterson, "but I think I begin to see daylight. Your master, Poole, is plainly seized with one of those maladies that both torture and deform the sufferer; hence, for aught I know, the alteration of his voice; hence the mask and the avoidance of his friends; hence his eagerness to find this drug, by means of which the poor soul retains some hope of ultimate recovery—God grant that he be not deceived! There is my explanation; it is sad enough, Poole, ay, and appalling to consider; but it is plain and natural, hangs well together, and delivers us from all exorbitant alarms."

"Sir," said the butler, turning to a sort of mottled pallor, "that thing was not my master, and there's the truth. My master"—here he looked round him and began to whisper—"is a tall, fine build of a man, and this was more of a dwarf." Utterson attempted to protest. "O, sir," cried Poole, "do you think I do not know my master after twenty years? Do you think I do not know where his head comes to in the cabinet door, where I saw him every morning of my life? No, sir, that thing in the mask was never Dr. Jekyll—God knows what it was, but it was never Dr. Jekyll; and it is the belief of my heart that there was murder done."

"Poole," replied the lawyer, "if you say that, it will become my duty to make certain. Much as I desire to spare your master's feelings, much as I am puzzled by this note which seems to prove him to be still alive, I shall consider it my duty to break in that door."

"Ah, Mr. Utterson, that's talking!" cried the butler.

"And now comes the second question," resumed Utterson: "Who is going to do it?"

"Why, you and me, sir," was the undaunted reply.

"That's very well said," returned the lawyer; "and whatever comes of it, I shall make it my business to see you are no loser."

"There is an axe in the theatre," continued Poole; "and you might take the kitchen poker for yourself."

The lawyer took that rude but weighty instrument into his hand, and balanced it. "Do you know, Poole," he said, looking up, "that you and I are about to place ourselves in a position of some peril?"

"You may say so, sir, indeed," returned the butler.

"It is well, then, that we should be frank," said the other. "We both think more than we have said; let us make a clean breast. This masked figure that you saw, did you recognise it?"

"Well, sir, it went so quick, and the creature was so doubled up, that I could hardly swear to that," was the answer. "But if you mean, was it Mr. Hyde?— why, yes, I think it was! You see, it was much of the same bigness; and it had the same quick, light way with it; and then who else could have got in by the laboratory door? You have not forgot, sir, that at the time of the murder he had still the key with him? But that's not all. I don't know, Mr. Utterson, if you ever met this Mr. Hyde?"

"Yes," said the lawyer, "I once spoke with him."

"Then you must know as well as the rest of us that there was something queer about that gentleman—something that gave a man a turn—I don't know rightly how to say it, sir, beyond this: that you felt in your marrow kind of cold and thin."

"I own I felt something of what you describe," said Mr. Utterson.

"Quite so, sir," returned Poole. "Well, when that masked thing like a monkey jumped from among the chemicals and whipped into the cabinet, it went down my spine like ice. O, I know it's not evidence, Mr. Utterson; I'm book-learned enough for that; but a man has his feelings, and I give you my bible-word it was Mr. Hyde!"

"Ay, ay," said the lawyer. "My fears incline to the same point. Evil, I fear, founded—evil was sure to come—of that connection. Ay truly, I believe you; I believe poor Harry is killed; and I believe his murderer (for what purpose, God alone can tell) is still lurking in his victim's room. Well, let our name be vengeance. Call Bradshaw."

The footman came at the summons, very white and nervous.

"Put yourself together, Bradshaw," said the lawyer. "This suspense, I know, is telling upon all of you; but it is now our intention to make an end of it. Poole, here, and I are going to force our way into the cabinet. If all is well, my shoulders are broad enough to bear the blame. Meanwhile, lest anything should really be amiss, or any malefactor seek to escape by the back, you and the boy must go round the corner with a pair of good sticks and take your post at the laboratory door. We give you ten minutes, to get to your stations."

As Bradshaw left, the lawyer looked at his watch. "And now, Poole, let us get to ours," he said; and taking the poker under his arm, led the way into the yard. The scud had banked over the moon, and it was now quite dark. The wind, which only broke in puffs and draughts into that deep well of building, tossed the light of the candle to and fro about their steps, until they came into the shelter of the theatre, where they sat down silently to wait. London hummed solemnly all around; but nearer at hand, the stillness was only broken by the sounds of a footfall moving to and fro along the cabinet floor.

"So it will walk all day, sir," whispered Poole; "ay, and the better part of the night. Only when a new sample comes from the chemist, there's a bit of a break. Ah, it's an ill conscience that's such an enemy to rest! Ah, sir, there's blood foully shed in every step of it! But hark again, a little closer—put your heart in your ears, Mr. Utterson, and tell me, is that the doctor's foot?"

The steps fell lightly and oddly, with a certain swing, for all they went so slowly; it was different indeed from the heavy creaking tread of Henry Jekyll. Utterson sighed. "Is there never anything else?" he asked.

Poole nodded. "Once," he said. "Once I heard it weeping!"

"Weeping? how that?" said the lawyer, conscious of a sudden chill of horror.

"Weeping like a woman or a lost soul," said the butler. "I came away with that upon my heart, that I could have wept too."

But now the ten minutes drew to an end. Poole disinterred the axe from under a stack of packing straw; the candle was set upon the nearest table to light them to the attack; and they drew near with bated breath to where that patient foot was still going up and down, up and down, in the quiet of the night. "Jekyll," cried Utterson, with a loud voice, "I demand to see you." He paused a moment, but there came no reply. "I give you fair warning, our suspicions are aroused, and I must and shall see you," he resumed; "if not by fair means, then by foul—if not of your consent, then by brute force!"

"Utterson," said the voice, "for God's sake, have mercy!"

"Ah, that's not Jekyll's voice—it's Hyde's!" cried Utterson. "Down with the door, Poole!"

Poole swung the axe over his shoulder; the blow shook the building, and the red baize door leaped against the lock and hinges. A dismal screech, as of mere animal terror, rang from the cabinet. Up went the axe again, and again the panels crashed and the frame bounded; four times the blow fell; but the wood was tough and the fittings were of excellent workmanship; and it was not until the fifth, that the lock burst and the wreck of the door fell inwards on the carpet.

The besiegers, appalled by their own riot and the stillness that had succeeded, stood back a little and peered in. There lay the cabinet before their eyes in the quiet lamplight, a good fire glowing and chattering on the hearth, the kettle singing its thin strain, a drawer or two open, papers neatly set forth on the business table, and nearer the fire, the things laid out for tea; the quietest room, you would have said, and, but for the glazed presses full of chemicals, the most commonplace that night in London.

Right in the midst there lay the body of a man sorely contorted and still twitching. They drew near on tiptoe, turned it on its back and beheld the face of Edward Hyde. He was dressed in clothes far too large for him, clothes of the doctor's bigness; the cords of his face still moved with a semblance of life, but life was quite gone: and by the crushed phial in the hand and the strong smell of kernels that hung upon the air, Utterson knew that he was looking on the body of a self-destroyer.

"We have come too late," he said sternly, "whether to save or punish. Hyde is gone to his account; and it only remains for us to find the body of your master."

The far greater proportion of the building was occupied by the theatre, which filled almost the whole ground storey and was lighted from above, and by the cabinet, which formed an upper storey at one end and looked upon the court. A corridor joined the theatre to the door on the by-street; and with this the cabinet communicated separately by a second flight of stairs. There were besides a few dark closets and a spacious cellar. All these they now thoroughly examined. Each closet needed but a glance, for all were empty, and all, by the dust that fell from their doors, had stood long unopened. The cellar, indeed, was filled with crazy lumber, mostly dating from the times of the surgeon who was Jekyll's predecessor; but even as they opened the door they were advertised of the uselessness of further search, by the fall of a perfect mat of cobweb which had for years sealed up the entrance. Nowhere was there any trace of Henry Jekyll, dead or alive.

Poole stamped on the flags of the corridor. "He must be buried here," he said, hearkening to the sound.

"Or he may have fled," said Utterson, and he turned to examine the door in the by-street. It was locked; and lying near by on the flags, they found the key, already stained with rust.

"This does not look like use," observed the lawyer.

"Use!" echoed Poole. "Do you not see, sir, it is broken? much as if a man had stamped on it."

"Ay," continued Utterson, "and the fractures, too, are rusty." The two men looked at each other with a scare. "This is beyond me, Poole," said the lawyer. "Let us go back to the cabinet."

They mounted the stair in silence, and still with an occasional awestruck glance at the dead body, proceeded more thoroughly to examine the contents of the cabinet. At one table, there were traces of chemical work, various measured heaps of some white salt being laid on glass saucers, as though for an experiment in which the unhappy man had been prevented.

"That is the same drug that I was always bringing him," said Poole; and even as he spoke, the kettle with a startling noise boiled over.

This brought them to the fireside, where the easychair was drawn cosily up, and the tea things stood ready to the sitter's elbow, the very sugar in the cup. There were several books on a shelf; one lay beside the tea things open, and Utterson was amazed to find it a copy of a pious work, for which Jekyll had several times expressed a great esteem, annotated, in his own hand, with startling blasphemies.

Next, in the course of their review of the chamber, the searchers came to the cheval-glass, into whose depths they looked with an involuntary horror. But it was so turned as to show them nothing but the rosy glow playing on the roof, the fire sparkling in a hundred repetitions along the glazed front of the presses, and their own pale and fearful countenances stooping to look in.

"This glass has seen some strange things, sir," whispered Poole.

"And surely none stranger than itself," echoed the lawyer in the same tones. "For what did Jekyll"—he caught himself up at the word with a start, and then conquering the weakness—"what could Jekyll want with it?" he said.

"You may say that!" said Poole.

Next they turned to the business table. On the desk, among the neat array of papers, a large envelope was uppermost, and bore, in the doctor's hand, the name of Mr. Utterson. The lawyer unsealed it, and several enclosures fell to the floor. The first was a will, drawn in the same eccentric terms as the one which he had returned six months before, to serve as a testament in case of death and as a deed of gift in case of disappearance; but in place of the name of Edward Hyde, the lawyer, with indescribable amazement, read the name of Gabriel John Utterson. He looked at Poole, and then back at the paper, and last of all at the dead malefactor stretched upon the carpet.

"My head goes round," he said. "He has been all these days in possession; he had no cause to like me; he must have raged to see himself displaced; and he has not destroyed this document."

He caught up the next paper; it was a brief note in the doctor's hand and dated at the top. "O Poole!" the lawyer cried, "he was alive and here this day. He cannot have been disposed of in so short a space; he must be still alive, he must have fled! And then, why fled? and how? and in that case, can we venture to declare this suicide? O, we must be careful. I foresee that we may yet involve your master in some dire catastrophe."

"Why don't you read it, sir?" asked Poole.

"Because I fear," replied the lawyer solemnly. God grant I have no cause for it!" And with that he brought the paper to his eyes and read as follows:

"My dear Utterson,—When this shall fall into your hands, I shall have disappeared, under what circumstances I have not the penetration to foresee, but my instinct and all the circumstances of my nameless situation tell me that the end is sure and must be early. Go then, and first read the narrative which Lanyon warned me he was to place in your hands; and if you care to hear more, turn to the confession of

"Your unworthy and unhappy friend,

"HENRY JEKYLL."

"There was a third enclosure?" asked Utterson.

"Here, sir," said Poole, and gave into his hands a considerable packet sealed in several places.

The lawyer put it in his pocket. "I would say nothing of this paper. If your master has fled or is dead, we may at least save his credit. It is now ten; I must go home and read these documents in quiet; but I shall be back before midnight, when we shall send for the police."

They went out, locking the door of the theatre behind them; and Utterson, once more leaving the servants gathered about the fire in the hall, trudged back to his office to read the two narratives in which this mystery was now to be explained.

DR. LANYON'S NARRATIVE

On the ninth of January, now four days ago, I received by the evening delivery a registered envelope, addressed in the hand of my colleague and old school companion, Henry Jekyll. I was a good deal surprised by this; for we were by no means in the habit of correspondence; I had seen the man, dined with him, indeed, the night before; and I could imagine nothing in our intercourse that should justify formality of registration. The contents increased my wonder; for this is how the letter ran:

"10th December, 18——.
"Dear Lanyon,—You are one of my oldest friends; and although we may have differed at times on scientific questions, I cannot remember, at least on my side, any break in our affection. There was never a day when, if you had said to me, 'Jekyll, my life, my honour, my reason, depend upon you,' I would not have sacrificed my left hand to help you. Lanyon, my life, my honour, my reason, are all at your mercy; if you fail me tonight, I am lost. You might suppose, after this preface, that I am going to ask you for something dishonourable to grant. Judge for yourself.

"I want you to postpone all other engagements for tonight—ay, even if you were summoned to the bedside of an emperor; to take a cab, unless your carriage should be actually at the door; and with this letter in your hand for consultation, to drive straight to my house.

Poole, my butler, has his orders; you will find him waiting your arrival with a locksmith. The door of my cabinet is then to be forced: and you are to go in alone; to open the glazed press (letter E) on the left hand, breaking the lock if it be shut; and to draw out, *with all its contents as they stand*, the fourth drawer from the top or (which is the same thing) the third from the bottom. In my extreme distress of mind, I have a morbid fear of misdirecting you; but even if I am in error, you may know the right drawer by its contents: some powders, a phial and a paper book. This drawer I beg of you to carry back with you to Cavendish Square exactly as it stands.

"That is the first part of the service: now for the second. You should be back, if you set out at once on the receipt of this, long before midnight; but I will leave you that amount of margin, not only in the fear of one of those obstacles that can neither be prevented nor foreseen, but because an hour when your servants are in bed is to be preferred for what will then remain to do. At midnight, then, I have to ask you to be alone in your consulting room, to admit with your own hand into the house a man who will present himself in my name, and to place in his hands the drawer that you will have brought with you from my cabinet. Then you will have played your part and earned my gratitude completely. Five minutes afterwards, if you insist upon an explanation, you will have understood that these arrangements are of capital importance; and that by the neglect of one of them, fantastic as they must appear, you might have charged your conscience with my death or the shipwreck of my reason.

"Confident as I am that you will not trifle with this appeal, my heart sinks and my hand trembles at the bare thought of such a possibility. Think of me at this hour, in a strange place, labouring under a blackness of distress that no fancy can exaggerate, and yet well aware that, if you will but punctually serve me, my troubles will roll away like a story that is told. Serve me, my dear Lanyon, and save

"Your friend,
"H. J.

"P.S.—I had already sealed this up when a fresh terror struck upon my soul. It is possible that the post-office may fail me, and this letter not come into your hands until tomorrow morning. In that case, dear Lanyon, do my errand when it shall be most convenient for you in the course of the day; and once more expect my messenger at midnight. It may then already be too late; and if that night passes without event, you will know that you have seen the last of Henry Jekyll."

Upon the reading of this letter, I made sure my colleague was insane; but till that was proved beyond the possibility of doubt, I felt bound to do as he requested. The less I understood of this farrago, the less I was in a position to judge of its importance; and an appeal so worded could not be set aside without a grave responsibility. I rose accordingly from table, got into a hansom,[1] and drove straight to Jekyll's house. The butler was awaiting my arrival; he had received by the same post as mine a registered letter of instruction, and had sent at once for a locksmith and a carpenter. The tradesmen came while we were yet speaking; and we moved in a body to old Dr. Denman's surgical theatre, from which (as you are doubtless aware) Jekyll's private cabinet is most conveniently entered. The door was very strong, the lock excellent; the carpenter avowed he would have great trouble and have to do much damage, if force were to be used; and the locksmith was near despair. But this last was a handy fellow, and after two hours' work, the door stood open. The press marked E was unlocked; and I took out the drawer, had it filled up with straw and tied in a sheet, and returned with it to Cavendish Square.

Here I proceeded to examine its contents. The powders were neatly enough made up, but not with the nicety of the dispensing chemist; so that it was plain they were of Jekyll's private manufacture: and when I opened one of the wrappers I found what seemed to me a simple crystalline salt of a white colour. The phial, to which I next turned my attention, might have been about half full of a blood-red liquor, which was highly pungent to the sense of smell and seemed to me to contain phosphorus and some volatile ether. At the other ingredients I could make no guess. The book was an ordinary version book and contained little but a series of dates. These covered a period of many years, but I observed that the entries ceased nearly a year ago and quite abruptly. Here and there a brief remark was appended to a date, usually no more than a single word: "double" occurring perhaps six times in a total of several hundred entries; and once very early in the list and followed by several marks of exclamation, "total failure!!!" All this, though it whetted my curiosity, told me little that was definite. Here were a phial of some salt, and the record of a series of experiments that had led (like too many of Jekyll's investigations) to no end of practical usefulness. How could the presence of these articles in my house affect either the honour, the sanity, or the life of my flighty colleague? If his messenger could go to one place, why could he not go to another? And even granting some impediment, why was this gentleman to be received by me in secret? The more I reflected the more convinced I grew that I was dealing with a case of cerebral disease; and though I dismissed my servants to bed, I loaded an old revolver, that I might be found in some posture of self-defence.

Twelve o'clock had scarce rung out over London, ere the knocker sounded very gently on the door. I went myself at the summons, and found a small man crouching against the pillars of the portico.

"Are you come from Dr. Jekyll?" I asked.

He told me "yes" by a constrained gesture; and when I had bidden him enter, he did not obey me without a searching backward glance into the darkness of the square. There was a policeman not far off, advancing with his bull's eye[2] open; and at the sight, I thought my visitor started and made greater haste.

These particulars struck me, I confess, disagreeably; and as I followed him into the bright light of the consulting room, I kept my hand ready on my weapon. Here, at last, I had a chance of clearly seeing him. I had never set eyes on him before, so much was certain. He was small, as I have said; I was struck besides with the shocking expression of his face, with his remarkable combination of great muscular activity and great apparent debility of constitution, and—last but not least—with the odd, subjective disturbance caused by his neighbourhood. This bore some resemblance to incipient rigour, and was accompanied by a marked sinking of the pulse. At the time, I set it down to some idiosyncratic, personal distaste, and merely wondered at the acuteness of the symptoms; but I have since had reason to believe the cause to lie much deeper in the nature of man, and to turn on some nobler hinge than the principle of hatred.

This person (who had thus, from the first moment of his entrance, struck in me what I can only describe as a disgustful curiosity) was dressed in a fashion that would have made an ordinary person laughable; his clothes, that is to say, although they were of rich and sober fabric, were enormously too large for him in every measurement—the trousers hanging on his legs and rolled up to keep them from the ground, the waist of the coat below his haunches, and the collar sprawling wide upon his shoulders. Strange to relate, this ludicrous accoutrement was far from moving me to laughter. Rather, as there was something abnormal and misbegotten in the very essence of the creature that now faced me—something seizing, surprising and revolting—this fresh disparity seemed but to fit in with and to reinforce it; so that to my interest in the man's nature and character, there was added a curiosity as to his origin, his life, his fortune and status in the world.

These observations, though they have taken so great a space to be set down in, were yet the work of a few seconds. My visitor was, indeed, on fire with sombre excitement.

"Have you got it?" he cried. "Have you got it?" And so lively was his impatience that he even laid his hand upon my arm and sought to shake me.

I put him back, conscious at his touch of a certain icy pang along my blood. "Come, sir," said I. "You forget that I have not yet the pleasure of your acquaintance. Be seated, if you please." And I showed him an example, and sat down myself in my customary seat and with as fair an imitation of my ordinary manner to a patient, as the lateness of the hour, the nature of my preoccupations, and the horror I had of my visitor, would suffer me to muster.

"I beg your pardon, Dr. Lanyon," he replied civilly enough. "What you say is very well founded; and my impatience has shown its heels to my politeness. I come here at the instance of your colleague, Dr. Henry Jekyll, on a piece of business of some moment; and I understood . . ." He paused and put his hand to his throat, and I could see, in spite of his collected manner, that he was wrestling against the approaches of the hysteria—"I understood, a drawer . . ."

But here I took pity on my visitor's suspense, and some perhaps on my own growing curiosity.

"There it is, sir," said I, pointing to the drawer, where it lay on the floor behind a table and still covered with the sheet.

He sprang to it, and then paused, and laid his hand upon his heart: I could hear his teeth grate with the convulsive action of his jaws; and his face was so ghastly to see that I grew alarmed both for his life and reason.

"Compose yourself," said I.

He turned a dreadful smile to me, and as if with the decision of despair, plucked away the sheet. At sight of the contents, he uttered one loud sob of such immense relief that I sat petrified. And the next moment, in a voice that was already fairly well under control, "Have you a graduated glass?"[1] he asked.

I rose from my place with something of an effort and gave him what he asked.

He thanked me with a smiling nod, measured out a few minims of the red tincture and added one of the powders. The mixture, which was at first of a reddish hue, began, in proportion as the crystals melted, to brighten in colour, to effervesce audibly, and to throw off small fumes of vapour. Suddenly and at the same moment, the ebullition ceased and the compound changed to a dark purple, which faded again more slowly to a watery green. My visitor, who had watched these metamorphoses with a keen eye, smiled, set down the glass upon the table, and then turned and looked upon me with an air of scrutiny.

"And now," said he, "to settle what remains. Will you be wise? will you be guided? will you suffer me to take this glass in my hand and to go forth from your house without further parley? or has the greed of curiosity too much command of you? Think before you answer, for it shall be done as you decide. As you decide, you shall be left as you were before, and neither richer nor wiser, unless the sense of service rendered to a man in mortal distress may be counted as a kind of riches of the soul. Or, if you shall so prefer to choose, a new province of knowledge and new avenues to fame and power shall be laid open to you, here, in this room, upon the instant; and your sight shall be blasted by a prodigy to stagger the unbelief of Satan."

"Sir," said I, affecting a coolness that I was far from truly possessing, "you speak enigmas, and you will perhaps not wonder that I hear you with no very strong impression of belief. But I have gone too far in the way of inexplicable services to pause before I see the end."

"It is well," replied my visitor. "Lanyon, you remember your vows: what follows is under the seal of our profession. And now, you who have so long been bound to the most narrow and material views, you who have denied the virtue of transcendental medicine, you who have derided your superiors—behold!"

He put the glass to his lips and drank at one gulp. A cry followed; he reeled, staggered, clutched at the table and held on, staring with injected eyes, gasping with open mouth; and as I looked there came, I thought, a change— he seemed to swell—his face became suddenly black and the features seemed to melt and alter—and the next moment, I had sprung to my feet and leaped back against the wall, my arm raised to shield me from that prodigy, my mind submerged in terror.

"O God!" I screamed, and "O God!" again and again; for there before my eyes—pale and shaken, and half fainting, and groping before him with his hands, like a man restored from death—there stood Henry Jekyll!

What he told me in the next hour, I cannot bring my mind to set on paper. I saw what I saw, I heard what I heard, and my soul sickened at it; and yet now when that sight has faded from my eyes, I ask myself if I believe it, and I cannot answer. My life is shaken to its roots; sleep has left me; the deadliest terror sits by me at all hours of the day and night; and I feel that my days are numbered, and that I must die; and yet I shall die incredulous. As for the moral turpitude that man unveiled to me, even with tears of penitence, I cannot, even in memory, dwell on it without a start of horror. I will say but one thing, Utterson, and that (if you can bring your mind to credit it) will be more than enough. The creature who crept into my house that night was, on Jekyll's own confession, known by the name of Hyde and hunted for in every corner of the land as the murderer of Carew.

Hastie Lanyon

HENRY JEKYLL'S FULL STATEMENT OF THE CASE

I was born in the year 18— to a large fortune, endowed besides with excellent parts, inclined by nature to industry, fond of the respect of the wise and good among my fellowmen, and thus, as might have been supposed, with every guarantee of an honourable and distinguished future. And indeed the worst of my faults was a certain impatient gaiety of disposition, such as has made the happiness of many, but such as I found it hard to reconcile with my imperious desire to carry my head high, and wear a more than commonly grave countenance before the public. Hence it came about that I concealed my pleasures; and that when I reached years of reflection, and began to look round me and take stock of my progress and position in the world, I stood already committed to a profound duplicity of life. Many a man would have even blazoned such irregularities as I was guilty of; but from the high views that I had set before me, I regarded and hid them with an almost morbid sense of shame. It was thus rather the exacting nature of my aspirations than any particular degradation in my faults, that made me what I was, and, with even a deeper trench than in the majority of men, severed in me those provinces of good and ill which divide and compound man's dual nature. In this case, I was driven to reflect deeply and inveterately on that hard law of life, which lies at the root of religion and is one of the most plentiful springs of distress. Though so profound a double-dealer, I was in no sense a hypocrite; both sides of me were in dead earnest; I was no more myself when I laid aside restraint and plunged in shame, than when I laboured, in the eye of day, at the furtherance of knowledge or the relief of sorrow and suffering. And it chanced that the direction of my scientific studies, which led wholly towards the mystic and the transcendental, reacted and shed a strong light on this consciousness of the perennial war among my members. With every day, and from both sides of my intelligence, the moral and the intellectual, I thus drew steadily nearer to that truth, by whose partial discovery I have been doomed to such a dreadful shipwreck: that man is not truly one, but truly two. I say two, because the state of my own knowledge does not pass beyond that point. Others will follow, others will outstrip me on the same lines; and I hazard the guess that man will be ultimately known for a mere polity of multifarious, incongruous and independent denizens. I, for my part, from the nature of my life, advanced infallibly in one direction and in one direction only. It was on the moral side, and in my own person, that I learned to recognise the thorough and primitive duality of man; I saw that, of the two natures that contended in the field of my consciousness, even if I could rightly be said to be either, it was only because I was radically both; and from an early date, even before the course of my scientific discoveries had begun to suggest the most naked possibility of such a miracle, I had learned to dwell with pleasure, as a beloved daydream, on the thought of the separation of these elements. If each, I told myself, could be housed in separate identities, life would be relieved of all that was unbearable; the unjust might go his way, delivered from the aspirations and remorse of his more upright twin; and the just could walk steadfastly and securely on his upward path, doing the good things in which he found his pleasure, and no longer exposed to disgrace and penitence by the hands of this extraneous evil. It was the curse of mankind that these incongruous faggots were thus bound together—that in the agonised womb of consciousness, these polar twins should be continuously struggling. How, then, were they dissociated?

I was so far in my reflections when, as I have said, a side light began to shine upon the subject from the laboratory table. I began to perceive more deeply than it has ever yet been stated, the trembling immateriality, the mistlike transience, of this seemingly so solid body in which we walk attired. Certain agents I found to have the power to shake and pluck back that fleshly vestment, even as a wind might toss the curtains of a pavilion. For two good reasons, I will not enter deeply into this scientific branch of my confession. First, because I have been made to learn that the doom and burthen of our life is bound for ever on man's shoulders, and when the attempt is made to cast it off, it but returns upon us with more unfamiliar and more awful pressure. Second, because, as my narrative will make, alas! too evident, my discoveries were incomplete. Enough then, that I not only recognised my natural body from the mere aura and effulgence of certain of the powers that made up my spirit, but managed to compound a drug by which these powers should be dethroned from their supremacy, and a second form and countenance substituted, none the less natural to me because they were the expression, and bore the stamp of lower elements in my soul.

I hesitated long before I put this theory to the test of practice. I knew well that I risked death; for any drug that so potently controlled and shook the very fortress of identity, might, by the least scruple of an overdose or at the least inopportunity in the moment of exhibition, utterly blot out that immaterial tabernacle which I looked to it to change. But the temptation of a discovery so singular and profound at last overcame the suggestions of alarm. I had long since prepared my tincture; I purchased at once, from a firm of wholesale chemists, a large quantity of a particular salt which I knew, from my experiments, to be the last ingredient required; and late one accursed night, I compounded the elements, watched them boil and smoke together in the glass, and when the ebullition had subsided, with a strong glow of courage, drank off the potion.

The most racking pangs succeeded: a grinding in the bones, deadly nausea, and a horror of the spirit that cannot be exceeded at the hour of birth or death. Then these agonies began swiftly to subside, and I came to myself as if out of a great sickness. There was something strange in my sensations, something indescribably new and, from its very novelty, incredibly sweet. I felt younger, lighter, happier in body; within I was conscious of a heady recklessness, a current of disordered sensual images running like a millrace in my fancy, a solution of the bonds of obligation, an unknown but not an innocent freedom of the soul. I knew myself, at the first breath of this new life, to be more wicked, tenfold more wicked, sold a slave to my original evil; and the thought, in that moment, braced and delighted me like wine. I stretched out my hands, exulting in the freshness of these sensations; and in the act, I was suddenly aware that I had lost in stature.

There was no mirror, at that date, in my room; that which stands beside me as I write, was brought there later on and for the very purpose of these transformations. The night, however, was far gone into the morning—the morning, black as it was, was nearly ripe for the conception of the day—the inmates of my house were locked in the most rigorous hours of slumber; and I determined, flushed as I was with hope and triumph, to venture in my new shape as far as to my bedroom. I crossed the yard, wherein the constellations looked down upon me, I could have thought, with wonder, the first creature of that sort that their unsleeping vigilance had yet disclosed to them; I stole through the corridors, a stranger in my own house; and coming to my room, I saw for the first time the appearance of Edward Hyde.

I must here speak by theory alone, saying not that which I know, but that which I suppose to be most probable. The evil side of my nature, to which I had now transferred the stamping efficacy, was less robust and less developed than the good which I had just deposed. Again, in the course of my life, which had been, after all, nine tenths a life of effort, virtue and control, it had been much less exercised and much less exhausted. And hence, as I think, it came about that Edward Hyde was so much smaller, slighter and younger than Henry Jekyll. Even as good shone upon the countenance of the one, evil was written broadly and plainly on the face of the other. Evil besides (which I must still believe to be the lethal side of man) had left on that body an imprint of deformity and decay. And yet when I looked upon that ugly idol in the glass, I was conscious of no repugnance, rather of a leap of welcome. This, too, was myself. It seemed natural and human. In my eyes it bore a livelier image of the spirit, it seemed more express and single, than the imperfect and divided countenance I had been hitherto accustomed to call mine. And in so far I was doubtless right. I have observed that when I wore the semblance of Edward Hyde, none could come near to me at first without a visible misgiving of the flesh. This, as I take it, was because all human beings, as we meet them, are commingled out of good and evil: and Edward Hyde, alone in the ranks of mankind, was pure evil.

I lingered but a moment at the mirror: the second and conclusive experiment had yet to be attempted; it yet remained to be seen if I had lost my identity beyond redemption and must flee before daylight from a house that was no longer mine; and hurrying back to my cabinet, I once more prepared and drank the cup, once more suffered the pangs of dissolution, and came to myself once more with the character, the stature and the face of Henry Jekyll.

That night I had come to the fatal cross-roads. Had I approached my discovery in a more noble spirit, had I risked the experiment while under the empire of generous or pious aspirations, all must have been otherwise, and from these agonies of death and birth, I had come forth an angel instead of a fiend. The drug had no discriminating action; it was neither diabolical nor divine; it but shook the doors of the prison-house of my disposition; and like the captives of Philippi, that which stood within ran forth.[2] At that time my virtue slumbered; my evil, kept awake by ambition, was alert and swift to seize the occasion; and the thing that was projected was Edward Hyde. Hence, although I had now two characters as well as two appearances, one was wholly evil, and the other was still the old Henry Jekyll, that incongruous compound of whose reformation and improvement I had already learned to despair. The movement was thus wholly toward the worse.

Even at that time, I had not conquered my aversions to the dryness of a life of study. I would still be merrily disposed at times; and as my pleasures were (to say the least) undignified, and I was not only well known and highly considered, but growing towards the elderly man, this incoherency of my life was daily growing more unwelcome. It was on this side that my new power tempted me until I fell in slavery. I had but to drink the cup, to doff at once the body of the noted professor, and to assume, like a thick cloak, that of Edward Hyde. I smiled at the notion; it seemed to me at the time to be humourous; and I made my preparations with the most studious care. I took and furnished that house in Soho, to which Hyde was tracked by the police; and engaged as a housekeeper a creature whom I knew well to be silent and unscrupulous. On the other side, I announced to my servants that a Mr. Hyde (whom I described) was to have full liberty and power about my house in the square; and to parry mishaps, I even called and made myself a familiar object, in my second character. I next drew up that will to which you so much objected; so that if anything befell me in the person of Dr. Jekyll, I could enter on that of Edward Hyde without pecuniary loss. And thus fortified, as I supposed, on every side, I began to profit by the strange immunities of my position.

Men have before hired bravos to transact their crimes, while their own person and reputation sat under shelter. I was the first that ever did so for his pleasures. I was the first that could plod in the public eye with a load of genial respectability, and in a moment, like a schoolboy, strip off these lendings and spring headlong into the sea of liberty. But for me, in my impenetrable mantle, the safety was complete. Think of it—I did not even exist! Let me but escape into my laboratory door, give me but a second or two to mix and swallow the draught that I had always standing ready; and whatever he had done, Edward Hyde would pass away like the stain of breath upon a mirror; and there in his stead, quietly at home, trimming the midnight lamp in his study, a man who could afford to laugh at suspicion, would be Henry Jekyll.

The pleasures which I made haste to seek in my disguise were, as I have said, undignified; I would scarce use a harder term. But in the hands of Edward Hyde, they soon began to turn toward the monstrous. When I would come back from these excursions, I was often plunged into a kind of wonder at my vicarious depravity. This familiar that I called out of my own soul, and sent forth alone to do his good pleasure, was a being inherently malign and villainous; his every act and thought centered on self; drinking pleasure with bestial avidity from any degree of torture to another; relentless like a man of stone. Henry Jekyll stood at times aghast before the acts of Edward Hyde; but the situation was apart from ordinary laws, and insidiously relaxed the grasp of conscience. It was Hyde, after all, and Hyde alone, that was guilty. Jekyll was no worse; he woke again to his good qualities seemingly unimpaired; he would even make haste, where it was possible, to undo the evil done by Hyde. And thus his conscience slumbered.

Into the details of the infamy at which I thus connived (for even now I can scarce grant that I committed it) I have no design of entering; I mean but to point out the warnings and the successive steps with which my chastisement approached. I met with one accident which, as it brought on no consequence, I shall no more than mention. An act of cruelty to a child aroused against me the anger of a passer-by, whom I recognised the other day in the person of your kinsman; the doctor and the child's family joined him; there were moments when I feared for my life; and at last, in order to pacify their too just resentment, Edward Hyde had to bring them to the door, and pay them in a cheque drawn in the name of Henry Jekyll. But this danger was easily eliminated from the future, by opening an account at another bank in the name of Edward Hyde himself; and when, by sloping my own hand backward, I had supplied my double with a signature, I thought I sat beyond the reach of fate.

Some two months before the murder of Sir Danvers, I had been out for one of my adventures, had returned at a late hour, and woke the next day in bed with somewhat odd sensations. It was in vain I looked about me; in vain I saw the decent furniture and tall proportions of my room in the square; in vain that I recognised the pattern of the bed curtains and the design of the mahogany frame; something still kept insisting that I was not where I was, that I had not wakened where I seemed to be, but in the little room in Soho where I was accustomed to sleep in the body of Edward Hyde. I smiled to myself, and, in my psychological way, began lazily to inquire into the elements of this illusion, occasionally, even as I did so, dropping back into a comfortable morning doze. I was still so engaged when, in one of my more wakeful moments, my eyes fell upon my hand. Now the hand of Henry Jekyll (as you have often remarked) was professional in shape and size: it was large, firm, white and comely. But the hand which I now saw, clearly enough, in the yellow light of a mid-London morning, lying half shut on the bedclothes, was lean, corded, knuckly, of a dusky pallor and thickly shaded with a swart growth of hair. It was the hand of Edward Hyde.

I must have stared upon it for near half a minute, sunk as I was in the mere stupidity of wonder, before terror woke up in my breast as sudden and startling as the crash of cymbals; and bounding from my bed, I rushed to the mirror. At the sight that met my eyes, my blood was changed into something exquisitely thin and icy. Yes, I had gone to bed Henry Jekyll, I had awakened Edward Hyde. How was this to be explained? I asked myself; and then, with another bound of terror—how was it to be remedied? It was well on in the morning; the servants were up; all my drugs were in the cabinet—a long journey down two pairs of stairs, through the back passage, across the open court and through the anatomical theatre, from where I was then standing horror-struck. It might indeed be possible to cover my face; but of what use was that, when I was unable to conceal the alteration in my stature? And then with an overpowering sweetness of relief, it came back upon my mind that the servants were already used to the coming and going of my second self. I had soon dressed, as well as I was able, in clothes of my own size: had soon passed through the house, where Bradshaw stared and drew back at seeing Mr. Hyde at such an hour and in such a strange array; and ten minutes later, Dr. Jekyll had returned to his own shape and was sitting down, with a darkened brow, to make a feint of breakfasting.

Small indeed was my appetite. This inexplicable incident, this reversal of my previous experience, seemed, like the Babylonian finger on the wall,[3] to be spelling out the letters of my judgment; and I began to reflect more seriously than ever before on the issues and possibilities of my double existence. That part of me which I had the power of projecting, had lately been much exercised and nourished; it had seemed to me of late as though the body of Edward Hyde had grown in stature, as though (when I wore that form) I were conscious of a more generous tide of blood; and I began to spy a danger that, if this were much prolonged, the balance of my nature might be permanently overthrown, the power of voluntary change be forfeited, and the character of Edward Hyde become irrevocably mine. The power of the drug had not been always equally displayed. Once, very early in my career, it had totally failed me; since then I had been obliged on more than one occasion to double, and once, with infinite risk of death, to treble the amount; and these rare uncertainties had cast hitherto the sole shadow on my contentment. Now, however, and in the light of that morning's accident, I was led to remark that whereas, in the beginning, the difficulty had been to throw off the body of Jekyll, it had of late gradually but decidedly transferred itself to the other side. All things therefore seemed to point to this; that I was slowly losing hold of my original and better self, and becoming slowly incorporated with my second and worse.

Between these two, I now felt I had to choose. My two natures had memory in common, but all other faculties were most unequally shared between them. Jekyll (who was composite) now with the most sensitive apprehensions, now with a greedy gusto, projected and shared in the pleasures and adventures of Hyde; but Hyde was indifferent to Jekyll, or but remembered him as the mountain bandit remembers the cavern in which he conceals himself from pursuit. Jekyll had more than a father's interest; Hyde had more than a son's indifference. To cast in my lot with Jekyll, was to die to those appetites which I had long secretly indulged and had of late begun to pamper. To cast it in with Hyde, was to die to a thousand interests and aspirations, and to become, at a blow and forever, despised and friendless. The bargain might appear unequal; but there was still another consideration in the scales; for while Jekyll would suffer smartingly in the fires of abstinence, Hyde would be not even conscious of all that he had lost. Strange as my circumstances were, the terms of this debate are as old and commonplace as man; much the same inducements and alarms cast the die for any tempted and trembling sinner; and it fell out with me, as it falls with so vast a majority of my fellows, that I chose the better part and was found wanting in the strength to keep to it.

Yes, I preferred the elderly and discontented doctor, surrounded by friends and cherishing honest hopes; and bade a resolute farewell to the liberty, the comparative youth, the light step, leaping impulses and secret pleasures, that I had enjoyed in the disguise of Hyde. I made this choice perhaps with some unconscious reservation, for I neither gave up the house in Soho, nor destroyed the clothes of Edward Hyde, which still lay ready in my cabinet. For two months, however, I was true to my determination; for two months, I led a life of such severity as I had never before attained to, and enjoyed the compensations of an approving conscience. But time began at last to obliterate the freshness of my alarm; the praises of conscience began to grow into a thing of course; I began to be tortured with throes and longings, as of Hyde struggling after freedom; and at last, in an hour of moral weakness, I once again compounded and swallowed the transforming draught.

I do not suppose that, when a drunkard reasons with himself upon his vice, he is once out of five hundred times affected by the dangers that he runs through his brutish, physical insensibility; neither had I, long as I had considered my position, made enough allowance for the complete moral insensibility and insensate readiness to evil, which were the leading characters of Edward Hyde. Yet it was by these that I was punished. My devil had been long caged, he came out roaring. I was conscious, even when I took the draught, of a more unbridled, a more furious propensity to ill. It must have been this, I suppose, that stirred in my soul that tempest of impatience with which I listened to the civilities of my unhappy victim; I declare, at last, before God, no man morally sane could have been guilty of that crime upon so pitiful a provocation; and that I struck in no more reasonable spirit than that in which a sick child may break a plaything. But I had voluntarily stripped myself of all those balancing instincts by which even the worst of us continues to walk with some degree of steadiness among temptations; and in my case, to be tempted, however slightly, was to fall.

Instantly the spirit of hell awoke in me and raged. With a transport of glee, I mauled the unresisting body, tasting delight from every blow; and it was not till weariness had begun to succeed, that I was suddenly, in the top fit of my delirium, struck through the heart by a cold thrill of terror. A mist dispersed; I saw my life to be forfeit; and fled from the scene of these excesses, at once glorying and trembling, my lust of evil gratified and stimulated, my love of life screwed to the topmost peg. I ran to the house in Soho, and (to make assurance doubly sure) destroyed my papers; thence I set out through the lamplit streets, in the same divided ecstasy of mind, gloating on my crime, light-headedly devising others in the future, and yet still hastening and still hearkening in my wake for the steps of the avenger. Hyde had a song upon his lips as he compounded the draught, and as he drank it, pledged the dead man. The pangs of transformation had not done tearing him, before Henry Jekyll, with streaming tears of gratitude and remorse, had fallen upon his knees and lifted his clasped hands to God. The veil of self-indulgence was rent from head to foot. I saw my life as a whole: I followed it up from the days of childhood, when I had walked with my father's hand, and through the self-denying toils of my professional life, to arrive again and again, with the same sense of unreality, at the damned horrors of the evening. I could have screamed aloud; I sought with tears and prayers to smother down the crowd of hideous images and sounds with which my memory swarmed against me; and still, between the petitions, the ugly face of my iniquity stared into my soul. As the acuteness of this remorse began to die away, it was succeeded by a sense of joy. The problem of my conduct was solved. Hyde was thenceforth impossible; whether I would or not, I was now confined to the better part of my existence; and O, how I rejoiced to think of it! with what willing humility I embraced anew the restrictions of natural life! with what sincere renunciation I locked the door by which I had so often gone and come, and ground the key under my heel!

The next day, came the news that the murder had been overlooked, that the guilt of Hyde was patent to the world, and that the victim was a man high in public estimation. It was not only a crime, it had been a tragic folly. I think I was glad to know it; I think I was glad to have my better impulses thus buttressed and guarded by the terrors of the scaffold. Jekyll was now my city of refuge; let but Hyde peep out an instant, and the hands of all men would be raised to take and slay him.

I resolved in my future conduct to redeem the past; and I can say with honesty that my resolve was fruitful of some good. You know yourself how earnestly, in the last months of the last year, I laboured to relieve suffering; you know that much was done for others, and that the days passed quietly, almost happily for myself. Nor can I truly say that I wearied of this beneficent and innocent life; I think instead that I daily enjoyed it more completely; but I was still cursed with my duality of purpose; and as the first edge of my penitence wore off, the lower side of me, so long indulged, so recently chained down, began to growl for license. Not that I dreamed of resuscitating Hyde; the bare idea of that would startle me to frenzy: no, it was in my own person that I was once more tempted to trifle with my conscience; and it was as an ordinary secret sinner that I at last fell before the assaults of temptation.

There comes an end to all things; the most capacious measure is filled at last; and this brief condescension to my evil finally destroyed the balance of my soul. And yet I was not alarmed; the fall seemed natural, like a return to the old days before I had made my discovery. It was a fine, clear, January day, wet under foot where the frost had melted, but cloudless overhead; and the Regent's Park was full of winter chirrupings and sweet with spring odours. I sat in the sun on a bench; the animal within me licking the chops of memory; the spiritual side a little drowsed, promising subsequent penitence, but not yet moved to begin. After all, I reflected, I was like my neighbours; and then I smiled, comparing myself with other men, comparing my active goodwill with the lazy cruelty of their neglect. And at the very moment of that vainglorious thought, a qualm came over me, a horrid nausea and the most deadly shuddering. These passed away, and left me faint; and then as in its turn faintness subsided, I began to be aware of a change in the temper of my thoughts, a greater boldness, a contempt of danger, a solution of the bonds of obligation. I looked down; my clothes hung formlessly on my shrunken limbs; the hand that lay on my knee was corded and hairy. I was once more Edward Hyde. A moment before I had been safe of all men's respect, wealthy, beloved—the cloth laying for me in the dining-room at home; and now I was the common quarry of mankind, hunted, houseless, a known murderer, thrall to the gallows.

My reason wavered, but it did not fail me utterly. I have more than once observed that, in my second character, my faculties seemed sharpened to a point and my spirits more tensely elastic; thus it came about that, where Jekyll perhaps might have succumbed, Hyde rose to the importance of the moment.

My drugs were in one of the presses of my cabinet; how was I to reach them? That was the problem that (crushing my temples in my hands) I set myself to solve. The laboratory door I had closed. If I sought to enter by the house, my own servants would consign me to the gallows. I saw I must employ another hand, and thought of Lanyon. How was he to be reached? how persuaded? Supposing that I escaped capture in the streets, how was I to make my way into his presence? and how should I, an unknown and displeasing visitor, prevail on the famous physician to rifle the study of his colleague, Dr. Jekyll? Then I remembered that of my original character, one part remained to me: I could write my own hand; and once I had conceived that kindling spark, the way that I must follow became lighted up from end to end.

Thereupon, I arranged my clothes as best I could, and summoning a passing hansom, drove to an hotel in Portland Street, the name of which I chanced to remember. At my appearance (which was indeed comical enough, however tragic a fate these garments covered) the driver could not conceal his mirth. I gnashed my teeth upon him with a gust of devilish fury; and the smile withered from his face—happily for him—yet more happily for myself, for in another instant I had certainly dragged him from his perch. At the inn, as I entered, I looked about me with so black a countenance as made the attendants tremble; not a look did they exchange in my presence; but obsequiously took my orders, led me to a private room, and brought me wherewithal to write. Hyde in danger of his life was a creature new to me; shaken with inordinate anger, strung to the pitch of murder, lusting to inflict pain. Yet the creature was astute; mastered his fury with a great effort of the will; composed his two important letters, one to Lanyon and one to Poole; and that he might receive actual evidence of their being posted, sent them out with directions that they should be registered. Thenceforward, he sat all day over the fire in the private room, gnawing his nails; there he dined, sitting alone with his fears, the waiter visibly quailing before his eye; and thence, when the night was fully come, he set forth in the corner of a closed cab, and was driven to and fro about the streets of the city. He, I say—I cannot say, I. That child of Hell had nothing human; nothing lived in him but fear and hatred. And when at last, thinking the driver had begun to grow suspicious, he discharged the cab and ventured on foot, attired in his misfitting clothes, an object marked out for observation, into the midst of the nocturnal passengers, these two base passions raged within him like a tempest. He walked fast, hunted by his fears, chattering to himself, skulking through the less frequented thoroughfares, counting the minutes that still divided him from midnight. Once a woman spoke to him, offering, I think, a box of lights. He smote her in the face, and she fled.

When I came to myself at Lanyon's, the horror of my old friend perhaps affected me somewhat: I do not know; it was at least but a drop in the sea to the abhorrence with which I looked back upon these hours. A change had come over me. It was no longer the fear of the gallows, it was the horror of being Hyde that racked me. I received Lanyon's condemnation partly in a dream; it was partly in a dream that I came home to my own house and got into bed. I slept after the prostration of the day, with a stringent and profound slumber which not even the nightmares that wrung me could avail to break. I awoke in the morning shaken, weakened, but refreshed. I still hated and feared the thought of the brute that slept within me, and I had not of course forgotten the appalling dangers of the day before; but I was once more at home, in my own house and close to my drugs; and gratitude for my escape shone so strong in my soul that it almost rivalled the brightness of hope.

I was stepping leisurely across the court after breakfast, drinking the chill of the air with pleasure, when I was seized again with those indescribable sensations that heralded the change; and I had but the time to gain the shelter of my cabinet, before I was once again raging and freezing with the passions of Hyde. It took on this occasion a double dose to recall me to myself; and alas! six hours after, as I sat looking sadly in the fire, the pangs returned, and the drug had to be re-administered. In short, from that day forth it seemed only by a great effort as of gymnastics, and only under the immediate stimulation of the drug, that I was able to wear the countenance of Jekyll. At all hours of the day and night, I would be taken with the premonitory shudder; above all, if I slept, or even dozed for a moment in my chair, it was always as Hyde that I awakened. Under the strain of this continually impending doom and by the sleeplessness to which I now condemned myself, ay, even beyond what I had thought possible to man, I became, in my own person, a creature eaten up and emptied by fever, languidly weak both in body and mind, and solely occupied by one thought: the horror of my other self. But when I slept, or when the virtue of the medicine wore off, I would leap almost without transition (for the pangs of transformation grew daily less marked) into the possession of a fancy brimming with images of terror, a soul boiling with causeless hatreds, and a body that seemed not strong enough to contain the raging energies of life. The powers of Hyde seemed to have grown with the sickliness of Jekyll. And certainly the hate that now divided them was equal on each side. With Jekyll, it was a thing of vital instinct. He had now seen the full deformity of that creature that shared with him some of the phenomena of consciousness, and was co-heir with him to death: and beyond these links of community, which in themselves made the most poignant part of his distress, he thought of Hyde, for all his energy of life, as of something not only hellish but inorganic. This was the shocking thing; that the slime of the pit seemed to utter cries and voices; that the amorphous dust gesticulated and sinned; that what was dead, and had no shape, should usurp the offices of life. And this again, that that insurgent horror was knit to him closer than a wife, closer than an eye; lay caged in his flesh, where he heard it mutter and felt it struggle to be born; and at every hour of weakness, and in the confidence of slumber, prevailed against him, and deposed him out of life. The hatred of Hyde for Jekyll was of a different order. His terror of the gallows drove him continually to commit temporary suicide, and return to his subordinate station of a part instead of a person; but he loathed the necessity, he loathed the despondency into which Jekyll was now fallen, and he resented the dislike with which he was himself regarded. Hence the ape-like tricks that he would play me, scrawling in my own hand blasphemies on the pages of my books, burning the letters and destroying the portrait of my father; and indeed, had it not been for his fear of death, he would long ago have ruined himself in order to involve me in the ruin. But his love of life is wonderful; I go further: I, who sicken and freeze at the mere thought of him, when I recall the abjection and passion of this attachment, and when I know how he fears my power to cut him off by suicide, I find it in my heart to pity him.

It is useless, and the time awfully fails me, to prolong this description; no one has ever suffered such torments, let that suffice; and yet even to these, habit brought—no, not alleviation—but a certain callousness of soul, a certain acquiescence of despair; and my punishment might have gone on for years, but for the last calamity which has now fallen, and which has finally severed me from my own face and nature. My provision of the salt, which had never been renewed since the date of the first experiment, began to run low. I sent out for a fresh supply and mixed the draught; the ebullition followed, and the first change of colour, not the second; I drank it and it was without efficiency. You will learn from Poole how I have had London ransacked; it was in vain; and I am now persuaded that my first supply was impure, and that it was that unknown impurity which lent efficacy to the draught.

About a week has passed, and I am now finishing this statement under the influence of the last of the old powders. This, then, is the last time, short of a miracle, that Henry Jekyll can think his own thoughts or see his own face (now how sadly altered!) in the glass. Nor must I delay too long to bring my writing to an end; for if my narrative has hitherto escaped destruction, it has been by a combination of great prudence and great good luck. Should the throes of change take me in the act of writing it, Hyde will tear it in pieces; but if some time shall have elapsed after I have laid it by, his wonderful selfishness and circumscription to the moment will probably save it once again from the action of his ape-like spite. And indeed the doom that is closing on us both has already changed and crushed him. Half an hour from now, when I shall again and forever reindue that hated personality, I know how I shall sit shuddering and weeping in my chair, or continue, with the most strained and fearstruck ecstasy of listening, to pace up and down this room (my last earthly refuge) and give ear to every sound of menace. Will Hyde die upon the scaffold? or will he find courage to release himself at the last moment? God knows; I am careless; this is my true hour of death, and what is to follow concerns another than myself. Here then, as I lay down the pen and proceed to seal up my confession, I bring the life of that unhappy Henry Jekyll to an end.

A Lodging for the Night

(1877)

A STORY OF FRANCIS VILLON

It was late in November, 1456. The snow fell over Paris with rigorous, relentless persistence; sometimes the wind made a sally and scattered it in flying vortices; sometimes there was a lull, and flake after flake descended out of the black night air, silent, circuitous, interminable. To poor people, looking up under moist eyebrows, it seemed a wonder where it all came from. Master Francis Villon had propounded an alternative that afternoon, at a tavern window: was it only Pagan Jupiter plucking geese upon Olympus? or were the holy angels moulting? He was only a poor Master of Arts, he went on; and as the question somewhat touched upon divinity, he durst not venture to conclude. A silly old priest from Montargis, who was among the company, treated the young rascal to a bottle of wine in honour of the jest and grimaces with which it was accompanied, and swore on his own white beard that he had been just such another irreverent dog when he was Villon's age.

The air was raw and pointed, but not far below freezing; and the flakes were large, damp, and adhesive. The whole city was sheeted up. An army might have marched from end to end and not a footfall given the alarm. If there were any belated birds in heaven, they saw the island like a large white patch, and the bridges like slim white spars, on the black ground of the river. High up overhead the snow settled among the tracery of the cathedral towers. Many a niche was drifted full; many a statue wore a long white bonnet on its grotesque or sainted head. The gargoyles had been transformed into great false noses, drooping towards the point. The crockets were like upright pillows swollen on one side. In the intervals of the wind, there was a dull sound of dripping about the precincts of the church.

The cemetery of St. John had taken its own share of the snow. All the graves were decently covered; tall white housetops stood around in grave array; worthy burghers were long ago in bed, benightcapped like their domiciles; there was no light in all the neighbourhood but a little peep from a lamp that hung swinging in the church choir, and tossed the shadows to and fro in time to its oscillations. The clock was hard on ten when the patrol went by with halberds and a lantern, beating their hands; and they saw nothing suspicious about the cemetery of St. John.

Yet there was a small house, backed up against the cemetery wall, which was still awake, and awake to evil purpose, in that snoring district. There was not much to betray it from without; only a stream of warm vapour from the chimney-top, a patch where the snow melted on the roof, and a few half-obliterated footprints at the door. But within, behind the shuttered windows, Master Francis Villon the poet, and some of the thievish crew with whom he consorted, were keeping the night alive and passing round the bottle.

A great pile of living embers diffused a strong and ruddy glow from the arched chimney. Before this straddled Dom Nicolas, the Picardy monk, with his skirts picked up and his fat legs bared to the comfortable warmth. His dilated shadow cut the room in half; and the firelight only escaped on either side of his broad person, and in a little pool between his outspread feet. His face had the beery, bruised appearance of the continual drinker's; it was covered with a network of congested veins, purple in ordinary circumstances, but now pale violet, for even with his back to the fire the cold pinched him on the other side. His cowl had half fallen back, and made a strange excrescence on either side of his bull neck. So he straddled, grumbling, and cut the room in half with the shadow of his portly frame.

On the right, Villon and Guy Tabary were huddled together over a scrap of parchment; Villon making a ballade which he was to call the "Ballade of Roast Fish," and Tabary spluttering admiration at his shoulder. The poet was a rag of a man, dark, little, and lean, with hollow cheeks and thin black locks. He carried his four-and-twenty years with feverish animation. Greed had made folds about his eyes, evil smiles had puckered his mouth. The wolf and pig struggled together in his face. It was an eloquent, sharp, ugly, earthly countenance. His hands were small and prehensile, with fingers knotted like a cord; and they were continually flickering in front of him in violent and expressive pantomime. As for Tabary, a broad, complacent, admiring imbecility breathed from his squash nose and slobbering lips: he had become a thief, just as he might have become the most decent of burgesses, by the imperious chance that rules the lives of human geese and human donkeys.

At the monk's other hand, Montigny and Thevenin Pensete played a game of chance. About the first there clung some flavour of good birth and training, as about a fallen angel; something long, lithe, and courtly in the person; something aquiline and darkling in the face. Thevenin, poor soul, was in great feather: he had done a good stroke of knavery that afternoon in the Faubourg St. Jacques, and all night he had been gaining from Montigny. A flat smile illuminated his face; his bald head shone rosily in a garland of red curls; his little protuberant stomach shook with silent chucklings as he swept in his gains.

"Doubles or quits?" said Thevenin.

Montigny nodded grimly.

"*Some may prefer to dine in state,*" wrote Villon, "*On bread and cheese on silver plate.* Or, or—help me out, Guido!"

Tabary giggled.

"*Or parsley on a golden dish,*" scribbled the poet.

The wind was freshening without; it drove the snow before it, and sometimes raised its voice in a victorious whoop, and made sepulchral grumblings in the chimney. The cold was growing sharper as the night went on. Villon, protruding his lips, imitated the gust with something between a whistle and a groan. It was an eerie, uncomfortable talent of the poet's, much detested by the Picardy monk.

"Can't you hear it rattle in the gibbet?" said Villon. "They are all dancing the devil's jig on nothing, up there. You may dance, my gallants, you'll be none the warmer! Whew! what a gust! Down went somebody just now! A medlar the fewer on the three-legged medlar-tree!—I say, Dom Nicolas, it'll be cold tonight on the St. Denis Road?" he asked.

Dom Nicolas winked both his big eyes, and seemed to choke upon his Adam's apple. Montfaucon, the great grisly Paris gibbet, stood hard by the St. Denis Road, and the pleasantry touched him on the raw. As for Tabary, he laughed immoderately over the medlars; he had never heard anything more light-hearted; and he held his sides and crowed. Villon fetched him a fillip on the nose, which turned his mirth into an attack of coughing.

"Oh, stop that row," said Villon, "and think of rhymes to 'fish.'"

"Doubles or quits," said Montigny doggedly.

"With all my heart," quoth Thevenin.

"Is there any more in that bottle?" asked the monk.

"Open another," said Villon. "How do you ever hope to fill that big hogs-head, your body, with little things like bottles? And how do you expect to get to heaven? How many angels, do you fancy, can be spared to carry up a single monk from Picardy? Or do you think yourself another Elias—and they'll send the coach for you?"[1]

"*Hominibus impossibile*,"[2] replied the monk as he filled his glass.

Tabary was in ecstasies.

Villon filliped his nose again.

"Laugh at my jokes, if you like," he said.

"It was very good," objected Tabary.

Villon made a face at him. "Think of rhymes to 'fish,'" he said. "What have you to do with Latin? You'll wish you knew none of it at the great assizes, when the devil calls for Guido Tabary, clericus—the devil with the hump-back and red-hot finger-nails. Talking of the devil," he added in a whisper, "look at Montigny!"

All three peered covertly at the gamester. He did not seem to be enjoying his luck. His mouth was a little to a side; one nostril nearly shut, and the other much inflated. The black dog was on his back, as people say, in terrifying nursery metaphor; and he breathed hard under the gruesome burthen.

"He looks as if he could knife him," whispered Tabary, with round eyes.

The monk shuddered, and turned his face and spread his open hands to the red embers. It was the cold that thus affected Dom Nicolas, and not any excess of moral sensibility.

"Come now," said Villon—"about this ballade. How does it run so far?" And beating time with his hand, he read it aloud to Tabary.

They were interrupted at the fourth rhyme by a brief and fatal movement among the gamesters. The round was completed, and Thevenin was just opening his mouth to claim another victory, when Montigny leaped up, swift as an adder, and stabbed him to the heart. The blow took effect before he had time to utter a cry, before he had time to move. A tremor or two convulsed his frame; his hands opened and shut, his heels rattled on the floor; then his head rolled backward over one shoulder with the eyes wide open; and Thevenin Pensete's spirit had returned to Him who made it.

Every one sprang to his feet; but the business was over in two twos. The four living fellows looked at each other in rather a ghastly fashion; the dead man contemplating a corner of the roof with a singular and ugly leer.

"My God!" said Tabary; and he began to pray in Latin.

Villon broke out into hysterical laughter. He came a step forward and ducked a ridiculous bow at Thevenin, and laughed still louder. Then he sat down suddenly, all of a heap, upon a stool, and continued laughing bitterly, as though he would shake himself to pieces.

Montigny recovered his composure first.

"Let's see what he has about him," he remarked, and he picked the dead man's pockets with a practised hand, and divided the money into four equal portions on the table. "There's for you," he said.

The monk received his share with a deep sigh, and a single stealthy glance at the dead Thevenin, who was beginning to sink into himself and topple sideways off the chair.

"We're all in for it," cried Villon, swallowing his mirth. "It's a hanging job for every man jack of us that's here—not to speak of those who aren't." He made a shocking gesture in the air with his raised right hand, and put out his tongue and threw his head on one side, so as to counterfeit the appearance of one who has been hanged. Then he pocketed his share of the spoil, and executed a shuffle with his feet as if to restore the circulation.

Tabary was the last to help himself; he made a dash at the money, and retired to the other end of the apartment.

Montigny stuck Thevenin upright in the chair, and drew out the dagger, which was followed by a jet of blood.

"You fellows had better be moving," he said, as he wiped the blade on his victim's doublet.

"I think we had," returned Villon, with a gulp. "Damn his fat head!" he broke out. "It sticks in my throat like phlegm. What right has a man to have red hair when he is dead?" And he fell all of a heap again upon the stool, and fairly covered his face with his hands.

Montigny and Dom Nicolas laughed aloud, even Tabary feebly chiming in.

"Cry baby," said the monk.

"I always said he was a woman," added Montigny, with a sneer. "Sit up, can't you?" he went on, giving another shake to the murdered body. "Tread out that fire, Nick!"

But Nick was better employed; he was quietly taking Villon's purse, as the poet sat, limp and trembling, on the stool where he had been making a ballade not three minutes before. Montigny and Tabary dumbly demanded a share of the booty, which the monk silently promised as he passed the little bag into the bosom of his gown. In many ways an artistic nature unfits a man for practical existence.

No sooner had the theft been accomplished than Villon shook himself, jumped to his feet, and began helping to scatter and extinguish the embers. Meanwhile Montigny opened the door and cautiously peered into the street. The coast was clear; there was no meddlesome patrol in sight. Still it was judged wiser to slip out severally; and as Villon was himself in a hurry to escape from the neighbourhood of the dead Thevenin, and the rest were in a still greater hurry to get rid of him before he should discover the loss of his money, he was the first by general consent to issue forth into the street.

The wind had triumphed and swept all the clouds from heaven. Only a few vapours, as thin as moonlight, fleeted rapidly across the stars. It was bitter cold; and by a common optical effect, things seemed almost more definite than in the broadest daylight. The sleeping city was absolutely still; a company of white hoods, a field full of little alps, below the twinkling stars. Villon cursed his fortune. Would it were still snowing! Now, wherever he went, he left an indelible trail behind him on the glittering streets; wherever he went he was still tethered to the house by the cemetery of St. John; wherever he went he must weave, with his own plodding feet, the rope that bound him to the crime and would bind him to the gallows. The leer of the dead man came back to him with a new significance. He snapped his fingers as if to pluck up his own spirits, and choosing a street at random, stepped boldly forward in the snow.

Two things preoccupied him as he went: the aspect of the gallows at Montfaucon in this bright, windy phase of the night's existence, for one; and for another, the look of the dead man with his bald head and garland of red curls. Both struck cold upon his heart, and he kept quickening his pace as if he could escape from unpleasant thoughts by mere fleetness of foot. Sometimes he looked back over his shoulder with a sudden nervous jerk; but he was the only moving thing in the white streets, except when the wind swooped round a corner and threw up the snow, which was beginning to freeze, in spouts of glittering dust.

Suddenly he saw, a long way before him, a black clump and a couple of lanterns. The clump was in motion, and the lanterns swung as though carried by men walking. It was a patrol. And though it was merely crossing his line of march he judged it wiser to get out of eyeshot as speedily as he could. He was not in the humour to be challenged, and he was conscious of making a very conspicuous mark upon the snow. Just on his left hand there stood a great hotel, with some turrets and a large porch before the door; it was half ruinous, he remembered, and had long stood empty; and so he made three steps of it, and jumped into the shelter of the porch. It was pretty dark inside, after the glimmer of the snowy streets, and he was groping forward with outspread hands, when he stumbled over some substance which offered an indescribable mixture of resistances, hard and soft, firm and loose. His heart gave a leap, and he sprang two steps back and stared dreadfully at the obstacle. Then he gave a little laugh of relief. It was only a woman, and she dead. He knelt beside her to make sure upon this latter point. She was freezing cold, and rigid like a stick. A little ragged finery fluttered in the wind about her hair, and her cheeks had been heavily rouged that same afternoon. Her pockets were quite empty; but in her stocking, underneath the garter, Villon found two of the small coins that went by the name of whites. It was little enough; but it was always something; and the poet was moved with a deep sense of pathos that she should have died before she had spent her money. That seemed to him a dark and pitiable mystery; and he looked from the coins in his hand to the dead woman, and back again to the coins, shaking his head over the riddle of man's life. Henry V. of England, dying at Vincennes just after he had conquered France, and this poor jade cut off by a cold draught in a great man's doorway, before she had time to spend her couple of whites—it seemed a cruel way to carry on the world. Two whites would have taken such a little while to squander; and yet it would have been one more good taste in the mouth, one more smack of the lips, before the devil got the soul, and the body was left to birds and vermin. He would like to use all his tallow before the light was blown out and the lantern broken.

While these thoughts were passing through his mind, he was feeling, half mechanically, for his purse. Suddenly his heart stopped beating; a feeling of cold scales passed up the back of his legs, and a cold blow seemed to fall upon his scalp. He stood petrified for a moment; then he felt again with one feverish movement; and then his loss burst upon him, and he was covered at once with perspiration. To spendthrifts money is so living and actual—it is such a thin veil between them and their pleasures! There is only one limit to their fortune— that of time; and a spendthrift with only a few crowns is the Emperor of Rome until they are spent. For such a person to lose his money is to suffer the most shocking reverse, and fall from heaven to hell, from all to nothing, in a breath. And all the more if he has put his head in the halter for it; if he may be hanged tomorrow for that same purse, so dearly earned, so foolishly departed! Villon stood and cursed; he threw the two whites into the street; he shook his fist at heaven; he stamped, and was not horrified to find himself trampling the poor corpse. Then he began rapidly to retrace his steps towards the house beside the cemetery. He had forgotten all fear of the patrol, which was long gone by at any rate, and had no idea but that of his lost purse. It was in vain that he looked right and left upon the snow: nothing was to be seen. He had not dropped it in the streets. Had it fallen in the house? He would have liked dearly to go in and see; but the idea of the grisly occupant unmanned him. And he saw besides, as he drew near, that their efforts to put out the fire had been unsuccessful; on the contrary, it had broken into a blaze, and a changeful light played in the chinks of door and window, and revived his terror for the authorities and Paris gibbet.

He returned to the hotel with the porch, and groped about upon the snow for the money he had thrown away in his childish passion. But he could only find one white; the other had probably struck sideways and sunk deeply in. With a single white in his pocket, all his projects for a rousing night in some wild tavern vanished utterly away. And it was not only pleasure that fled laughing from his grasp; positive discomfort, positive pain, attacked him as he stood ruefully before the porch. His perspiration had dried upon him; and although the wind had now fallen, a binding frost was setting in stronger with every hour, and he felt benumbed and sick at heart. What was to be done? Late as was the hour, improbable as was success, he would try the house of his adopted father, the chaplain of St. Benoît.

He ran there all the way, and knocked timidly. There was no answer. He knocked again and again, taking heart with every stroke; and at last steps were heard approaching from within. A barred wicket fell open in the iron-studded door, and emitted a gush of yellow light.

"Hold up your face to the wicket," said the chaplain from within.

"It's only me," whimpered Villon.

"Oh, it's only you, is it?" returned the chaplain; and he cursed him with foul unpriestly oaths for disturbing him at such an hour, and bade him be off to hell, where he came from.

"My hands are blue to the wrist," pleaded Villon; "my feet are dead and full of twinges; my nose aches with the sharp air; the cold lies at my heart. I may be dead before morning. Only this once, father, and before God, I will never ask again!"

"You should have come earlier," said the ecclesiastic coolly. "Young men require a lesson now and then." He shut the wicket and retired deliberately into the interior of the house.

Villon was beside himself; he beat upon the door with his hands and feet, and shouted hoarsely after the chaplain.

"Wormy old fox!" he cried. "If I had my hand under your twist, I would send you flying headlong into the bottomless pit."

A door shut in the interior, faintly audible to the poet down long passages. He passed his hand over his mouth with an oath. And then the humour of the situation struck him, and he laughed and looked lightly up to heaven, where the stars seemed to be winking over his discomfiture.

What was to be done? It looked very like a night in the frosty streets. The idea of the dead woman popped into his imagination, and gave him a hearty fright; what had happened to her in the early night might very well happen to him before morning. And he so young! and with such immense possibilities of disorderly amusement before him! He felt quite pathetic over the notion of his own fate, as if it had been some one else's, and made a little imaginative vignette of the scene in the morning when they should find his body.

He passed all his chances under review, turning the white between his thumb and forefinger. Unfortunately he was on bad terms with some old friends who would once have taken pity on him in such a plight. He had lampooned them in verses; he had beaten and cheated them; and yet now, when he was in so close a pinch, he thought there was at least one who might perhaps relent. It was a chance. It was worth trying at least, and he would go and see.

On the way, two little accidents happened to him which coloured his musings in a very different manner. For, first, he fell in with the track of a patrol, and walked in it for some hundred yards, although it lay out of his direction. And this spirited him up; at least he had confused his trail; for he was still possessed with the idea of people tracking him all about Paris over the snow, and collaring him next morning before he was awake. The other matter affected him quite differently. He passed a street corner, where, not so long before, a woman and her child had been devoured by wolves. This was just the kind of weather, he reflected, when wolves might take it into their heads to enter Paris again; and a lone man in these deserted streets would run the chance of something worse than a mere scare. He stopped and looked upon the place with an unpleasant interest—it was a centre where several lanes intersected each other; and he looked down them all, one after another, and held his breath to listen, lest he should detect some galloping black things on the snow or hear the sound of howling between him and the river. He remembered his mother telling him the story and pointing out the spot, while he was yet a child. His mother! If he only knew where she lived, he might make sure at least of shelter. He determined he would inquire upon the morrow; nay, he would go and see her too, poor old girl! So thinking, he arrived at his destination—his last hope for the night.

The house was quite dark, like its neighbours; and yet after a few taps, he heard a movement overhead, a door opening, and a cautious voice asking who was there. The poet named himself in a loud whisper, and waited, not without some trepidation, the result. Nor had he to wait long. A window was suddenly opened, and a pailful of slops splashed down upon the doorstep. Villon had not been unprepared for something of the sort, and had put himself as much in shelter as the nature of the porch admitted; but for all that, he was deplorably drenched below the waist. His hose began to freeze almost at once. Death from cold and exposure stared him in the face; he remembered he was of phthisical tendency,[3] and began coughing tentatively. But the gravity of the danger steadied his nerves. He stopped a few hundred yards from the door where he had been so rudely used, and reflected with his finger to his nose. He could only see one way of getting a lodging, and that was to take it. He had noticed a house not far away, which looked as if it might be easily broken into, and thither he betook himself promptly, entertaining himself on the way with the idea of a room still hot, with a table still loaded with the remains of supper, where he might pass the rest of the black hours and whence he should issue, on the morrow, with an armful of valuable plate. He even considered on what viands and what wines he should prefer; and as he was calling the roll of his favourite dainties, roast fish presented itself to his mind with an odd mixture of amusement and horror.

"I shall never finish that ballade," he thought to himself; and then, with another shudder at the recollection, "Oh, damn his fat head!" he repeated fervently, and spat upon the snow.

The house in question looked dark at first sight; but as Villon made a preliminary inspection in search of the handiest point of attack, a little twinkle of light caught his eye from behind a curtained window.

"The devil!" he thought. "People awake! Some student or some saint, confound the crew! Can't they get drunk and lie in bed snoring like their neighbours? What's the good of curfew, and poor devils of bell-ringers jumping at a rope's end in bell-towers? What's the use of day, if people sit up all night? The gripes to them!" He grinned as he saw where his logic was leading him. "Every man to his business, after all," added he, "and if they're awake, by the Lord, I may come by a supper honestly for once, and cheat the devil."

He went boldly to the door and knocked with an assured hand. On both previous occasions, he had knocked timidly and with some dread of attracting notice; but now when he had just discarded the thought of a burglarious entry, knocking at a door seemed a mighty simple and innocent proceeding. The sound of his blows echoed through the house with thin, phantasmal reverberations, as though it were quite empty; but these had scarcely died away before a measured tread drew near, a couple of bolts were withdrawn, and one wing was opened broadly, as though no guile or fear of guile were known to those within. A tall figure of a man, muscular and spare, but a little bent, confronted Villon. The head was massive in bulk, but finely sculptured; the nose blunt at the bottom, but refining upward to where it joined a pair of strong and honest eyebrows; the mouth and eyes surrounded with delicate markings, and the whole face based upon a thick white beard, boldly and squarely trimmed. Seen as it was by the light of a flickering hand-lamp, it looked perhaps nobler than it had a right to do; but it was a fine face, honourable rather than intelligent, strong, simple, and righteous.

"You knock late, sir," said the old man in resonant, courteous tones.

Villon cringed and brought up many servile words of apology; at a crisis of this sort the beggar was uppermost in him, and the man of genius hid his head with confusion.

"You are cold," repeated the old man, "and hungry? Well, step in." And he ordered him into the house with a noble enough gesture.

"Some great seigneur," thought Villon, as his host, setting down the lamp on the flagged pavement of the entry, shot the bolts once more into their places.

"You will pardon me if I go in front," he said, when this was done; and he preceded the poet upstairs into a large apartment, warmed with a pan of charcoal and lit by a great lamp hanging from the roof. It was very bare of furniture: only some gold plate on a sideboard; some folios; and a stand of armour between the windows. Some smart tapestry hung upon the walls, representing the crucifixion of our Lord in one piece, and in another a scene of shepherds and shepherdesses by a running stream. Over the chimney was a shield of arms.

"Will you seat yourself," said the old man, "and forgive me if I leave you? I am alone in my house tonight, and if you are to eat I must forage for you myself."

No sooner was his host gone than Villon leaped from the chair on which he had just seated himself, and began examining the room, with the stealth and passion of a cat. He weighed the gold flagons in his hand, opened all the folios, and investigated the arms upon the shield, and the stuff with which the seats were lined. He raised the window curtains, and saw that the windows were set with rich stained glass in figures, so far as he could see, of martial import. Then he stood in the middle of the room, drew a long breath, and retaining it with puffed cheeks, looked round and round him, turning on his heels, as if to impress every feature of the apartment on his memory.

"Seven pieces of plate," he said. "If there had been ten, I would have risked it. A fine house, and a fine old master, so help me all the saints!"

And just then, hearing the old man's tread returning along the corridor, he stole back to his chair, and began humbly toasting his wet legs before the charcoal pan.

His entertainer had a plate of meat in one hand and a jug of wine in the other. He set down the plate upon the table, motioning Villon to draw in his chair, and going to the sideboard, brought back two goblets which he filled.

"I drink your better fortune," he said, gravely touching Villon's cup with his own.

"To our better acquaintance," said the poet, growing bold. A mere man of the people would have been awed by the courtesy of the old seigneur, but Villon was hardened in that matter; he had made mirth for great lords before now, and found them as black rascals as himself. And so he devoted himself to the viands with a ravenous gusto, while the old man, leaning backward, watched him with steady, curious eyes.

"You have blood on your shoulder, my man," he said.

Montigny must have laid his wet right hand upon him as he left the house. He cursed Montigny in his heart.

"It was none of my shedding," he stammered.

"I had not supposed so," returned his host quietly. "A brawl?"

"Well, something of that sort," Villon admitted with a quaver.

"Perhaps a fellow murdered?"

"Oh, no, not murdered," said the poet, more and more confused. "It was all fair play—murdered by accident. I had no hand in it, God strike me dead!" he added fervently.

"One rogue the fewer, I dare say," observed the master of the house.

"You may dare to say that," agreed Villon, infinitely relieved. "As big a rogue as there is between here and Jerusalem. He turned up his toes like a lamb. But it was a nasty thing to look at. I dare say you've seen dead men in your time, my lord?" he added, glancing at the armour.

"Many," said the old man. "I have followed the wars, as you imagine."

Villon laid down his knife and fork, which he had just taken up again.

"Were any of them bald?" he asked.

"Oh, yes, and with hair as white as mine."

"I don't think I should mind the white so much," said Villon. "His was red." And he had a return of his shuddering and tendency to laughter, which he drowned with a great draught of wine. "I'm a little put out when I think of it," he went on. "I knew him—damn him! And then the cold gives a man fancies— or the fancies give a man cold, I don't know which."

"Have you any money?" asked the old man.

"I have one white," returned the poet, laughing. "I got it out of a dead jade's stocking in a porch. She was as dead as Cæsar, poor wench, and as cold as a church, with bits of ribbon sticking in her hair. This is a hard world in winter for wolves and wenches and poor rogues like me."

"I," said the old man, "am Enguerrand de la Feuillée, seigneur de Brisetout, bailly du Patatrac. Who and what may you be?"

Villon rose and made a suitable reverence. "I am called Francis Villon," he said, "a poor Master of Arts of this university. I know some Latin, and a deal of vice. I can make chansons, ballades, lais, virelais, and roundels, and I am very fond of wine. I was born in a garret, and I shall not improbably die upon the gallows. I may add, my lord, that from this night forward I am your lordship's very obsequious servant to command."

"No servant of mine," said the knight; "my guest for this evening, and no more."

"A very grateful guest," said Villon politely, and he drank in dumb show to his entertainer.

"You are shrewd," began the old man, tapping his forehead, "very shrewd; you have learning; you are a clerk; and yet you take a small piece of money off a dead woman in the street. Is it not a kind of theft?"

"It is a kind of theft much practised in the wars, my lord."

"The wars are the field of honour," returned the old man proudly. "There a man plays his life upon the cast; he fights in the name of his lord the king, his Lord God, and all their lordships the holy saints and angels."

"Put it," said Villon, "that I were really a thief, should I not play my life also, and against heavier odds?"

"For gain but not for honour."

"Gain?" repeated Villon with a shrug. "Gain! The poor fellow wants supper, and takes it. So does the soldier in a campaign. Why, what are all these requisitions we hear so much about? If they are not gain to those who take them, they are loss enough to the others. The men-at-arms drink by a good fire, while the burgher bites his nails to buy them wine and wood. I have seen a good many ploughmen swinging on trees about the country; ay, I have seen thirty on one elm, and a very poor figure they made; and when I asked some one how all these came to be hanged, I was told it was because they could not scrape together enough crowns to satisfy the men-at-arms."

"These things are a necessity of war, which the low-born must endure with constancy. It is true that some captains drive overhard; there are spirits in every rank not easily moved by pity; and indeed many follow arms who are no better than brigands."

"You see," said the poet, "you cannot separate the soldier from the brigand; and what is a thief but an isolated brigand with circumspect manners? I steal a couple of mutton chops, without so much as disturbing people's sleep; the farmer grumbles a bit, but sups none the less wholesomely on what remains. You come up blowing gloriously on a trumpet, take away the whole sheep, and beat the farmer pitifully into the bargain. I have no trumpet; I am only Tom, Dick, or Harry; I am a rogue and a dog, and hanging's too good for me—with all my heart; but just ask the farmer which of us he prefers, just find out which of us he lies awake to curse on cold nights."

"Look at us two," said his lordship. "I am old, strong, and honoured. If I were turned from my house tomorrow, hundreds would be proud to shelter me. Poor people would go out and pass the night in the streets with their children, if I merely hinted that I wished to be alone. And I find you up, wandering homeless, and picking farthings off dead women by the wayside! I fear no man and nothing; I have seen you tremble and lose countenance at a word. I wait God's summons contentedly in my own house, or, if it please the king to call me out again, upon the field of battle. You look for the gallows; a rough, swift death, without hope or honour. Is there no difference between these two?"

"As far as to the moon," Villon acquiesced. "But if I had been born lord of Brisetout, and you had been the poor scholar Francis, would the difference have been any the less? Should not I have been warming my knees at this charcoal pan, and would not you have been groping for farthings in the snow? Should not I have been the soldier, and you the thief?"

"A thief?" cried the old man. "I a thief! If you understood your words, you would repent them."

Villon turned out his hands with a gesture of inimitable impudence. "If your lordship had done me the honour to follow my argument!" he said.

"I do you too much honour in submitting to your presence," said the knight. "Learn to curb your tongue when you speak with old and honourable men, or some one hastier than I may reprove you in a sharper fashion." And he rose and paced the lower end of the apartment, struggling with anger and antipathy. Villon surreptitiously refilled his cup, and settled himself more comfortably in the chair, crossing his knees and leaning his head upon one hand and the elbow against the back of the chair. He was now replete and warm; and he was in nowise frightened for his host, having gauged him as justly as was possible between two such different characters. The night was far spent, and in a very comfortable fashion after all; and he felt morally certain of a safe departure on the morrow.

"Tell me one thing," said the old man, pausing in his walk. "Are you really a thief?"

"I claim the sacred rights of hospitality," returned the poet. "My lord, I am."

"You are very young," the knight continued.

"I should never have been so old," replied Villon, showing his fingers, "if I had not helped myself with these ten talents. They have been my nursing mothers and my nursing fathers."

"You may still repent and change."

"I repent daily," said the poet. "There are few people more given to repentance than poor Francis. As for change, let somebody change my circumstances. A man must continue to eat, if it were only that he may continue to repent."

"The change must begin in the heart," returned the old man solemnly.

"My dear lord," answered Villon, "do you really fancy that I steal for pleasure? I hate stealing, like any other piece of work or of danger. My teeth chatter when I see a gallows. But I must eat, I must drink, I must mix in society of some sort. What the devil! Man is not a solitary animal—*Cui Deus fœminam tradit.*[4] Make me king's pantler—make me abbot of St. Denis; make me bailly of the Patatrac; and then I shall be changed indeed. But as long as you leave me the poor scholar Francis Villon, without a farthing, why, of course, I remain the same."

"The grace of God is all-powerful."

"I should be a heretic to question it," said Francis. "It has made you lord of Brisetout and bailly of the Patatrac; it has given me nothing but the quick wits under my hat and these ten toes upon my hands. May I help myself to wine? I thank you respectfully. By God's grace, you have a very superior vintage."

The lord of Brisetout walked to and fro with his hands behind his back. Perhaps he was not yet quite settled in his mind about the parallel between thieves and soldiers; perhaps Villon had interested him by some cross-thread of sympathy; perhaps his wits were simply muddled by so much unfamiliar reasoning; but whatever the cause, he somehow yearned to convert the young man to a better way of thinking, and could not make up his mind to drive him forth again into the street.

"There is something more than I can understand in this," he said at length. "Your mouth is full of subtleties, and the devil has led you very far astray; but the devil is only a very weak spirit before God's truth, and all his subtleties vanish at a word of true honour, like darkness at morning. Listen to me once more. I learned long ago that a gentleman should live chivalrously and lovingly to God, and the king, and his lady; and though I have seen many strange things done, I have still striven to command my ways upon that rule. It is not only written in all noble histories, but in every man's heart, if he will take care to read. You speak of food and wine, and I know very well that hunger is a difficult trial to endure; but you do not speak of other wants; you say nothing of honour, of faith to God and other men, of courtesy, of love without reproach. It may be that I am not very wise—and yet I think I am—but you seem to me like one who has lost his way and made a great error in life. You are attending to the little wants, and you have totally forgotten the great and only real ones, like a man who should be doctoring toothache on the Judgment Day. For such things as honour and love and faith are not only nobler than food and drink, but indeed I think we desire them more, and suffer more sharply for their absence. I speak to you as I think you will most easily understand me. Are you not, while careful to fill your belly, disregarding another appetite in your heart, which spoils the pleasure of your life and keeps you continually wretched?"

Villon was sensibly nettled under all this sermonising. "You think I have no sense of honour!" he cried. "I'm poor enough, God knows! It's hard to see rich people with their gloves, and you blowing in your hands. An empty belly is a bitter thing, although you speak so lightly of it. If you had had as many as I, perhaps you would change your tune. Anyway I'm a thief—make the most of that—but I'm not a devil from hell, God strike me dead. I would have you to know I've an honour of my own, as good as yours, though I don't prate about it all day long, as if it was a God's miracle to have any. It seems quite natural to me; I keep it in its box till it's wanted. Why now, look you here, how long have I been in this room with you? Did you not tell me you were alone in the house? Look at your gold plate! You're strong, if you like, but you're old and unarmed, and I have my knife. What did I want but a jerk of the elbow and here would have been you with the cold steel in your bowels, and there would have been me, linking in the streets, with an armful of golden cups! Did you suppose I hadn't wit enough to see that? And I scorned the action. There are your damned goblets, as safe as in a church; there are you, with your heart ticking as good as new; and here am I, ready to go out again as poor as I came in, with my one white that you threw in my teeth! And you think I have no sense of honour—God strike me dead!"

The old man stretched out his right arm. "I will tell you what you are," he said. "You are a rogue, my man, an impudent and black-hearted rogue and vagabond. I have passed an hour with you. Oh! believe me, I feel myself disgraced! And you have eaten and drunk at my table. But now I am sick at your presence; the day has come, and the night-bird should be off to his roost. Will you go before, or after?"

"Which you please," returned the poet, rising. "I believe you to be strictly honourable." He thoughtfully emptied his cup. "I wish I could add you were intelligent," he went on, knocking on his head with his knuckles. "Age! age! the brains stiff and rheumatic."

The old man preceded him from a point of self-respect. Villon followed, whistling, with his thumbs in his girdle.

"God pity you," said the lord of Brisetout at the door.

"Good-bye, papa," returned Villon with a yawn. "Many thanks for the cold mutton."

The door closed behind him. The dawn was breaking over the white roofs. A chill, uncomfortable morning ushered in the day. Villon stood and heartily stretched himself in the middle of the road.

"A very dull old gentleman," he thought. "I wonder what his goblets may be worth."

The Suicide Club

(1878)

STORY OF THE YOUNG MAN
WITH THE CREAM TARTS

During his residence in London, the accomplished Prince Florizel of Bohemia[1] gained the affection of all classes by the seduction of his manner and by a well-considered generosity. He was a remarkable man even by what was known of him; and that was but a small part of what he actually did. Although of a placid temper in ordinary circumstances, and accustomed to take the world with as much philosophy as any ploughman, the Prince of Bohemia was not without a taste for ways of life more adventurous and eccentric than that to which he was destined by his birth. Now and then, when he fell into a low humour, when there was no laughable play to witness in any of the London theatres, and when the season of the year was unsuitable to those field sports in which he excelled all competitors, he would summon his confidant and Master of the Horse, Colonel Geraldine, and bid him prepare himself against an evening ramble. The Master of the Horse was a young officer of a brave and even temerarious disposition. He greeted the news with delight, and hastened to make ready. Long practice and a varied acquaintance of life had given him a singular facility in disguise; he could adapt not only his face and bearing, but his voice and almost his thoughts, to those of any rank, character, or nation; and in this way he diverted attention from the Prince, and sometimes gained admission for the pair into strange societies. The civil authorities were never taken into the secret of these adventures; the imperturbable courage of the one and the ready invention and chivalrous devotion of the other had brought them through a score of dangerous passes; and they grew in confidence as time went on.

One evening in March they were driven by a sharp fall of sleet into an Oyster Bar in the immediate neighborhood of Leicester Square.[2] Colonel Geraldine was dressed and painted to represent a person connected with the Press in reduced circumstances; while the Prince had, as usual, travestied his appearance by the addition of false whiskers and a pair of large adhesive eyebrows. These lent him a shaggy and weather-beaten air, which, for one of his urbanity, formed the most impenetrable disguise. Thus equipped, the commander and his satellite sipped their brandy and soda in security.

The bar was full of guests, both male and female; but though more than one of these offered to fall into talk with our adventurers, none of them promised to grow interesting upon a nearer acquaintance. There was nothing present but the lees of London and the commonplace of disrespectability; and the Prince had already fallen to yawning, and was beginning to grow weary of the whole excursion, when the swing doors were pushed violently open, and a young man, followed by a couple of commissionaires, entered the bar. Each of the commissionaires carried a large dish of cream tarts under a cover, which they at once removed; and the young man made the round of the company, and pressed these confections upon everyone's acceptance with an exaggerated courtesy. Sometimes his offer was laughingly accepted; sometimes it was firmly, or even harshly, rejected. In these latter cases the newcomer always ate the tart himself, with some more or less humourous commentary.

At last he accosted Prince Florizel.

"Sir," said he, with a profound obeisance, proffering the tart at the same time between his thumb and forefinger, "will you so far honour an entire stranger? I can answer for the quality of the pastry, having eaten two dozen and three of them myself since five o'clock."

"I am in the habit," replied the Prince, "of looking not so much to the nature of a gift as to the spirit in which it is offered."

"The spirit, sir," returned the young man, with another bow, "is one of mockery."

"Mockery?" repeated Florizel. "And whom do you propose to mock?"

"I am not here to expound my philosophy," replied the other, "but to distribute these cream tarts. If I mention that I heartily include myself in the ridicule of the transaction, I hope you will consider honour satisfied and condescend. If not, you will constrain me to eat my twenty-eighth, and I own to being weary of the exercise."

"You touch me," said the Prince, "and I have all the will in the world to rescue you from this dilemma, but upon one condition. If my friend and I eat your cakes—for which we have neither of us any natural inclination—we shall expect you to join us at supper by way of recompense."

The young man seemed to reflect.

"I have still several dozen upon hand," he said at last; "and that will make it necessary for me to visit several more bars before my great affair is concluded. This will take some time; and if you are hungry——"

The Prince interrupted him with a polite gesture.

"My friend and I will accompany you," he said: "for we have already a deep interest in your very agreeable mode of passing an evening. And now that the preliminaries of peace are settled, allow me to sign the treaty for both."

And the Prince swallowed the tart with the best grace imaginable.

"It is delicious," said he.

"I perceive you are a connoisseur," replied the young man.

Colonel Geraldine likewise did honour to the pastry; and every one in that bar having now either accepted or refused his delicacies, the young man with the cream tarts led the way to another and similar establishment. The two commissionaires, who seemed to have grown accustomed to their absurd employment, followed immediately after; and the Prince and the Colonel brought up the rear, arm in arm, and smiling to each other as they went. In this order the company visited two other taverns, where scenes were enacted of a like nature to that already described—some refusing, some accepting, the favours of this vagabond hospitality, and the young man himself eating each rejected tart.

On leaving the third saloon the young man counted his store. There were but nine remaining, three in one tray and six in the other.

"Gentlemen," said he, addressing himself to his two new followers, "I am unwilling to delay your supper. I am positively sure you must be hungry.

I feel that I owe you a special consideration. And on this great day for me, when I am closing a career of folly by my most conspicuously silly action, I wish to behave handsomely to all who give me countenance. Gentlemen, you shall wait no longer. Although my constitution is shattered by previous excesses, at the risk of my life I liquidate the suspensory condition."

With these words he crushed the nine remaining tarts into his mouth, and swallowed them at a single movement each. Then, turning to the commissionaires, he gave them a couple of sovereigns.

"I have to thank you," said he, "for your extraordinary patience."

And he dismissed them with a bow apiece. For some seconds he stood looking at the purse from which he had just paid his assistants, then, with a laugh, he tossed it into the middle of the street, and signified his readiness for supper.

In a small French restaurant in Soho, which had enjoyed an exaggerated reputation for some little while, but had already begun to be forgotten, and in a private room up two pairs of stairs, the three companions made a very elegant supper, and drank three or four bottles of champagne, talking the while upon indifferent subjects. The young man was fluent and gay, but he laughed louder than was natural in a person of polite breeding; his hands trembled violently, and his voice took sudden and surprising inflections, which seemed to be independent of his will. The dessert had been cleared away, and all three had lighted their cigars, when the Prince addressed him in these words:—

"You will, I am sure, pardon my curiosity. What I have seen of you has greatly pleased but even more puzzled me. And though I should be loath to seem indiscreet, I must tell you that my friend and I are persons very well worthy to be entrusted with a secret. We have many of our own, which we are continually revealing to improper ears. And if, as I suppose, your story is a silly one, you need have no delicacy with us, who are two of the silliest men in England. My name is Godall, Theophilus Godall; my friend is Major Alfred Hammersmith—or at least, such is the name by which he chooses to be known. We pass our lives entirely in the search for extravagant adventures; and there is no extravagance with which we are not capable of sympathy."

"I like you, Mr. Godall," returned the young man; "you inspire me with a natural confidence; and I have not the slightest objection to your friend, the

Major; whom I take to be a nobleman in masquerade. At least, I am sure he is no soldier."

The Colonel smiled at this compliment to the perfection of his art; and the young man went on in a more animated manner.

"There is every reason why I should not tell you my story. Perhaps that is just the reason why I am going to do so. At least, you seem so well prepared to hear a tale of silliness that I cannot find it in my heart to disappoint you. My name, in spite of your example, I shall keep to myself. My age is not essential to the narrative. I am descended from my ancestors by ordinary generation, and from them I inherited the very eligible human tenement which I still occupy and a fortune of three hundred pounds a year. I suppose they also handed on to me a hare-brain humour, which it has been my chief delight to indulge. I received a good education. I can play the violin nearly well enough to earn money in the orchestra of a penny gaff, but not quite. The same remark applies to the flute and the French horn. I learned enough of whist to lose about a hundred a year at that scientific game. My acquaintance with French was sufficient to enable me to squander money in Paris with almost the same facility as in London. In short, I am a person full of manly accomplishments. I have had every sort of adventure, including a duel about nothing. Only two months ago I met a young lady exactly suited to my taste in mind and body; I found my heart melt; I saw that I had come upon my fate at last, and was in the way to fall in love. But when I came to reckon up what remained to me of my capital, I found it amounted to something less than four hundred pounds! I ask you fairly—can a man who respects himself fall in love on four hundred pounds? I concluded, certainly not; left the presence of my charmer, and slightly accelerating my usual rate of expenditure, came this morning to my last eighty pounds. This I divided into two equal parts; forty I reserved for a particular purpose; the remaining forty I was to dissipate before the night. I have passed a very entertaining day, and played many farces besides that of the cream tarts which procured me the advantage of your acquaintance; for I was determined, as I told you, to bring a foolish career to a still more foolish conclusion; and when you saw me throw my purse into the street, the forty pounds were at an end. Now you know me as well as I know myself: a fool, but consistent in his folly; and, as I will ask you to believe, neither a whimperer nor a coward."

From the whole tone of the young man's statement it was plain that he harboured very bitter and contemptuous thoughts about himself. His auditors were led to imagine that his love affair was nearer his heart than he admitted, and that he had a design on his own life. The farce of the cream tarts began to have very much the air of a tragedy in disguise.

"Why, is this not odd," broke out Geraldine, giving a look to Prince Florizel, "that we three fellows should have met by the merest accident in so large a wilderness as London, and should be so nearly in the same condition?"

"How?" cried the young man. "Are you, too, ruined? Is this supper a folly like my cream tarts? Has the devil brought three of his own together for a last carouse?"

"The devil, depend upon it, can sometimes do a very gentlemanly thing," returned Prince Florizel; "and I am so much touched by this coincidence, that, although we are not entirely in the same case, I am going to put an end to the disparity. Let your heroic treatment of the last cream tarts be my example."

So saying, the Prince drew out his purse and took from it a small bundle of bank-notes.

"You see, I was a week or so behind you, but I mean to catch you up and come neck and neck into the winning-post," he continued. "This," laying one of the notes upon the table, "will suffice for the bill. As for the rest——"

He tossed them into the fire, and they went up the chimney in a single blaze.

The young man tried to catch his arm, but as the table was between them his interference came too late.

"Unhappy man," he cried, "you should not have burned them all! You should have kept forty pounds."

"Forty pounds!" repeated the Prince. "Why, in Heaven's name, forty pounds?"

"Why not eighty?" cried the Colonel; "for to my certain knowledge there must have been a hundred in the bundle."

"It was only forty pounds he needed," said the young man gloomily. "But without them there is no admission. The rule is strict. Forty pounds for each. Accursed life, where a man cannot even die without money!"

The Prince and the Colonel exchanged glances.

"Explain yourself," said the latter. "I have still a pocket-book tolerably well lined, and I need not say how readily I would share my wealth with Godall. But I must know to what end: you must certainly tell us what you mean."

The young man seemed to awaken; he looked uneasily from one to the other, and his face flushed deeply.

"You are not fooling me?" he asked. "You are indeed ruined men like me?"

"Indeed, I am for my part," replied the Colonel.

"And for mine," said the Prince, "I have given you proof. Who but a ruined man would throw his notes into the fire? The action speaks for itself."

"A ruined man—yes," returned the other suspiciously, "or else a millionaire."

"Enough, sir," said the Prince; "I have said so, and I am not accustomed to have my word remain in doubt."

"Ruined?" said the young man. "Are you ruined, like me? Are you, after a life of indulgence, come to such a pass that you can only indulge yourself in one thing more? Are you"—he kept lowering his voice as he went on—"are you going to give yourselves that last indulgence! Are you going to avoid the consequences of your folly by the one infallible and easy path? Are you going to give the slip to the sheriff's officers of conscience by the one open door?"

Suddenly he broke off and attempted to laugh.

"Here is your health!" he cried, emptying his glass, "and good night to you, my merry ruined men."

Colonel Geraldine caught him by the arm as he was about to rise.

"You lack confidence in us," he said, "and you are wrong. To all your questions I make answer in the affirmative. But I am not so timid, and can speak the Queen's English plainly. We too, like yourself, have had enough of life, and are determined to die. Sooner or later, alone or together, we meant to seek out death and beard him where he lies ready. Since we have met you, and your case is more pressing, let it be tonight—and at once—and, if you will, all three together. Such a penniless trio," he cried, "should go arm in arm into the halls of Pluto, and give each other some countenance among the shades!"

Geraldine had hit exactly on the manners and intonations that became the part he was playing. The Prince himself was disturbed, and looked over at his confidant with a shade of doubt. As for the young man, the flush came back darkly into his cheek, and his eyes threw out a spark of light.

"You are the men for me!" he cried, with an almost terrible gayety. "Shake hands upon the bargain!" (his hand was cold and wet). "You little know in what a company you will begin the march! You little know in what a happy moment for yourselves you partook of my cream tarts! I am only a unit, but I am a unit in an army. I know Death's private door. I am one of his familiars, and can show you into eternity without ceremony and yet without scandal."

They called upon him eagerly to explain his meaning.

"Can you muster eighty pounds between you?" he demanded.

Geraldine ostentatiously consulted his pocket-book, and replied in the affirmative.

"Fortunate beings!" cried the young man. "Forty pounds is the entry money of the Suicide Club."

"The Suicide Club," said the Prince, "why, what the devil is that?"

"Listen," said the young man; "this is the age of conveniences, and I have to tell you of the last perfection of the sort. We have affairs in different places; and hence railways were invented. Railways separated us infallibly from our friends; and so telegraphs were made that we might communicate speedily at great distances. Even in hotels we have lifts to spare us a climb of some hundred steps. Now, we know that life is only a stage to play the fool upon as long as the part amuses us. There was one more convenience lacking to modern comfort; a decent, easy way to quit that stage; the back stairs to liberty; or, as I said this moment, Death's private door. This, my two fellow-rebels, is supplied by the Suicide Club. Do not suppose that you and I are alone, or even exceptional, in the highly reasonable desire that we profess. A large number of our fellow-men, who have grown heartily sick of the performance in which they are expected to join daily and all their lives long, are only kept from flight by one or two considerations. Some have families who would be shocked, or even blamed, if the matter became public; others have a weakness at heart and recoil from the circumstances of death. That is, to some extent, my own experience. I cannot put a pistol to my head and draw the trigger; for something stronger than myself withholds the act; and although I loathe life, I have not strength enough in my body to take hold of death and be done with it. For such as I, and for all who desire to be out of the coil[3] without posthumous scandal, the Suicide Club has been inaugurated. How this has been managed, what is its history, or what may be its ramifications in other lands, I am myself uninformed; and what I know of its constitution, I am not at liberty to communicate to you. To this extent, however, I am at your service. If you are truly tired of life, I will introduce you tonight to a meeting; and if not tonight, at least some time within the week, you will be easily relieved of your existences. It is now (consulting his watch) eleven; by half-past, at latest, we must leave this place; so that you have half an hour before you to consider my proposal. It is more serious than a cream tart," he added, with a smile; "and I suspect more palatable."

"More serious, certainly," returned Colonel Geraldine; "and as it is so much more so, will you allow me five minutes' speech in private with my friend, Mr. Godall?"

"It is only fair," answered the young man. "If you will permit, I will retire."

"You will be very obliging," said the Colonel.

As soon as the two were alone—"What," said Prince Florizel, "is the use of this confabulation, Geraldine? I see you are flurried, whereas my mind is very tranquilly made up. I will see the end of this."

"Your Highness," said the Colonel turning pale; "let me ask you to consider the importance of your life, not only to your friends, but to the public interest. 'If not tonight,' said this madman; but supposing that tonight some irreparable disaster were to overtake your Highness's person, what, let me ask you, what would be my despair, and what the concern and disaster of a great nation?"

"I will see the end of this," repeated the Prince in his most deliberate tones; "and have the kindness, Colonel Geraldine, to remember and respect your word of honour as a gentleman. Under no circumstances, recollect, nor without my special authority, are you to betray the incognito under which I choose to go abroad. These were my commands, which I now reiterate. And now," he added, "let me ask you to call for the bill."

Colonel Geraldine bowed in submission; but he had a very white face as he summoned the young man of the cream tarts, and issued his directions to the waiter. The Prince preserved his undisturbed demeanor, and described a Palais Royal farce to the young suicide with great humour and gusto. He avoided the Colonel's appealing looks without ostentation, and selected another cheroot with more than usual care. Indeed, he was now the only man of the party who kept any command over his nerves.

The bill was discharged, the Prince giving the whole change of the note to the astonished waiter; and the three drove off in a four wheeler. They were not long upon the way before the cab stopped at the entrance to a rather dark court. Here all descended.

After Geraldine had paid the fare, the young man turned, and addressed Prince Florizel as follows:

"It is still time, Mr. Godall, to make good your escape into thralldom. And for you too, Major Hammersmith. Reflect well before you take another step; and if your hearts say no—here are the crossroads."

"Lead on, sir," said the Prince. "I am not the man to go back from a thing once said."

"Your coolness does me good," replied their guide. "I have never seen anyone so unmoved at this conjuncture; and yet you are not the first whom I have escorted to this door. More than one of my friends has preceded me, where I knew I must shortly follow. But this is of no interest to you. Wait me here for only a few moments; I shall return as soon as I have arranged the preliminaries of your introduction."

And with that the young man, waving his hand to his companions, turned into the court, entered a doorway and disappeared.

"Of all our follies," said Colonel Geraldine in a low voice, "this is the wildest and most dangerous."

"I perfectly believe so," returned the Prince.

"We have still," pursued the Colonel, "a moment to ourselves. Let me beseech your Highness to profit by the opportunity and retire. The consequences of this step are so dark, and may be so grave, that I feel myself justified in pushing a little farther than usual the liberty which your Highness is so condescending as to allow me in private."

"Am I to understand that Colonel Geraldine is afraid?" asked his Highness, taking his cheroot from his lips, and looking keenly into the other's face.

"My fear is certainly not personal," replied the other proudly; "of that your Highness may rest well assured."

"I had supposed as much," returned the Prince, with undisturbed good humour; "but I was unwilling to remind you of the difference in our stations. No more—no more," he added, seeing Geraldine about to apologize, "you stand excused."

And he smoked placidly, leaning against a railing, until the young man returned.

"Well," he asked, "has our reception been arranged?"

"Follow me," was the reply. "The President will see you in the cabinet. And let me warn you to be frank in your answers. I have stood your guarantee; but the club requires a searching inquiry before admission; for the indiscretion of a single member would lead to the dispersion of the whole society forever."

The Prince and Geraldine put their heads together for a moment. "Bear me out in this," said the one; and "bear me out in that," said the other; and by boldly taking up the characters of men with whom both were acquainted, they had come to an agreement in a twinkling, and were ready to follow their guide into the President's cabinet.

There were no formidable obstacles to pass. The outer door stood open; the door of the cabinet was ajar; and there, in a small but very high apartment, the young man left them once more.

"He will be here immediately," he said with a nod, as he disappeared.

Voices were audible in the cabinet through the folding doors which formed one end; and now and then the noise of a champagne cork, followed by a burst of laughter, intervened among the sounds of conversation. A single tall window looked out upon the river and the embankment; and by the disposition of the lights they judged themselves not far from Charing Cross station.[4] The furniture was scanty, and the coverings worn to the thread; and there was nothing movable except a hand-bell in the centre of a round table, and the hats and coats of a considerable party hung round the wall on pegs.

"What sort of a den is this?" said Geraldine.

"That is what I have come to see," replied the Prince. "If they keep live devils on the premises, the thing may grow amusing."

Just then the folding door was opened no more than necessary for the passage of a human body; and there entered at the same moment a louder buzz of talk, and the redoubtable President of the Suicide Club. The President was a man of fifty or upwards; large and rambling in his gait, with shaggy side-whiskers, a bald top to his head, and a veiled gray eye, which now and then emitted a twinkle. His mouth, which embraced a large cigar, he kept continually screwing round and round and from side to side, as he looked sagaciously and coldly at the strangers. He was dressed in light tweeds, with his neck very open, in a striped shirt collar; and carried a minute book under one arm.

"Good evening," said he, after he had closed the door behind him. "I am told you wish to speak with me."

"We have a desire, sir, to join the Suicide Club," replied the Colonel.

The President rolled his cigar about in his mouth.

"What is that?" he said abruptly.

"Pardon me," returned the Colonel, "but I believe you are the person best qualified to give us information on that point."

"I?" cried the President. "A Suicide Club? Come, come! this is a frolic for All Fools' Day. I can make allowances for gentlemen who get merry in their liquor; but let there be an end to this."

"Call your Club what you will," said the Colonel, "you have some company behind these doors, and we insist on joining it."

"Sir," returned the President, curtly, "you have made a mistake. This is a private house, and you must leave it instantly."

The Prince had remained quietly in his seat throughout this little colloquy; but now, when the Colonel looked over to him, as much as to say, "Take your answer and come away, for God's sake!" he drew his cheroot from his mouth, and spoke—

"I have come here," said he, "upon the invitation of a friend of yours. He has doubtless informed you of my intention in thus intruding on your party. Let me remind you that a person in my circumstances has exceedingly little to bind him, and is not at all likely to tolerate much rudeness. I am a very quiet man, as a usual thing; but, my dear sir, you are either going to oblige me in the little matter of which you are aware, or you shall very bitterly repent that you ever admitted me to your ante-chamber."

The President laughed aloud.

"That is the way to speak," said he. "You are a man who is a man. You know the way to my heart, and can do what you like with me. Will you," he continued, addressing Geraldine, "will you step aside for a few minutes? I shall finish first with your companion, and some of the club's formalities require to be fulfilled in private."

With these words he opened the door of a small closet, into which he shut the Colonel.

"I believe in you," he said to Florizel, as soon as they were alone; "but are you sure of your friend?"

"Not so sure as I am of myself, though he has more cogent reasons," answered Florizel, "but sure enough to bring him here without alarm. He has had enough to cure the most tenacious man of life. He was cashiered the other day for cheating at cards."[5]

"A good reason, I daresay," replied the President; "at least, we have another in the same case, and I feel sure of him. Have you also been in the Service, may I ask?"

"I have," was the reply; "but I was too lazy, I left it early."

"What is your reason for being tired of life?" pursued the President.

"The same, as near as I can make out," answered the Prince; "unadulterated laziness."

The President started. "D——n it," said he, "you must have something better than that."

"I have no more money," added Florizel. "That is also a vexation, without doubt. It brings my sense of idleness to an acute point."

The President rolled his cigar round in his mouth for some seconds, directing his gaze straight into the eyes of this unusual neophyte; but the Prince supported his scrutiny with unabashed good temper.

"If I had not a deal of experience," said the President at last, "I should turn you off. But I know the world; and this much any way, that the most frivolous excuses for a suicide are often the toughest to stand by. And when I downright like a man, as I do you, sir, I would rather strain the regulation than deny him."

The Prince and the Colonel, one after the other, were subjected to a long and particular interrogatory: the Prince alone; but Geraldine in the presence of the Prince, so that the President might observe the countenance of the one while the other was being warmly cross-examined. The result was satisfactory; and the President, after having booked a few details of each case, produced a form of oath to be accepted. Nothing could be conceived more passive than the obedience promised, or more stringent than the terms by which the juror bound himself. The man who forfeited a pledge so awful could scarcely have a rag of honour or any of the consolations of religion left to him. Florizel signed the document, but not without a shudder; the Colonel followed his example with an air of great depression. Then the President received the entry money; and without more ado, introduced the two friends into the smoking-room of the Suicide Club.

The smoking-room of the Suicide Club was the same height as the cabinet into which it opened, but much larger, and papered from top to bottom with an imitation of oak wainscot. A large and cheerful fire and a number of gas-jets illuminated the company. The Prince and his follower made the number up to eighteen. Most of the party were smoking, and drinking champagne; a feverish hilarity reigned, with sudden and rather ghastly pauses.

"Is this a full meeting?" asked the Prince.

"Middling," said the President. "By the way," he added, "if you have any money, it is usual to offer some champagne. It keeps up a good spirit, and is one of my own little perquisites."

"Hammersmith," said Florizel, "I may leave the champagne to you."

And with that he turned away and began to go round among the guests. Accustomed to play the host in the highest circles, he charmed and dominated all whom he approached; there was something at once winning and authoritative in his address; and his extraordinary coolness gave him yet another distinction in this half maniacal society. As he went from one to another he kept both his eyes and ears open, and soon began to gain a general idea of the people among whom he found himself. As in all other places of resort, one type predominated: people in the prime of youth, with every show of intelligence and sensibility in their appearance, but with little promise of strength or the quality that makes success. Few were much above thirty, and not a few were still in their teens. They stood, leaning on tables and shifting on their feet; sometimes they smoked extraordinarily fast, and sometimes they let their cigars go out; some talked well, but the conversation of others was plainly the result of nervous tension, and was equally without wit or purport. As each new bottle of champagne was opened, there was a manifest improvement in gaiety. Only two were seated—one in a chair in the recess of the window, with his head hanging and his hands plunged deep into his trouser pockets, pale, visibly moist with perspiration, saying never a word, a very wreck of soul and body; the other sat on the divan close by the chimney, and attracted notice by a trenchant dissimilarity from all the rest. He was probably upwards of forty, but he looked fully ten years older; and Florizel thought he had never seen a man more naturally hideous, nor one more ravaged by disease and ruinous excitements. He was no more than skin and bone, was partly paralyzed, and wore spectacles of such unusual power, that his eyes appeared through the glasses greatly magnified and distorted in shape. Except the Prince and the President, he was the only person in the room who preserved the composure of ordinary life.

There was little decency among the members of the club. Some boasted of the disgraceful actions, the consequences of which had reduced them to seek refuge in death; and the others listened without disapproval. There was a tacit understanding against moral judgments; and whoever passed the club doors enjoyed already some of the immunities of the tomb. They drank to each other's memories, and to those of notable suicides in the past. They compared and developed their different views of death—some declaring that it was no more than blackness and cessation; others full of a hope that that very night they should be scaling the stars and commercing with the mighty dead.

"To the eternal memory of Baron Trenck,[6] the type of suicides!" cried one. "He went out of a small cell into a smaller, that he might come forth again to freedom."

"For my part," said a second, "I wish no more than a bandage for my eyes and cotton for my ears. Only they have no cotton thick enough in this world."

A third was for reading the mysteries of life in a future state; and a fourth professed that he would never have joined the club, if he had not been induced to believe in Mr. Darwin.

"I could not bear," said this remarkable suicide, "to be descended from an ape."[7]

Altogether, the Prince was disappointed by the bearing and conversation of the members.

"It does not seem to me," he thought, "a matter for so much disturbance. If a man has made up his mind to kill himself, let him do it, in God's name, like a gentleman. This flutter and big talk is out of place."

In the meanwhile Colonel Geraldine was a prey to the blackest apprehensions; the club and its rules were still a mystery, and he looked round the room for some one who should be able to set his mind at rest. In this survey his eye lighted on the paralytic person with the strong spectacles; and seeing him so exceedingly tranquil, he besought the President, who was going in and out of the room under a pressure of business, to present him to the gentleman on the divan.

The functionary explained the needlessness of all such formalities within the club, but nevertheless presented Mr. Hammersmith to Mr. Malthus.[8]

Mr. Malthus looked at the Colonel curiously, and then requested him to take a seat upon his right.

"You are a newcomer," he said, "and wish information? You have come to the proper source. It is two years since I first visited this charming club."

The Colonel breathed again. If Mr. Malthus had frequented the place for two years there could be little danger for the Prince in a single evening. But Geraldine was none the less astonished, and began to suspect a mystification.

"What!" cried he, "two years! I thought—but indeed I see I have been made the subject of a pleasantry."

"By no means," replied Mr. Malthus mildly. "My case is peculiar. I am not, properly speaking, a suicide at all; but, as it were, an honourary member. I rarely visit the club twice in two months. My infirmity and the kindness of the President have procured me these little immunities, for which besides I pay at an advanced rate. Even as it is my luck has been extraordinary."

"I am afraid," said the Colonel, "that I must ask you to be more explicit. You must remember that I am still most imperfectly acquainted with the rules of the club."

"An ordinary member who comes here in search of death like yourself," replied the paralytic, "returns every evening until fortune favours him. He can, even if he is penniless, get board and lodging from the President: very fair, I believe, and clean, although, of course, not luxurious; that could hardly be, considering the exiguity (if I may so express myself) of the subscription. And then the President's company is a delicacy in itself."

"Indeed!" cried Geraldine, "he had not greatly prepossessed me."

"Ah!" said Mr. Malthus, "you do not know the man: the drollest fellow! What stories! What cynicism! He knows life to admiration and, between ourselves, is probably the most corrupt rogue in Christendom."

"And he also," asked the Colonel, "is a permanency—like yourself, if I may say so without offence?"

"Indeed, he is a permanency in a very different sense from me," replied Mr. Malthus. "I have been graciously spared, but I must go at last. Now he never plays. He shuffles and deals for the club, and makes the necessary arrangements. That man, my dear Mr. Hammersmith, is the very soul of ingenuity. For three years he has pursued in London his useful and, I think I may add, his artistic calling; and not so much as a whisper of suspicion has been once aroused. I believe him myself to be inspired. You doubtless remember the celebrated case, six months ago, of the gentleman who was accidentally poisoned in a chemist's shop? That was one of the least rich, one of the least racy, of his notions; but then, how simple! and how safe!"

"You astound me," said the Colonel. "Was that unfortunate gentleman one of the——" He was about to say "victims"; but bethinking himself in time, he substituted—"members of the club?"

In the same flash of thought, it occurred to him that Mr. Malthus himself had not at all spoken in the tone of one who is in love with death; and he added hurriedly:

"But I perceive I am still in the dark. You speak of shuffling and dealing; pray for what end? And since you seem rather unwilling to die than otherwise, I must own that I cannot conceive what brings you here at all."

"You say truly that you are in the dark," replied Mr. Malthus with more animation. "Why, my dear sir, this club is the temple of intoxication. If my enfeebled health could support the excitement more often, you may depend upon it I should be more often here. It requires all the sense of duty engendered by a long habit of ill-health and careful regimen, to keep me from excess in this, which is, I may say, my last dissipation. I have tried them all, sir," he went on, laying his hand on Geraldine's arm, "all without exception, and I declare to you, upon my honour, there is not one of them that has not been grossly and untruthfully overrated. People trifle with love. Now, I deny that love is a strong passion. Fear is the strong passion; it is with fear that you must trifle, if you wish to taste the intense joys of living. Envy me—envy me, sir," he added with a chuckle, "I am a coward!"

Geraldine could scarcely repress a movement of repulsion for this deplorable wretch; but he commanded himself with an effort, and continued his inquiries.

"How, sir," he asked, "is the excitement so artfully prolonged? and where is there any element of uncertainty?"

"I must tell you how the victim for every evening is selected," returned Mr. Malthus; "and not only the victim, but another member, who is to be the instrument in the club's hands, and death's high priest of that occasion."

"Good God!" said the Colonel, "do they then kill each other?"

"The trouble of suicide is removed in that way," returned Malthus with a nod.

"Merciful Heavens!" ejaculated the Colonel, "and may you—may I—may the—my friend, I mean—may any of us be pitched upon this evening as the slayer of another man's body and immortal spirit? Can such things be possible among men born of women? Oh! infamy of infamies!"

He was about to rise in his horror, when he caught the Prince's eye. It was fixed upon him from across the room with a frowning and angry stare. And in a moment Geraldine recovered his composure.

"After all," he added, "why not? And since you say the game is interesting, *vogue la galère*—I follow the club!"

Mr. Malthus had keenly enjoyed the Colonel's amazement and disgust. He had the vanity of wickedness; and it pleased him to see another man give way to a generous movement, while he felt himself, in his entire corruption, superior to such emotions.

"You now, after your first moment of surprise," said he, "are in a position to appreciate the delights of our society. You can see how it combines the excitement of a gaming-table, a duel, and a Roman amphitheatre. The Pagans did well enough; I cordially admire the refinement of their minds; but it has been reserved for a Christian country to attain this extreme, this quintessence, this absolute of poignancy. You will understand how vapid are all amusements to a man who has acquired a taste for this one. The game we play," he continued, "is one of extreme simplicity. A full pack—but I perceive you are about to see the thing in progress. Will you lend me the help of your arm? I am unfortunately paralyzed."

Indeed, just as Mr. Malthus was beginning his description, another pair of folding-doors was thrown open, and the whole club began to pass, not without some hurry, into the adjoining room. It was similar in every respect to the one from which it was entered, but somewhat differently furnished. The centre was occupied by a long green table, at which the President sat shuffling a pack of cards with great particularity. Even with the stick and the Colonel's arm, Mr. Malthus walked with so much difficulty that everyone was seated before this pair and the Prince, who had waited for them, entered the apartment; and, in consequence, the three took seats close together at the lower end of the board.

"It is a pack of fifty-two," whispered Mr. Malthus. "Watch for the ace of spades, which is the sign of death, and the ace of clubs, which designates the official of the night. Happy, happy young men!" he added. "You have good eyes, and can follow the game. Alas! I cannot tell an ace from a deuce across the table."

And he proceeded to equip himself with a second pair of spectacles.

"I must at least watch the faces," he explained.

The Colonel rapidly informed his friend of all that he had learned from the honourary member, and of the horrible alternative that lay before them. The Prince was conscious of a deadly chill and a contraction about his heart; he swallowed with difficulty, and looked from side to side like a man in a maze.

"One bold stroke," whispered the Colonel, "and we may still escape."

But the suggestion recalled the Prince's spirits.

"Silence!" said he. "Let me see that you can play like a gentleman for any stake, however serious."

And he looked about him, once more to all appearance at his ease, although his heart beat thickly, and he was conscious of an unpleasant heat in his bosom. The members were all very quiet and intent; everyone was pale, but none so pale as Mr. Malthus. His eyes protruded; his head kept nodding involuntarily upon his spine; his hands found their way, one after the other, to his mouth, where they made clutches at his tremulous and ashen lips. It was plain that the honourary member enjoyed his membership on very startling terms.

"Attention, gentlemen!" said the President.

And he began slowly dealing the cards about the table in the reverse direction, pausing until each man had shown his card. Nearly everyone hesitated; and sometimes you would see a player's fingers stumble more than once before he could turn over the momentous slip of pasteboard. As the Prince's turn drew nearer, he was conscious of a growing and almost suffocating excitement; but he had somewhat of the gambler's nature, and recognized almost with astonishment that there was a degree of pleasure in his sensations. The nine of clubs fell to his lot; the three of spades was dealt to Geraldine; and the queen of hearts to Mr. Malthus, who was unable to suppress a sob of relief. The young man of the cream tarts almost immediately afterwards turned over the ace of clubs, and remained frozen with horror, the card still resting on his finger; he had not come there to kill, but to be killed; and the Prince, in his generous sympathy with his position, almost forgot the peril that still hung over himself and his friend.

The deal was coming round again, and still Death's card had not come out. The players held their respiration, and only breathed by gasps. The Prince received another club; Geraldine had a diamond; but when Mr. Malthus turned up his card a horrible noise, like that of something breaking, issued from his mouth; and he rose from his seat and sat down again, with no sign of his paralysis. It was the ace of spades. The honourary member had trifled once too often with his terrors.

Conversation broke out again almost at once. The players relaxed their rigid attitudes, and began to rise from the table and stroll back by twos and threes into the smoking-room. The President stretched his arms and yawned, like a man who had finished his day's work. But Mr. Malthus sat in his place, with his head in his hands, and his hands upon the table, drunk and motionless—a thing stricken down.

The Prince and Geraldine made their escape at once. In the cold night air their horror of what they had witnessed was redoubled.

"Alas!" cried the Prince, "to be bound by an oath in such a matter! to allow this wholesale trade in murder to be continued with profit and impunity! If I but dared to forfeit my pledge!"

"That is impossible for your Highness," replied the Colonel, "whose honour is the honour of Bohemia. But I dare, and may with propriety, forfeit mine."

"Geraldine," said the Prince, "if your honour suffers in any of the adventures into which you follow me, not only will I never pardon you, but—what I believe will much more sensibly affect you—I should never forgive myself."

"I receive your Highness's commands," replied the Colonel. "Shall we go from this accursed spot?"

"Yes," said the Prince. "Call a cab in Heaven's name, and let me try to forget in slumber the memory of this night's disgrace."

But it was notable that he carefully read the name of the court before he left it.

The next morning, as soon as the Prince was stirring, Colonel Geraldine brought him a daily newspaper, with the following paragraph marked:—

"MELANCHOLY ACCIDENT.—This morning, about two o'clock, Mr. Bartholomew Malthus, of 16 Chepstow Place, Westbourne Grove, on his way home from a party at a friend's house, fell over the upper parapet in Trafalgar Square, fracturing his skull and breaking a leg and an arm. Death was instantaneous. Mr. Malthus, accompanied by a friend, was engaged in looking for a cab at the time of the unfortunate occurrence. As Mr. Malthus was paralytic, it is thought that his fall may have been occasioned by another seizure. The unhappy gentleman was well known in the most respectable circles, and his loss will be widely and deeply deplored."

"If ever a soul went straight to Hell," said Geraldine solemnly, "it was that paralytic man's."

The Prince buried his face in his hands, and remained silent.

"I am almost rejoiced," continued the Colonel, "to know that he is dead. But for our young man of the cream tarts I confess my heart bleeds."

"Geraldine," said the Prince, raising his face, "that unhappy lad was last night as innocent as you and I; and this morning the guilt of blood is on his soul. When I think of the President, my heart grows sick within me. I do not know how it shall be done, but I shall have that scoundrel at my mercy as there is a God in Heaven. What an experience, what a lesson, was that game of cards!"

"One," said the Colonel, "never to be repeated."

The Prince remained so long without replying, that Geraldine grew alarmed.

"You cannot mean to return," he said. "You have suffered too much and seen too much horror already. The duties of your high position forbid the repetition of the hazard."

"There is much in what you say," replied Prince Florizel, "and I am not altogether pleased with my own determination. Alas! in the clothes of the greatest potentate, what is there but a man? I never felt my weakness more acutely than now, Geraldine, but it is stronger than I. Can I cease to interest myself in the fortunes of the unhappy young man who supped with us some hours ago? Can I leave the President to follow his nefarious career unwatched? Can I begin an adventure so entrancing, and not follow it to an end? No, Geraldine; you ask of the Prince more than the man is able to perform. Tonight, once more, we take our places at the table of the Suicide Club."

Colonel Geraldine fell upon his knees.

"Will your Highness take my life?" he cried. "It is his—his freely; but do not, Oh, do not! let him ask me to countenance so terrible a risk."

"Colonel Geraldine," replied the Prince, with some haughtiness of manner, "your life is absolutely your own. I only looked for obedience; and when that is unwillingly rendered, I shall look for that no longer. I add one word: your importunity in this affair has been sufficient."

The Master of the Horse regained his feet at once. "Your Highness," he said, "may I be excused in my attendance this afternoon? I dare not, as an honourable man, venture a second time into that fatal house until I have perfectly ordered my affairs. Your Highness shall meet, I promise him, with no more opposition from the most devoted and grateful of his servants."

"My dear Geraldine," returned Prince Florizel, "I always regret when you oblige me to remember my rank. Dispose of your day as you think fit, but be here before eleven in the same disguise."

The club, on this second evening, was not so fully attended; and when Geraldine and the Prince arrived, there were not above half a dozen persons in the smoking-room. His Highness took the President aside and congratulated him warmly on the demise of Mr. Malthus.

"I like," he said, "to meet with capacity, and certainly find much of it in you. Your profession is of a very delicate nature, but I see you are well qualified to conduct it with success and secrecy."

The President was somewhat affected by these compliments from one of his Highness's superior bearing. He acknowledged them almost with humility.

"Poor Malthy!" he added, "I shall hardly know the club without him. The most of my patrons are boys, sir, and poetical boys, who are not much company for me. Not but what Malthy had some poetry, too; but it was of a kind that I could understand."

"I can readily imagine you should find yourself in sympathy with Mr. Malthus," returned the Prince. "He struck me as a man of a very original disposition."

The young man of the cream tarts was in the room, but painfully depressed and silent. His late companions sought in vain to lead him into conversation.

"How bitterly I wish," he cried, "that I had never brought you to this infamous abode! Begone, while you are clean-handed. If you could have heard the old man scream as he fell, and the noise of his bones upon the pavement! Wish me, if you have any kindness to so fallen a being—wish the ace of spades for me tonight!"

A few more members dropped in as the evening went on, but the club did not muster more than the devil's dozen when they took their places at the table. The Prince was again conscious of a certain joy in his alarms; but he was astonished to see Geraldine so much more self-possessed than on the night before.

"It is extraordinary," thought the Prince, "that a will, made or unmade, should so greatly influence a young man's spirit."

"Attention, gentlemen!" said the President, and he began to deal.

Three times the cards went all round the table, and neither of the marked cards had yet fallen from his hand. The excitement as he began the fourth distribution was overwhelming. There were just cards enough to go once more entirely round. The Prince, who sat second from the dealer's left, would receive, in the reverse mode of dealing practiced at the club, the second last card. The third player turned up a black ace—it was the ace of clubs. The next received a diamond, the next a heart, and so on; but the ace of spades was still undelivered. At last Geraldine, who sat upon the Prince's left, turned his card; it was an ace, but the ace of hearts.

When Prince Florizel saw his fate upon the table in front of him, his heart stood still. He was a brave man, but the sweat poured off his face. There were exactly fifty chances out of a hundred that he was doomed. He reversed the card; it was the ace of spades. A loud roaring filled his brain, and the table swam before his eyes. He heard the player on his right break into a fit of laughter that sounded between mirth and disappointment; he saw the company rapidly dispersing, but his mind was full of other thoughts. He recognized how foolish, how criminal, had been his conduct. In perfect health, in the prime of his years, the heir to a throne, he had gambled away his future and that of a brave and loyal country. "God," he cried, "God forgive me!" And with that, the confusion of his senses passed away, and he regained his self-possession in a moment.

To his surprise Geraldine had disappeared. There was no one in the card-room but his destined butcher consulting with the President, and the young man of the cream tarts, who slipped up to the Prince and whispered in his ear:

"I would give a million, if I had it, for your luck."

His Highness could not help reflecting, as the young man departed, that he would have sold his opportunity for a much more moderate sum.

The whispered conference now came to an end. The holder of the ace of clubs left the room with a look of intelligence, and the President, approaching the unfortunate Prince, proffered him his hand.

"I am pleased to have met you, sir," said he, "and pleased to have been in a position to do you this trifling service. At least, you cannot complain of delay. On the second evening—what a stroke of luck!"

The Prince endeavored in vain to articulate something in response, but his mouth was dry and his tongue seemed paralyzed.

"You feel a little sickish?" asked the President, with some show of solicitude. "Most gentlemen do. Will you take a little brandy?"

The Prince signified in the affirmative, and the other immediately filled some of the spirit into a tumbler.

"Poor old Malthy!" ejaculated the President, as the Prince drained the glass. "He drank near upon a pint, and little enough good it seemed to do him!"

"I am more amenable to treatment," said the Prince, a good deal revived. "I am my own man again at once, as you perceive. And so, let me ask you, what are my directions?"

"You will proceed along the Strand in the direction of the City, and on the left-hand pavement, until you meet the gentleman who has just left the room. He will continue your instructions, and him you will have the kindness to obey; the authority of the club is vested in his person for the night. And now," added the President, "I wish you a pleasant walk."

Florizel acknowledged the salutation rather awkwardly, and took his leave. He passed through the smoking-room, where the bulk of the players were still consuming champagne, some of which he had himself ordered and paid for; and he was surprised to find himself cursing them in his heart. He put on his hat and great coat in the cabinet, and selected his umbrella from a corner. The familiarity of these acts, and the thought that he was about them for the last time, betrayed him into a fit of laughter which sounded unpleasantly in his own ears. He conceived a reluctance to leave the cabinet, and turned instead to the window. The sight of the lamps and the darkness recalled him to himself.

"Come, come, I must be a man," he thought, "and tear myself away."

At the corner of Box Court three men fell upon Prince Florizel and he was unceremoniously thrust into a carriage, which at once drove rapidly away. There was already an occupant.

"Will your Highness pardon my zeal?" said a well-known voice.

The Prince threw himself upon the Colonel's neck in a passion of relief.

"How can I ever thank you?" he cried. "And how was this effected?"

Although he had been willing to march upon his doom, he was overjoyed to yield to friendly violence, and return once more to life and hope.

"You can thank me effectually enough," replied the Colonel, "by avoiding all such dangers in the future. And as for your second question, all has been managed by the simplest means. I arranged this afternoon with a celebrated detective. Secrecy has been promised and paid for. Your own servants have been principally engaged in the affair. The house in Box Court has been surrounded since nightfall, and this, which is one of your own carriages, has been awaiting you for nearly an hour."

"And the miserable creature who was to have slain me—what of him?" inquired the Prince.

"He was pinioned as he left the club," replied the Colonel, "and now awaits your sentence at the Palace, where he will soon be joined by his accomplices."

"Geraldine," said the Prince, "you have saved me against my explicit orders, and you have done well. I owe you not only my life, but a lesson; and I should be unworthy of my rank if I did not show myself grateful to my teacher. Let it be yours to choose the manner."

There was a pause, during which the carriage continued to speed through the streets, and the two men were each buried in his own reflections. The silence was broken by Colonel Geraldine.

"Your Highness," said he, "has by this time a considerable body of prisoners. There is at least one criminal among the number to whom justice should be dealt. Our oath forbids us all recourse to law; and discretion would forbid it equally if the oath were loosened. May I inquire your Highness's intention?"

"It is decided," answered Florizel; "the President must fall in duel. It only remains to choose his adversary."

"Your Highness has permitted me to name my own recompense," said the Colonel. "Will he permit me to ask the appointment of my brother? It is an honourable post, but I dare assure your Highness that the lad will acquit himself with credit."

"You ask me an ungracious favour," said the Prince, "but I must refuse you nothing."

The Colonel kissed his hand with the greatest affection; and at that moment the carriage rolled under the archway of the Prince's splendid residence.

An hour after, Florizel in his official robes, and covered with all the orders of Bohemia, received the members of the Suicide Club.

"Foolish and wicked men," said he, "as many of you as have been driven into this strait by the lack of fortune shall receive employment and remuneration from my officers. Those who suffer under a sense of guilt must have recourse to a higher and more generous Potentate than I. I feel pity for all of you, deeper than you can imagine; tomorrow you shall tell me your stories; and as you answer more frankly, I shall be the more able to remedy your misfortunes. As for you," he added, turning to the President, "I should only offend a person of your parts by any offer of assistance; but I have instead a piece of diversion to propose to you. Here," laying his hand on the shoulder of Colonel Geraldine's young brother, "is an officer of mine who desires to make a little tour upon the Continent; and I ask you, as a favour, to accompany him on this excursion. Do you," he went on, changing his tone, "do you shoot well with the pistol? Because you may have need of that accomplishment. When two men go traveling together, it is best to be prepared for all. Let me add that, if by any chance you should lose young Mr. Geraldine upon the way, I shall always have another member of my household to place at your disposal; and I am known, Mr. President, to have long eyesight, and as long an arm."

With these words, said with much sternness, the Prince concluded his address. Next morning the members of the club were suitably provided for by his munificence, and the President set forth upon his travels, under the supervision of Mr. Geraldine, and a pair of faithful and adroit lackeys, well trained in the Prince's household. Not content with this, discreet agents were put in possession of the house of Box Court, and all letters of visitors for the Suicide Club or its officials were to be examined by Prince Florizel in person.

Here (says my Arabian author)[9] *ends the* STORY OF THE YOUNG MAN WITH THE CREAM TARTS, *who is now a comfortable householder in Wigmore Street, Cavendish Square. The number, for obvious reasons, I suppress. Those who care to pursue the adventures of Prince Florizel and the President of the Suicide Club, may read the* STORY OF THE PHYSICIAN AND THE SARATOGA TRUNK.

STORY OF THE PHYSICIAN AND THE
SARATOGA TRUNK

Mr. Silas Q. Scuddamore was a young American of a simple and harmless disposition, which was the more to his credit as he came from New England—a quarter of the New World not precisely famous for those qualities. Although he was exceedingly rich, he kept a note of all his expenses in a little paper pocketbook; and he had chosen to study the attractions of Paris from the seventh story of what is called a furnished hotel, in the Latin Quarter. There was a great deal of habit in his penuriousness; and his virtue, which was very remarkable among his associates, was principally founded upon diffidence and youth.

The next room to his was inhabited by a lady, very attractive in her air and very elegant in toilette, whom, on his first arrival, he had taken for a Countess. In course of time he had learned that she was known by the name of Madame Zéphyrine, and that whatever station she occupied in life it was not that of a person of title. Madame Zéphyrine, probably in the hope of enchanting the young American, used to flaunt by him on the stairs with a civil inclination, a word of course, and a knock-down look out of her black eyes, and disappear in a rustle of silk, and with the revelation of an admirable foot and ankle. But these advances, so far from encouraging Mr. Scuddamore, plunged him into the depths of depression and bashfulness. She had come to him several times for a light, or to apologize for the imaginary depredations of her poodle, but his mouth was closed in the presence of so superior a being, his French promptly left him, and he could only stare and stammer until she was gone. The slenderness of their intercourse did not prevent him from throwing out insinuations of a very glorious order when he was safely alone with a few males.

The room on the other side of the American's—for there were three rooms on a floor in the hotel—was tenanted by an old English physician of rather doubtful reputation. Dr. Noel, for that was his name, had been forced to leave London, where he enjoyed a large and increasing practice; and it was hinted that the police had been the instigators of this change of scene. At least he, who had made something of a figure in earlier life, now dwelt in the Latin Quarter in great simplicity and solitude, and devoted much of his time to study. Mr. Scuddamore had made his acquaintance, and the pair would now and then dine together frugally in a restaurant across the street.

Silas Q. Scuddamore had many little vices of the more respectable order, and was not restrained by delicacy from indulging them in many rather doubtful ways. Chief among his foibles stood curiosity. He was a born gossip; and life, and especially those parts of it in which he had no experience, interested him to the degree of passion. He was a pert, invincible questioner, pushing his inquiries with equal pertinacity and indiscretion; he had been observed, when he took a letter to the post, to weigh it in his hand, to turn it over and over, and to study the address with care; and when he found a flaw in the partition between his room and Madame Zéphyrine's, instead of filling it up, he enlarged and improved the opening, and made use of it as a spy-hole on his neighbor's affairs.

One day, in the end of March, his curiosity grew as it was indulged and he enlarged the hole a little further, so that he might command another corner of the room. That evening, when he went as usual to inspect Madame Zéphyrine's movements, he was astonished to find the aperture obscured in an odd manner on the other side, and still more abashed when the obstacle was suddenly withdrawn and a titter of laughter reached his ears. Some of the plaster had evidently betrayed the secret of his spy-hole, and his neighbor had been returning the compliment in kind. Mr. Scuddamore was moved to a very acute feeling of annoyance; he condemned Madame Zéphyrine unmercifully; he even blamed himself; but when he found, next day, that she had taken no means to baulk him of his favourite pastime, he continued to profit by her carelessness, and gratify his idle curiosity.

That next day Madame Zéphyrine received a long visit from a tall, loosely built man of fifty or upwards, whom Silas had not hitherto seen. His tweed suit and colored shirt, no less than his shaggy side-whiskers, identified him as a Britisher, and his dull gray eye affected Silas with a sense of cold. He kept screwing his mouth from side to side and round and round during the whole colloquy, which was carried on in whispers. More than once it seemed to the young New Englander as if their gestures indicated his own apartment; but the only thing definite he could gather by the most scrupulous attention was this remark made by the Englishman in a somewhat higher key, as if in answer to some reluctance or opposition.

"I have studied his taste to a nicety, and I tell you again and again you are the only woman of the sort that I can lay my hands on."

In answer to this, Madame Zéphyrine sighed, and appeared by a gesture to resign herself, like one yielding to unqualified authority.

That afternoon the observatory was finally blinded, a wardrobe having been drawn in front of it upon the other side, and while Silas was still lamenting over this misfortune, which he attributed to the Britisher's malign suggestion, the concierge brought him up a letter in a female handwriting. It was conceived in French of no very rigorous orthography, bore no signature, and in the most encouraging terms invited the young American to be present in a certain part of the Bullier Ball at eleven o'clock that night. Curiosity and timidity fought a long battle in his heart; sometimes he was all virtue, sometimes all fire and daring; and the result of it was that, long before ten, Mr. Silas Q. Scuddamore presented himself in unimpeachable attire at the door of the Bullier Ball Rooms, and paid his entry money with a sense of reckless deviltry that was not without its charm.

It was Carnival time, and the Ball was very full and noisy. The lights and the crowd at first rather abashed our young adventurer, and then, mounting to his brain with a sort of intoxication, put him in possession of more than his own share of manhood. He felt ready to face the devil, and strutted in the ballroom with the swagger of a cavalier. While he was thus parading, he became aware of Madame Zéphyrine and her Britisher in conference behind a pillar. The cat-like spirit of eaves-dropping overcame him at once. He stole nearer and nearer on the couple from behind, until he was within earshot.

"That is the man," the Britisher was saying; "there—with the long blond hair—speaking to a girl in green."

Silas identified a very handsome young fellow of small stature, who was plainly the object of this designation.

"It is well," said Madame Zéphyrine. "I shall do my utmost. But, remember, the best of us may fail in such a matter."

"Tut!" returned her companion; "I answer for the result. Have I not chosen you from thirty? Go; but be wary of the Prince. I cannot think what cursed accident has brought him here tonight. As if there were not a dozen balls in Paris better worth his notice than this riot of students and counter-jumpers! See him where he sits, more like a reigning Emperor at home than a Prince upon his holidays!"

Silas was again lucky. He observed a person of rather a full build, strikingly handsome, and of a very stately and courteous demeanor, seated at table with another handsome young man, several years his junior, who addressed him with conspicuous deference. The name of Prince struck gratefully on Silas's republican hearing, and the aspect of the person to whom that name was applied exercised its usual charm upon his mind. He left Madame Zéphyrine and her Englishman to take care of each other, and threading his way through the assembly, approached the table which the Prince and his confidant had honoured with their choice.

"I tell you, Geraldine," the former was saying, "the action is madness. Yourself (I am glad to remember it) chose your brother for this perilous service, and you are bound in duty to have a guard upon his conduct. He has consented to delay so many days in Paris; that was already an imprudence, considering the character of the man he has to deal with; but now, when he is within eight and forty hours of his departure, when he is within two or three days of the decisive trial, I ask you, is this a place for him to spend his time? He should be in a gallery at practice; he should be sleeping long hours and taking moderate exercise on foot; he should be on a rigorous diet, without white wines or brandy. Does the dog imagine we are all playing comedy? The thing is deadly earnest, Geraldine."

"I know the lad too well to interfere," replied Colonel Geraldine, "and well enough not to be alarmed. He is more cautious than you fancy, and of an indomitable spirit. If it had been a woman I should not say so much, but I trust the President to him and the two valets without an instant's apprehension."

"I am gratified to hear you say so," replied the Prince; "but my mind is not at rest. These servants are well-trained spies, and already has not this miscreant succeeded three times in eluding their observation and spending several hours on end in private, and most likely dangerous, affairs? An amateur might have lost him by accident, but if Rudolph and Jérome were thrown off the scent, it must have been done on purpose, and by a man who had a cogent reason and exceptional resources."

"I believe the question is now one between my brother and myself," replied Geraldine, with a shade of offense in his tone.

"I permit it to be so, Colonel Geraldine," returned Prince Florizel. "Perhaps, for that very reason, you should be all the more ready to accept my counsels. But enough. That girl in yellow dances well."

And the talk veered into the ordinary topics of a Paris ballroom in the Carnival.

Silas remembered where he was, and that the hour was already near at hand when he ought to be upon the scene of his assignation. The more he reflected the less he liked the prospect, and as at that moment an eddy in the crowd began to draw him in the direction of the door, he suffered it to carry him away without resistance. The eddy stranded him in a corner under the gallery, where his ear was immediately struck with the voice of Madame Zéphyrine. She was speaking in French with the young man of the blond locks who had been pointed out by the strange Britisher not half an hour before.

"I have a character at stake," she said, "or I would put no other condition than my heart recommends. But you have only to say so much to the porter, and he will let you go by without a word."

"But why this talk of debt?" objected her companion.

"Heavens!" said she, "do you think I do not understand my own hotel?"

And she went by, clinging affectionately to her companion's arm.

This put Silas in mind of his billet.

"Ten minutes hence," thought he, "and I may be walking with as beautiful a woman as that, and even better dressed—perhaps a real lady, possibly a woman of title."

And then he remembered the spelling, and was a little downcast.

"But it may have been written by her maid," he imagined.

The clock was only a few minutes from the hour, and this immediate prox-imity set his heart beating at a curious and rather disagreeable speed. He reflected with relief that he was in no way bound to put in an appearance. Vir-tue and cowardice were together, and he made once more for the door, but this time of his own accord, and battling against the stream of people which was now moving in a contrary direction. Perhaps this prolonged resistance wearied him, or perhaps he was in that frame of mind when merely to con-tinue in the same determination for a certain number of minutes produces a reaction and a different purpose. Certainly, at least, he wheeled about for a third time, and did not stop until he had found a place of concealment within a few yards of the appointed place.

Here he went through an agony of spirit, in which he several times prayed to God for help, for Silas had been devoutly educated. He had now not the least inclination for the meeting; nothing kept him from flight but a silly fear lest he should be thought unmanly; but this was so powerful that it kept head against all other motives; and although it could not decide him to advance, prevented him from definitely running away. At last the clock indicated ten minutes past the hour. Young Scuddamore's spirit began to rise; he peered round the corner and saw no one at the place of meeting; doubtless his unknown correspondent had wearied and gone away. He became as bold as he had formerly been timid. It seemed to him that if he came at all to the appoint-ment, however late, he was clear from the charge of cowardice. Nay, now he began to suspect a hoax, and actually complimented himself on his shrewd-ness in having suspected and out-manœuvred his mystifiers. So very idle a thing is a boy's mind!

Armed with these reflections, he advanced boldly from his corner; but he had not taken above a couple of steps before a hand was laid upon his arm. He turned and beheld a lady cast in a very large mould and with somewhat stately features, but bearing no mark of severity in her looks.

"I see that you are a very self-confident lady-killer," said she; "for you make yourself expected. But I was determined to meet you. When a woman has once so far forgotten herself as to make the first advance, she has long ago left behind her all considerations of petty pride."

Silas was overwhelmed by the size and attractions of his correspondent and the suddenness with which she had fallen upon him. But she soon set him at his ease. She was very towardly and lenient in her behaviour; she led him on to make pleasantries, and then applauded him to the echo; and in a very short time, between blandishments and a liberal exhibition of warm brandy, she had not only induced him to fancy himself in love, but to declare his passion with the greatest vehemence.

"Alas!" she said; "I do not know whether I ought not to deplore this moment, great as is the pleasure you give me by your words. Hitherto I was alone to suffer; now, poor boy, there will be two. I am not my own mistress. I dare not ask you to visit me at my own house, for I am watched by jealous eyes. Let me see," she added; "I am older than you, although so much weaker; and while I trust in your courage and determination, I must employ my own knowledge of the world for our mutual benefit. Where do you live?"

He told her that he lodged in a furnished hotel, and named the street and number.

She seemed to reflect for some minutes, with an effort of mind.

"I see," she said at last. "You will be faithful and obedient, will you not?"

Silas assured her eagerly of his fidelity.

"Tomorrow night, then," she continued, with an encouraging smile, "you must remain at home all the evening; and if any friends should visit you, dismiss them at once on any pretext that most readily presents itself. Your door is probably shut by ten?" she asked.

"By eleven," answered Silas.

"At a quarter past eleven," pursued the lady, "leave the house. Merely cry for the door to be opened, and be sure you fall into no talk with the porter, as that might ruin everything. Go straight to the corner where the Luxembourg Gardens join the Boulevard; there you will find me waiting you. I trust you to follow my advice from point to point: and remember, if you fail me in only one particular, you will bring the sharpest trouble on a woman whose only fault is to have seen and loved you."

"I cannot see the use of all these instructions," said Silas.

"I believe you are already beginning to treat me as a master," she cried, tapping him with her fan upon the arm. "Patience, patience! that should come in time. A woman loves to be obeyed at first, although afterwards she finds her pleasure in obeying. Do as I ask you, for Heaven's sake, or I will answer for nothing. Indeed, now I think of it," she added, with the manner of one who had just seen further into a difficulty, "I find a better plan of keeping importunate visitors away. Tell the porter to admit no one for you, except a person who may come that night to claim a debt; and speak with some feeling, as though you feared the interview, so that he may take your words in earnest."

"I think you may trust me to protect myself against intruders," he said, not without a little pique.

"That is how I should prefer the thing arranged," she answered, coldly. "I know you men; you think nothing of a woman's reputation."

Silas blushed and somewhat hung his head; for the scheme he had in view had involved a little vain-glorying before his acquaintances.

"Above all," she added, "do not speak to the porter as you come out."

"And why?" said he. "Of all your instructions, that seems to me the least important."

"You at first doubted the wisdom of some of the others, which you now see to be very necessary," she replied. "Believe me, this also has its uses; in time you will see them; and what am I to think of your affection, if you refuse me such trifles at our first interview?"

Silas confounded himself in explanations and apologies; in the middle of these she looked up at the clock and clapped her hands together with a suppressed scream.

"Heavens!" she cried, "is it so late? I have not an instant to lose. Alas, we poor women, what slaves we are! What have I not risked for you already?"

And after repeating her directions, which she artfully combined with caresses and the most abandoned looks, she bade him farewell and disappeared among the crowd.

The whole of the next day Silas was filled with a sense of great importance; he was now sure she was a countess; and when evening came he minutely obeyed her orders and was at the corner of the Luxembourg Gardens by the hour appointed. No one was there. He waited nearly half an hour, looking in the face of everyone who passed or loitered near the spot; he even visited the neighboring corners of the Boulevard and made a complete circuit of the garden railings; but there was no beautiful countess to throw herself into his arms. At last, and most reluctantly, he began to retrace his steps towards his hotel. On the way he remembered the words he had heard pass between Madame Zéphyrine and the blond young man, and they gave him an indefinite uneasiness.

"It appears," he reflected, "that everyone has to tell lies to our porter."

He rang the bell, the door opened before him, and the porter in his bedclothes came to offer him a light.

"Has he gone?" inquired the porter.

"He? Whom do you mean?" asked Silas, somewhat sharply, for he was irritated by his disappointment.

"I did not notice him go out," continued the porter, "but I trust you paid him. We do not care, in this house, to have lodgers who cannot meet their liabilities."

"What the devil do you mean?" demanded Silas, rudely. "I cannot understand a word of this farrago."

"The short, blond young man who came for his debt," returned the other. "Him it is I mean. Who else should it be, when I had your orders to admit no one else?"

"Why, good God, of course he never came," retorted Silas.

"I believe what I believe," retorted the porter, putting his tongue into his cheek with a most roguish air.

"You are an insolent scoundrel," cried Silas, and, feeling that he had made a ridiculous exhibition of asperity, and at the same time bewildered by a dozen alarms, he turned and began to run upstairs.

"Do you not want a light then?" cried the porter.

But Silas only hurried the faster, and did not pause until he had reached the seventh landing and stood in front of his own door. There he waited a moment to recover his breath, assailed by the worst forebodings and almost dreading to enter the room.

When at last he did so he was relieved to find it dark, and to all appearance, untenanted. He drew a long breath. Here he was, home again in safety, and this should be his last folly as certainly as it had been his first. The matches stood on a little table by the bed, and he began to grope his way in that direction. As he moved, his apprehensions grew upon him once more, and he was pleased, when his foot encountered an obstacle, to find it nothing more alarming than a chair. At last he touched curtains. From the position of the window, which was faintly visible, he knew he must be at the foot of the bed, and had only to feel his way along it in order to reach the table in question.

He lowered his hand, but what he touched was not simply a counterpane— it was a counterpane with something underneath it like the outline of a human leg. Silas withdrew his arm and stood a moment petrified.

"What, what," he thought, "can this betoken?"

He listened intently, but there was no sound of breathing. Once more, with a great effort, he reached out the end of his finger to the spot he had already touched; but this time he leaped back half a yard, and stood shivering and fixed with terror. There was something in his bed. What it was he knew not, but there was something there.

It was some seconds before he could move. Then, guided by an instinct, he fell straight upon the matches, and keeping his back toward the bed, lighted a candle. As soon as the flame had kindled, he turned slowly round and looked for what he feared to see. Sure enough, there was the worst of his imaginations realized. The coverlid was drawn carefully up over the pillow, but it moulded the outline of a human body lying motionless; and when he dashed forward and flung aside the sheets, he beheld the blond young man whom he had seen in the Bullier Ball the night before, his eyes open and without speculation, his face swollen and blackened, and a thin stream of blood trickling from his nostrils.

Silas uttered a long, tremulous wail, dropped the candle, and fell on his knees beside the bed.

Silas was awakened from the stupor into which his terrible discovery had plunged him, by a prolonged but discreet tapping at the door. It took him some seconds to remember his position; and when he hastened to prevent anyone from entering it was already too late. Dr. Noel, in a tall nightcap, carrying a lamp which lighted up his long white countenance, sidling in his gait, and peering and cocking his head like some sort of bird, pushed the door slowly open, and advanced into the middle of the room.

"I thought I heard a cry," began the Doctor, "and fearing you might be unwell, I did not hesitate to offer this intrusion."

Silas, with a flushed face and a fearful beating heart, kept between the Doctor and the bed; but he found no voice to answer.

"You are in the dark," pursued the Doctor; "and yet you have not even begun to prepare for rest. You will not easily persuade me against my own eyesight; and your face declares most eloquently that you require either a friend or a physician—which is it to be? Let me feel your pulse, for that is often a just reporter of the heart."

He advanced to Silas, who still retreated before him backwards, and sought to take him by the wrist; but the strain on the young American's nerves had become too great for endurance. He avoided the Doctor with a febrile movement, and, throwing himself upon the floor, burst into a flood of weeping.

As soon as Dr. Noel perceived the dead man in the bed his face darkened; and hurrying back to the door which he had left ajar, he hastily closed and double-locked it.

"Up!" he cried, addressing Silas in strident tones. "This is no time for weeping. What have you done? How came this body in your room. Speak freely to one who may be helpful. Do you imagine I would ruin you? Do you think this piece of dead flesh on your pillow can alter in any degree the sympathy with which you have inspired me? Credulous youth, the horror with which blind and unjust law regards an action never attaches to the doer in the eyes of those who love him; and if I saw the friend of my heart return to me out of seas of blood he would be in no way changed in my affection. Raise yourself," he said; "good and ill are a chimera; there is naught in life except destiny, and however you may be circumstanced there is one at your side who will help you to the last."

Thus encouraged, Silas gathered himself together, and in a broken voice, and helped out by the Doctor's interrogation, contrived at last to put him in possession of the facts. But the conversation between the Prince and Geraldine he altogether omitted, as he had understood little of its purport, and had no idea that it was in any way related to his own misadventure.

"Alas!" cried Dr. Noel, "I am much abused, or you have fallen innocently into the most dangerous hands in Europe. Poor boy, what a pit has been dug for your simplicity! into what a deadly peril have your unwary feet been conducted! This man," he said, "this Englishman, whom you twice saw, and whom I suspect to be the soul of the contrivance, can you describe him? Was he young or old? tall or short?"

But Silas, who, for all his curiosity, had not a seeing eye in his head, was able to supply nothing but meagre generalities, which it was impossible to recognize.

"I would have it a piece of education in all schools!" cried the Doctor angrily. "Where is the use of eyesight and articulate speech if a man cannot observe and recollect the features of his enemy? I, who know all the gangs of Europe, might have identified him, and gained new weapons for your defence. Cultivate this art in future, my poor boy; you may find it of momentous service."

"The future!" repeated Silas. "What future is there left for me except the gallows?"

"Youth is but a cowardly season," returned the Doctor; "and a man's own troubles look blacker than they are. I am old, and yet I never despair."

"Can I tell such a story to the police?" demanded Silas.

"Assuredly not," replied the Doctor. "From what I see already of the machination in which you have been involved, your case is desperate upon that side; and for the narrow eye of the authorities you are infallibly the guilty person. And remember that we only know a portion of the plot; and the same infamous contrivers have doubtless arranged many other circumstances which would be elicited by a police inquiry, and help to fix the guilt more certainly upon your innocence."

"I am then lost, indeed!" cried Silas.

"I have not said so," answered Dr. Noel, "for I am a cautious man."

"But look at this!" objected Silas, pointing to the body. "Here is this object in my bed: not to be explained, not to be disposed of, not to be regarded without horror."

"Horror?" replied the Doctor. "No. When this sort of clock has run down, it is no more to me than an ingenious piece of mechanism, to be investigated with the bistery.[1] When blood is once cold and stagnant, it is no longer human blood; when flesh is once dead, it is no longer that flesh which we desire in our lovers and respect in our friends. The grace, the attraction, the terror, have all gone from it with the animating spirit. Accustom yourself to look upon it with composure; for if my scheme is practicable you will have to live in constant proximity to that which now so greatly horrifies you."

"Your scheme?" cried Silas. "What is that? Tell me speedily, Doctor; for I have scarcely courage enough to continue to exist."

Without replying, Dr. Noel turned towards the bed, and proceeded to examine the corpse.

"Quite dead," he murmured. "Yes, as I had supposed, the pockets empty. Yes, and the name cut off the shirt. Their work has been done thoroughly and well. Fortunately he is of small stature."

Silas followed these words with an extreme anxiety. At last the Doctor, his autopsy completed, took a chair and addressed the young American with a smile.

"Since I came into your room," said he, "although my ears and my tongue have been so busy, I have not suffered my eyes to remain idle. I noted a little while ago that you have there, in the corner, one of those monstrous constructions which your fellow-countrymen carry with them into all quarters of the globe—in a word, a Saratoga trunk.[2] Until this moment I have never been able to conceive the utility of these erections; but then I began to have a glimmer. Whether it was for convenience in the slave trade, or to obviate the results of too ready an employment of the bowie-knife, I cannot bring myself to decide. But one thing I see plainly—the object of such a box is to contain a human body."

"Surely," cried Silas, "surely this is not a time for jesting."

"Although I may express myself with some degree of pleasantry," replied the Doctor, "the purport of my words is entirely serious. And the first thing we have to do, my young friend, is to empty your coffer of all it contains."

Silas, obeying the authority of Doctor Noel, put himself at his disposition. The Saratoga trunk was soon gutted of its contents, which made a considerable litter on the floor; and then—Silas taking the heels and the Doctor supporting the shoulders—the body of the murdered man was carried from the bed, and, after some difficulty, doubled up and inserted whole into the empty box. With an effort on the part of both, the lid was forced down upon this unusual baggage, and the trunk was locked and corded by the Doctor's own hand, while Silas disposed of what had been taken out between the closet and a chest of drawers.

"Now," said the Doctor, "the first step has been taken on the way to your deliverance. Tomorrow, or rather today, it must be your task to allay the suspicions of your porter, paying him all that you owe; while you may trust me to make the arrangements necessary to a safe conclusion. Meantime, follow me to my room, where I shall give you a safe and powerful opiate; for, whatever you do you must have rest."

The next day was the longest in Silas's memory; it seemed as if it would never be done. He denied himself to his friends, and sat in a corner with his eyes fixed upon the Saratoga trunk in dismal contemplation. His own former indiscretions were now returned upon him in kind; for the observatory had been once more opened, and he was conscious of an almost continual study from Madame Zéphyrine's apartment. So distressing did this become, that he was at last obliged to block up the spy-hole from his own side; and when he was thus secured from observation he spent a considerable portion of his time in contrite tears and prayer.

Late in the evening Dr. Noel entered the room carrying in his hand a pair of sealed envelopes without address, one somewhat bulky, and the other so slim as to seem without enclosure.

"Silas," he said, seating himself at the table, "the time has now come for me to explain my plan for your salvation. Tomorrow morning, at an early hour, Prince Florizel of Bohemia returns to London, after having diverted himself for a few days with the Parisian Carnival. It was my fortune, a good while ago, to do Colonel Geraldine, his Master of the Horse, one of those services so common in my profession, which are never forgotten upon either side. I have no need to explain to you the nature of the obligation under which he was laid; suffice it to say that I knew him ready to serve me in any practicable manner. Now, it was necessary for you to gain London with your trunk unopened. To this the Custom House seemed to oppose a fatal difficulty; but I bethought me that the baggage of so considerable a person as the Prince is, as a matter of courtesy, passed without examination by the officers of Custom. I applied to Colonel Geraldine, and succeeded in obtaining a favourable answer. Tomorrow, if you go before six to the hotel where the Prince lodges, your baggage will be passed over as a part of his, and you yourself will make the journey as a member of his suite."

"It seems to me, as you speak, that I have already seen both the Prince and Colonel Geraldine; I even overheard some of their conversation the other evening at the Bullier Ball."

"It is probable enough; for the Prince loves to mix with all societies," replied the Doctor. "Once arrived in London," he pursued, "your task is nearly ended. In this more bulky envelope I have given you a letter which I dare not address; but in the other you will find the designation of the house to which you must carry it along with your box, which will there be taken from you and not trouble you any more."

"Alas!" said Silas, "I have every wish to believe you; but how is it possible? You open up to me a bright prospect, but, I ask you, is my mind capable of receiving so unlikely a solution? Be more generous, and let me farther understand your meaning."

The Doctor seemed painfully impressed.

"Boy," he answered, "you do not know how hard a thing you ask of me. But be it so. I am now inured to humiliation; and it would be strange if I refused you this, after having granted you so much. Know, then, that although I now make so quiet an appearance—frugal, solitary, addicted to study—when I was younger, my name was once a rallying-cry among the most astute and dangerous spirits of London; and while I was outwardly an object for respect and consideration, my true power resided in the most secret, terrible, and criminal relations. It is to one of the persons who then obeyed me that I now address myself to deliver you from your burden. They were men of many different nations and dexterities, all bound together by a formidable oath, and working to the same purposes; the trade of the association was in murder; and I who speak to you, innocent as I appear, was the chieftain of this redoubtable crew."

"What?" cried Silas. "A murderer? And one with whom murder was a trade? Can I take your hand? Ought I to so much as accept your services? Dark and criminal old man, would you make an accomplice of my youth and my distress?"

The Doctor bitterly laughed.

"You are difficult to please, Mr. Scuddamore," said he; "but I now offer you your choice of company between the murdered man and the murderer. If your conscience is too nice to accept my aid, say so, and I will immediately leave you. Thenceforward you can deal with your trunk and its belongings as best suits your upright conscience."

"I own myself wrong," replied Silas. "I should have remembered how generously you offered to shield me, even before I had convinced you of my innocence, and I continue to listen to your counsels with gratitude."

"That is well," returned the Doctor; "and I perceive you are beginning to learn some of the lessons of experience."

"At the same time," resumed the New Englander, "as you confess yourself accustomed to this tragical business, and the people to whom you recommend me are your own former associates and friends, could you not yourself undertake the transport of the box, and rid me at once of its detested presence?"

"Upon my word," replied the Doctor, "I admire you cordially. If you do not think I have already meddled sufficiently in your concerns, believe me, from my heart I think the contrary. Take or leave my services as I offer them; and trouble me with no more words of gratitude, for I value your consideration even more lightly than I do your intellect. A time will come, if you should be spared to see a number of years in health and mind, when you will think differently of all this, and blush for your tonight's behaviour."

So saying, the Doctor arose from his chair, repeated his directions briefly and clearly, and departed from the room without permitting Silas any time to answer.

The next morning Silas presented himself at the hotel, where he was politely received by Colonel Geraldine, and relieved, from that moment, of all immediate alarm about his trunk and its grisly contents. The journey passed over without much incident, although the young man was horrified to overhear the sailors and railway porters complaining among themselves about the unusual weight of the Prince's baggage. Silas traveled in a carriage with the valets, for Prince Florizel chose to be alone with his Master of the Horse. On board the steamer, however, Silas attracted his Highness's attention by the melancholy of his air and attitude as he stood gazing at the pile of baggage; for he was still full of disquietude about the future.

"There is a young man," observed the Prince, "who must have some cause for sorrow."

"That," replied Geraldine, "is the American for whom I obtained permission to travel with your suite."

"You remind me that I have been remiss in courtesy," said Prince Florizel, and advancing to Silas, he addressed him with the most exquisite condescension in these words:

"I was charmed, young sir, to be able to gratify the desire you made known to me through Colonel Geraldine. Remember, if you please, that I shall be glad at any future time to lay you under a more serious obligation."

And then he put some questions as to the political condition of America, which Silas answered with sense and propriety.

"You are still a young man," said the Prince; "but I observe you to be very serious for your years. Perhaps you allow your attention to be too much occupied with grave studies. But, perhaps, on the other hand, I am myself indiscreet and touch upon a painful subject."

"I have certainly cause to be the most miserable of men," said Silas; "never has a more innocent person been more dismally abused."

"I will not ask you for your confidence," returned Prince Florizel. "But do not forget that Colonel Geraldine's recommendation is an unfailing passport; and that I am not only willing, but possibly more able than many others, to do you a service."

Silas was delighted with the amiability of this great personage; but his mind soon returned upon its gloomy preoccupations; for not even the favour of a Prince to a republican can discharge a brooding spirit of its cares.

The train arrived at Charing Cross, where the officers of the Revenue respected the baggage of Prince Florizel in the usual manner. The most elegant equipages were in waiting; and Silas was driven, along with the rest, to the Prince's residence. There Colonel Geraldine sought him out, and expressed himself pleased to have been of any service to a friend of the physician's, for whom he professed a great consideration.

"I hope," he added, "that you will find none of your porcelain injured. Special orders were given along the line to deal tenderly with the Prince's effects."

And then, directing the servants to place one of the carriages at the young gentleman's disposal, and at once to charge the Saratoga trunk upon the dickey, the Colonel shook hands and excused himself on account of his occupations in the princely household.

Silas now broke the seal of the envelope containing the address, and directed the stately footman to drive him to Box Court, opening off the Strand. It seemed as if the place were not at all unknown to the man, for he looked startled and begged a repetition of the order. It was with a heart full of alarms, that Silas mounted into the luxurious vehicle, and was driven to his destination. The entrance to Box Court was too narrow for the passage of a coach; it was a mere footway between railings, with a post at either end. On one of these posts was seated a man, who at once jumped down and exchanged a friendly sign with the driver, while the footman opened the door and inquired of Silas whether he should take down the Saratoga trunk, and to what number it should be carried.

"If you please," said Silas. "To number three."

The footman and the man who had been sitting on the post, even with the aid of Silas himself, had hard work to carry in the trunk; and before it was deposited at the door of the house in question, the young American was horrified to find a score of loiterers looking on. But he knocked with as good a countenance as he could muster up, and presented the other envelope to him who opened.

"He is not at home," said he, "but if you will leave your letter and return tomorrow early, I shall be able to inform you whether and when he can receive your visit. Would you like to leave your box?" he added.

"Dearly," cried Silas; and the next moment he repented his precipitation, and declared, with equal emphasis, that he would rather carry the box along with him to the hotel.

The crowd jeered at his indecision and followed him to the carriage with insulting remarks; and Silas, covered with shame and terror, implored the servants to conduct him to some quiet and comfortable house of entertainment in the immediate neighbourhood.

The Prince's equipage deposited Silas at the Craven Hotel in Craven Street, and immediately drove away, leaving him alone with the servants of the inn. The only vacant room, it appeared, was a little den up four pairs of stairs, and looking towards the back. To this hermitage, with infinite trouble and complaint, a pair of stout porters carried the Saratoga trunk. It is needless to mention that Silas kept closely at their heels throughout the ascent, and had his heart in his mouth at every corner. A single false step, he reflected, and the box might go over the banisters and land its fatal contents, plainly discovered, on the pavement of the hall.

Arrived in the room, he sat down on the edge of his bed to recover from the agony that he had just endured; but he had hardly taken his position when he was recalled to a sense of his peril by the action of the boots, who had knelt beside the trunk, and was proceeding officiously to undo its elaborate fastenings.

"Let it be!" cried Silas. "I shall want nothing from it while I stay here."

"You might have let it lie in the hall then," growled the man; "a thing as big and heavy as a church. What you have inside, I cannot fancy. If it is all money, you are a richer man than me."

"Money?" repeated Silas, in a sudden perturbation. "What did you mean by money? I have no money, and you are speaking like a fool."

"All right, Captain," retorted the boots with a wink. "There's nobody will touch your lordship's money. I'm as safe as the bank," he added; "but as the box is heavy, I shouldn't mind drinking something to your lordship's health."

Silas pressed two Napoleons upon his acceptance, apologizing, at the same time, for being obliged to trouble him with foreign money, and pleading his recent arrival for excuse. And the man, grumbling with even greater fervor, and looking contemptuously from the money in his hand to the Saratoga trunk and back again from the one to the other, at last consented to withdraw.

For nearly two days the dead body had been packed into Silas's box; and as soon as he was alone the unfortunate New Englander nosed all the cracks and openings with the most passionate attention. But the weather was cool, and the trunk still managed to contain his shocking secret.

He took a chair beside it, and buried his face in his hands, and his mind in the most profound reflection. If he were not speedily relieved, no question but he must be speedily discovered. Alone in a strange city, without friends or accomplices, if the Doctor's introduction failed him, he was indubitably a lost New Englander. He reflected pathetically over his ambitious designs for the future; he should not now become the hero and spokesman of his native place of Bangor, Maine; he should not, as he had fondly anticipated, move on from office to office, from honour to honour; he might as well divest himself at once of all hope of being acclaimed President of the United States, and leaving behind him a statue, in the worst possible style of art, to adorn the Capitol at Washington. Here he was, chained to a dead Englishman doubled up inside a Saratoga trunk; whom he must get rid of, or perish from the rolls of national glory!

I should be afraid to chronicle the language employed by this young man to the Doctor, to the murdered man, to Madame Zéphyrine, to the boots of the hotel, to the Prince's servants, and, in a word, to all who had been ever so remotely connected with his horrible misfortune.

He slunk down to dinner about seven at night; but the yellow coffee-room appalled him, the eyes of the other diners seemed to rest on his with suspicion, and his mind remained upstairs with the Saratoga trunk. When the waiter came to offer him cheese, his nerves were already so much on edge that he leaped half-way out of his chair and upset the remainder of a pint of ale upon the table-cloth.

The fellow offered to show him the smoking-room when he had done; and although he would have much preferred to return at once to his perilous treasure, he had not the courage to refuse, and was shown downstairs, to the black, gas-lit cellar, which formed, and possibly still forms, the divan of the Craven Hotel.

Two very sad betting men were playing billiards, attended by a moist, consumptive marker; and for the moment Silas imagined that these were the only occupants of the apartment. But at the next glance his eye fell upon a person smoking in the farthest corner, with lowered eyes and a most respectable and modest aspect. He knew at once that he had seen the face before; and in spite of the entire change of clothes, recognized the man whom he had found seated on a post at the entrance to Box Court, and who had helped him to carry the trunk to and from the carriage. The New Englander simply turned and ran, nor did he pause until he had locked and bolted himself into his bedroom.

There, all night long, a prey to the most terrible imaginations, he watched beside the fatal boxful of dead flesh. The suggestion of the boots that his trunk was full of gold inspired him with all manner of new terrors, if he so much as dared to close an eye; and the presence in the smoking-room, and under an obvious disguise, of the loiterer from Box Court convinced him that he was once more the centre of obscure machination.

Midnight had sounded some time, when, impelled by uneasy suspicions, Silas opened his bedroom door and peered into the passage. It was dimly illuminated by a single jet of gas; and some distance off he perceived a man sleeping on the floor in the costume of an hotel under-servant. Silas drew near the man on tip-toe. He lay partly on his back, partly on his side, and his right forearm concealed his face from recognition. Suddenly, while the American was still bending over him, the sleeper removed his arm and opened his eyes, and Silas found himself once more face to face with the loiterer of Box Court.

"Good night, sir," said the man, pleasantly.

But Silas was too profoundly moved to find an answer, and regained his room in silence.

Towards morning, worn out by apprehension, he fell asleep on his chair, with his head forward on the trunk. In spite of so constrained an attitude and such a grisly pillow, his slumber was sound and prolonged, and he was only awakened at a late hour and by a sharp tapping at the door.

He hurried to open, and found the boots without.

"You are the gentleman who called yesterday at Box Court?" he asked.

Silas, with a quaver, admitted that he had done so.

"Then this note is for you," added the servant, proffering a sealed envelope.

Silas tore it open, and found inside the words: "Twelve o'clock."

He was punctual to the hour; the trunk was carried before him by several stout servants; and he was himself ushered into a room, where a man sat warming himself before the fire with his back towards the door. The sound of so many persons entering and leaving, and the scraping of the trunk as it was deposited upon the bare boards, were alike unable to attract the notice of the occupant; and Silas stood waiting, in an agony of fear, until he should deign to recognize his presence.

Perhaps five minutes had elapsed before the man turned leisurely about, and disclosed the features of Prince Florizel of Bohemia.

"So, sir," he said with great severity, "this is the manner in which you abuse my politeness. You join yourself to persons of condition, I perceive, for no other purpose than to escape the consequences of your crimes; and I can readily understand your embarrassment when I addressed myself to you yesterday."

"Indeed," cried Silas, "I am innocent of everything except misfortune."

And in a hurried voice, and with the greatest ingenuousness, he recounted to the Prince the whole history of his calamity.

"I see I have been mistaken," said his Highness, when he had heard him to an end. "You are no other than a victim, and since I am not to punish you, you may be sure I shall do my utmost to help. And now," he continued, "to business. Open your box at once, and let me see what it contains."

Silas changed color.

"I almost fear to look upon it," he exclaimed.

"Nay," replied the Prince, "have you not looked at it already? This is a form of sentimentality to be resisted. The sight of a sick man, whom we can still help, should appeal more directly to the feelings than that of a dead man who is equally beyond help or harm, love or hatred. Nerve yourself, Mr. Scuddamore," and then, seeing that Silas still hesitated, "I do not desire to give another name to my request," he added.

The young American awoke as if out of a dream, and with a shiver of repugnance addressed himself to loose the straps and open the lock of the Saratoga trunk. The Prince stood by, watching with a composed countenance and his hands behind his back. The body was quite stiff, and it cost Silas a great effort, both moral and physical, to dislodge it from its position, and discover the face.

Prince Florizel started back with an exclamation of painful surprise.

"Alas!" he cried, "you little know, Mr. Scuddamore, what a cruel gift you have brought me. This is a young man of my own suite, the brother of my trusted friend; and it was upon matters of my own service that he has thus perished at the hands of violent and treacherous men. Poor Geraldine," he went on, as if to himself, "in what words am I to tell you of your brother's fate? How can I excuse myself in your eyes, or in the eyes of God, for the presumptuous schemes that led him to this bloody and unnatural death? Ah, Florizel! Florizel! when will you learn the discretion that suits mortal life, and be no longer dazzled with the image of power at your disposal? Power!" he cried; "who is more powerless? I look upon this young man whom I have sacrificed, Mr. Scuddamore, and feel how small a thing it is to be a Prince."

Silas was moved at the sight of his emotion. He tried to murmur some consolatory words, and burst into tears. The Prince, touched by his obvious intention, came up to him and took him by the hand.

"Command yourself," said he. "We have both much to learn and we shall both be better men for today's meeting."

Silas thanked him in silence with an affectionate look.

"Write me the address of Doctor Noel on this piece of paper," continued the Prince, leading him towards the table; "and let me recommend you, when you are again in Paris, to avoid the society of that dangerous man. He has acted in this matter on a generous inspiration; that I must believe; had he been privy to young Geraldine's death he would never have despatched the body to the care of the actual criminal."

"The actual criminal!" repeated Silas in astonishment.

"Even so," returned the Prince. "This letter, which the disposition of Almighty Providence has so strangely delivered into my hands, was addressed to no less a person than the criminal himself, the infamous President of the Suicide Club. Seek to pry no further in these perilous affairs, but content yourself with your own miraculous escape, and leave this house at once. I have pressing affairs, and must arrange at once about this poor clay, which was so lately a gallant and handsome youth."

Silas took a grateful and submissive leave of Prince Florizel, but he lingered in Box Court until he saw him depart in a splendid carriage on a visit to Colonel Henderson of the police. Republican as he was, the young American took off his hat with almost a sentiment of devotion to the retreating carriage. And the same night he started by rail on his return to Paris.

Here (observes my Arabian Author) *is the end of the* STORY OF THE PHYSICIAN AND THE SARATOGA TRUNK. *Omitting some reflections on the power of Providence, highly pertinent in the original, but little suited to our occidental taste, I shall only add that Mr. Scudda-more has already begun to mount the ladder of political fame, and by last advices was the Sheriff of his native town.*

The Adventure of the Hansom Cab

Lieutenant Brackenbury Rich had greatly distinguished himself in one of the lesser Indian hill wars.[1] He it was who took the chieftain prisoner with his own hand; his gallantry was universally applauded; and when he came home, prostrated by an ugly sabre cut and a protracted jungle fever, society was prepared to welcome the Lieutenant as a celebrity of minor luster. But his was a character remarkable for unaffected modesty; adventure was dear to his heart, but he cared little for adulation; and he waited at foreign watering-places and in Algiers until the fame of his exploits had run through its nine days' vitality and begun to be forgotten. He arrived in London at last, in the early season, with as little observation as he could desire; and as he was an orphan and had none but distant relatives who lived in the provinces, it was almost as a foreigner that he installed himself in the capital of the country for which he had shed his blood.

On the day following his arrival he dined alone at a military club. He shook hands with a few old comrades, and received their congratulations; but as one and all had some engagement for the evening, he found himself left entirely to his own resources. He was in dress, for he had entertained the notion of visiting a theater. But the great city was new to him; he had gone from a provincial school to a military college, and thence direct to the Eastern Empire; and he promised himself a variety of delights in this world for exploration. Swinging his cane, he took his way westward. It was a mild evening, already dark, and now and then threatening rain. The succession of faces in the lamplight stirred the Lieutenant's imagination; and it seemed to him as if he could walk for ever in that stimulating city atmosphere and surrounded by the mystery of four million private lives. He glanced at the houses, and marvelled what was passing behind those warmly lighted windows; he looked into face after face, and saw them each intent upon some unknown interest, criminal or kindly.

"They talk of war," he thought, "but this is the great battlefield of mankind."

And then he began to wonder that he should walk so long in this complicated scene, and not chance upon so much as the shadow of an adventure for himself.

"All in good time," he reflected. "I am still a stranger, and perhaps wear a strange air. But I must be drawn into the eddy before long."

The night was already well advanced, when a plump of cold rain fell suddenly out of the darkness. Brackenbury paused under some trees, and as he did so he caught sight of a hansom cabman making him a sign that he was disengaged. The circumstance fell in so happily to the occasion that he at once raised his cane in answer, and had soon ensconced himself in the London gondola.

"Where to, sir?" asked the driver.

"Where you please," said Brackenbury.

And immediately, at a pace of surprising swiftness, the hansom drove off through the rain into a maze of villas. One villa was so like another, each with its front garden, and there was so little to distinguish the deserted lamp-lit streets and crescents through which the flying hansom took its way, that Brackenbury soon lost all idea of direction. He would have been contented to believe that the cabman was amusing himself by driving him round and round and in and out about a small quarter, but there was something businesslike in the speed which convinced him of the contrary. The man had an object in view, he was hastening towards a definite end and Brackenbury was at once astonished at the fellow's skill in picking a way through such a labyrinth, and a little concerned to imagine what was the occasion of his hurry. He had heard tales of strangers falling ill in London. Did the driver belong to some bloody and treacherous association? and was he himself being whirled to a murderous death?

The thought had scarcely presented itself, when the cab swung sharply round a corner and pulled up before the garden gate of a villa in a long and wide road. The house was brilliantly lighted up. Another hansom had just driven away, and Brackenbury could see a gentleman being admitted at the front door and received by several liveried servants. He was surprised that the cabman should have stopped so immediately in front of a house where a reception was being held; but he did not doubt it was the result of accident, and sat placidly smoking where he was, until he heard the trap thrown open over his head.

"Here we are, sir," said the driver.

"Here!" repeated Brackenbury. "Where?"

"You told me to take you where I pleased, sir," returned the man with a chuckle, "and here we are."

It struck Brackenbury that the voice was wonderfully smooth and courteous for a man in so inferior a position; he remembered the speed at which he had been driven; and now it occurred to him that the hansom was more luxuriously appointed than the common run of public conveyances.

"I must ask you to explain," said he. "Do you mean to turn me out into the rain? My good man, I suspect the choice is mine."

"The choice is certainly yours," replied the driver, "but when I tell you all, I believe I know how a gentleman of your figure will decide. There is a gentlemen's party in this house. I do not know whether the master be a stranger to London and without acquaintances of his own; or whether he is a man of odd notions. But certainly I was hired to kidnap single gentlemen in evening dress, as many as I pleased, but military officers by preference. You have simply to go in and say that Mr. Morris invited you."

"Are you Mr. Morris?" inquired the Lieutenant.

"Oh, no," replied the cabman. "Mr. Morris is the person of the house."

"It is not a common way of collecting guests," said Brackenbury; "but an eccentric man might very well indulge the whim without any intention to offend. And suppose that I refuse Mr. Morris's invitation," he went on, "what then?"

"My orders are to drive you back where I took you from," replied the man, "and set out to look for others up to midnight. Those who have no fancy for such an adventure, Mr. Morris said, were not the guests for him."

These words decided the Lieutenant on the spot.

"After all," he reflected, as he descended from the hansom, "I have not had long to wait for my adventure."

He had hardly found footing on the side-walk, and was still feeling in his pocket for the fare, when the cab swung about and drove off by the way it came at the former break-neck velocity. Brackenbury shouted after the man, who paid no heed, and continued to drive away; but the sound of his voice was overheard in the house, the door was again thrown open, emitting a flood of light upon the garden, and a servant ran down to meet him holding an umbrella.

"The cabman has been paid," observed the servant in a very civil tone; and he proceeded to escort Brackenbury along the path and up the steps. In the hall several other attendants relieved him of his hat, cane, and paletot,[2] gave him a ticket with a number in return, and politely hurried him up a stair adorned with tropical flowers, to the door of an apartment on the first story. Here a grave butler inquired his name, and announcing "Lieutenant Brackenbury Rich," ushered him into the drawing-room of the house.

A young man, slender and singularly handsome, came forward and greeted him with an air at once courtly and affectionate. Hundreds of candles, of the finest wax, lit up a room perfumed, like the staircase, with a profusion of rare and beautiful flowering shrubs. A side-table was loaded with tempting viands. Several servants went to and fro with fruits and goblets of champagne. The company was perhaps sixteen in number, all men, few beyond the prime of life, and with hardly an exception, of a dashing and capable exterior.

They were divided into two groups, one about a roulette board, and the other surrounding a table at which one of their number held a bank of baccarat.

"I see," thought Brackenbury, "I am in a private gambling saloon, and the cabman was a tout."

His eye had embraced the details, and his mind formed the conclusion, while his host was still holding him by the hand; and to him his looks returned from this rapid survey. At a second view Mr. Morris surprised him still more than on the first. The easy elegance of his manners, the distinction, amiability, and courage that appeared upon his features, fitted very ill with the Lieutenant's preconceptions on the subject of the proprietor of a hell;[3] and the tone of his conversation seemed to mark him out for a man of position and merit. Brackenbury found he had an instinctive liking for his entertainer and though he chid himself for the weakness he was unable to resist a sort of friendly attraction for Mr. Morris's person and character.

"I have heard of you, Lieutenant Rich," said Mr. Morris, lowering his tone; "and believe me I am gratified to make your acquaintance. Your looks accord with the reputation that has preceded you from India. And if you will forget for a while the irregularity of your presentation in my house, I shall feel it not only an honour, but genuine pleasure besides. A man who makes a mouthful of barbarian cavaliers," he added with a laugh, "should not be appalled by a breach of etiquette, however serious."

And he led him towards the sideboard and pressed him to partake of some refreshments.

"Upon my word," the Lieutenant reflected, "this is one of the pleasantest fellows and, I do not doubt, one of the most agreeable societies in London."

He partook of some champagne, which he found excellent; and observing that many of the company were already smoking, he lit one of his own Manilas, and strolled up to the roulette board, where he sometimes made a stake and sometimes looked on smilingly on the fortune of others. It was while he was thus idling that he became aware of a sharp scrutiny to which the whole of the guests were subjected. Mr. Morris went here and there, ostensibly busied on hospitable concerns; but he had ever a shrewd glance at disposal; not a man of the party escaped his sudden, searching looks; he took stock of the bearing of heavy losers, he valued the amount of the stakes, he paused behind couples who were deep in conversation; and, in a word, there was hardly a characteristic of anyone present but he seemed to catch and make a note of it. Brackenbury began to wonder if this were indeed a gambling hell: it had so much the air of a private inquisition. He followed Mr. Morris in all his movements; and although the man had a ready smile, he seemed to perceive, as it were under a mask, a haggard, careworn, and preoccupied spirit. The fellows around him laughed and made their game; but Brackenbury had lost interest in the guests.

"This Morris," thought he, "is no idler in the room. Some deep purpose inspires him; let it be mine to fathom it."

Now and then Mr. Morris would call one of his visitors aside; and after a brief colloquy in an ante-room, he would return alone, and the visitors in question reappeared no more. After a certain number of repetitions, this performance excited Brackenbury's curiosity to a high degree. He determined to be at the bottom of this minor mystery at once; and strolling into the anteroom, found a deep window recess concealed by curtains of the fashionable green. Here he hurriedly ensconced himself; nor had he to wait long before the sound of steps and voices drew near him from the principal apartment. Peering through the division, he saw Mr. Morris escorting a fat and ruddy personage, with somewhat the look of a commercial traveler, whom Brackenbury had already remarked for his coarse laugh and under-bred behaviour at the table. The pair halted immediately before the window, so that Brackenbury lost not a word of the following discourse:—

"I beg you a thousand pardons!" began Mr. Morris, with the most conciliatory manner; "and, if I appear rude, I am sure you will readily forgive me. In a place so great as London accidents must continually happen; and the best that we can hope is to remedy them with as small delay as possible. I will not deny that I fear you have made a mistake and honoured my poor house by inadvertence; for, to speak openly, I cannot at all remember your appearance. Let me put the question without unnecessary circumlocution—between gentlemen of honour a word will suffice—Under whose roof do you suppose yourself to be?"

"That of Mr. Morris," replied the other, with a prodigious display of confusion, which had been visibly growing upon him throughout the last few words.

"Mr. John or Mr. James Morris?" inquired the host.

"I really cannot tell you," returned the unfortunate guest. "I am not personally acquainted with the gentleman, any more than I am with yourself."

"I see," said Mr. Morris. "There is another person of the same name farther down the street; and I have no doubt the policeman will be able to supply you with his number. Believe me, I felicitate myself on the misunderstanding which has procured me the pleasure of your company for so long; and let me express a hope that we may meet again upon a more regular footing. Meantime, I would not for the world detain you longer from your friends. John," he added, raising his voice, "will you see that the gentleman finds his great-coat?"

And with the most agreeable air Mr. Morris escorted his visitor as far as the ante-room door, where he left him under conduct of the butler. As he passed the window, on his return to the drawing-room, Brackenbury could hear him utter a profound sigh, as though his mind was loaded with great anxiety, and his nerves already fatigued with the task on which he was engaged.

For perhaps an hour the hansoms kept arriving with such frequency, that Mr. Morris had to receive a new guest for every old one that he sent away, and the company preserved its number undiminished. But towards the end of that time the arrivals grew few and far between, and at length ceased entirely, while the process of elimination was continued with unimpaired activity. The drawing-room began to look empty: the baccarat was discontinued for lack of a banker; more than one person said good night of his own accord, and was suffered to depart without expostulation: and in the meanwhile Mr. Morris redoubled in agreeable attentions to those who stayed behind. He went from group to group and from person to person with looks of the readiest sympathy and the most pertinent and pleasing talk; he was not so much like a host as like a hostess, and there was a feminine coquetry and condescension in his manner which charmed the hearts of all.

As the guests grew thinner, Lieutenant Rich strolled for a moment out of the drawing-room into the hall in quest of fresher air. But he had no sooner passed the threshold of the ante-chamber than he was brought to a dead halt by a discovery of the most surprising nature. The flowering shrubs had disappeared from the staircase; three large furniture wagons stood before the garden gate; the servants were busy dismantling the house upon all sides; and some of them had already donned their great-coats and were preparing to depart. It was like the end of a country ball, where everything has been supplied by contract. Brackenbury had indeed some matter for reflection. First, the guests, who were no real guests after all, had been dismissed; and now the servants, who could hardly be genuine servants, were actively dispersing.

"Was the whole establishment a sham?" he asked himself. "The mushroom of a single night which should disappear before morning?"

Watching a favourable opportunity, Brackenbury dashed upstairs to the higher regions of the house. It was as he had expected. He ran from room to room, and saw not a stick of furniture nor so much as a picture on the walls. Although the house had been painted and papered, it was not only uninhabited at present, but plainly had never been inhabited at all. The young officer remembered with astonishment its specious, settled, and hospitable air on his arrival. It was only at a prodigious cost that the imposture could have been carried out upon so great a scale.

Who, then, was Mr. Morris? What was his intention in thus playing the householder for a single night in the remote west of London? And why did he collect his visitors at hazard from the streets?

Brackenbury remembered that he had already delayed too long, and hastened to join the company. Many had left during his absence; and counting the Lieutenant and his host, there were not more than five persons in the drawing-room—recently so thronged. Mr. Morris greeted him, as he re-entered the apartment, with a smile, and immediately rose to his feet.

"It is now time, gentlemen," said he, "to explain my purpose in decoying you from your amusements. I trust you did not find the evening hang very dully on your hands; but my object, I will confess it, was not to entertain your leisure, but to help myself in an unfortunate necessity. You are all gentlemen," he continued, "your appearance does you that much justice, and I ask for no better security. Hence, I speak it without concealment, I ask you to render me a dangerous and delicate service; dangerous because you may run the hazard of your lives, and delicate because I must ask an absolute discretion upon all that you shall see or hear. From an utter stranger the request is almost comically extravagant; I am well aware of this; and I would add at once, if there be anyone present who has heard enough, if there be one among the party who recoils from a dangerous confidence and a piece of Quixotic devotion to he knows not whom—here is my hand ready, and I shall wish him good night and Godspeed, with all the sincerity in the world."

A very tall, black man, with a heavy stoop, immediately responded to this appeal.

"I commend your frankness, sir," said he; "and, for my part, I go. I make no reflections; but I cannot deny that you fill me with suspicious thoughts. I go myself, as I say; and perhaps you will think I have no right to add words to my example."

"On the contrary," replied Mr. Morris, "I am obliged to you for all you say. It would be impossible to exaggerate the gravity of my proposal."

"Well, gentlemen, what do you say?" said the tall man, addressing the others. "We have had our evening's frolic; shall we go homeward peaceably in a body? You will think well of my suggestion in the morning, when you see the sun again in innocence and safety."

The speaker pronounced the last words with an intonation which added to their force; and his face wore a singular expression, full of gravity and significance. Another of the company rose hastily, and, with some appearance of alarm, prepared to take his leave. There were only two who held their ground, Brackenbury and an old red-nosed cavalry Major; but these two preserved a nonchalant demeanor, and, beyond a look of intelligence which they rapidly exchanged, appeared entirely foreign to the discussion that had just been terminated.

Mr. Morris conducted the deserters as far as the door, which he closed upon their heels; then he turned round disclosing a countenance of mingled relief and animation, and addressed the two officers as follows:

"I have chosen my men like Joshua in the Bible,"[4] said Mr. Morris, "and I now believe I have the pick of London. Your appearance pleased my hansom cabmen; then it delighted me; I watched your behaviour in a strange company, and under the most unusual circumstances: I have studied how you played and how you bore your losses; lastly, I have put you to the test of a staggering announcement, and you received it like an invitation to dinner. It is not for nothing," he cried, "that I have been for years the companion and the pupil of the bravest and wisest potentate in Europe."

"At the affair of Bunderchang," observed the Major, "I asked for twelve volunteers, and every trooper in the ranks replied to my appeal. But a gaming party is not the same thing as a regiment under fire. You may be pleased, I suppose, to have found two, and two who will not fail you at a push. As for the pair who ran away, I count them among the most pitiful hounds I ever met with. Lieutenant Rich," he added, addressing Brackenbury, "I have heard much of you of late; and I cannot doubt but you have also heard of me. I am Major O'Rooke."

And the veteran tendered his hand, which was red and tremulous, to the young Lieutenant.

"Who has not?" answered Brackenbury.

"When this little matter is settled," said Mr. Morris, "you will think I have sufficiently rewarded you; for I could offer neither a more valuable service than to make him acquainted with the other."

"And now," said Major O'Rooke, "is it a duel?"

"A duel after a fashion," replied Mr. Morris, "a duel with unknown and dangerous enemies, and, as I gravely fear, a duel to the death. I must ask you," he continued, "to call me Morris no longer; call me, if you please,

Hammersmith; my real name, as well as that of another person to whom I hope to present you before long, you will gratify me by not asking and not seeking to discover for yourselves. Three days ago the person of whom I speak disappeared suddenly from home; and, until this morning, I received no hint of his situation. You will fancy my alarm when I tell you that he is engaged upon a work of private justice. Bound by an unhappy oath, too lightly sworn, he finds it necessary, without the help of law, to rid the earth of an insidious and bloody villain. Already two of our friends, and one of them my own born brother, have perished in the enterprise. He himself, or I am much deceived, is taken in the same fatal toils. But at least he still lives and still hopes, as this billet sufficiently proves."

And the speaker, no other than Colonel Geraldine, proffered a letter, thus conceived:——

"Major Hammersmith,——On Wednesday, at 3 A.M., you will be admitted by the small door to the gardens of Rochester House, Regent's Park, by a man who is entirely in my interest. I must request you not to fail me by a second. Pray bring my case of swords, and, if you can find them, one or two gentlemen of conduct and discretion to whom my person is unknown. My name must not be used in this affair.

"T. GODALL."

"From his wisdom alone, if he had no other title," pursued Colonel Geraldine, when the others had each satisfied his curiosity, "my friend is a man whose directions should implicitly be followed. I need not tell you, therefore, that I have not so much as visited the neighborhood of Rochester House; and that I am still as wholly in the dark as either of yourselves as to the nature of my friend's dilemma. I betook myself, as soon as I had received this order, to a furnishing contractor, and, in a few hours, the house in which we now are had assumed its late air of festival. My scheme was at least original; and I am far from regretting an action which has procured me the services of Major O'Rooke and Lieutenant Brackenbury Rich. But the servants in the street will have a strange awakening. The house which this evening was full of lights and visitors they will find uninhabited and for sale tomorrow morning. Thus even the most serious concerns," added the Colonel, "have a merry side."

"And let us add a merry ending," said Brackenbury.

The Colonel consulted his watch.

"It is now hard on two," he said. "We have an hour before us, and a swift cab is at the door. Tell me if I may count upon your help."

"During a long life," replied Major O'Rooke, "I never took back my hand from anything, nor so much as hedged a bet."

Brackenbury signified his readiness in the most becoming terms; and after they had drunk a glass or two of wine, the Colonel gave each of them a loaded revolver, and the three mounted into the cab and drove off for the address in question.

Rochester House was a magnificent residence on the banks of the canal. The large extent of the garden isolated it in an unusual degree from the annoyances of neighbourhood. It seemed the *parc aux cerfs*[5] of some great nobleman or millionaire. As far as could be seen from the street, there was not a glimmer of light in any of the numerous windows of the mansion; and the place had a look of neglect, as though the master had been long from home.

The cab was discharged, and the three gentlemen were not long in discovering the small door, which was a sort of postern in a lane between two garden walls. It still wanted ten or fifteen minutes of the appointed time, the rain fell heavily, and the adventurers sheltered themselves below some pendent ivy, and spoke in low tones of the approaching trial.

Suddenly Geraldine raised his finger to command silence, and all three bent their hearing to the utmost. Through the continuous noise of the rain, the steps and voices of two men became audible from the other side of the wall; and, as they drew nearer, Brackenbury, whose sense of hearing was remarkably acute, could even distinguish some fragments of their talk.

"Is the grave dug?" asked one

"It is," replied the other; "behind the laurel hedge. When the job is done, we can cover it with a pile of stakes."

The first speaker laughed, and the sound of his merriment was shocking to the listeners on the other side.

"In an hour from now," he said.

And by the sound of the steps it was obvious that the pair had separated, and were proceeding in contrary directions.

Almost immediately after the postern door was cautiously opened, a white face was protruded into the lane, and a hand was seen beckoning to the watchers. In dead silence the three passed the door, which was immediately locked behind them, and followed their guide through several garden alleys to the kitchen entrance of the house. A single candle burned in the great paved kitchen, which was destitute of the customary furniture; and as the party proceeded to ascend from thence by a flight of winding stairs, a prodigious noise of rats testified still more plainly to the dilapidation of the house.

Their conductor preceded them, carrying the candle. He was a lean man, much bent, but still agile; and he turned from time to time and admonished silence and caution by his gestures. Colonel Geraldine followed on his heels, the case of swords under one arm, and a pistol ready in the other. Brackenbury's heart beat thickly. He perceived that they were still in time; but he judged from the alacrity of the old man that the hour of action must be near at hand; the circumstances of this adventure were so obscure and menacing, the place seemed so well chosen for the darkest acts, that an older man than Brackenbury might have been pardoned a measure of emotion as he closed the procession up the winding stair.

At the top the guide threw open a door and ushered the three officers before him into a small apartment, lighted by a smoky lamp and the glow of a modest fire. At the chimney corner sat a man in the early prime of life, and of a stout but courtly and commanding appearance. His attitude and expression were those of the most unmoved composure; he was smoking a cheroot with much enjoyment and deliberation, and on a table by his elbow stood a long glass of some effervescing beverage which diffused an agreeable odor through the room.

"Welcome," said he, extending his hand to Colonel Geraldine. "I knew I might count on your exactitude."

"On my devotion," replied the Colonel, with a bow.

"Present me to your friends," continued the first; and, when that ceremony had been performed, "I wish, gentlemen," he added, with the most exquisite affability, "that I could offer you a more cheerful programme; it is ungracious to inaugurate an acquaintance upon serious affairs; but the compulsion of events is stronger than the obligations of good-fellowship. I hope and believe you will be able to forgive me this unpleasant evening; and for men of your stamp it will be enough to know that you are conferring a considerable favour."

"Your Highness," said the Major, "must pardon my bluntness. I am unable to hide what I know. For some time back I have suspected Major Hammersmith, but Mr. Godall is unmistakable. To seek two men in London unacquainted with Prince Florizel of Bohemia was to ask too much at Fortune's hands."

"Prince Florizel!" cried Brackenbury in amazement.

And he gazed with the deepest interest on the features of the celebrated personage before him.

"I shall not lament the loss of my incognito," remarked the Prince, "for it enables me to thank you with the more authority. You would have done as much for Mr. Godall, I feel sure, as for the Prince of Bohemia; but the latter can perhaps do more for you. The gain is mine," he added, with a courteous gesture.

And the next moment he was conversing with the two officers about the Indian army and the native troops, a subject on which, as on all others, he had a remarkable fund of information and the soundest views.

There was something so striking in this man's attitude at a moment of deadly peril that Brackenbury was overcome with respectful admiration; nor was he less sensible to the charm of his conversation or the surprising amenity of his address. Every gesture, every intonation, was not only noble in itself, but seemed to ennoble the fortunate mortal for whom it was intended; and Brackenbury confessed to himself with enthusiasm that this was a sovereign for whom a brave man might thankfully lay down his life.

Many minutes had thus passed, when the person who had introduced them into the house, and who had sat ever since in a corner, and with his watch in his hand, arose and whispered a word into the Prince's ear.

"It is well, Dr. Noel," replied Florizel, aloud; and then addressing the others, "You will excuse me, gentlemen," he added, "if I have to leave you in the dark. The moment now approaches."

Dr. Noel extinguished the lamp. A faint, gray light, premonitory to the dawn, illuminated the window, but was not sufficient to illuminate the room; and when the Prince rose to his feet, it was impossible to distinguish his features or to make a guess at the nature of the emotion which obviously affected him as he spoke. He moved towards the door, and placed himself at one side of it in an attitude of the wariest attention.

"You will have the kindness," he said, "to maintain the strictest silence, and to conceal yourselves in the densest of the shadow."

The three officers and the physician hastened to obey, and for nearly ten minutes the only sound in Rochester House was occasioned by the excursions of the rats behind the woodwork. At the end of that period, a loud creak of a hinge broke in with surprising distinctness on the silence; and shortly after, the watchers could distinguish a slow and cautious tread approaching up the kitchen stair. At every second step the intruder seemed to pause and lend an ear, and during these intervals, which seemed of an incalculable duration, a profound disquiet possessed the spirit of the listeners. Dr. Noel, accustomed as he was to dangerous emotions, suffered an almost pitiful physical prostration; his breath whistled in his lungs, his teeth grated one upon another, and his joints cracked aloud as he nervously shifted his position.

At last a hand was laid upon the door, and the bolt shot back with a slight report. There followed another pause, during which Brackenbury could see the Prince draw himself together noiselessly as if for some unusual exertion. Then the door opened, letting in a little more of the light of the morning; and the figure of a man appeared upon the threshold and stood motionless. He was tall, and carried a knife in his hand. Even in the twilight they could see his upper teeth bare and glistening, for his mouth was open like that of a hound about to leap. The man had evidently been over the head in water but a minute or two before; and even while he stood there the drops kept falling from his wet clothes and pattered on the floor.

The next moment he crossed the threshold. There was a leap, a stifled cry, an instantaneous struggle; and before Colonel Geraldine could spring to his aid, the Prince held the man, disarmed and helpless, by the shoulders.

"Dr. Noel," he said, "you will be so good as to relight the lamp."

And relinquishing the charge of his prisoner to Geraldine and Brackenbury, he crossed the room and set his back against the chimney-piece. As soon as the lamp had kindled, the party beheld an unaccustomed sternness on the Prince's features. It was no longer Florizel, the careless gentleman; it was the Prince of

Bohemia, justly incensed and full of deadly purpose, who now raised his head and addressed the captive President of the Suicide Club.

"President," he said, "you have laid your last snare, and your own feet are taken in it. The day is beginning; it is your last morning. You have just swum the Regent's Canal; it is your last bath in this world. Your old accomplice, Dr. Noel, so far from betraying me, has delivered you into my hands for judgment. And the grave you had dug for me this afternoon shall serve, in God's almighty providence, to hide your own just doom from the curiosity of mankind. Kneel and pray, sir, if you have a mind that way; for your time is short, and God is weary of your iniquities."

The President made no answer either by word or sign; but continued to hang his head and gaze sullenly on the floor, as though he were conscious of the Prince's prolonged and unsparing regard.

"Gentlemen," continued Florizel, resuming the ordinary tone of his conversation, "this is a fellow who has long eluded me, but whom, thanks to Dr. Noel, I now have tightly by the heels. To tell the story of his misdeeds would occupy more time than we can now afford; but if the canal had contained nothing but the blood of his victims, I believe the wretch would have been no drier than you see him. Even in an affair of this sort I desire to preserve the forms of honour. But I make you the judges, gentlemen—this is more an execution than a duel; and to give the rogue his choice of weapons would be to push too far a point of etiquette. I cannot afford to lose my life in such a business," he continued, unlocking the case of swords, "and as a pistol-bullet travels so often on the wings of chance, and skill and courage may fall by the most trembling marksman, I have decided, and I feel sure you will approve my determination, to put this question to the touch of swords."

When Brackenbury and Major O'Rooke, to whom these remarks were particularly addressed, had each intimated his approval, "Quick, sir," added Prince Florizel to the President, "choose a blade and do not keep me waiting; I have an impatience to be done with you for ever."

For the first time since he was captured and disarmed the President raised his head, and it was plain that he began instantly to pluck up courage.

"Is it to be stand up?" he asked eagerly, "and between you and me?"

"I mean so far to honour you," replied the Prince.

"Oh, come," cried the President. "With a fair field, who knows how things may happen? I must add that I consider it handsome behaviour on your Highness's part; and if the worst comes to the worst I shall die by one of the most gallant gentlemen in Europe."

And the President, liberated by those who had detained him, stepped up to the table and began, with minute attention, to select a sword. He was highly elated, and seemed to feel no doubt that he should issue victorious from the contest. The spectators grew alarmed in the face of so entire a confidence, and adjured Prince Florizel to reconsider his intention.

"It is but a farce," he answered; "and I think I can promise you, gentlemen, that it will not be long a-playing."

"Your Highness will be careful not to overreach," said Colonel Geraldine.

"Geraldine," returned the Prince, "did you ever know me fail in a debt of honour? I owe you this man's death, and you shall have it."

The President at last satisfied himself with one of the rapiers, and signified his readiness by a gesture that was not devoid of a rude nobility. The nearness of peril, and the sense of courage, even to this obnoxious villain, lent an air of manhood and a certain grace.

The Prince helped himself at random to a sword.

"Colonel Geraldine and Doctor Noel," he said, "will have the goodness to await me in this room. I wish no personal friend of mine to be involved in this transaction. Major O'Rooke, you are a man of some years and a settled reputation—let me recommend the President to your good graces. Lieutenant Rich will be so good as to lend me his attentions: a young man cannot have too much experience in such affairs."

"Your Highness," replied Brackenbury, "it is an honour I shall prize extremely."

"It is well," returned Prince Florizel; "I shall hope to stand your friend in more important circumstances."

And so saying he led the way out of the apartment and down the kitchen stairs.

The two men who were thus left alone threw open the window and leaned out, straining every sense to catch an indication of the tragical events that were about to follow. The rain was now over; day had almost come, and the birds were piping in the shrubbery and on the forest trees of the garden. The Prince and his companions were visible for a moment as they followed an alley

between two flowering thickets; but at the first corner a clump of foliage intervened, and they were again concealed from view. This was all that the Colonel
and the physician had an opportunity to see, and the garden was so vast, and
the place of combat evidently so remote from the house that not even the
noise of sword-play reached their ears.

"He has taken him towards the grave," said Dr. Noel, with a shudder.

"God," cried the Colonel, "God defend the right!"

And they awaited the event in silence, the Doctor shaking with fear, the
Colonel in an agony of sweat. Many minutes must have elapsed, the day was
sensibly broader, and the birds were singing more heartily in the garden
before a sound of returning footsteps recalled their glances towards the door.
It was the Prince and the two Indian officers who entered. God had defended
the right.

"I am ashamed of my emotion," said Prince Florizel; "I feel it a weakness
unworthy of my station, but the continued existence of that hound of hell had
begun to play upon me like a disease, and his death has more refreshed me
than a night of slumber. Look, Geraldine," he continued, throwing his sword
upon the floor, "there is the blood of the man who killed your brother. It
should be a welcome sight. And yet," he added, "see how strangely we men are
made! my revenge is not yet five minutes old, and already I am beginning to ask
myself if even revenge be attainable on this precarious stage of life. The ill he
did, who can undo it? The career in which he amassed a huge fortune (for the
house itself in which he stayed belonged to him)—that career is now a part of
the destiny of mankind forever; and I might weary myself making thrusts in
carte until the crack of judgment, and Geraldine's brother would be none the
less dead, and a thousand other innocent persons would be none the less dis-
honoured and debauched! The existence of a man is so small a thing to take, so
mighty a thing to employ! Alas!" he cried, "is there anything in life so disen-
chanting as attainment?"

"God's justice has been done," replied the Doctor. "So much I behold. The
lesson, your Highness, has been a cruel one for me; and I await my own turn
with deadly apprehension."

"What was I saying?" cried the Prince. "I have punished, and here is the man
beside us who can help me to undo. Ah, Dr. Noel! you and I have before us

many a day of hard and honourable toil; and perhaps, before we have done, you may have more than redeemed your early errors."

"And in the meantime," said the Doctor, "let me go and bury my oldest friend."

(*And this,* observes the erudite Arabian, *is the fortunate conclusion of the tale. The Prince, it is superfluous to mention, forgot none of those who served him in this great exploit; and to this day his authority and influence help them forward in their public career, while his condescending friendship adds a charm to their private life. To collect,* continues the author, *all the strange events in which this Prince has played the part of Providence were to fill the habitable globe with books. But the stories which relate to the fortunes of* THE RAJAH'S DIAMOND *are of too entertaining a description,* says he, *to be omitted. Following prudently in the footsteps of this Oriental, we shall now begin the series to which he refers with the* STORY OF THE BANDBOX.)

THE BODY-SNATCHER

(1881)

THE BODY-SNATCHER

Every night in the year, four of us sat in the small parlour of the George at Debenham—the undertaker, and the landlord, and Fettes, and myself. Sometimes there would be more; but blow high, blow low, come rain or snow or frost, we four would be each planted in his own particular arm-chair. Fettes was an old drunken Scotchman, a man of education obviously, and a man of some property, since he lived in idleness. He had come to Debenham years ago, while still young, and by a mere continuance of living had grown to be an adopted townsman. His blue camlet cloak was a local antiquity, like the church-spire. His place in the parlour at the George, his absence from church, his old, crapulous, disreputable vices, were all things of course in Debenham. He had some vague Radical opinions and some fleeting infidelities, which he would now and again set forth and emphasise with tottering slaps upon the table. He drank rum—five glasses regularly every evening; and for the greater portion of his nightly visit to the George sat, with his glass in his right hand, in a state of melancholy alcoholic saturation. We called him the Doctor, for he was supposed to have some special knowledge of medicine, and had been known, upon a pinch, to set a fracture or reduce a dislocation; but beyond these slight particulars, we had no knowledge of his character and antecedents.

One dark winter night—it had struck nine some time before the land-lord joined us—there was a sick man in the George, a great neighbouring proprietor suddenly struck down with apoplexy on his way to Parliament; and the great man's still greater London doctor had been telegraphed to his bedside. It was the first time that such a thing had happened in Debenham, for the railway was but newly open, and we were all proportionately moved by the occurrence.

"He's come," said the landlord, after he had filled and lighted his pipe.

"He?" said I. "Who?—not the doctor?"

"Himself," replied our host.

"What is his name?"

"Dr. Macfarlane," said the landlord.

Fettes was far through his third tumbler, stupidly fuddled, now nodding over, now staring mazily around him; but at the last word he seemed to awaken, and repeated the name "Macfarlane" twice, quietly enough the first time, but with sudden emotion at the second.

"Yes," said the landlord, "that's his name, Doctor Wolfe Macfarlane."

Fettes became instantly sober; his eyes awoke, his voice became clear, loud, and steady, his language forcible and earnest. We were all startled by the transformation, as if a man had risen from the dead.

"I beg your pardon," he said, "I am afraid I have not been paying much attention to your talk. Who is this Wolfe Macfarlane?" And then, when he had heard the landlord out, "It cannot be, it cannot be," he added; "and yet I would like well to see him face to face."

"Do you know him, Doctor?" asked the undertaker, with a gasp.

"God forbid!" was the reply. "And yet the name is a strange one; it were too much to fancy two. Tell me, landlord, is he old?"

"Well," said the host, "he's not a young man, to be sure, and his hair is white; but he looks younger than you."

"He is older, though; years older. But," with a slap upon the table, "it's the rum you see in my face—rum and sin. This man, perhaps, may have an easy conscience and a good digestion. Conscience! Hear me speak. You would think I was some good, old, decent Christian, would you not? But no, not I; I never canted. Voltaire might have canted if he'd stood in my shoes,[1] but the brains"— with a rattling fillip on his bald head—"the brains were clear and active, and I saw and made no deductions."

"If you know this doctor," I ventured to remark, after a somewhat awful pause, "I should gather that you do not share the landlord's good opinion."

Fettes paid no regard to me.

"Yes," he said, with sudden decision, "I must see him face to face."

There was another pause, and then a door was closed rather sharply on the first floor, and a step was heard upon the stair.

"That's the doctor," cried the landlord. "Look sharp, and you can catch him."

It was but two steps from the small parlour to the door of the old George Inn; the wide oak staircase landed almost in the street; there was room for a Turkey rug and nothing more between the threshold and the last round of the descent; but this little space was every evening brilliantly lit up, not only by the light upon the stair and the great signal-lamp below the sign, but by the warm radiance of the barroom window. The George thus brightly advertised itself to passers-by in the cold street. Fettes walked steadily to the spot, and we, who were hanging behind, beheld the two men meet, as one of them had phrased it, face to face. Dr. Macfarlane was alert and vigorous. His white hair set off his pale and placid, although energetic, countenance. He was richly dressed in the finest of broadcloth and the whitest of linen, with a great gold watchchain, and studs and spectacles of the same precious material. He wore a broad-folded tie, white and speckled with lilac, and he carried on his arm a comfortable driving-coat of fur. There was no doubt but he became his years, breathing, as he did, of wealth and consideration; and it was a surprising contrast to see our parlour sot—bald, dirty, pimpled, and robed in his old camlet cloak—confront him at the bottom of the stairs.

"Macfarlane!" he said somewhat loudly, more like a herald than a friend.

The great doctor pulled up short on the fourth step, as though the familiarity of the address surprised and somewhat shocked his dignity.

"Toddy Macfarlane!" repeated Fettes.

The London man almost staggered. He stared for the swiftest of seconds at the man before him, glanced behind him with a sort of scare, and then in a startled whisper, "Fettes!" he said, "you!"

"Ay," said the other, "me! Did you think I was dead too? We are not so easy shut of our acquaintance."

"Hush, hush!" exclaimed the doctor. "Hush, hush! this meeting is so unexpected—I can see you are unmanned. I hardly knew you, I confess, at first; but I am overjoyed—overjoyed to have this opportunity. For the present it must be howd'ye-do and good-bye in one, for my fly is waiting, and I must not fail the train; but you shall—let me see—yes—you shall give me your address, and you can count on early news of me. We must do something for you, Fettes. I fear you are out at elbows; but we must see to that for auld lang syne, as once we sang at suppers."

"Money!" cried Fettes; "money from you! The money that I had from you is lying where I cast it in the rain."

Dr. Macfarlane had talked himself into some measure of superiority and confidence, but the uncommon energy of this refusal cast him back into his first confusion.

A horrible, ugly look came and went across his almost venerable countenance. "My dear fellow," he said, "be it as you please; my last thought is to offend you. I would intrude on none. I will leave you my address, however——"

"I do not wish it—I do not wish to know the roof that shelters you," interrupted the other. "I heard your name; I feared it might be you; I wished to know if, after all, there were a God; I know now that there is none. Begone!"

He still stood in the middle of the rug, between the stair and doorway; and the great London physician, in order to escape, would be forced to step to one side. It was plain that he hesitated before the thought of this humiliation. White as he was, there was a dangerous glitter in his spectacles; but while he still paused uncertain, he became aware that the driver of his fly was peering in from the street at this unusual scene and caught a glimpse at the same time of our little body from the parlour, huddled by the corner of the bar. The presence of so many witnesses decided him at once to flee. He crouched together, brushing on the wainscot, and made a dart like a serpent, striking for the door. But his tribulation was not yet entirely at an end, for even as he was passing Fettes clutched him by the arm and these words came in a whisper, and yet painfully distinct, "Have you seen it again?"

The great rich London doctor cried out aloud with a sharp, throttling cry; he dashed his questioner across the open space, and, with his hands over his head, fled out of the door like a detected thief. Before it had occurred to one of us to make a movement the fly was already rattling toward the station. The scene was over like a dream, but the dream had left proofs and traces of its passage. Next day the servant found the fine gold spectacles broken on the threshold, and that very night we were all standing breathless by the barroom window, and Fettes at our side, sober, pale and resolute in look.

"God protect us, Mr. Fettes!" said the landlord, coming first into possession of his customary senses. "What in the universe is all this? These are strange things you have been saying."

Fettes turned toward us; he looked us each in succession in the face. "See if you can hold your tongues," said he. "That man Macfarlane is not safe to cross; those that have done so already have repented it too late."

And then, without so much as finishing his third glass, far less waiting for the other two, he bade us good-bye and went forth, under the lamp of the hotel, into the black night.

We three turned to our places in the parlour, with the big red fire and four clear candles; and as we recapitulated what had passed the first chill of our surprise soon changed into a glow of curiosity. We sat late; it was the latest session I have known in the old George. Each man, before we parted, had his theory that he was bound to prove; and none of us had any nearer business in this world than to track out the past of our condemned companion, and surprise the secret that he shared with the great London doctor. It is no great boast, but I believe I was a better hand at worming out a story than either of my fellows at the George; and perhaps there is now no other man alive who could narrate to you the following foul and unnatural events.

In his young days Fettes studied medicine in the schools of Edinburgh. He had talent of a kind, the talent that picks up swiftly what it hears and readily retails it for its own. He worked little at home; but he was civil, attentive, and intelligent in the presence of his masters. They soon picked him out as a lad who listened closely and remembered well; nay, strange as it seemed to me when I first heard it, he was in those days well favoured, and pleased by his exterior. There was, at that period, a certain extramural teacher of anatomy, whom I shall here designate by the letter K. His name was subsequently too well known. The man who bore it skulked through the streets of Edinburgh in disguise, while the mob that applauded at the execution of Burke[2] called loudly for the blood of his employer. But Mr. K—— was then at the top of his vogue; he enjoyed a popularity due partly to his own talent and address, partly to the incapacity of his rival, the university professor. The students, at least, swore by his name, and Fettes believed himself, and was believed by others, to have laid the foundations of success when he had acquired the favour of this meteorically famous man. Mr. K—— was a *bon vivant*[3] as well as an accomplished teacher; he liked a sly illusion no less than a careful preparation. In both capacities Fettes enjoyed and deserved his notice, and by the second year of his attendance he held the half-regular position of second demonstrator or sub-assistant in his class.

In this capacity, the charge of the theatre and lecture-room devolved in particular upon his shoulders. He had to answer for the cleanliness of the premises and the conduct of the other students, and it was a part of his duty to supply, receive, and divide the various subjects. It was with a view to this last— at that time very delicate—affair that he was lodged by Mr. K—— in the same wynd,[4] and at last in the same building, with the dissecting-rooms. Here, after a night of turbulent pleasures, his hand still tottering, his sight still misty and confused, he would be called out of bed in the black hours before the winter dawn by the unclean and desperate interlopers who supplied the table. He would open the door to these men, since infamous throughout the land. He would help them with their tragic burden, pay them their sordid price, and remain alone, when they were gone, with the unfriendly relics of humanity. From such a scene he would return to snatch another hour or two of slumber, to repair the abuses of the night, and refresh himself for the labours of the day.

Few lads could have been more insensible to the impressions of a life thus passed among the ensigns of mortality. His mind was closed against all general considerations. He was incapable of interest in the fate and fortunes of another, the slave of his own desires and low ambitions. Cold, light, and selfish in the last resort, he had that modicum of prudence, miscalled morality, which keeps a man from inconvenient drunkenness or punishable theft. He coveted, besides, a measure of consideration from his masters and his fellow-pupils, and he had no desire to fail conspicuously in the external parts of life. Thus he made it his pleasure to gain some distinction in his studies, and day after day rendered unimpeachable eye-service to his employer, Mr. K——. For his day of work he indemnified himself by nights of roaring, blackguardly enjoyment; and when that balance had been struck, the organ that he called his conscience declared itself content.

The supply of subjects was a continual trouble to him as well as to his master. In that large and busy class, the raw material of the anatomists kept perpetually running out; and the business thus rendered necessary was not only unpleasant in itself, but threatened dangerous consequences to all who were concerned. It was the policy of Mr. K—— to ask no questions in his dealings with the trade. "They bring the body, and we pay the price," he used to say, dwelling on the alliteration—"*quid pro quo.*" And, again, and somewhat profanely, "Ask no questions," he would tell his assistants, "for conscience sake." There was no understanding that the subjects were provided by the crime of murder. Had that idea been broached to him in words, he would have recoiled in horror; but the lightness of his speech upon so grave a matter was, in itself, an offence against good manners, and a temptation to the men with whom he dealt. Fettes, for instance, had often remarked to himself upon the singular freshness of the bodies. He had been struck again and again by the hang-dog, abominable looks of the ruffians who came to him before the dawn; and putting things together clearly in his private thoughts, he perhaps attributed a meaning too immoral and too categorical to the unguarded counsels of his master. He understood his duty, in short, to have three branches: to take what was brought, to pay the price, and to avert the eye from any evidence of crime.

One November morning this policy of silence was put sharply to the test. He had been awake all night with a racking toothache—pacing his room like a caged beast or throwing himself in fury on his bed—and had fallen at last into that profound, uneasy slumber that so often follows on a night of pain, when he was awakened by the third or fourth angry repetition of the concerted signal. There was a thin, bright moonshine; it was bitter cold, windy, and frosty; the town had not yet awakened, but an indefinable stir already preluded the noise and business of the day. The ghouls had come later than usual, and they seemed more than usually eager to be gone. Fettes, sick with sleep, lighted them upstairs. He heard their grumbling Irish voices through a dream; and as they stripped the sack from their sad merchandise he leaned dozing, with his shoulder propped against the wall; he had to shake himself to find the men their money. As he did so his eyes lighted on the dead face. He started; he took two steps nearer, with the candle raised.

"God Almighty!" he cried. "That is Jane Galbraith!"

The men answered nothing, but they shuffled nearer the door.

"I know her, I tell you," he continued. "She was alive and hearty yesterday. It's impossible she can be dead; it's impossible you should have got this body fairly."

"Sure, sir, you're mistaken entirely," said one of the men.

But the other looked Fettes darkly in the eyes, and demanded the money on the spot.

It was impossible to misconceive the threat or to exaggerate the danger. The lad's heart failed him. He stammered some excuses, counted out the sum, and saw his hateful visitors depart. No sooner were they gone than he hastened to confirm his doubts. By a dozen unquestionable marks he identified the girl he had jested with the day before. He saw, with horror, marks upon her body that might well betoken violence. A panic seized him, and he took refuge in his room. There he reflected at length over the discovery that he had made; considered soberly the bearing of Mr. K——'s instructions and the danger to himself of interference in so serious a business, and at last, in sore perplexity, determined to wait for the advice of his immediate superior, the class assistant.

This was a young doctor, Wolfe Macfarlane, a high favourite among all the reckless students, clever, dissipated, and unscrupulous to the last degree. He had travelled and studied abroad. His manners were agreeable and a little forward. He was an authority on the stage, skilful on the ice or the links with skate or golf-club; he dressed with nice audacity, and, to put the finishing touch upon his glory, he kept a gig and a strong trotting-horse. With Fettes he was on terms of intimacy; indeed, their relative positions called for some community of life; and when subjects were scarce the pair would drive far into the country in Macfarlane's gig, visit and desecrate some lonely graveyard, and return before dawn with their booty to the door of the dissecting-room.

On that particular morning Macfarlane arrived somewhat earlier than his wont. Fettes heard him, and met him on the stairs, told him his story, and showed him the cause of his alarm. Macfarlane examined the marks on her body.

"Yes," he said with a nod, "it looks fishy."

"Well, what should I do?" asked Fettes.

"Do?" repeated the other. "Do you want to do anything? Least said soonest mended, I should say."

"Some one else might recognise her," objected Fettes. "She was as well known as the Castle Rock."

"We'll hope not," said Macfarlane, "and if anybody does—well, you didn't, don't you see, and there's an end. The fact is, this has been going on too long. Stir up the mud, and you'll get K—— into the most unholy trouble; you'll be in a shocking box yourself. So will I, if you come to that. I should like to know how any one of us would look, or what the devil we should have to say for ourselves, in any Christian witness-box. For me, you know there's one thing certain—that, practically speaking, all our subjects have been murdered."

"Macfarlane!" cried Fettes.

"Come now!" sneered the other. "As if you hadn't suspected it yourself!"

"Suspecting is one thing——"

"And proof another. Yes, I know; and I'm as sorry as you are this should have come here," tapping the body with his cane. "The next best thing for me is not to recognise it; and," he added coolly, "I don't. You may, if you please. I don't dictate, but I think a man of the world would do as I do; and I may add, I fancy that is what K—— would look for at our hands. The question is, Why did he choose us two for his assistants? And I answer, because he didn't want old wives."

This was the tone of all others to affect the mind of a lad like Fettes. He agreed to imitate Macfarlane. The body of the unfortunate girl was duly dissected, and no one remarked or appeared to recognise her.

One afternoon, when his day's work was over, Fettes dropped into a popular tavern and found Macfarlane sitting with a stranger. This was a small man, very pale and dark, with coal-black eyes. The cut of his features gave a promise of intellect and refinement which was but feebly realised in his manners, for he proved, upon a nearer acquaintance, coarse, vulgar, and stupid. He exercised, however, a very remarkable control over Macfarlane; issued orders like the Great Bashaw; became inflamed at the least discussion or delay, and commented rudely on the servility with which he was obeyed. This most offensive person took a fancy to Fettes on the spot, plied him with drinks, and honoured him with unusual confidences on his past career. If a tenth part of what he confessed were true, he was a very loathsome rogue; and the lad's vanity was tickled by the attention of so experienced a man.

"I'm a pretty bad fellow myself," the stranger remarked, "but Macfarlane is the boy—Toddy Macfarlane I call him. Toddy, order your friend another glass." Or it might be, "Toddy, you jump up and shut the door." "Toddy hates me," he said again. "Oh, yes, Toddy, you do!"

"Don't you call me that confounded name," growled Macfarlane.

"Hear him! Did you ever see the lads play knife? He would like to do that all over my body," remarked the stranger.

"We medicals have a better way than that," said Fettes. "When we dislike a dead friend of ours, we dissect him."

Macfarlane looked up sharply, as though this jest were scarcely to his mind.

The afternoon passed. Gray, for that was the stranger's name, invited Fettes to join them at dinner, ordered a feast so sumptuous that the tavern was thrown in commotion, and when all was done commanded Macfarlane to settle the bill. It was late before they separated; the man Gray was incapably drunk. Macfarlane, sobered by his fury, chewed the cud of the money he had been forced to squander and the slights he had been obliged to swallow. Fettes, with various liquors singing in his head, returned home with devious footsteps and a mind entirely in abeyance. Next day Macfarlane was absent from the class, and Fettes smiled to himself as he imagined him still squiring the intolerable Gray from tavern to tavern. As soon as the hour of liberty had struck he posted from place to place in quest of his last night's companions. He could find them, however, nowhere; so returned early to his rooms, went early to bed, and slept the sleep of the just.

At four in the morning he was awakened by the well-known signal. Descending to the door, he was filled with astonishment to find Macfarlane with his gig, and in the gig one of those long and ghastly packages with which he was so well acquainted.

"What?" he cried. "Have you been out alone? How did you manage?"

But Macfarlane silenced him roughly, bidding him turn to business. When they had got the body upstairs and laid it on the table, Macfarlane made at first as if he were going away. Then he paused and seemed to hesitate; and then,

"You had better look at the face," said he, in tones of some constraint. "You had better," he repeated, as Fettes only stared at him in wonder.

"But where, and how, and when did you come by it?" cried the other.

"Look at the face," was the only answer.

Fettes was staggered; strange doubts assailed him. He looked from the young doctor to the body, and then back again. At last, with a start, he did as he was bidden. He had almost expected the sight that met his eyes, and yet the shock was cruel. To see, fixed in the rigidity of death and naked on that coarse layer of sack-cloth, the man whom he had left well clad and full of meat and sin upon the threshold of a tavern, awoke, even in the thoughtless Fettes, some of the terrors of the conscience. It was a *cras tibi*[5] which re-echoed in his soul, that two whom he had known should have come to lie upon these icy tables. Yet these were only secondary thoughts. His first concern regarded Wolfe. Unprepared for a challenge so momentous, he knew not how to look his comrade in the face. He durst not meet his eye, and he had neither words nor voice at his command.

It was Macfarlane himself who made the first advance. He came up quietly behind and laid his hand gently but firmly on the other's shoulder.

"Richardson," said he, "may have the head."

Now Richardson was a student who had long been anxious for that portion of the human subject to dissect. There was no answer, and the murderer resumed: "Talking of business, you must pay me; your accounts, you see, must tally."

Fettes found a voice, the ghost of his own: "Pay you!" he cried. "Pay you for that?"

"Why, yes, of course you must. By all means and on every possible account, you must," returned the other. "I dare not give it for nothing, you dare not take it for nothing; it would compromise us both. This is another case like Jane Galbraith's. The more things are wrong the more we must act as if all were right. Where does old K—— keep his money?"

"There," answered Fettes hoarsely, pointing to a cupboard in the corner.

"Give me the key, then," said the other, calmly, holding out his hand.

There was an instant's hesitation, and the die was cast. Macfarlane could not suppress a nervous twitch, the infinitesimal mark of an immense relief, as he felt the key between his fingers. He opened the cupboard, brought out pen and ink and a paper-book that stood in one compartment, and separated from the funds in a drawer a sum suitable to the occasion.

"Now, look here," he said, "there is the payment made—first proof of your good faith: first step to your security. You have now to clinch it by a second. Enter the payment in your book, and then you for your part may defy the devil."

The next few seconds were for Fettes an agony of thought; but in balancing his terrors it was the most immediate that triumphed. Any future difficulty seemed almost welcome if he could avoid a present quarrel with Macfarlane. He set down the candle which he had been carrying all this time, and with a steady hand entered the date, the nature, and the amount of the transaction.

"And now," said Macfarlane, "it's only fair that you should pocket the lucre. I've had my share already. By the bye, when a man of the world falls into a bit of luck, has a few shillings extra in his pocket—I'm ashamed to speak of it, but there's a rule of conduct in the case. No treating, no purchase of expensive class-books, no squaring of old debts; borrow, don't lend."

"Macfarlane," began Fettes, still somewhat hoarsely, "I have put my neck in a halter to oblige you."[6]

"To oblige me?" cried Wolfe. "Oh, come! You did, as near as I can see the matter, what you downright had to do in self-defence. Suppose I got into trouble, where would you be? This second little matter flows clearly from the first. Mr. Gray is the continuation of Miss Galbraith. You can't begin and then stop. If you begin, you must keep on beginning; that's the truth. No rest for the wicked."

A horrible sense of blackness and the treachery of fate seized hold upon the soul of the unhappy student.

"My God!" he cried, "but what have I done? and when did I begin? To be made a class assistant—in the name of reason, where's the harm in that? Service wanted the position; Service might have got it. Would *he* have been where *I* am now?"

"My dear fellow," said Macfarlane, "what a boy you are! What harm *has* come to you? What harm *can* come to you if you hold your tongue? Why, man, do you know what this life is? There are two squads of us—the lions and the lambs. If you're a lamb, you'll come to lie upon these tables like Gray or Jane

Galbraith; if you're a lion, you'll live and drive a horse like me, like K——, like all the world with any wit or courage. You're staggered at the first. But look at K——! My dear fellow, you're clever, you have pluck. I like you, and K—— likes you. You were born to lead the hunt; and I tell you, on my honour and my experience of life, three days from now you'll laugh at all these scarecrows like a high school boy at a farce."

And with that Macfarlane took his departure and drove off up the wynd in his gig to get under cover before daylight. Fettes was thus left alone with his regrets. He saw the miserable peril in which he stood involved. He saw, with inexpressible dismay, that there was no limit to his weakness, and that, from concession to concession, he had fallen from the arbiter of Macfarlane's destiny to his paid and helpless accomplice. He would have given the world to have been a little braver at the time, but it did not occur to him that he might still be brave. The secret of Jane Galbraith and the cursed entry in the daybook closed his mouth.

Hours passed; the class began to arrive; the members of the unhappy Gray were dealt out to one and to another, and received without remark. Richardson was made happy with the head; and before the hour of freedom rang Fettes trembled with exultation to perceive how far they had already gone toward safety.

For two days he continued to watch, with increasing joy, the dreadful process of disguise.

On the third day Macfarlane made his appearance. He had been ill, he said; but he made up for lost time by the energy with which he directed the students. To Richardson in particular he extended the most valuable assistance and advice, and that student, encouraged by the praise of the demonstrator, burned high with ambitious hopes, and saw the medal already in his grasp.

Before the week was out Macfarlane's prophecy had been fulfilled. Fettes had outlived his terrors and had forgotten his baseness. He began to plume himself upon his courage, and had so arranged the story in his mind that he could look back on these events with an unhealthy pride. Of his accomplice he saw but little. They met, of course, in the business of the class; they received their orders together from Mr. K——. At times they had a word or two in private, and Macfarlane was from first to last particularly kind and jovial. But it was plain that he avoided any reference to their common secret; and even when Fettes whispered to him that he had cast in his lot with the lions and foresworn the lambs, he only signed to him smilingly to hold his peace.

At length an occasion arose which threw the pair once more into a closer union. Mr. K—— was again short of subjects; pupils were eager, and it was a part of this teacher's pretensions to be always well supplied. At the same time there came the news of a burial in the rustic graveyard of Glencorse. Time has little changed the place in question. It stood then, as now, upon a cross road, out of call of human habitations, and buried fathom deep in the foliage of six cedar trees. The cries of the sheep upon the neighbouring hills, the streamlets upon either hand, one loudly singing among pebbles, the other dripping furtively from pond to pond, the stir of the wind in mountainous old flowering chestnuts, and once in seven days the voice of the bell and the old tunes of the precentor, were the only sounds that disturbed the silence around the rural church. The Resurrection Man[7]—to use a byname of the period—was not to be deterred by any of the sanctities of customary piety. It was part of his trade to despise and desecrate the scrolls and trumpets of old tombs, the paths worn by the feet of worshippers and mourners, and the offerings and the inscriptions of bereaved affection. To rustic neighbour-hoods, where love is more than commonly tenacious, and where some bonds of blood or fellowship unite the entire society of a parish, the body-snatcher, far from being repelled by natural respect, was attracted by the ease and safety of the task. To bodies that had been laid in earth, in joyful expectation of a far different awakening, there came that hasty, lamp-lit, terror-haunted resurrection of the spade and mattock. The coffin was forced, the cerements torn, and the melancholy relics, clad in sackcloth, after being rattled for hours on moonless byways, were at length exposed to uttermost indignities before a class of gaping boys.

Somewhat as two vultures may swoop upon a dying lamb, Fettes and Mac-farlane were to be let loose upon a grave in that green and quiet resting-place. The wife of a farmer, a woman who had lived for sixty years, and been known for nothing but good butter and a godly conversation, was to be rooted from her grave at midnight and carried, dead and naked, to that faraway city that she had always honoured with her Sunday's best; the place beside her family was to be empty till the crack of doom; her innocent and almost venerable members to be exposed to that last curiosity of the anatomist.

Late one afternoon the pair set forth, well wrapped in cloaks and furnished with a formidable bottle. It rained without remission—a cold, dense, lashing rain. Now and again there blew a puff of wind, but these sheets of falling water kept it down. Bottle and all, it was a sad and silent drive as far as Penicuik, where they were to spend the evening. They stopped once, to hide their implements in a thick bush not far from the churchyard, and once again at the Fisher's Tryst, to have a toast before the kitchen fire and vary their nips of whisky with a glass of ale. When they reached their journey's end the gig was housed, the horse was fed and comforted, and the two young doctors in a private room sat down to the best dinner and the best wine the house afforded. The lights, the fire, the beating rain upon the window, the cold, incongruous work that lay before them, added zest to their enjoyment of the meal. With every glass their cordiality increased. Soon Macfarlane handed a little pile of gold to his companion.

"A compliment," he said. "Between friends these little d——d accommodations ought to fly like pipe-lights."

Fettes pocketed the money, and applauded the sentiment to the echo. "You are a philosopher," he cried. "I was an ass till I knew you. You and K—— between you, by the Lord Harry! but you'll make a man of me."

"Of course, we shall," applauded Macfarlane. "A man? I tell you, it required a man to back me up the other morning. There are some big, brawling, forty-year-old cowards who would have turned sick at the look of the d——d thing; but not you—you kept your head. I watched you."

"Well, and why not?" Fettes thus vaunted himself. "It was no affair of mine. There was nothing to gain on the one side but disturbance, and on the other I could count on your gratitude, don't you see?" And he slapped his pocket till the gold pieces rang.

Macfarlane somehow felt a certain touch of alarm at these unpleasant words. He may have regretted that he had taught his young companion so successfully, but he had no time to interfere, for the other noisily continued in this boastful strain:

"The great thing is not to be afraid. Now, between you and me, I don't want to hang—that's practical; but for all cant, Macfarlane, I was born with a contempt. Hell, God, Devil, right, wrong, sin, crime, and all the old gallery of curiosities—they may frighten boys, but men of the world, like you and me, despise them. Here's to the memory of Gray!"

It was by this time growing somewhat late. The gig, according to order, was brought round to the door with both lamps brightly shining, and the young men had to pay their bill and take the road. They announced that they were bound for Peebles, and drove in that direction till they were clear of the last houses of the town; then, extinguishing the lamps, returned upon their course, and followed a by-road toward Glencorse. There was no sound but that of their own passage, and the incessant, strident pouring of the rain. It was pitch dark; here and there a white gate or a white stone in the wall guided them for a short space across the night; but for the most part it was at a foot pace, and almost groping, that they picked their way through that resonant blackness to their solemn and isolated destination. In the sunken woods that traverse the neighbourhood of the burying-ground the last glimmer failed them, and it became necessary to kindle a match and reillumine one of the lanterns of the gig. Thus, under the dripping trees, and environed by huge and moving shadows, they reached the scene of their unhallowed labours.

They were both experienced in such affairs, and powerful with the spade; and they had scarce been twenty minutes at their task before they were rewarded by a dull rattle on the coffin lid. At the same moment Macfarlane, having hurt his hand upon a stone, flung it carelessly above his head. The grave, in which they now stood almost to the shoulders, was close to the edge of the plateau of the graveyard; and the gig lamp had been propped, the better to illuminate their labours, against a tree, and on the immediate verge of the steep bank descending to the stream. Chance had taken a sure aim with the stone. Then came a clang of broken glass; night fell upon them; sounds alternately dull and ringing announced the bounding of the lantern down the bank, and its occasional collision with the trees. A stone or two, which it had dislodged in its descent, rattled behind it into the profundities of the glen; and then silence, like night, resumed its sway; and they might bend their hearing to its utmost pitch, but naught was to be heard except the rain, now marching to the wind, now steadily falling over miles of open country.

They were so nearly at an end of their abhorred task that they judged it wisest to complete it in the dark. The coffin was exhumed and broken open; the body inserted in the dripping sack and carried between them to the gig; one mounted to keep it in its place, and the other, taking the horse by the mouth, groped along by wall and bush until they reached the wider road by the Fisher's Tryst. Here was a faint, diffused radiancy, which they hailed like daylight; by that they pushed the horse to a good pace and began to rattle along merrily in the direction of the town.

They had both been wetted to the skin during their operations, and now, as the gig jumped among the deep ruts, the thing that stood propped between them fell now upon one and now upon the other. At every repetition of the horrid contact each instinctively repelled it with the greater haste; and the process, natural although it was, began to tell upon the nerves of the companions. Macfarlane made some ill-favoured jest about the farmer's wife, but it came hollowly from his lips, and was allowed to drop in silence. Still their unnatural burden bumped from side to side; and now the head would be laid, as if in confidence, upon their shoulders, and now the drenching sackcloth would flap icily about their faces. A creeping chill began to possess the soul of Fettes. He peered at the bundle, and it seemed somehow larger than at first. All over the countryside, and from every degree of distance, the farm dogs accompanied their passage with tragic ululations; and it grew and grew upon his mind that some unnatural miracle had been accomplished, that some nameless change had befallen the dead body, and that it was in fear of their unholy burden that the dogs were howling.

"For God's sake," said he, making a great effort to arrive at speech, "for God's sake, let's have a light!"

Seemingly Macfarlane was affected in the same direction; for, though he made no reply, he stopped the horse, passed the reins to his companion, got down, and proceeded to kindle the remaining lamp. They had by that time got no farther than the cross-road down to Auchenclinny. The rain still poured as though the deluge were returning, and it was no easy matter to make a light in such a world of wet and darkness. When at last the flickering blue flame had been transferred to the wick and began to expand and clarify, and shed a wide circle of misty brightness round the gig, it became possible for the two young men to see each other and the thing they had along with them. The rain had moulded the rough sacking to the outlines of the body underneath; the head was distinct from the trunk, the shoulders plainly modelled; something at once spectral and human riveted their eyes upon the ghastly comrade of their drive.

For some time Macfarlane stood motionless, holding up the lamp. A nameless dread was swathed, like a wet sheet, about the body, and tightened the white skin upon the face of Fettes; a fear that was meaningless, a horror of what could not be, kept mounting to his brain. Another beat of the watch, and he had spoken. But his comrade forestalled him.

"That is not a woman," said Macfarlane, in a hushed voice.

"It was a woman when we put her in," whispered Fettes.

"Hold that lamp," said the other. "I must see her face."

And as Fettes took the lamp his companion untied the fastenings of the sack and drew down the cover from the head. The light fell very clear upon the dark, well-moulded features and smooth-shaven cheeks of a too familiar countenance, often beheld in dreams of both of these young men. A wild yell rang up into the night; each leaped from his own side into the roadway; the lamp fell, broke, and was extinguished; and the horse, terrified by this unusual commotion, bounded and went off toward Edinburgh at a gallop, bearing along with it, sole occupant of the gig, the body of the dead and long-dissected Gray.

THE BOTTLE IMP

(1891)

THE BOTTLE IMP

Note.—Any student of that very unliterary product, the English drama of the early part of the century, will here recognize the name and the root idea of a piece once rendered popular by the redoubtable B. Smith. The root idea is there and identical, and yet I believe I have made it a new thing. And the fact that the tale has been designed and written for a Polynesian audience may lend it some extraneous interest nearer home.—R. L. S.

There was a man of the island of Hawaii, whom I shall call Keawe; for the truth is, he still lives, and his name must be kept secret; but the place of his birth was not far from Honaunau, where the bones of Keawe the Great lie hidden in a cave. This man was poor, brave, and active; he could read and write like a schoolmaster; he was a first-rate mariner besides, sailed for some time in the island steamers, and steered a whaleboat on the Hamakua coast. At length it came in Keawe's mind to have a sight of the great world and foreign cities, and he shipped on a vessel bound to San Francisco.

This is a fine town, with a fine harbor, and rich people uncountable; and, in particular, there is one hill which is covered with palaces. Upon this hill Keawe was one day taking a walk with his pocket full of money, viewing the great houses upon either hand with pleasure. "What fine houses there are!" he was thinking, "and how happy must these people be who dwell in them, and take no care for the morrow!" The thought was in his mind when he came abreast of a house that was smaller than some others, but all finished and beautified like a toy; the steps of that house shone like silver, and the borders of the garden bloomed like garlands, and the windows were bright like diamonds; and Keawe stopped and wondered at the excellence of all he saw. So stopping, he was aware of a man that looked forth upon him through a window, so clear, that Keawe could see him as you see a fish in a pool upon the reef. The man was elderly, with a bald head and a black beard; and his face was heavy with sorrow, and he bitterly sighed. And the truth of it is, that as Keawe looked in upon the man, and the man looked out upon Keawe, each envied the other.

All of a sudden the man smiled and nodded, and beckoned Keawe to enter, and met him at the door of the house.

"This is a fine house of mine," said the man, and bitterly sighed. "Would you not care to view the chambers?"

So he led Keawe all over it, from the cellar to the roof, and there was nothing there that was not perfect of its kind, and Keawe was astonished.

"Truly," said Keawe, "this is a beautiful house; if I lived in the like of it, I should be laughing all day long. How comes it, then, that you should be sighing?"

"There is no reason," said the man, "why you should not have a house in all points similar to this, and finer, if you wish. You have some money, I suppose?"

"I have fifty dollars," said Keawe; "but a house like this will cost more than fifty dollars."

The man made a computation. "I am sorry you have no more," said he, "for it may raise you trouble in the future; but it shall be yours at fifty dollars."

"The house?" asked Keawe.

"No, not the house," replied the man; "but the bottle. For, I must tell you, although I appear to you so rich and fortunate, all my fortune, and this house itself and its garden, came out of a bottle not much bigger than a pint. This is it."

And he opened a lockfast place, and took out a round-bellied bottle with a long neck; the glass of it was white like milk, with changing rainbow colors in the grain. Within-sides something obscurely moved, like a shadow and a fire.

"This is the bottle," said the man; and, when Keawe laughed, "You do not believe me?" he added. "Try, then, for yourself. See if you can break it."

So Keawe took the bottle up and dashed it on the floor till he was weary; but it jumped on the floor like a child's ball, and was not injured.

"This is a strange thing," said Keawe. "For by the touch of it, as well as by the look, the bottle should be of glass."

"Of glass it is," replied the man, sighing more heavily than ever; "but the glass of it was tempered in the flames of hell. An imp lives in it, and that is the shadow we behold there moving; or, so I suppose. If any man buy this bottle the imp is at his command; all that he desires—love, fame, money, houses like this house, ay, or a city like this city—all are his at the word uttered. Napoleon had this bottle, and by it he grew to be the king of the world; but he sold it at the last and fell. Captain Cook had this bottle, and by it he found his way to so many islands; but he, too, sold it, and was slain upon Hawaii. For, once it is sold, the power goes and the protection; and unless a man remain content with what he has, ill will befall him."

"And yet you talk of selling it yourself?" Keawe said.

"I have all I wish, and I am growing elderly," replied the man. "There is one thing the imp cannot do—he cannot prolong life; and, it would not be fair to conceal from you there is a drawback to the bottle; for if a man die before he sells it, he must burn in hell forever."

"To be sure, that is a drawback and no mistake," cried Keawe. "I would not meddle with the thing. I can do without a house, thank God; but there is one thing I could not be doing with one particle, and that is to be damned."

"Dear me, you must not run away with things," returned the man. "All you have to do is to use the power of the imp in moderation, and then sell it to someone else, as I do to you, and finish your life in comfort."

"Well, I observe two things," said Keawe. "All the time you keep sighing like a maid in love, that is one; and, for the other, you sell this bottle very cheap."

"I have told you already why I sigh," said the man. "It is because I fear my health is breaking up; and, as you said yourself, to die and go to the devil is a pity for anyone. As for why I sell so cheap, I must explain to you there is a peculiarity about the bottle. Long ago, when the devil brought it first upon earth, it was extremely expensive, and was sold first of all to Prester John for many millions of dollars; but it cannot be sold at all, unless sold at a loss. If you sell it for as much as you paid for it, back it comes to you again like a homing pigeon. It follows that the price has kept falling in these centuries, and the bottle is now remarkably cheap. I bought it myself from one of my great neighbors on this hill, and the price I paid was only ninety dollars. I could sell it for as high as eighty-nine dollars and ninety-nine cents, but not a penny dearer, or back the thing must come to me. Now, about this there are two bothers. First, when you offer a bottle so singular for eighty odd dollars, people suppose you to be jesting. And second—but there is no hurry about that—and I need not go into it. Only remember it must be coined money that you sell it for."

"How am I to know that this is all true?" asked Keawe.

"Some of it you can try at once," replied the man. "Give me your fifty dollars, take the bottle, and wish your fifty dollars back into your pocket. If that does not happen, I pledge you my honor I will cry off the bargain and restore your money."

"You are not deceiving me?" said Keawe.

The man bound himself with a great oath.

"Well, I will risk that much," said Keawe, "for that can do no harm," and he paid over his money to the man, and the man handed him the bottle.

"Imp of the bottle," said Keawe, "I want my fifty dollars back." And sure enough he had scarce said the word before his pocket was as heavy as ever.

"To be sure this is a wonderful bottle," said Keawe.

"And now good-morning to you, my fine fellow, and the devil go with you for me," said the man.

"Hold on," said Keawe, "I don't want any more of this fun. Here, take your bottle back."

"You have bought it for less than I paid for it," replied the man, rubbing his hands. "It is yours now; and, for my part, I am only concerned to see the back of you." And with that he rang for his Chinese servant, and had Keawe shown out of the house.

Now, when Keawe was in the street, with the bottle under his arm, he began to think. "If all is true about this bottle, I may have made a losing bargain," thinks he. "But, perhaps the man was only fooling me." The first thing he did was to count his money; the sum was exact—forty-nine dollars American money, and one Chili piece. "That looks like the truth," said Keawe. "Now I will try another part."

The streets in that part of the city were as clean as a ship's decks, and though it was noon, there were no passengers. Keawe set the bottle in the gutter and walked away. Twice he looked back, and there was the milky, round-bellied bottle where he left it. A third time he looked back, and turned a corner; but he had scarce done so, when something knocked upon his elbow, and behold! It was the long neck sticking up; and, as for the round belly, it was jammed into the pocket of his pilot-coat.

"And that looks like the truth," said Keawe.

The next thing he did was to buy a corkscrew in a shop, and go apart into a secret place in the fields. And there he tried to draw the cork, but as often as he put the screw in, out it came again, and the cork as whole as ever.

"This is some new sort of cork," said Keawe, and all at once he began to shake and sweat, for he was afraid of that bottle.

On his way back to the port-side he saw a shop where a man sold shells and clubs from the wild islands, old heathen deities, old coined money, pictures from China and Japan, and all manner of things that sailors bring in their sea-chests. And here he had an idea. So he went in and offered the bottle for a hundred dollars. The man of the shop laughed at him at the first, and offered him five; but, indeed, it was a curious bottle, such glass was never blown in any human glassworks, so prettily the colors shone under the milky white, and so strangely the shadow hovered in the midst; so, after he had disputed awhile after the manner of his kind, the shopman gave Keawe sixty silver dollars for the thing and set it on a shelf in the midst of his window.

"Now," said Keawe, "I have sold that for sixty which I bought for fifty—or, to say truth, a little less, because one of my dollars was from Chili. Now I shall know the truth upon another point."

So he went back on board his ship, and when he opened his chest, there was the bottle, and had come more quickly than himself. Now Keawe had a mate on board whose name was Lopaka.

"What ails you?" said Lopaka, "that you stare in your chest?"

They were alone in the ship's forecastle, and Keawe bound him to secrecy, and told all.

"This is a very strange affair," said Lopaka; "and I fear you will be in trouble about this bottle. But there is one point very clear—that you are sure of the trouble, and you had better have the profit in the bargain. Make up your mind what you want with it; give the order, and if it is done as you desire, I will buy the bottle myself; for I have an idea of my own to get a schooner, and go trading through the islands."

"That is not my idea," said Keawe; "but to have a beautiful house and garden on the Kona Coast, where I was born, the sun shining in at the door, flowers in the garden, glass in the windows, pictures on the walls, and toys and fine carpets on the tables, for all the world like the house I was in this day—only a story higher, and with balconies all about like the King's palace; and to live there without care and make merry with my friends and relatives."

"Well," said Lopaka, "let us carry it back with us to Hawaii; and if all comes true, as you suppose, I will buy the bottle, as I said, and ask a schooner."

Upon that they were agreed, and it was not long before the ship returned to Honolulu, carrying Keawe and Lopaka, and the bottle. They were scarce come ashore when they met a friend upon the beach, who began at once to condole with Keawe.

"I do not know what I am to be condoled about," said Keawe.

"Is possible you have not heard," said the friend, "your uncle—that good old man—is dead, and your cousin—that beautiful boy—was drowned at sea?"

Keawe was filled with sorrow, and, beginning to weep and to lament, he forgot about the bottle. But Lopaka was thinking to himself, and presently, when Keawe's grief was a little abated, "I have been thinking," said Lopaka, "had not your uncle lands in Hawaii, in the district of Kau?"

"No," said Keawe, "not in Kau: they are on the mountain-side—a little be south Hookena."

"These lands will now be yours?" asked Lopaka.

"And so they will," says Keawe, and began again to lament for his relatives.

"No," said Lopaka, "do not lament at present. I have a thought in my mind. How if this should be the doing of the bottle? For here is the place ready for your house."

"If this be so," cried Keawe, "it is a very ill way to serve me by killing my relatives. But it may be, indeed; for it was in just such a station that I saw the house with my mind's eye."

"The house, however, is not yet built," said Lopaka.

"No, nor like to be!" said Keawe; "for though my uncle has some coffee and ava and bananas, it will not be more than will keep me in comfort; and the rest of that land is the black lava."

"Let us go to the lawyer," said Lopaka; "I have still this idea in my mind."

Now, when they came to the lawyer's, it appeared Keawe's uncle had grown monstrous rich in the last days, and there was a fund of money.

"And here is the money for the house!" cried Lopaka.

"If you are thinking of a new house," said the lawyer, "here is the card of a new architect, of whom they tell me great things."

"Better and better!" cried Lopaka. "Here is all made plain for us. Let us continue to obey orders."

So they went to the architect, and he had drawings of houses on his table.

"You want something out of the way," said the architect. "How do you like this?" and he handed a drawing to Keawe.

Now, when Keawe set eyes on the drawing, he cried out aloud, for it was the picture of his thought exactly drawn.

"I am in for this house," thought he. "Little as I like the way it comes to me, I am in for it now, and I may as well take the good along with the evil."

So he told the architect all that he wished, and how he would have that house furnished, and about the pictures on the wall and the knick-knacks on the tables; and he asked the man plainly for how much he would undertake the whole affair.

The architect put many questions, and took his pen and made a computation; and when he had done he named the very sum that Keawe had inherited.

Lopaka and Keawe looked at one another and nodded.

"It is quite clear," thought Keawe, "that I am to have this house, whether or no. It comes from the devil, and I fear I will get little good by that; and of one thing I am sure, I will make no more wishes as long as I have this bottle. But with the house I am saddled, and I may as well take the good along with the evil."

So he made his terms with the architect, and they signed a paper; and Keawe and Lopaka took ship again and sailed to Australia; for it was concluded between them they should not interfere at all, but leave the architect and the bottle-imp to build and to adorn that house at their own pleasure.

The voyage was a good voyage, only all the time Keawe was holding in his breath, for he had sworn he would utter no more wishes, and take no more favors, from the devil. The time was up when they got back. The architect told them that the house was ready, and Keawe and Lopaka took a passage in the

Hall, and went down Kona way to view the house, and see if all had been done fitly according to the thought that was in Keawe's mind.

Now, the house stood on the mountain side, visible to ships. Above, the forest ran up into the clouds of rain; below, the black lava fell in cliffs, where the kings of old lay buried. A garden bloomed about that house with every hue of flowers; and there was an orchard of papaia on the one hand and an orchard of herdprint on the other, and right in front, toward the sea, a ship's mast had been rigged up and bore a flag. As for the house, it was three stories high, with great chambers and broad balconies on each. The windows were of glass, so excellent that it was as clear as water and as bright as day. All manner of furniture adorned the chambers. Pictures hung upon the wall in golden frames—pictures of ships, and men fighting, and of the most beautiful women, and of singular places; nowhere in the world are there pictures of so bright a color as those Keawe found hanging in his house. As for the knick-knacks, they were extraordinarily fine; chiming clocks and musical boxes, little men with nodding heads, books filled with pictures, weapons of price from all quarters of the world, and the most elegant puzzles to entertain the leisure of a solitary man. And as no one would care to live in such chambers, only to walk through and view them, the balconies were made so broad that a whole town might have lived upon them in delight; and Keawe knew not which to prefer, whether the back porch, where you get the land breeze, and looked upon the orchards and the flowers, or the front balcony, where you could drink the wind of the sea, and look down the steep wall of the mountain and see the Hall going by once a week or so between Hookena and the hills of Pele, or the schooners plying up the coast for wood and ava and bananas.

When they had viewed all, Keawe and Lopaka sat on the porch.

"Well," asked Lopaka, "is it all as you designed?"

"Words cannot utter it," said Keawe. "It is better than I dreamed, and I am sick with satisfaction."

"There is but one thing to consider," said Lopaka, "all this may be quite natural, and the bottle-imp have nothing whatever to say to it. If I were to buy the bottle, and got no schooner after all, I should have put my hand in the fire for nothing. I gave you my word, I know; but yet I think you would not grudge me one more proof."

"I have sworn I would take no more favors," said Keawe. "I have gone already deep enough."

"This is no favor I am thinking of," replied Lopaka. "It is only to see the imp himself. There is nothing to be gained by that, and so nothing to be ashamed of, and yet, if I once saw him, I should be sure of the whole matter. So indulge me so far, and let me see the imp; and, after that, here is the money in my hand, and I will buy it."

"There is only one thing I am afraid of," said Keawe. "The imp may be very ugly to view, and if you once set eyes upon him you might be very undesirous of the bottle."

"I am a man of my word," said Lopaka. "And here is the money betwixt us."

"Very well," replied Keawe, "I have a curiosity myself. So come, let us have one look at you, Mr. Imp."

Now as soon as that was said, the imp looked out of the bottle, and in again, swift as a lizard; and there sat Keawe and Lopaka turned to stone. The night had quite come, before either found a thought to say or voice to say it with; and then Lopaka pushed the money over and took the bottle.

"I am a man of my word," said he, "and had need to be so, or I would not touch this bottle with my foot. Well, I shall get my schooner and a dollar or two for my pocket; and then I will be rid of this devil as fast as I can. For to tell you the plain truth, the look of him has cast me down."

"Lopaka," said Keawe, "do not you think any worse of me than you can help; I know it is night, and the roads bad, and the pass by the tombs an ill place to go by so late, but I declare since I have seen that little face, I cannot eat or sleep or pray till it is gone from me. I will give you a lantern, and a basket to put the bottle in, and any picture or fine thing in all my house that takes your fancy; and be gone at once, and go sleep at Hookena with Nahinu."

"Keawe," said Lopaka, "many a man would take this ill; above all, when I am doing you a turn so friendly, as to keep my word and buy the bottle; and for that matter, the night and the dark, and the way by the tombs, must be all tenfold more dangerous to a man with such a sin upon his conscience, and such a bottle under his arm. But for my part, I am so extremely terrified myself, I have not the heart to blame you. Here I go, then; and I pray God you may be happy in your house, and I fortunate with my schooner, and both get to heaven in the end in spite of the devil and his bottle.

So Lopaka went down the mountain; and Keawe stood in his front balcony, and listened to the clink of the horse's shoes, and watched the lantern go shining down the path, and along the cliff of caves where the old dead are buried; and all the time he trembled and clasped his hands, and prayed for his friend, and gave glory to God that he himself was escaped out of that trouble.

But the next day came very brightly, and that new house of his was so delightful to behold that he forgot his terrors. One day followed another, and Keawe dwelt there in perpetual joy. He had his place on the back porch; it was there he ate and lived, and read the stories in the Honolulu newspapers; but when anyone came by they would go in and view the chambers and the pictures. And the fame of the house went far and wide; it was called *Ka-Hale Nui*—the Great House—in all Kona; and sometimes the Bright House, for Keawe kept a Chinaman, who was all day dusting and furbishing; and the glass, and the gilt, and the fine stuffs, and the pictures, shone as bright as the morning. As for Keawe himself, he could not walk in the chambers without singing, his heart was so enlarged; and when ships sailed by upon the sea, he would fly his colors on the mast.

So time went by, until one day Keawe went upon a visit as far as Kailua to certain of his friends. There he was well feasted; and left as soon as he could the next morning, and rode hard, for he was impatient to behold his beautiful house; and, besides, the night then coming on was the night in which the dead of old days go abroad in the sides of Kona; and having already meddled with the devil, he was the more chary of meeting with the dead. A little beyond Houaunau, looking far ahead, he was aware of a woman bathing in the edge of the sea; and she seemed a well-grown girl, but he thought no more of it. Then he saw her white shift flutter as she put it on, and then her red holoku; and by the time he came abreast of her she was done with her toilet, and had come up from the sea, and stood by the track-side in her red holoku, and she was all freshened with the bath, and her eyes shone and were kind. Now Keawe no sooner beheld her than he drew rein.

"I thought I knew everyone in this country," said he. "How comes it that I do not know you?"

"I am Kokua, daughter of Kiano," said the girl, "and I have just returned from Oahu. Who are you?"

"I will tell you who I am in a little," said Keawe, dismounting from his horse, "but not now. For I have a thought in my mind, and if you knew who I was, you might have heard of me, and would not give me a true answer. But tell me, first of all, one thing: are you married?"

At this Kokua laughed out loud. "It is you who ask questions," she said. "Are you married yourself?"

"Indeed, Kokua, I am not," replied Keawe, "and never thought to be until this hour. But here is the plain truth. I have met you here at the road-side, and I saw your eyes, which are like the stars, and my heart went to you as swift as a bird. And so now, if you want none of me, say so, and I will go on to my own place; but if you think me no worse than any other young man, say so, too, and I will turn aside to your father's for the night, and tomorrow I will talk with the good man."

Kokua said never a word, but she looked at the sea and laughed.

"Kokua," said Keawe, "if you say nothing, I will take that for the good answer; so let us be stepping to your father's door."

She went on ahead of him, still without speech; only sometimes she glanced back and glanced away again, and she kept the strings of her hat in her mouth.

Now, when they had come to the door, Kiano came out on his veranda, and cried out and welcomed Keawe by name. At that the girl looked over, for the fame of the great house had come to her ears; and, to be sure, it was a great temptation. All that evening they were very merry together; and the girl was as bold as brass under the eyes of her parents, and made a mark of Keawe, for she had a quick wit. The next day he had a word with Kiano, and found the girl alone.

"Kokua," said he, "you made a mark of me all the evening; and it is still time to bid me go. I would not tell you who I was, because I have so fine a house, and I feared you would think too much of that house and too little of the man that loves you. Now you know all, and if you wish to have seen the last of me, say so at once."

"No," said Kokua, but this time she did not laugh, nor did Keawe ask for more.

This was the wooing of Keawe; things had gone quickly; but so an arrow goes, and the ball of a rifle swifter still, and yet both may strike the target.

Things had gone fast, but they had gone far also, and the thought of Keawe rang in the maiden's head; she heard his voice in the breach of the surf upon the lava, and for this young man that she had seen but twice she would have left father and mother and her native islands. As for Keawe himself, his horse flew up the path of the mountain under the cliff of tombs, and the sound of the hoofs, and the sound of Keawe singing to himself for pleasure, echoed in the caverns of the dead. He came to the Bright House, and still he was singing. He sat and ate in the broad balcony, and the Chinaman wondered at his master, to hear how he sang between the mouthfuls. The sun went down into the sea, and the night came; and Keawe walked the balconies by lamplight, high on the mountains, and the voice of his singing startled men on ships.

"Here am I now upon my high place," he said to himself. "Life may be no better; this is the mountain top; and all shelves about me toward the worse. For the first time I will light up the chambers, and bathe in my fine bath with the hot water and the cold, and sleep above in the bed of my bridal chamber."

So the Chinaman had word, and he must rise from sleep and light the furnaces; and as he walked below, beside the boilers, he heard his master singing and rejoicing above him in the lighted chambers. When the water began to be hot the Chinaman cried to his master: and Keawe went into the bathroom; and the Chinaman heard him sing as he filled the marble basin; and heard him sing, and the singing broken, as he undressed; until of a sudden, the song ceased. The Chinaman listened, and listened; he called up the house to Keawe to ask if all were well, and Keawe answered him "Yes," and bade him go to bed; but there was no more singing in the Bright House; and all night long the Chinaman heard his master's feet go round and round the balconies without repose.

Now, the truth of it was this: as Keawe undressed for his bath, he spied upon his flesh a patch like a patch of lichen on a rock, and it was then that he stopped singing. For he knew the likeness of that patch, and knew that he was fallen in the Chinese Evil.

Now, it is a sad thing for any man to fall into this sickness. And it would be a sad thing for anyone to leave a house so beautiful and so commodious, and depart from all his friends to the north coast of Molokai, between the mighty cliff and the sea-breakers. But what was that to the case of the man Keawe, he who had met his love but yesterday, and won her but that morning, and now saw all his hopes break, in a moment, like a piece of glass?

Awhile he sat upon the edge of the bath, then sprang, with a cry, and ran outside; and to and fro, to and fro, along the balcony, like one despairing.

"Very willingly could I leave Hawaii, the home of my fathers," Keawe was thinking. "Very lightly could I leave my house, the high-placed, the many-windowed, here upon the mountains. Very bravely could I go to Molokai, to Kalaupapa by the cliffs, to live with the smitten and to sleep there, far from my fathers. But what wrong have I done, what sin lies upon my soul, that I should have encountered Kokua coming cool from the seawater in the evening? Kokua, the soul ensnarer! Kokua, the light of my life! Her may I never wed, her may I look upon no longer, her may I no more handle with my loving hand; and it is for this, it is for you, O Kokua! that I pour my lamentations!"

Now you are to observe what sort of a man Keawe was, for he might have dwelt there in the Bright House for years, and no one been the wiser of his sickness; but he reckoned nothing of that, if he must lose Kokua. And again he might have wed Kokua even as he was; and so many would have done, because they have the souls of pigs; but Keawe loved the maid manfully, and he would do her no hurt and bring her in no danger.

A little beyond the midst of the night, there came in his mind the recollection of that bottle. He went round to the back porch, and called to memory the day when the devil had looked forth; and at the thought ice ran in his veins.

"A dreadful thing is the bottle," thought Keawe, "and dreadful is the imp, and it is a dreadful thing to risk the flames of hell. But what other hope have I to cure my sickness or to wed Kokua? What!" he thought, "would I beard the devil once, only to get me a house, and not face him again to win Kokua?"

Thereupon he called to mind it was the next day the Hall went by on her return to Honolulu. "There must I go first," he thought, "and see Lopaka. For the best hope that I have now is to find that same bottle I was so pleased to be rid of."

Never a wink could he sleep; the food stuck in his throat; but he sent a letter to Kiano, and about the time when the steamer would be coming, rode down beside the cliff of the tombs. It rained; his horse went heavily; he looked up at the black mouths of the caves, and he envied the dead that slept there and were done with trouble; and called to mind how he had galloped by the day before, and was astonished. So he came down to Hookena, and there was all the country gathered for the steamer as usual. In the shed before the store they sat and jested and passed the news; but there was no matter of speech in Keawe's bosom, and he sat in their midst and looked without on the rain falling on the houses, and the surf beating among the rocks, and the sighs arose in his throat.

"Keawe of the Bright House is out of spirits," said one to another. Indeed, and so he was, and little wonder.

Then the Hall came, and the whaleboat carried him on board. The after-part of the ship was full of Haoles—whites—who had been to visit the volcano, as their custom is; and the midst was crowded with Kanakas, and the fore-part with wild bulls from Hilo and horses from Kau; but Keawe sat apart from all in his sorrow, and watched for the house of Kiano. There it sat low upon the shore in the black rocks, and shaded by the coron palms, and there by the door was a red holoku, no greater than a fly, and going to and fro with a fly's busyness. "Ah, queen of my heart," he cried, "I'll venture my dear soul to win you!"

Soon after darkness fell and the cabins were lit up, and the Haoles sat and played at the cards and drank whiskey as their custom is; but Keawe walked the deck all night; and all the next day, as they steamed under the lee of Maui or of Molokai, he was still pacing to and fro like a wild animal in a menagerie.

Toward evening they passed Diamond Head, and came to the pier of Honolulu. Keawe stepped out among the crowd and began to ask for Lopaka. It seemed he had become the owner of a schooner—none better in the islands—and was gone upon an adventure as far as Pola-Pola or Kahiki; so there was no help to be looked for from Lopaka. Keawe called to mind a friend of his, a lawyer in the town (I must not tell his name), and inquired of him. They said he was grown suddenly rich, and had a fine new house upon Waikiki shore; and this put a thought in Keawe's head, and he called a hack and drove to the lawyer's house.

The house was all brand new, and the trees in the garden no greater than walking-sticks, and the lawyer, when he came, had the air of a man well pleased.

"What can I do to serve you?" said the lawyer.

"You are a friend of Lopaka's," replied Keawe, "and Lopaka purchased from me a certain piece of goods that I thought you might enable me to trace."

The lawyer's face became very dark. "I do not profess to misunderstand you, Mr. Keawe," said he, "though this is an ugly business to be stirring in. You may be sure I know nothing, but yet I have a guess, and if you would apply in a certain quarter I think you might have news."

And he named the name of a man, which, again, I had better not repeat. So it was for days, and Keawe went from one to another, finding everywhere new clothes and carriages, and fine new houses and men everywhere in great contentment, although, to be sure, when he hinted at his business their faces would cloud over.

"No doubt I am upon the track," thought Keawe. "These new clothes and carriages are all the gifts of the little imp, and these glad faces are the faces of men who have taken their profit and got rid of the accursed thing in safety. When I see pale cheeks and hear sighing, I shall know that I am near the bottle."

So it befell at last that he was recommended to a Haole in Beritania Street. When he came to the door, about the hour of the evening meal, there were the usual marks of the new house, and the young garden, and the electric light shining in the windows; but when the owner came, a shock of hope and fear ran through Keawe; for here was a young man, white as a corpse, and black about the eyes, the hair shedding from his head, and such a look in his countenance as a man may have when he is waiting for the gallows.

"Here it is, to be sure," thought Keawe, and so with this man he noways veiled his errand. "I am come to buy the bottle," said he.

At the word, the young Haole of Beritania Street reeled against the wall.

"The bottle!" he gasped. "To buy the bottle!" Then he seemed to choke, and seizing Keawe by the arm, carried him into a room and poured out wine in two glasses.

"Here is my respects," said Keawe, who had been much about with Haoles in his time. "Yes," he added, "I am come to buy the bottle. What is the price by now?"

At that word the young man let his glass slip through his fingers, and looked upon Keawe like a ghost.

"The price," says he; "the price! You do not know the price?"

"It is for that I am asking you," returned Keawe. "But why are you so much concerned? Is there anything wrong about the price?"

"It has dropped a great deal in value since your time, Mr. Keawe," said the young man, stammering.

"Well, well, I shall have the less to pay for it," says Keawe. "How much did it cost you?"

The young man was as white as a sheet. "Two cents," said he.

"What?" cried Keawe, "two cents? Why, then, you can only sell it for one. And he who buys it——" The words died upon Keawe's tongue; he who bought it could never sell it again, the bottle and the bottle imp must abide with him until he died, and when he died must carry him to the red end of hell.

The young man of Beritania Street fell upon his knees. "For God's sake, buy it!" he cried. "You can have all my fortune in the bargain. I was mad when I bought it at that price. I had embezzled money at my store; I was lost else; I must have gone to jail."

"Poor creature," said Keawe, "you would risk your soul upon so desperate an adventure, and to avoid the proper punishment of your own disgrace; and you think I could hesitate with love in front of me. Give me the bottle, and the change which I make sure you have all ready. Here is a five-cent piece."

It was as Keawe supposed; the young man had the change ready in a drawer; the bottle changed hands, and Keawe's fingers were no sooner clasped upon the stalk than he had breathed his wish to be a clean man. And, sure enough, when he got home to his room, and stripped himself before a glass, his flesh was whole like an infant's. And here was the strange thing: he had no sooner seen this miracle than his mind was changed within him, and he cared naught for the Chinese Evil, and little enough for Kokua; and had but the one thought, that here he was bound to the bottle imp for time and for eternity, and had no better hope but to be a cinder forever in the flames of hell. Away ahead of him he saw them blaze with his mind's eye, and his soul shrank, and darkness fell upon the light.

When Keawe came to himself a little, he was aware it was the night when the band played at the hotel. Thither he went, because he feared to be alone; and there, among happy faces, walked to and fro, and heard the tunes go up and down, and saw Berger beat the measure, and all the while he heard the flames crackle, and saw the red fire burning in the bottomless pit. Of a sudden the band played *Hiki-ao-ao*; that was a song that he had sung with Kokua, and at the strain courage returned to him.

"It is done now," he thought, "and once more let me take the good along with the evil."

So it befell that he returned to Hawaii by the first steamer, and as soon as it could be managed he was wedded to Kokua, and carried her up the mountain side to the Bright House.

Now it was so with these two, that when they were together Keawe's heart was stilled; but so soon as he was alone he fell into a brooding horror, and heard the flames crackle, and saw the red fire burn in the bottomless pit. The girl, indeed, had come to him wholly; her heart leaped in her side at sight of him, her hand clung to his; and she was so fashioned, from the hair upon her head to the nails upon her toes, that none could see her without joy. She was pleasant in her nature. She had the good word always. Full of song she was, and went to and fro in the Bright House, the brightest thing in its three stories, carolling like the birds. And Keawe beheld and heard her with delight, and then must shrink upon one side, and weep and groan to think upon the price that he had paid for her; and then he must dry his eyes, and wash his face, and go and sit with her on the broad balconies, joining in her songs, and, with a sick spirit, answering her smiles.

There came a day when her feet began to be heavy and her songs more rare; and now it was not Keawe only that would weep apart, but each would sunder from the other and sit in opposite balconies with the whole width of the Bright House betwixt. Keawe was so sunk in his despair, he scarce observed the change, and was only glad he had more hours to sit alone and brood upon his destiny, and was not so frequently condemned to pull a smiling face on a sick heart. But one day, coming softly through the house, he heard the sound of a child sobbing, and there was Kokua rolling her face upon the balcony floor, and weeping like the lost.

"You do well to weep in this house, Kokua," he said. "And yet I would give the head off my body that you (at least) might have been happy."

"Happy!" she cried. "Keawe, when you lived alone in your Bright House you were the word of the island for a happy man; laughter and song were in your mouth, and your face was as bright as the sunrise. Then you wedded poor Kokua; and the good God knows what is amiss in her—but from that day you have not smiled. Oh!" she cried, "what ails me? I thought I was pretty, and I knew I loved him. What ails me, that I throw this cloud upon my husband?"

"Poor Kokua," said Keawe. He sat down by her side, and sought to take her hand; but that she plucked away. "Poor Kokua," he said, again. "My poor child—my pretty. And I had thought all this while to spare you! Well, you shall know all. Then, at least, you will pity poor Keawe; then you will understand how much he loved you in the past—that he dared hell for your possession—and how much he loves you still (the poor condemned one), that he can yet call up a smile when he beholds you."

With that, he told her all, even from the beginning.

"You have done this for me?" she cried. "Ah, well, then what do I care!" and she clasped and wept upon him.

"Ah, child!" said Keawe, "and yet, when I consider of the fire of hell, I care a good deal!"

"Never tell me," said she, "no man can be lost because he loved Kokua, and no other fault. I tell you, Keawe, I shall save you with these hands, or perish in your company. What! you loved me and gave your soul, and you think I will not die to save you in return?"

"Ah, my dear, you might die a hundred times, and what difference would that make?" he cried, "except to leave me lonely till the time comes of my damnation?"

"You know nothing," said she. "I was educated in a school in Honolulu; I am no common girl. And I tell you I shall save my lover. What is this you say about a cent? But all the world is not American. In England they have a piece they call a farthing, which is about half a cent. Ah! sorrow!" she cried, "that makes it scarcely better, for the buyer must be lost, and we shall find none so brave as my Keawe! But, then, there is France; they have a small coin there which they call a centime, and these go five to the cent or thereabout. We could not do better. Come, Keawe, let us go to the French islands; let us go to Tahiti, as fast as ships can bear us. There we have four centimes, three centimes, two centimes, one centime; four possible sales to come and go on; and two of us to push the bargain. Come, my Keawe! kiss me, and banish care. Kokua will defend you."

"Gift of God!" he cried. "I cannot think that God will punish me for desiring aught so good! Be it as you will, then, take me where you please: I put my life and my salvation in your hands."

Early the next day Kokua was about her preparations. She took Keawe's chest that he went with sailoring; and first she put the bottle in a corner, and then packed it with the richest of their clothes and the bravest of the knick-knacks in the house. "For," said she, "we must seem to be rich folks, or who will believe in the bottle?" All the time of her preparation she was as gay as a bird; only when she looked upon Keawe the tears would spring in her eye, and she must run and kiss him. As for Keawe, a weight was off his soul; now that he had his secret shared, and some hope in front of him, he seemed like a new man, his feet went lightly on the earth, and his breath was good to him again. Yet was terror still at his elbow; and ever and again, as the wind blows out a taper, hope died in him, and he saw the flames toss and the red fire burn in hell.

It was given out in the country they were gone pleasuring to the States, which was thought a strange thing, and yet not so strange as the truth, if any could have guessed it. So they went to Honolulu in the Hall, and thence in the Umatilla to San Francisco with a crowd of Haoles, and at San Francisco took their passage by the mail brigantine, the Tropic Bird, for Papeete, the chief place of the French in the south islands. Thither they came, after a pleasant voyage, on a fair day of the Trade wind, and saw the reef with the surf breaking and Motuiti with its palms, and the schooner riding within-side, and the white houses of the town low down along the shore among green trees, and overhead the mountains and the clouds of Tahiti, the wise island.

It was judged the most wise to hire a house, which they did accordingly, opposite the British Consul's, to make a great parade of money, and themselves conspicuous with carriages and horses. This it was very easy to do, so long as they had the bottle in their possession; for Kokua was more bold than Keawe, and, whenever she had a mind, called on the imp for twenty or a hundred dollars. At this rate they soon grew to be remarked in the town; and the strangers from Hawaii, their riding and their driving, the fine holokus, and the rich lace of Kokua, became the matter of much talk.

They got on well after the first with the Tahitian language, which is indeed like to the Hawaiian, with a change of certain letters; and as soon as they had any freedom of speech, began to push the bottle. You are to consider it was not an easy subject to introduce; it was not easy to persuade people you were in earnest, when you offered to sell them for four centimes the spring of health and riches inexhaustible. It was necessary besides to explain the dangers of the bottle; and either people disbelieved the whole thing and laughed, or they thought the more of the darker part, became overcast with gravity, and drew away from Keawe and Kokua, as from persons who had dealings with the devil. So far from gaining ground, these two began to find they were avoided in the town; the children ran away from them screaming, a thing intolerable to Kokua; Catholics crossed themselves as they went by; and all persons began with one accord to disengage themselves from their advances.

Depression fell upon their spirits. They would sit at night in their new house, after a day's weariness, and not exchange one word, or the silence would be broken by Kokua bursting suddenly into sobs. Sometimes they would pray together; sometimes they would have the bottle out upon the floor, and sit all evening watching how the shadow hovered in the midst. At such times they would be afraid to go to rest. It was long ere slumber came to them, and, if either dozed off, it would be to wake and find the other silently weeping in the dark, or, perhaps, to wake alone, the other having fled from the house and the neighborhood of that bottle, to pace under the bananas in the little garden, or to wander on the beach by moonlight.

One night it was so when Kokua awoke. Keawe was gone. She felt in the bed and his place was cold. Then fear fell upon her, and she sat up in bed. A little moonshine filtered through the shutters. The room was bright, and she could spy the bottle on the floor. Outside it blew high, the great trees of the avenue cried aloud, and the fallen leaves rattled in the veranda. In the midst of this Kokua was aware of another sound; whether of a beast or of a man she could scarce tell, but it was as sad as death, and cut her to the soul. Softly she arose, set the door ajar, and looked forth into the moonlit yard. There, under the bananas, lay Keawe, his mouth in the dust, and as he lay he moaned.

It was Kokua's first thought to run forward and console him; her second potently withheld her. Keawe had borne himself before his wife like a brave man; it became her little in the hour of weakness to intrude upon his shame. With the thought she drew back into the house.

"Heaven," she thought, "how careless have I been—how weak! It is he, not I, that stands in this eternal peril; it was he, not I, that took the curse upon his soul. It is for my sake, and for the love of a creature of so little worth and such poor help, that he now beholds so close to him the flames of hell—ay, and smells the smoke of it, lying without there in the wind and moonlight. Am I so dull of spirit that never till now I have surmised my duty, or have I seen it before and turned aside? But now, at least, I take up my soul in both the hands of my affection; now I say farewell to the white steps of heaven and the waiting faces of my friends. A love for a love, and let mine be equalled with Keawe's! A soul for a soul, and be it mine to perish!"

She was a deft woman with her hands, and was soon apparelled. She took in her hands the change—the precious centimes they kept ever at their side; for this coin is little used, and they had made provision at a government office. When she was forth in the avenue clouds came on the wind, and the moon was blackened. The town slept, and she knew not whither to turn till she heard one coughing in the shadow of the trees.

"Old man," said Kokua, "what do you here abroad in the cold night?"

The old man could scarce express himself for coughing, but she made out that he was old and poor, and a stranger in the island.

"Will you do me a service?" said Kokua. "As one stranger to another, and as an old man to a young woman, will you help a daughter of Hawaii?"

"Ah," said the old man. "So you are the witch from the eight islands, and even my old soul you seek to entangle. But I have heard of you, and defy your wickedness."

"Sit down here," said Kokua, "and let me tell you a tale." And she told him the story of Keawe from the beginning to the end.

"And now," said she, "I am his wife, whom he bought with his soul's welfare. And what should I do? If I went to him myself and offered to buy it, he will refuse. But if you go, he will sell it eagerly; I will await you here; you will buy it for four centimes, and I will buy it again for three. And the Lord strengthen a poor girl!"

"If you meant falsely," said the old man, "I think God would strike you dead."

"He would!" cried Kokua. "Be sure he would. I could not be so treacherous, God would not suffer it."

"Give me the four centimes and await me here," said the old man.

Now, when Kokua stood alone in the street, her spirit died. The wind roared in the trees, and it seemed to her the rushing of the flames of hell; the shadows towered in the light of the street lamp, and they seemed to her the snatching hands of evil ones. If she had had the strength, she must have run away, and if she had had the breath she must have screamed aloud; but, in truth, she could do neither, and stood and trembled in the avenue, like an affrighted child.

Then she saw the old man returning, and he had the bottle in his hand.

"I have done your bidding," said he, "I left your husband weeping like a child; tonight he will sleep easy." And he held the bottle forth.

"Before you give it me," Kokua panted, "take the good with the evil—ask to be delivered from your cough."

"I am an old man," replied the other, "and too near the gate of the grave to take a favor from the devil. But what is this? Why do you not take the bottle? Do you hesitate?"

"Not hesitate!" cried Kokua. "I am only weak. Give me a moment. It is my hand resists, my flesh shrinks back from the accursed thing. One moment only!"

The old man looked upon Kokua kindly. "Poor child!" said he, "you fear: your soul misgives you. Well, let me keep it. I am old, and can never more be happy in this world, and as for the next——"

"Give it me!" gasped Kokua. "There is your money. Do you think I am so base as that? Give me the bottle."

"God bless you child," said the old man.

Kokua concealed the bottle under her holoku, said farewell to the old man, and walked off along the avenue, she cared not whither. For all roads were now the same to her, and led equally to hell. Sometimes she walked, and sometimes ran; sometimes she screamed out loud in the night, and sometimes lay by the wayside in the dust and wept. All that she had heard of hell came back to her; she saw the flames blaze, and she smelled the smoke, and her flesh withered on the coals.

Near day she came to her mind again, and returned to the house. It was even as the old man said—Keawe slumbered like a child. Kokua stood and gazed upon his face.

"Now, my husband," said she, "it is your turn to sleep. When you wake it will be your turn to sing and laugh. But for poor Kokua, alas! that meant no evil—for poor Kokua no more sleep, no more singing, no more delight, whether in earth or Heaven."

With that she lay down in the bed by his side, and her misery was so extreme that she fell in a deep slumber instantly.

Late in the morning her husband woke her and gave her the good news. It seemed he was silly with delight, for he paid no heed to her distress, ill though she dissembled it. The words stuck in her mouth, it mattered not; Keawe did the speaking. She ate not a bite, but who was to observe it? For Keawe cleared the dish. Kokua saw and heard him, like some strange thing in a dream; there were times when she forgot or doubted, and put her hands to her brow; to know herself doomed and hear her husband babble, seemed so monstrous.

All the while Keawe was eating and talking, and planning the time of their return, and thanking her for saving him, and fondling her, and calling her the true helper after all. He laughed at the old man that was fool enough to buy that bottle.

"A worthy old man he seemed," Keawe said. "But no one can judge by appearances. For why did the old reprobate require the bottle?"

"My husband," said Kokua, humbly, "his purpose may have been good."

Keawe laughed like an angry man.

"Fiddle-de-dee!" cried Keawe. "An old rogue, I tell you; and an old ass to boot. For the bottle was hard enough to sell at four centimes; and at three it will be quite impossible. The margin is not broad enough, the thing begins to smell of scorching—brrr!" said he, and shuddered. "It is true I bought it myself at a cent, when I knew not there were smaller coins. I was a fool for my pains; there will never be found another, and whoever has that bottle now will carry it to the pit."

"O my husband!" said Kokua. "Is it not a terrible thing to save oneself by the eternal ruin of another? It seems to me I could not laugh. I would be humbled. I would be filled with melancholy. I would pray for the poor holder."

Then Keawe, because he felt the truth of what she said, grew the more angry. "Heighty-teighty!" cried he. "You may be filled with melancholy if you please. It is not the mind of a good wife. If you thought at all of me, you would sit shamed."

Thereupon he went out, and Kokua was alone.

What chance had she to sell that bottle at two centimes? None, she perceived. And if she had any, here was her husband hurrying her away to a country where there was nothing lower than a cent. And here—on the morrow of her sacrifice—was her husband leaving her and blaming her.

She would not even try to profit by what time she had, but sat in the house, and now had the bottle out and viewed it with unutterable fear, and now, with loathing, hid it out of sight.

By and by, Keawe came back, and would have her take a drive.

"My husband, I am ill," she said. "I am out of heart. Excuse me, I can take no pleasure."

Then was Keawe more wroth than ever. With her, because he thought she was brooding over the case of the old man; and with himself, because he thought she was right, and was ashamed to be so happy.

"This is your truth," cried he, "and this your affection! Your husband is just saved from eternal ruin, which he encountered for the love of you—and you can take no pleasure! Kokua, you have a disloyal heart."

He went forth again furious, and wandered in the town all day. He met friends, and drank with them; they hired a carriage and drove into the country, and there drank again. All the time Keawe was ill at ease, because he was taking this pastime while his wife was sad, and because he knew in his heart that she was more right than he; and the knowledge made him drink the deeper.

Now, there was an old brutal Haole drinking with him, one that had been a boatswain of a whaler—a runaway, a digger in gold mines, a convict in prisons. He had a low mind and a foul mouth; he loved to drink and to see others drunken; and he pressed the glass upon Keawe. Soon there was no more money in the company.

"Here, you!" says the boatswain, "you are rich, you have been always saying. You have a bottle or some foolishness."

"Yes," says Keawe, "I am rich; I will go back and get some money from my wife, who keeps it."

"That's a bad idea, mate," said the boatswain. "Never you trust a petticoat with dollars. They're all as false as water; you keep an eye on her."

Now, this word struck in Keawe's mind; for he was muddled with what he had been drinking.

"I should not wonder but she was false, indeed," thought he. "Why else should she be so cast down at my release? But I will show her I am not the man to be fooled. I will catch her in the act."

Accordingly, when they were back in town, Keawe bade the boatswain wait for him at the corner, by the old calaboose, and went forward up the avenue alone to the door of his house. The night had come again; there was a light within, but never a sound; and Keawe crept about the corner, opened the back door softly, and looked in.

There was Kokua on the floor, the lamp at her side; before her was a milk-white bottle, with a round belly and a long neck; and as she viewed it, Kokua wrung her hands.

A long time Keawe stood and looked in the doorway. At first he was struck stupid; and then fear fell upon him that the bargain had been made amiss, and the bottle had come back to him as it came at San Francisco; and at that his knees were loosened, and the fumes of the wine departed from his head like mists off a river in the morning. And then he had another thought; and it was a strange one, that made his cheeks to burn.

"I must make sure of this," thought he.

So he closed the door, and went softly round the corner again, and then came noisily in, as though he were but now returned. And, lo! by the time he opened the front door no bottle was to be seen; and Kokua sat in a chair and started up like one awakened out of sleep.

"I have been drinking all day and making merry," said Keawe. "I have been with good companions, and now I only come back for money, and return to drink and carouse with them again."

Both his face and voice were as stern as judgment, but Kokua was too troubled to observe.

"You do well to use your own, my husband," said she, and her words trembled.

"Oh, I do well in all things," said Keawe, and he went straight to the chest and took out money. But he looked besides in the corner where they kept the bottle, and there was no bottle there.

At that the chest heaved upon the floor like a sea-billow, and the house span about him like a wreath of smoke, for he saw she was lost now, and there was no escape. "It is what I feared," he thought. "It is she who has bought it."

And then he came to himself a little and rose up; but the sweat streamed on his face as thick as the rain and as cold as the well-water.

"Kokua," said he, "I said to you today what ill became me. Now I return to house with my jolly companions," and at that he laughed a little quietly. "I will take more pleasure in the cup if you forgive me."

She clasped his knees in a moment; she kissed his knees with flowing tears.

"Oh," she cried, "I asked but a kind word!"

"Let us never one think hardly of the other," said Keawe, and was gone out of the house.

Now, the money that Keawe had taken was only some of that store of centime pieces they had laid in at their arrival. It was very sure he had no mind to be drinking. His wife had given her soul for him, now he must give his for hers; no other thought was in the world with him.

At the corner, by the old calaboose, there was the boatswain waiting.

"My wife has the bottle," said Keawe, "and, unless you help me to recover it, there can be no more money and no more liquor tonight."

"You do not mean to say you are serious about that bottle?" cried the boatswain.

"There is the lamp," said Keawe. "Do I look as if I was jesting?"

"That is so," said the boatswain. "You look as serious as a ghost."

"Well, then," said Keawe, "here are two centimes; you must go to my wife in the house, and offer her these for the bottle, which (if I am not much mistaken) she will give you instantly. Bring it to me here, and I will buy it back from you for one; for that is the law with this bottle, that it still must be sold for a less sum. But whatever you do, never breathe a word to her that you have come from me."

"Mate, I wonder are you making a fool of me?" asked the boatswain.

"It will do you no harm if I am," returned Keawe.

"That is so, mate," said the boatswain.

"And if you doubt me," added Keawe, "you can try. As soon as you are clear of the house, wish to have your pocket full of money, or a bottle of the best rum, or what you please, and you will see the virtue of the thing."

"Very well, Kanaka," says the boatswain. "I will try; but if you are having your fun out of me, I will take my fun out of you with a belaying-pin."

So the whaler-man went off up the avenue; and Keawe stood and waited. It was near the same spot where Kokua had waited the night before; but Keawe was more resolved, and never faltered in his purpose; only his soul was bitter with despair.

It seemed a long time he had to wait before he heard a voice singing in the darkness of the avenue. He knew the voice to be the boatswain's; but it was strange how drunken it appeared upon a sudden.

Next the man himself came stumbling into the light of the lamp. He had the devil's bottle buttoned in his coat; another bottle was in his hand; and even as he came in view he raised it to his mouth and drank.

"You have it," said Keawe. "I see that."

"Hands off!" cried the boatswain, jumping back. "Take a step near me, and I'll smash your mouth. You thought you could make a cat's paw of me, did you?"

"What do you mean?" cried Keawe.

"Mean?" cried the boatswain. "This is a pretty good bottle, this is; that's what I mean. How I got it for two centimes I can't make out; but I'm sure you sha'n't have it for one."

"You mean you won't sell?" gasped Keawe.

"No, sir," cried the boatswain. "But I'll give you a drink of the rum, if you like."

"I tell you," said Keawe, "the man who has that bottle goes to hell."

"I reckon I'm going anyway," returned the sailor; "and this bottle's the best thing to go with I've struck yet. No, sir!" he cried again, "this is my bottle now, and you can go and fish for another."

"Can this be true?" Keawe cried. "For your own sake, I beseech you, sell it me!"

"I don't value any of your talk," replied the boatswain. "You thought I was a flat, now you see I'm not; and there's an end. If you won't have a swallow of the rum, I'll have one myself. Here's your health, and good night to you!"

So off he went down the avenue toward town, and there goes the bottle out of the story.

But Keawe ran to Kokua light as the wind; and great was their joy that night; and great, since then, has been the peace of all their days in the Bright House.

The Isle of Voices

(1892)

The Isle of Voices

Keola was married with Lehua, daughter of Kalamake, the wise man Molokai, and he kept his dwelling with the father of his wife. There was no man more cunning than that prophet; he read the stars, he could divine by the bodies of the dead, and by the means of evil creatures: he could go alone into the highest parts of the mountain, into the region of the hobgoblins, and there he would lay snares to entrap the spirits of ancient.

For this reason no man was more consulted in all the Kingdom of Hawaii. Prudent people bought, and sold, and married, and laid out their lives by his counsels; and the King had him twice to Kona to seek the treasures of Kamehameha. Neither was any man more feared: of his enemies, some had dwindled in sickness by the virtue of his incantations, and some had been spirited away, the life and the clay both, so that folk looked in vain for so much as a bone of their bodies. It was rumored that he had the art or the gift of the old heroes. Men had seen him at night upon the mountains, stepping from one cliff to the next; they had seen him walking in the high forest, and his head and shoulders were above the trees.

This Kalamake was a strange man to see. He was come of the best blood in Molokai and Maui, of a pure descent; and yet he was more white to look upon than any foreigner; his hair the color of dry grass, and his eyes red and very blind, so that "Blind as Kalamake that can see across tomorrow," was a byword in the islands.

Of all these doings of his father-in-law, Keola knew a little by the common repute, a little more he suspected, and the rest he ignored. But there was one thing troubled him. Kalamake was a man that spared for nothing, whether to eat or to drink, or to wear; and for all he paid in bright new dollars. "Bright as Kalamake's dollars," was another saying in the Eight Isles. Yet he neither sold, nor planted, nor took hire—only now and then from his sorceries—and there was no source conceivable for so much silver coin.

It chanced one day Keola's wife was gone upon a visit to Kaunakakai on the lee side of the island, and the men were forth at the sea-fishing. But Keola was an idle dog, and he lay in the veranda and watched the surf beat on the shore and the birds fly about the cliff. It was a chief thought with him always—the thought of the bright dollars. When he lay down to bed he would be wondering why they were so many, and when he woke at morn he would be wondering why they were all new; and the thing was never absent from his mind. But this day of all days he made sure in his heart of some discovery. For it seems he had observed the place where Kalamake kept his treasure, which was a lock-fast desk against the parlor wall, under the print of Kamehameha the fifth, and a photograph of Queen Victoria with her crown; and it seems again that, no later than the night before, he found occasion to look in, and behold! the bag lay there empty. And this was the day of the steamer; he could see her smoke off Kalaupapa; and she must soon arrive with a month's goods, tinned salmon and gin, and all manner of rare luxuries for Kalamake.

"Now if he can pay for his goods today," Keola thought, "I shall know for certain that the man is a warlock, and the dollars come out of the Devil's pocket."

While he was so thinking, there was his father-in-law behind him, looking vexed.

"Is that the steamer?" he asked.

"Yes," said Keola. "She has but to call at Pelekunu, and then she will be here."

"There is no help for it then," returned Kalamake, "and I must take you in my confidence, Keola, for the lack of anyone better. Come here within the house."

So they stepped together into the parlor, which was a very fine room, papered and hung with prints, and furnished with a rocking-chair, and a table and a sofa in the European style. There was a shelf of books besides, and a family Bible in the midst of the table, and the lock-fast writing-desk against the wall; so that anyone could see it was the house of a man of substance.

Kalamake made Keola close the shutters of the windows, while he himself locked all the doors and set open the lid of the desk. From this he brought forth a pair of necklaces hung with charms and shells, a bundle of dried herbs, and the dried leaves of trees, and a green branch of palm.

"What I am about," said he, "is a thing beyond wonder. The men of old were wise; they wrought marvels, and this among the rest; but that was at night, in the dark, under the fit stars and in the desert. The same will I do here in my own house, and under the plain eye of day." So saying, he put the Bible under the cushion of the sofa so that it was all covered, brought out from the same place a mat of a wonderfully fine texture, and heaped the herbs and leaves on sand in a tin pan. And then he and Keola put on the necklaces, and took their stand upon the opposite corners of the mat.

"The time comes," said the warlock; "be not afraid."

With that he set flame to the herbs, and began to mutter and wave the branch of palm. At first the light was dim because of the closed shutters; but the herbs caught strongly afire, and the flames beat upon Keola, and the room glowed with the burning; and next the smoke rose and made his head swim and his eyes darken, and the sound of Kalamake muttering ran in his ears. And suddenly, to the mat on which they were standing came a snatch or twitch, that seemed to be more swift than lightning. In the same wink the room was gone, and the house, the breath all beaten from Keola's body. Volumes of sun rolled upon his eyes and head, and he found himself transported to a beach of the sea, under a strong sun, with a great surf roaring: he and the warlock standing there on the same mat, speechless, gasping and grasping at one another, and passing their hands before their eyes.

"What was this?" cried Keola, who came to himself the first, because he was the younger. "The pang of it was like death."

"It matters not," panted Kalamake. "It is now done."

"And, in the name of God, where are we?" cried Keola.

"That is not the question," replied the sorcerer. "Being here, we have matter in our hands, and that we must attend to. Go, while I recover my breath, into the borders of the wood, and bring me the leaves of such and such a herb, and such and such a tree, which you will find to grow there plentifully—three handfuls of each. And be speedy. We must be home again before the steamer comes; it would seem strange if we had disappeared." And he sat on the sand and panted.

Keola went up the beach, which was of shining sand and coral, strewn with singular shells; and he thought in his heart——

"How do I not know this beach? I will come here again and gather shells."

"How do I not know this beach? I will come here again and gather shells."

In front of him was a line of palms against the sky; not like the palms of the Eight Islands, but tall and fresh and beautiful, and hanging out withered fans like gold among the green, and he thought in his heart——

"It is strange I should not have found this grove. I will come here again, when it is warm, to sleep." And he thought, "How warm it has grown suddenly!" For it was winter in Hawaii, and the day had been chill. And he thought also, "Where are the gray mountains? And where is the high cliff with the hanging forest and the wheeling birds?" And the more he considered, the less he might conceive in what quarter of the islands he was fallen.

In the border of the grove, where it met the beach, the herb was growing, but the tree further back. Now, as Keola went toward the tree, he was aware of a young woman who had nothing on her body but a belt of leaves.

"Well!" thought Keola, "they are not very particular about their dress in this part of the country." And he paused, supposing she would observe him and escape; and seeing that she still looked before her, stood and hummed aloud. Up she leaped at the sound. Her face was ashen; she looked this way and that, and her mouth gaped with the terror of her soul. But it was a strange thing that her eyes did not rest upon Keola.

"Good-day," said he. "You need not be so frightened, I will not eat you." And he had scarce opened his mouth before the young woman fled into the bush.

"These are strange manners," thought Keola. And, not thinking what he did, ran after her.

As she ran, the girl kept crying in some speech that was not practiced in Hawaii, yet some of the words were the same, and he knew she kept calling and warning others. And presently he saw more people running—men, women, and children, one with another, all running and crying like people at a fire. And with that he began to grow afraid himself, and returned to Kalamake bringing the leaves. Him he told what he had seen.

"You must pay no heed," said Kalamake. "All this is like a dream and shadows. All will disappear and be forgotten."

"It seemed none saw me," said Keola.

"And none did," replied the sorcerer. "We walk here in the broad sun invisible by reason of these charms. Yet they hear us; and therefore it is well to speak softly, as I do."

With that he made a circle round the mat with stones, and in the midst he set the leaves.

"It will be your part," said he, "to keep the leaves alight, and feed the fire slowly. While they blaze (which is but for a little moment) I must do my errand; and before the ashes blacken, the same power that brought us carries us away. Be ready now with the match; and do you call me in good time lest the flames burn out and I be left."

As soon as the leaves caught, the sorcerer leaped like a deer out of the circle, and began to race along the beach like a hound that has been bathing. As he ran, he kept stooping to snatch shells; and it seemed to Keola that they glittered as he took them. The leaves blazed with a clear flame that consumed them swiftly; and presently Keola had but a handful left, and the sorcerer was far off, running and stopping.

"Back!" cried Keola. "Back! The leaves are near done."

At that Kalamake turned, and if he had run before, now he flew. But fast as he ran, the leaves burned faster. The flame was ready to expire when, with a great leap, he bounded on the mat. The wind of his leaping blew it out; and with that the beach was gone, and the sun and the sea; and they stood once more in the dimness of the shuttered parlor, and were once more shaken and blinded; and on the mat betwixt them lay a pile of shining dollars. Keola ran to the shutters; and there was the steamer tossing in the swell close in.

The same night Kalamake took his son-in-law apart, and gave him five dollars in his hand.

"Keola," said he; "if you are a wise man (which I am doubtful of) you will think you slept this afternoon on the veranda, and dreamed as you were sleeping. I am a man of few words, and I have for my helpers people of short memories."

Never a word more said Kalamake, nor referred again to that affair. But it ran all the while in Keola's head—if he were lazy before, he would now do nothing.

"Why should I work," thought he, "when I have a father-in-law who makes dollars of seashells?"

Presently his share was spent. He spent it all upon fine clothes. And then he was sorry:

"For," thought he, "I had done better to have bought a concertina, with which I might have entertained myself all day long." And then he began to grow vexed with Kalamake.

"This man has the soul of a dog," thought he. "He can gather dollars when he pleases on the beach, and he leaves me to pine for a concertina! Let him beware: I am no child, I am as cunning as he, and hold his secret." With that he spoke to his wife Lehua, and complained of her father's manners.

"I would let my father be," said Lehua. "He is a dangerous man to cross."

"I care that for him!" cried Keola; and snapped his fingers. "I have him by the nose. I can make him do what I please." And he told Lehua the story.

But she shook her head.

"You may do what you like," said she; "but as sure as you thwart my father, you will be no more heard of. Think of this person, and that person; think of Hua, who was a noble of the House of Representatives, and went to Honolulu every year; and not a bone or a hair of him was found. Remember Kamau, and how he wasted to a thread, so that his wife lifted him with one hand. Keola, you are a baby in my father's hands; he will take you with his thumb and finger and eat you like a shrimp."

Now Keola was truly afraid of Kalamake, but he was vain too; and these words of his wife's incensed him.

"Very well," said he, "if that is what you think of me, I will show how much you are deceived." And he went straight to where his father-in-law was sitting in the parlor.

"Kalamake," said he, "I want a concertina."

"Do you, indeed?" said Kalamake.

"Yes," said he, "and I may as well tell you plainly, I mean to have it. A man who picks up dollars on the beach can certainly afford a concertina."

"I had no idea you had so much spirit," replied the sorcerer. "I thought you were a timid, useless lad, and I cannot describe how much pleased I am to find I was mistaken. Now I begin to think I may have found an assistant and successor in my difficult business. A concertina? You shall have the best in Honolulu. And tonight, as soon as it is dark, you and I will go and find the money."

"Shall we return to the beach?" asked Keola.

"No, no!" replied Kalamake; "you must begin to learn more of my secrets. Last time I taught you to pick shells; this time I shall teach you to catch fish. Are you strong enough to launch Pili's boat?"

"I think I am," returned Keola. "But why should we not take your own, which is afloat already?"

"I have a reason which you will understand thoroughly before tomorrow," said Kalamake. "Pili's boat is the better suited for my purpose. So, if you please, let us meet there as soon as it dark; and in the meanwhile, let us keep our own counsel, for there is no cause to let the family into our business."

Honey is not more sweet than was the voice of Kalamake, and Keola could scarce contain his satisfaction.

"I might have had my concertina weeks ago," thought he, "and there is nothing needed in this world but a little courage."

Presently after he spied Lehua weeping, and was half in a mind to tell her all was well.

"But no," thinks he; "I shall wait till I can show her the concertina; we shall see what the chit will do then. Perhaps she will understand in the future that her husband is a man of some intelligence."

As soon as it was dark father and son-in-law launched Pili's boat and set the sail. There was a great sea, and it blew strong from the leeward; but the boat was swift and light and dry, and skimmed the waves. The wizard had a lantern, which he lit and held with his finger through the ring; and the two sat in the stern and smoked cigars, of which Kalamake had always a provision, and spoke like friends of magic and the great sums of money which they could make by its exercise, and what they should buy first, and what second; and Kalamake talked like a father.

Presently he looked all about, and above him at the stars, and back at the island, which was already three parts sunk under the sea, and he seemed to consider ripely his position.

"Look!" says he, "there is Molokai already far behind us, and Maui like a cloud; and by the bearing of these three stars I know I am come where I desire. This part of the sea is called the Sea of the Dead. It is in this place extraordinarily deep, and the floor is all covered with the bones of men, and in the holes of this part gods and goblins keep their habitation. The flow of the sea is to the north, stronger than a shark can swim, and any man who shall here be thrown out of a ship it bears away like a wild horse into the uttermost ocean. Presently he is spent and goes down, and his bones are scattered with the rest, and the gods devour his spirit."

Fear came on Keola at the words, and he looked, and by the light of the stars and the lantern, the warlock seemed to change.

"What ails you?" cried Keola, quick and sharp.

"It is not I who am ailing," said the wizard; "but there is one here very sick."

With that he changed his grasp upon the lantern, and, behold! as he drew his finger from the ring, the finger stuck and the ring was burst, and his hand was grown to be of the bigness of three.

At that sight Keola screamed and covered his face.

But Kalamake held up the lantern. "Look rather at my face!" said he—and his head was huge as a barrel; and still he grew and grew as a cloud grows on a mountain, and Keola sat before him screaming, and the boat raced on the great seas.

"And now," said the wizard, "what do you think about that concertina? and are you sure you would not rather have a flute? No?" says he; "that is well, for I do not like my family to be changeable of purpose. But I begin to think I had better get out of this paltry boat, for my bulk swells to a very unusual degree, and if we are not the more careful, she will presently be swamped."

With that he threw his legs over the side. Even as he did so, the greatness of the man grew thirtyfold and fortyfold as swift as sight or thinking, so that he stood in the deep seas to the armpits, and his head and shoulders rose like a high isle, and the swell beat and burst upon his bosom, as it beats and breaks against a cliff. The boat ran still to the north, but he reached out his hand, and took the gunwale by the finger and thumb, and broke the side like a biscuit, and Keola was spilled into the sea. And the pieces of the boat the sorcerer crushed in the hollow of his hand and flung miles away into the night.

"Excuse me taking the lantern," said he; "for I have a long wade before me, and the land is far, and the bottom of the sea uneven, and I feel the bones under my toes."

And he turned and went off walking with great strides; and as often as Keola sank in the trough he could see him no longer; but as often as he was heaved upon the crest, there he was striding and dwindling, and he held the lamp high over his head, and the waves broke white about him as he went.

Since first the islands were fished out of the sea, there was never a man so terrified as this Keola. He swam indeed, but he swam as puppies swim when they are cast in to drown, and knew not wherefore. He could but think of the hugeness of the swelling of the warlock, of that face which was great as a mountain, of those shoulders that were broad as an isle, and of the seas that beat on them in vain. He thought, too, of the concertina, and shame took hold upon him; and of the dead men's bones, and fear shook him.

Of a sudden he was aware of something dark against the stars that tossed, and a light below, and a brightness of the cloven sea; and he heard speech of men. He cried out aloud and a voice answered; and in a twinkling the bows of a ship hung above him on a wave like a thing balanced, and swooped down. He caught with his two hands in the chains of her, and the next moment was buried in the rushing seas, and the next hauled on board by seamen.

They gave him gin and biscuit and dry clothes, and asked him how he came where they found him, and whether the light which they had seen was the lighthouse, Lae o Ka Laau. But Keola knew white men are like children and only believe their own stories; so about himself he told them what he pleased, and as for the light (which was Kalamake's lantern) he vowed he had seen none.

This ship was a schooner bound for Honolulu, and then to trade in the low islands; and by a very good chance for Keola she had lost a man off the bowsprit in a squall. It was no use talking. Keola durst not stay in the Eight Islands. Word goes so quickly, and all men are so fond to talk and carry news, that if he hid in the north end of Kauai or in the south end of Kaü, the wizard would have wind of it before a month, and he must perish. So he did what seemed the most prudent, and shipped sailor in the place of the man who had been drowned.

In some ways the ship was a good place. The food was extraordinarily rich and plenty, with biscuits and salt beef every day, and pea-soup and puddings made of flour and suet twice a week, so that Keola grew fat. The captain also was a good man, and the crew no worse than other whites. The trouble was the mate, who was the most difficult man to please Keola had ever met with, and beat and cursed him daily, both for what he did and what he did not. The blows that he dealt were very sure, for he was strong; and the words he used were very unpalatable, for Keola was come of a good family and accustomed to respect. And what was the worst of all, whenever Keola found a chance to sleep, there was the mate awake and stirring him up with a rope's end. Keola saw it would never do; and he made up his mind to run away.

They were about a month out from Honolulu when they made the land. It was a fine starry night, the sea was smooth as well as the sky fair; it blew a steady trade; and there was the island on their weather bow, a ribbon of palm trees lying flat along the sea. The captain and the mate looked at it with the night glass, and named the name of it, and talked of it, beside the wheel where Keola was steering. It seemed it was an isle where no traders came. By the captain's way, it was an isle besides where no man dwelt; but the mate thought otherwise.

"I don't give a cent for the directory," said he. "I've been past here one night in the schooner *Eugenie*: it was just such a night as this; they were fishing with torches, and the beach was thick with lights like a town."

"Well, well," says the captain, "its steep-to, that's the great point; and there ain't any outlying dangers by the chart, so we'll just hug the lee side of it. Keep her ramping full, don't I tell you!" he cried to Keola, who was listening so hard that he forgot to steer.

And the mate cursed him, and swore that Kanaka was for no use in the world, and if he got started after him with a belaying pin, it would be a cold day for Keola.

And so the captain and mate lay down on the house together, and Keola was left to himself.

"This island will do very well for me," he thought; "if no traders deal there, the mate will never come. And as for Kalamake, it is not possible he can ever get as far as this."

With that he kept edging the schooner nearer in. He had to do this quietly, for it was the trouble with these white men, and above all with the mate, that you could never be sure of them; they would all be sleeping sound, or else pretending, and if a sail shook, they would jump to their feet and fall on you with a rope's end. So Keola edged her up little by little, and kept all drawing. And presently the land was close on board, and the sound of the sea on the sides of it grew loud.

With that, the mate sat up suddenly upon the house.

"What are you doing?" he roars. "You'll have the ship ashore!"

And he made one bound for Keola, and Keola made another clean over the rail and plump into the starry sea. When he came up again, the schooner had payed off on her true course, and the mate stood by the wheel himself, and Keola heard him cursing. The sea was smooth under the lee of the island; it was warm besides, and Keola had his sailor's knife, so he had no fear of sharks. A little way before him the trees stopped; there was a break in the line of the land like the mouth of a harbor; and the tide, which was then flowing, took him up and carried him through. One minute he was without, and the next within, had floated there in a wide shallow water, bright with ten thousand stars, and all about him was the ring of the land, with its string of palm-trees. And he was amazed, because this was a kind of island he had never heard of.

The time of Keola in that place was in two periods—the period when he was alone, and the period when he was there with the tribe. At first he sought everywhere and found no man; only some houses standing in a hamlet, and the marks of fires. But the ashes of the fires were cold and the rains had washed them away; and the winds had blown, and some of the huts were overthrown. It was here he took his dwelling; and he made a fire drill, and a shell hook, and fished and cooked his fish, and climbed after green cocoanuts, the juice of which he drank, for in all the isle there was no water. The days were long to him, and the nights terrifying. He made a lamp of cocoa-shell, and drew the oil of the ripe nuts, and made a wick of fibre; and when evening came he closed up his hut, and lit his lamp, and lay and trembled till morning. Many a time he thought in his heart he would have been better in the bottom of the sea, his bones rolling there with the others.

All this while he kept by the inside of the island, for the huts were on the shore of the lagoon, and it was there the palms grew best, and the lagoon itself abounded with good fish. And to the outer side he went once only, and he looked but once at the beach of the ocean, and came away shaking. For the look of it, with its bright sand, and strewn shells, and strong sun and surf, went sore against his inclination.

"It cannot be," he thought, "and yet it is very like. And how do I know? These white men, although they pretend to know where they are sailing, must take their chance like other people. So that after all we may have sailed in a circle, and I may be quite near to Molokai, and this may be the very beach where my father-in-law gathers his dollars."

So after that he was prudent, and kept to the land side.

It was perhaps a month later, when the people of the place arrived—the fill of six great boats. They were a fine race of men, and spoke a tongue that sounded very different from the tongue of Hawaii, but so many of the words were the same that it was not difficult to understand. The men besides were very courteous, and the women very towardly; and they made Keola welcome, and built him a house, and gave him a wife; and what surprised him the most, he was never sent to work with the young men.

And now Keola had three periods. First he had a period of being very sad, and then he had a period when he was pretty merry. Last of all came the third, when he was the most terrified man in the four oceans.

The cause of the first period was the girl he had to wife. He was in doubt about the island, and he might have been in doubt about the speech, of which he had heard so little when he came there with the wizard on the mat. But about his wife there was no mistake conceivable, for she was the same girl that ran from him crying in the wood. So he had sailed all this way, and might as well have stayed in Molokai; and had left home and wife and all his friends for no other cause but to escape his enemy, and the place he had come to was that wizard's hunting ground, and the place where he walked invisible. It was at this period when he kept the most close to the lagoon side, and as far as he dared, abode in the cover of his hut.

The cause of the second period was talk he heard from his wife and the chief islanders. Keola himself said little. He was never so sure of his new friends, for he judged they were too civil to be wholesome, and since he had grown better acquainted with his father-in-law the man had grown more cautious. So he told them nothing of himself, but only his name and descent, and that he came from the Eight Islands, and what fine islands they were; and about the king's palace in Honolulu, and how he was a chief friend of the king and the missionaries. But he put many questions and learned much. The island where he was was called the Isle of Voices; it belonged to the tribe, but they made their home upon another, three hour's sail to the southward. There they lived and had their permanent houses, and it was a rich island where were eggs and chickens and pigs, and ships came trading with rum and tobacco. It was there the schooner had gone after Keola deserted; there, too, the mate had died, like the fool of a white man as he was. It seems, when the ship came, it was the beginning of the sickly season in that isle, when the fish of the lagoon are poisonous, and all who eat of them swell up and die. The mate was told of it; he saw the boats preparing, because in that season the people leave that island and sail to the Isle of Voices; but he was a fool of a white man, who would believe no stories but his own, and he caught one of these fish, cooked it and ate it, and swelled up and died, which was good news to Keola. As for the Isle of Voices, it lay solitary the most part of the year; only now and then a boat's crew came for copra, and in the bad season, when the fish at the main isle were poisonous, the tribe dwelt there in a body. It had its name from a marvel, for it seemed the seaside of it was all beset with invisible devils; day and night you heard them talking one with another in strange tongues; day and night little fires blazed up and were extinguished on the beach; and what was the cause of these doings no man might conceive. Keola asked them if it were the same in their own island where they stayed, and they told him no, not there; nor yet in any other of some hundred isles that lay all about them in that sea; but it was a thing peculiar to the Isle of Voices. They told him also that these fires and voices were ever on the seaside and in the seaward fringes of the wood, and a man might dwell by the lagoon two thousand years (if he could live so long) and never be any way troubled; and even on the seaside the devils did no harm if let alone. Only once a chief had cast a spear at one of the voices, and the same night he fell out of a cocoanut-palm and was killed.

Keola thought a good bit with himself. He saw he would be all right when the tribe returned to the main island, and right enough where he was, if he kept by the lagoon, yet he had a mind to make things righter if he could. So he told the high chief he had once been in an isle that was pestered the same way, and the folk had found a means to cure that trouble.

"There was a tree growing in the bush there," says he, "and it seems these devils came to get the leaves of it. So the people of the isle cut down the tree wherever it was found, and the devils came no more."

They asked what kind of a tree this was, and he showed them the tree of which Kalamake burned the leaves. They found it hard to believe, yet the idea tickled them. Night after night the old men debated it in their councils, but the high chief (though he was a brave man) was afraid of the matter, and reminded them daily of the chief who cast a spear against the voices and was killed, and the thought of that brought all to a stand again.

Though he could not yet bring about the destruction of the trees, Keola was well enough pleased, and began to look about him and take pleasure in his days;

and, among other things, he was the kinder to his wife, so that the girl began to love him greatly. One day he came to the hut, and she lay on the ground lamenting.

"Why," said Keola, "what is wrong with you now?"

She declared it was nothing.

The same night she woke him. The lamp burned very low, but he saw by her face she was in sorrow.

"Keola," she said, "put your ear to my mouth that I may whisper, for no one must hear us. Two days before the boats begin to be got ready, go you to the seaside of the isle and lie in a thicket. We shall choose that place beforehand, you and I; and hide food; and every night I shall come near by there singing. So when a night comes and you do not hear me, you shall know we are clean gone out of the island, and you may come forth again in safety."

The soul of Keola died within him.

"What is this?" he cried. "I cannot live among devils. I will not be left behind upon this isle. I am dying to leave it."

"You will never leave it alive, my poor Keola," said the girl; "for to tell you the truth, my people are eaters of men; but this they keep secret. And the reason they will kill you before we leave is because in our island ships come, and Donat-Kimaran comes and talks for the French, and there is a white trader there in a house with a veranda, and a catechist. Oh, that is a fine place indeed! The trader has barrels filled with flour; and a French warship once came in the lagoon and gave everybody wine and biscuit. Ah, my poor Keola, I wish I could take you there, for great is my love to you, and it is the finest place in the seas except Papeete."

So now Keola was the most terrified man in the four oceans. He had heard tell of eaters of men in the south islands, and the thing had always been a fear to him; and here it was knocking at his door. He had heard besides, by travellers, of their practices, and how when they are in a mind to eat a man, they cherish and fondle him like a mother with a favorite baby. And he saw this must be his own case; and that was why he had been housed, and fed, and wived, and liberated from all work; and why the old men and the chiefs discoursed with him like a person of weight. So he lay on his bed and railed upon his destiny; and the flesh curdled on his bones.

The next day the people of the tribe were very civil, as their way was. They were elegant speakers, and they made beautiful poetry, and jested at meals, so that a missionary must have died laughing. It was little enough Keola cared for their fine ways; all he saw was the white teeth shining in their mouths, and his gorge rose at the sight; and when they were done eating, he went and lay in the bush like a dead man.

The next day it was the same, and then his wife followed him.

"Keola," she said, "if you do not eat, I tell you plainly you will be killed and cooked tomorrow. Some of the old chiefs are murmuring already. They think you are fallen sick and must lose flesh."

With that Keola got to his feet, and anger burned in him.

"It is little I care one way or the other," said he. "I am between the devil and the deep sea. Since die I must, let me die the quickest way; and since I must be eaten at the best of it, let me rather be eaten by hobgoblins than by men. Farewell," said he, and he left her standing, and walked to the sea-side of that island.

It was all bare in the strong sun; there was no sign of man, only the beach was trodden, and all about him as he went, the voices talked and whispered, and the little fires sprang up and burned down. All tongues of the earth were spoken there: the French, the Dutch, the Russian, the Tamil, the Chinese. Whatever land knew sorcery, there were some of its people whispering in Keola's ear. That beach was thick as a cried fair, yet no man seen; and as he walked he saw the shells vanish before him, and no man to pick them up. I think the devil would have been afraid to be alone in such a company; but Keola was past fear and courted death. When the fires sprang up, he charged for them like a bull. Bodiless voices called to and fro; unseen hands poured sand upon the flames; and they were gone from the beach before he reached them.

"It is plain Kalamake is not here," he thought, "as I must have been killed long since."

With that he sat him down in the margin of the wood, for he was tired, and put his chin upon his hands. The business before his eyes continued; the beach babbled with voices, and the fires sprang up and sank, and the shells vanished and were renewed again even while he looked.

"It was a by-day when I was here before," he thought, "for it was nothing to this."

And his head was dizzy with the thought of these millions and millions of dollars, and all these hundreds and hundreds of persons culling them upon the beach and flying in the air higher and swifter than eagles.

"And to think how they have fooled me with their talk of mints," says he, "and that money was made there, when it is clear that all the new coin in all the world is gathered on these sands! But I will know better the next time!" said he.

And at last, he knew not very well how or when, sleep fell on Keola, and he forgot the island and all his sorrows.

Early the next day, before the sun was yet up, a bustle woke him. He awoke in fear, for he thought the tribe had caught him napping; but it was no such matter. Only, on the beach in front of him, the bodiless voices called and shouted one upon another, and it seemed they all passed and swept beside him up the coast of the island.

"What is afoot now?" thinks Keola. And it was plain to him it was something beyond ordinary, for the fires were not lighted nor the shells taken, but the bodiless voices kept posting up the beach, and hailing and dying away; and others following, and by the sound of them these wizards should be angry.

"It is not me they are angry at," thought Keola, "for they pass me close."

As when hounds go by, or horses in a race, or city folk coursing to a fire, and all men join and follow after, so it was now with Keola; and he knew not what he did, nor why he did it, but there, lo and behold! he was running with the voices.

So he turned one point of the island, and this brought him in view of a second; and there he remembered the wizard trees to have been growing by the score together in a wood. From this point there went up a hubbub of men crying not to be described; and by the sound of them, those that he ran with shaped their course for the same quarter. A little nearer, and there began to mingle with the outcry the crash of many axes. And at this a thought came at last into his mind that the high chief had consented; that the men of the tribe had set-to cutting down these trees; that word had gone about the isle from sorcerer to sorcerer, and these were all now assembling to defend their trees. Desire of strange things swept him on. He posted with the voices, crossed the beach, and came into the borders of the wood, and stood astonished. One tree had fallen, others were part hewed away. There was the tribe clustered. They were back to back, and bodies lay, and blood flowed among their feet. The hue of fear was on all their faces; their voices went up to heaven shrill as a weasel's cry.

Have you seen a child when he is all alone and has a wooden sword, and fights, leaping and hewing with the empty air? Even so the man-eaters huddled back to back, and heaved up their axes, and laid on, and screamed as they laid on, and behold! no man to contend with them! only here and there Keola saw an axe swinging over against them without hands; and time and again a man of the tribe would fall before it, clove in twain or burst asunder, and his soul sped howling.

For awhile Keola looked upon this prodigy like one that dreams, and then fear took him by the midst as sharp as death, that he should behold such doings. Even in that same flash the high chief of the clan espied him standing, and pointed and called out his name. Thereat the whole tribe saw him also, and their eyes flashed, and their teeth clashed.

"I am too long here," thought Keola, and ran farther out of the wood and down the beach, not caring whither.

"Keola!" said a voice close by upon the empty sand.

"Lehua! is that you!" he cried, and gasped, and looked in vain for her; but by the eyesight he was stark alone.

"I saw you pass before," the voice answered; "but you would not hear me. Quick! get the leaves and the herbs, and let us free."

"You are there with the mat?" he asked.

"Here, at your side," said she. And he felt her arms about him. "Quick! the leaves and the herbs, before my father can get back!"

So Keola ran for his life, and fetched the wizard fuel; and Lehua guided him back, and set his feet upon the mat, and made the fire. All the time of its burning, the sound of the battle towered out of the wood; the wizards and the man-eaters hard at fight; the wizards, the viewless ones, roaring out aloud like bulls upon a mountain, and the men of the tribe replying shrill and savage out of the terror of their souls. And all the time of the burning, Keola stood there and listened, and shook, and watched how the unseen hands of Lehua poured the leaves. She poured them fast, and the flame burned high, and scorched Keola's hands; and she speeded and blew the burning with her breath. The last leaf was eaten, the flame fell, and the shock followed, and there were Keola and Lehua in the room at home.

Now, when Keola could see his wife at last he was mighty pleased, and he was mighty pleased to be home again in Molokai and sit down beside a bowl of poi— for they make no poi on board ships, and there was none in the Isle of Voices—and he was out of the body with pleasure to be clean escaped out of the hands of the eaters of men. But there was another matter not so clear, and Lehua and Keola talked of it all night and were troubled. There was Kalamake left upon the isle. If, by the blessing of God, he could but stick there, all were well; but should he escape and return to Molokai, it would be an ill day for his daughter and her husband. They spoke of his gift of swelling, and whether he could wade that distance in the seas. But Keola knew by this time where that island was—and that is to say, in the Low or Dangerous Archipelago. So they fetched the atlas and looked upon the distance in the map, and by what they could make of it, it seemed a far way for an old gentleman to walk. Still, it would not do to make too sure of a warlock like Kalamake, and they determined at last to take counsel of a white missionary.

So the first one that came by Keola told him everything. And the missionary was very sharp on him for taking the second wife in the low island; but for all the rest, he vowed he could make neither head nor tail of it.

"However," says he, "if you think this money of your father's ill gotten, my advice to you would be give some of it to the lepers and some to the missionary fund. And as for this extraordinary rigmarole, you cannot do better than keep it to yourselves."

But he warned the police at Honolulu that, by all he could make out, Kalamake and Keola had been coining false money, and it would not be amiss to watch them.

Keola and Lehua took his advice, and gave many dollars to the lepers and the fund. And no doubt the advice must have been good, for from that day to this, Kalamake has never more been heard of. But whether he was slain in the battle by the trees, or whether he is still kicking his heels upon the Isle of Voices, who shall say?

THE LIFE AND TIMES OF
ROBERT LOUIS STEVENSON

1837	20 June	*King William IV dies at Windsor Castle and Princess Victoria of Kent is proclaimed queen*
1838	28 June	*Victoria is coronated queen at Westminster Abbey*
1847	14 December	*Emily Brontë's novel* Wuthering Heights *(under the pseudonym Ellis Bell) is published by Thomas Cautley Newby, London*
1850	13 November	Robert Louis Balfour Stevenson is born to Margaret Isabella Balfour and Thomas Stevenson at 8 Howard Place, Edinburgh, Scotland
1851	1 February	*Mary Shelley dies in London; the cause of death is reported to be a brain tumor*
		The Stevenson family moves to 1 Inverleith Terrance, Edinburgh
1853	23 October	*The Crimean War, in which Great Britain and France fight Russia, begins with a declaration of war by the Sultan of the Ottoman Empire against the Tsar of Russia*
1856		The Stevensons move to 17 Heriot Row, Edinburgh
1857		Robert begin his schooling at Mr. Henderson's school in Edinburgh, but returns home in a few weeks and alternates between home schooling and traditional private schooling for the next seven years due to poor health

1859	30 April	*The first issue of Charles Dickens's weekly magazine,* All the Year Round, *is published in London*
	22 May	*Arthur Ignatius Conan Doyle is born in Edinburgh, Scotland*
	2 November	*Charles Darwin's* On the Origin of Species *is published by John Murray, London*
	26 November	*Wilkie Collins's* The Woman in White *begins its serialization in Charles Dickens's weekly literary magazine,* All the Year Round
1861	14 December	*Prince Albert dies of typhoid fever in the Blue Room at Windsor Castle*
1863	10 January	*The London Underground first opens for business offering service between Paddington and Farringdon Street*
	26 October	*The Football Association is formed*
1864	October	Stevenson attends a private school in Edinburgh until he entered university
1865	December	*Lewis Carroll's* Alice's Adventures in *Wonderland is published by Macmillan & Co., London*
1867	5 March	*Fenian Rising in Ireland*
	November	Stevenson enters the University of Edinburgh as a chemistry student
1868	26 May	*The last public hanging in Britain occurs outside Newgate Prison*
	Autumn	*Wilkie Collins's* The Moonstone *is published in three volumes by Tinsley Brothers, London*
1869	Summer	Stevenson joins his father on an inspection of the lighthouses on the Orkney and Shetland Islands
1870	9 June	*Charles Dickens dies at Gads Hill Place in Higham, Kent, England*
	19 July	The Franco-Prussian War begins and results in the end of the Second French Empire the following year and the beginning of the Third French Republic
1871	26 January	*Rugby Football Union established*
	Fall	Stevenson begins to study law at the University of Edinburgh
	1 November	*The sale of commissions in the British Army is abolished*
1875	July	Stevenson is admitted to the Scottish bar, though he Nevers practices law

1876	September	Stevenson first meets Fanny Van de Grift Osbourne
1877	1 January	*Queen Victoria is proclaimed Empress of India*
1878	7 April	*The Metropolitan Police Service's Criminal Investigations Department is established by Charles Howard Vincent*
	25 May	*Gilbert & Sullivan's* "H.M.S. Pinafore," *performed by the D'Oyly Carte Opera Company opens at the Opera Comique, London, and runs for 571 performances*
	21 November	*Second Afghan War begins*
1879	1 January	*Benjamin Henry Blackwell opens his first bookshop in Oxford*
	22 January	*British troops are massacred by Zulu warriors at the Battle of Isandlwana while a small detachment from the 2nd Battalion of the 24th Foot and a Native Natal Contingent hold off Zulu forces at Rorke's Drift*
	August	Stevenson follows Fanny to California
	21 December	*Henrik Ibsen's play* Doll House *opens at the Royal Theatre, Copenhagen*
1880	May	Stevenson and Fanny are married in California, honeymooning at an abandoned mining camp on the slopes of Mount Saint Helena
	August	Stevenson, Fanny, and her son Lloyd return to Britain, though his ill health causes him to move frequently in search of a satisfactory place to call home
	2 August	*Greenwich Mean Time (GMT) is adopted as the standard time throughout Great Britain*
	16 December	*The Boers declare independence in the Transvaal, initiating the First Boer War*
1881	4 March	*As Conan Doyle tells us, this is the day Dr. Watson and Sherlock Holmes begin their first case together. At 221B Baker Street,* A Study in Scarlet *commences . . .*
	26 July	*The first issue of the* London Evening News *appears*
	3 August	*The Pretoria Convention is signed, ending the First Boer War*
	10 October	*The D'Oyly Carte Savoy Theatre opens and is the first building in Britain fully lit by electricity*
1882	August	*British forces occupy Egypt and declare it a protectorate*

1883	23 May	Stevenson's adventure novel *Treasure Island* is published by Cassell, Petter & Galpin, London
1884	1 February	*The first fascicle of* A New English Dictionary *is published by Oxford University Press, under the editorship of James Murray*
	13 October	*General Charles George Gordon is besieged in Khartoum in the Mahdist War*
1885	1 January	*The first volume of the* Dictionary of National Biography *is published by Smith, Elder, London, under the editorship of Leslie Stephen*
	14 March	*Gilbert & Sullivan's* "Mikado" *performed by the D'Oyly Carte Opera Company opens at the Opera Comique, London, and runs for 672 performances*
	June	Stevenson's collection of children's poetry A Child's Garden of Verses is published by Longmans, Green & Co., London
	September	*H. Rider Haggard's* King Solomon's Mines *is published by Cassell & Co., London*
	November	Stevenson's romance, *Prince Otto*, is published by Chatto & Windus, London
1886	5 January	Stevenson's novella *The Strange Case of Dr. Jekyll and Mr. Hyde* is published by Longmans, Green & Co., London
	July	Stevenson's adventure novel *Kidnaped* is published by Cassell and Co. Ltd., London
1887	21 June	*Queen Victoria's Golden Jubilee Thanksgiving service is held at Westminster Abbey*
	November	*Arthur Conan Doyle's* A Study in Scarlet *appears in Beeton's Christmas Annual and introduces Sherlock Holmes and Dr. Watson to the world*
	Winter	Stevenson and his family spend the winter at Saranac Lake, New York
1888	June	Stevenson charters the yacht *Casco* and sets sail from San Francisco to Hawaiian Islands
	July	Stevenson's historical novel *The Black Arrow: A Tale of the Two Roses* is published by Cassell and Co. Ltd., London

	September	The Stevensons travel extensively throughout the South Pacific
1889	July	Stevenson's novel *The Master of Ballentrae* is published by Cassell and Co. Ltd., London
		Jerome K. Jerome's Three Men in a *Boat is published by J. W. Arrowsmith, 11 Quay Street, Bristol*
	6 August	*London's Savoy Hotel opens*
1890	April	The Stevensons leave Sydney for Samoa where Robert purchases land on the Samoan island of Upolu
	July	Oscar *Wilde's* The Picture of Dorian Gray *appears in* Lippincott's Monthly Magazine
1891	20 April	Ibsen's Hedda Gabler premières in English at the Vaudeville Theatre, London
	April	The Picture of Dorian Gray *is published by Ward Lock & Co., London*
1892	14 January	*Prince Albert Victor, Duke of Clarence, dies*
	October	*Conan Doyle's* The Adventures of Sherlock *Holmes is published by George Newnes, Ltd., London*
1893	July	Stevenson's novel *Catriona*, a sequel to *Kidnapped* is published by Cassell and Co. Ltd., London
1894	30 June	*London's Tower Bridge opens for traffic*
	3 December	Stevenson dies in the village of Vailima on Upolu at the age of 44 and is buried on Mount Vaea
1895	14 February	*Oscar Wilde's play* The Importance of Being Earnest *opens at the St. James Theatre and is a critical and commercial success*
1901	22 January	*Queen Victoria dies at Osborne House, on the Isle of Wight*

REVIEWS AND NOTICES

Our children and grandchildren shall rejoice in his books; but we of this generation possessed in the living man something that they will not know. So long as he lived, though it were far from Britain—though we had never spoken to him and he, perhaps, had barely heard our names—we always wrote our best for Stevenson. To him each writer amongst us—small or more than small—had been proud to have carried his best. That best might be poor enough. So long as it was not slipshod, Stevenson could forgive. While he lived, he moved men to put their utmost even into writings that quite certainly would never meet his eye. Surely another age will wonder over this curiosity of letters—that for five years the needle of literary endeavour in Great Britain has quivered towards a little island in the South Pacific, as to its magnetic pole.—QUILLER-COUCH, A. T., 1894, *Adventures in Criticism, p.* 184.

Stevenson's early school days do not bulk largely in the "Memories." In fact he was not much at school. His father had a terror of education (so called), and often plumed himself on having been the author of Louis' success in life, by keeping him as much as possible from pedagogic influence. That the paternal efforts met with filial support, Stevenson's own confession assures us. "All through my boyhood and youth," he writes, "I was known and pointed out for the pattern of an idler"; and this was highly probable, for his industry was by no means the sort to be recognised in scholastic high places. He was a day pupil first at Henderson's, Inverleith Row, and then, for a year, at the Edinburgh Academy. While at the latter he edited a MS school magazine, called the

"Sunbeam." A water-color sketch by him in connection with this is still extant. . . . But, ere long, memory is busy again with the old haunts. Edinburgh University, in all innocence, inscribes a new classic on her roll. In the self-likeness he has left us of this period, he is a "lean, ugly, idle, unpopular student." He takes care here, too, that his education shall not be interfered with, by acting upon "an extensive and highly rational system of truancy." In the intervals, however, of his serious work—scribbling in penny version books, noting down features and scenes, and commemorating halting stanzas—his professors get some of his attention. But even then it is more as men than teachers. He could have written much better papers on themselves than on their subjects. Indeed he has done so.—ARMOUR, MARGARET, 1895, *The Home and Early Haunts of Robert Louis Stevenson, pp.* 22, 63, 72.

We first knew Louis Stevenson when his schooldays and teens were past, and he was facing what he called "the equinoctial gales of youth," and beginning to put his self-taught art of writing into print. . . . He would frequently drop in to dinner with us, and of an evening he had the run of our smoking-room. After 10 P.M., when a stern old servant went to bed, the "open sesame" to our door was a rattle on the letter-box. He liked this admittance by secret sign, and we liked to hear his special rat-a-tat, for we knew we would then enjoy an hour or two of talk which, he said, "is the harmonious speech of two or more, and is by far the most accessible of pleasures." He always adhered to the same dress for all entertainments, a shabby, short, velveteen jacket, a loose, Byronic, collared shirt (for a brief space he adopted black flannel ones), and meagre, shabby-looking trousers. His straight hair he wore long, and he looked like an unsuccessful artist, or a poorly clad but eager student. He was then fragile in figure and, to use a Scottish expression, *shilpit* looking. There is no English equivalent for *shilpit*, being lean, starving, ill-thriven, in one. His dark, bright eyes were his most noticeable and attractive feature;—wide apart, almost Japanese in their shape, and above them a fine brow. He was pale and sallow, and there was a foreign, almost gipsy look about him, despite his long-headed Scotch ancestry.—SIMPSON, EVA BLANTYRE, 1895, *Some Edinburgh Notes; Class-Book, Essays; pp.* 196, 197.

> Her breast is old, it will not rise,
> Her tearless sobs in anguish choke,
> God put His finger on her eyes,

And then it was her tears that spoke.
"I've ha'en o' brawer sons a flow,
My Walter mair renown could win,
And he that followed at the plough,
But Louis was my Benjamin!
Ye sons wha do your little best,
Ye writing Scots, put by the pen,
He's deid, the ane abune the rest,
I winna look at write again!

.   .   .   .

And when he had to cross the sea,
He wouldna lat his een grow dim,
He bravely dree'd his weird for me,
I tried to do the same for him.
Ahint his face his pain was sair,
Ahint hers grat his waefu' mither
We kent that we should meet nae mair,
The ane saw easy thro' the ither."

.   .   .   .

A star that shot across the night
Struck fire on Pala's mourning head,
And left for aye a steadfast light,
By which the mother guards her dead.
The lad was mine! Erect she stands,
No more by vain regrets oppress't,
Once more her eyes are clear; her hands
Are proudly crossed upon her breast.

—BARRIE, JAMES MATTHEW, 1895; *Scotland's Lament, McClure's Magazine, vol. 4, p. 286.*

Perhaps no one was ever quicker to make deep friends when the true metal was found, or surer to grapple them "with hooks of steel." A witty, ever-ready talker, a charmingly responsive listener, he was the best of company, even when he was in his bed-prison. His eager vivacity seemed to show no abatement save in the total eclipses of health.—LANIER, CHARLES D. 1895, *Robert Louis Stevenson, Review of Reviews, American Ed., vol. 2, p. 185.*

I came home dazzled with my new friend, saying as Constance does of Arthur, "Was ever such a gracious creature born?" That impression of ineffable mental charm was formed at the first moment of acquaintance, [about 1877] and it never lessened or became modified. Stevenson's rapidity in the sympathetic interchange of ideas was, doubtless, the source of it. He has been described as an "egotist" but I challenge the description. If ever there was an altruist, it was Louis Stevenson; he seemed to feign an interest in himself merely to stimulate you to be liberal in your confidences. Those who have written about him from later impressions than these of which I speak seem to me to give insufficient prominence to the gaiety of Stevenson. It was his cardinal quality in those early days. A childlike mirth leaped and danced in him; he seemed to skip the hills of life. He was simply bubbling with quips and jests; his inherent earnestness or passion about abstract things was incessantly relieved by jocosity; and when he had built one of his intellectual castles in the sand, a wave of humor was certain to sweep in and destroy it. I cannot, for the life of me, recall any of his jokes; and written down in cold blood, they might not be funny if I did. They were not wit so much as humanity, the many-sided-outlook upon life. I am anxious that his laughter-loving mood should not be forgotten, because later on it was partly, but I think never wholly, quenched by ill health, responsibility, and the advance of years. He was often, in the old days, excessively and delightfully silly—silly with the silliness of an inspired school-boy; and I am afraid that our laughter sometimes sounded ill in the ears of age.—GOSSE, EDMUND, 1895, *Personal Memories of Robert Louis Stevenson, Century Magazine, vol. 50, p.* 448.

I never had heard of his existence till, in 1873, I think, I was at Mentone, in the interests of my health. Here I met Mr. Sidney Colvin, now of the British Musuem, and, with Mr. Colvin, Stevenson. He looked as, in my eyes, he always did look, more like a lass than a lad, with a rather long, smooth oval face, brown hair worn at greater length than is common, large lucid eyes, but whether blue or brown I cannot remember, if brown, certainly light brown. On appealing to the authority of a lady, I learn that brown *was* the hue. His color was a trifle hectic, as is not unusual at Mentone, but he seemed, under his big blue cloak, to be of slender, yet agile frame. He was like nobody else whom I ever met. There was a sort of uncommon celerity in changing expression, in thought and speech. I shall not deny that my first impression was not wholly favorable. "Here," I thought, "is one of your æsthetic young men, though a very clever one." What the talk was about I do not remember; probably of books. Mr. Stevenson afterwards told me that I had spoken of Monsieur Paul de St. Victor, as a fine writer, but added that "he was not a British sportsman." Mr. Stevenson himself, to my surprise, was unable to walk beyond a very short distance, and, as it soon appeared, he thought his thread of life was nearly spun. He had just written his essay, "Ordered South," the first of his published works, for his "Pentland Rising" pamphlet was unknown, a boy's performance. On reading "Ordered South," I saw, at once, that here was a new writer, a writer indeed; one who could do what none of us, *nous autres*, could rival, or approach. I was instantly "sealed of the Tribe of Louis," an admirer, a devotee, a fanatic, if you please. . . . I have known no man in whom the pre-eminently manly virtues of kindness, courage, sympathy, generosity, helpfulness, were more beautifully conspicuous than in Mr. Stevenson, none so much loved—it is not too strong a word—by so many and such various people. He was as unique in character as in literary genius.—LANG, ANDREW, 1895, *Recollections of Robert Louis Stevenson, North American Review, vol.* 160, *pp.* 186, 194.

> Son of a race nomadic, finding still
> Its home in regions furthest from its home,
> Ranging untired the borders of the world,
> And resting but to roam;
> Loved of his land, and making all his boast
> The birthright of the blood from which he came,
> Heir to those lights that guard the Scottish coast,
> And caring only for a filial fame;
> Proud, if a poet, he was Scotsman most,
> And bore a Scottish name.

—LEGALLIENNE, RICHARD, 1895, *Robert Louis Stevenson, an Elegy, p.* 1.

Stevenson calls himself "ugly" in his student days, but I think that is a term that never at any time fitted him. Certainly to him as a boy about fourteen (with the creed which he propounded to me, that at sixteen one was a man) it would not apply. In body Stevenson was assuredly badly set up. His limbs were long and lean and spidery, and his chest flat, so as almost to suggest some malnutrition, such sharp angles and corners did his joints make under his clothes. But in his face this was belied. His brow was oval and full, over soft brown eyes, that seemed already to have drunk the sunlight under southern vines. The whole face had a tendency to an oval Madonna-like type. But about the mouth and in the mirthful, mocking light of the eyes, there lingered ever a ready Autolycus roguery, that rather suggested the sly god Hermes masquerading as a mortal. Yet the eyes were always genial, however gaily the lights danced in them; but about the mouth there was something tricksy and mocking, as of a spirit that had already peeped behind the scenes of Life's pageant and more than guessed its unrealities.—BAILDON, H. BELLYSE, 1901, *Robert Louis Stevenson, a Life Study in Criticism, pp.* 20, 21.

TREASURE ISLAND

1883

To whom we could almost have raised a statue in the market-place for having written "Treasure Island."—BIRRELL, AUGUSTINE, 1887, *Obiter Dicta, Second Series, p.* 217.

The best boys' story since Marryatt, and one of a literary excellence to which Marryatt could make no pretensions.—SAINTSBURY, GEORGE, 1896, *A History of Nineteenth Century Literature, p.* 339.

"Treasure Island" is a piece of astounding ingenuity, in which the manner is taken from "Robinson Crusoe," and the plot belongs to the era of the detective story.—CHAPMAN, JOHN JAY, 1898, *Emerson and Other Essays, p.* 229.

"Treasure Island" is, properly speaking, a boy's book, but, like "Robinson Crusoe" (the only book with which it ought to be compared, though "Reuben Davidger" runs it close), children of a larger growth are fascinated by it. There is not a dull page in it, and every incident seems to be, in turn, more effective than the other. We hurry through it, eager to be in at the death; we feel, at the end, as if we had been among the pirates and endured many a strange adventure; and then we read it again, rolling it, like a sweet morsel, under the tongue.—MACCULLOCH, J. A., 1898, *R. L. Stevenson, Westminster Review, vol.* 149, *p.* 642.

KIDNAPPED

1886

Kidnapped is the outstanding boy's book of its generation.

James Matthew Barrie, 1889, *An Edinburgh Eleven,* p. 120

The whole of *Kidnapped* is written with so much salt and piquancy, such happy invention, and fullest measure of the author's spirit of dexterity and finish, of his power of humorously graphic portraiture, as to make it stand out preeminent even among Mr. Stevenson's own works.

Mrs. (Janetta) C. E. Newton-Robinson, 1893, "Some Aspects of the Work of Mr. Robert Louis Stevenson," *Westminster Review,* vol. 139, p. 603.

THE STRANGE CASE OF DR. JEKYLL AND MR. HYDE

1886

The subject is one which has haunted literature and men's minds for ages; and perhaps Mr. Stevenson, by transferring the ghost to a living and comfortable *bourgeois,* may have done something to allay its wanderings. It seems, however, as if the possibilities of the theme would have admitted of a treatment a trifle finer and more subtle than he has chosen to give it. It may be misreading the intention of the book, with its hint of unfathomed depths in the soul, to suggest that the evil of Mr. Hyde is hardly that which would belong to Dr. Jekyll; but its effect as a tale of situation and moral would scarcely have been marred if the link of connection between the two characters had been a little more delicate, and the individuality of each more carefully worked out. As it is, its gruesomeness has just a touch of the perfunctory: it does not thrill with so poetic a terror as that stirred by the inimitable one-legged sailor in *Treasure Island,* or by the ghastliness of Thrawn Janet.

Sophia Kirk, 1887, "Mr. Stevenson as a Story-teller," *Atlantic Monthly,* vol. 60, p. 753.

If *The Pavillion of the Links* has claims to be considered a masterpiece, and may confidently hope to stand the merciless test of time, the same must also be conceded to *Dr. Jekyll*. In fact, of the two, *Dr. Jekyll*, though slightly inferior as a work of art, has the greater certainty of longevity. The allegory within it would lengthen its days, even should new methods and changes of taste take the charm from the story. As long as man remains a dual being, as long as he is in danger of being conquered by his worse self, and, with every defeat, finds it the more difficult to make a stand, so long *Dr. Jekyll* will have a personal and most vital meaning to every poor, struggling human being. *Mutato nomine de te fabula narratur,* so craftily is the parable worked out that it never obtrudes itself upon the reader or clogs the action of the splendid story. It is only on looking back, after he has closed the book, that he sees how close is the analogy and how direct the application.

Conan Doyle, 1890, "Mr. Stevenson's Methods in Fiction,"
National Review, vol. 14, p. 647.

What piece of prose fiction is less likely to be forgotten? To begin with, the central idea, strange as it is, at once comes home to everybody....This is the only case where Mr. Stevenson, working by himself, has used a mystery; and most skilfully it is used in the opening chapters to stimulate curiosity....In the third part, when the mystery has been solved, nothing but consummate art could have saved the interest from collapsing. But Jekyll's own written statement gives the crowning emotion when it recites the drama that passed in the study behind the locked door; the appalling conflict between the two personages in the same outwardly changing breast. Other writers have approached the same idea. Gautier, for instance, has a curious story of a gentleman who gets translated into another man's body to court the other's wife; but Mr. Stevenson has everything to gain by the comparison.

Stephen Gwynn, 1894, "Mr. Robert Louis Stevenson,"
Fortnightly Review, vol. 62, p. 787.

FURTHER READING

Jekyll and Hyde Contexts

ARATA, STEPHEN. *Fictions of Loss in the Victorian Fin de Siècle: Identity and Empire.* Cambridge University Press. 2009.

BATHURST, BELLA. *The Lighthouse Stevensons.* Harper Perennial. 2000.

BELL, IAN. *Dreams of Exile: Robert Louis Stevenson.* Henry Holt. 1993.

DONLOP, EILEEN. *The Travelling Mind.* NMS Enterprises. 2008.

HARMAN, CLAIRE. *Myself and the Other Fellow: A Life of Robert Louis Stevenson.* Harper Collins. 2005.

RANKIN, NICHOLAS. *Dead Man's Chest: Travels after R.L.S.* Faber & Faber. 1987.

REED, THOMAS L., JR. *The Transforming Draught: Jekyll and Hyde, Robert Louis Stevenson and the Victorian Alcohol Debate.* McFarland. 2006.

SHOWALTER, ELAINE. *Sexual Anarchy: Gender and Culture at the Fin de Siècle.* Penguin. 1990.

TERRY, R.C. *Robert Louis Stevenson: Interviews and Recollections.* University of Iowa Press. 1995.

Works Inspired by Jekyll and Hyde

ESTLEMAN, LOREN D. *Dr. Jekyll and Mr. Holmes.* Doubleday. 1979.

HORAN, NANCY. *Under the Wide and Starry Sky.* Ballantine Books. 2014.

KELLER, ELIAS. *Strange Case of Mr. Bodkin and Father Whitechapel.* GZI Productions. 2012.

LEVINE, DANIEL. *Hyde.* Houghton Mifflin Harcourt. 2014.

MARTIN, VALERIE. *Mary Reilly.* Doubleday. 1990.

MOORE, ALAN AND KEVIN O'NEILL. *The League of Extraordinary Gentlemen.* America's Best Comics. 1999.

SANFORD, JOHN A. *The Strange Trial of Mr. Hyde: A New Look at the Nature of Human Evil.* Harper and Row. 1987.

WIEDERANDERS, MARK. *Stevenson's Treasure.* Fireship Press. 2014